JUBILEE YEAR

Hi, Yvette –
I hope you like this one –
Joanne

JUBILEE YEAR

JOANNE GREENBERG

Joanne Greenberg

MCMANIA PUBLISHING

McMania Publishing

McMANIA

Printed in the United States of America

ISBN-13: 978-1-54567-815-2

LCCN: 2019918534

DEDICATION

To Albert, again and still

Many thanks to the people who have taken the time and trouble to help in my researches—to Maris (Ria) Brunhart-Lupo for the geology underlying my mountain's fall; to Jack Reed for help with the water problems; to Lois Wallace, and for the encouragement of Albert, David, and Alan. Thank you to the McManis family and McMania Publishing for working to save its life once born, and to Denise Johnson for that and more.

4. "In the 7th year you shall be a complete rest for the land... it shall be a Jubilee year for you."
10. "You shall return each man to his ancestral heritage and you shall return each man to his family."

—Leviticus 25: 4, 10

CHAPTER 1

IT WAS JANUARY FOURTH, AND SHERIFF JAY ISAACS was sitting in his patrol car outside the main doors of Callan High School, waiting for the three kids to come out. When they did, he would arrest them for the break-in at one of the ski condos in the new development. Many of those condos were unoccupied, even during ski season. The three had been caught on camera and easily identified. He would take them to the town hall back in Gold Flume, where there was a small lockup. He would call their parents and recover the items the kids had taken. There had been some vandalism. Later, he would go to each of their homes for a chat. There were advantages to Gold Flume being as small as it was. He and the parents might get the matter taken care of without a record, even a juvenile one, if the items were returned and restitution made, and if the owners of the condo could be talked out of pressing charges.

Isaacs had been sheriff for sixteen years, seeing the population grow and the condos and developments come in, the mall and the old high school closing. The school his kids had gone to had been in town, small and close. They had been well known and looked after. This place seemed huge and impersonal to him. He lived in Gold Flume and was technically under-sheriff to Sheriff McMasters in Aureole, the county seat, thirty miles away and over Victory Pass. He and AnneMarie had

1

just had their thirtieth anniversary—he wouldn't say celebrated—noted would be more accurate.

He reminded himself of his good luck, being happy in his job and being good at it. His work made up for—he was pushing that thought away when the doors opened and kids burst out in a torrent, flowing toward the five waiting school buses that would take them back to each of the four towns in this narrow, mountain-belted valley.

He watched them, seeing how tribal they still were, as he had been, and as his kids had been. School life was cut into bands, like a plaid with cross-threads of age, wealth and gender: rich-poor, jock-nerd, local-away. Being local meant being from Gold Flume or Callan; being away meant being from Bluebank or Granite City, poorer towns where workers who couldn't afford to live in the high-priced ski and tourist towns stayed. The physical distance between the ski towns and the two near the pass was six and eleven miles, respectively. The social distance was in the hundreds.

Out they came, the three together. Jay got out of the patrol car and walked toward them.

"Mike, Chris: you know why I'm here. Hello, Angela. The building won't be closed for another hour or so. Suppose we go back in there and talk for a while."

They looked at him out of their anxious eyes, caught, until the personas they were trying to cultivate showed up and slipped over their heads—street smart, the viewers of years of police shows on TV. The sight made him all but lose face in laughter. Angela's model was savvy street whore. She and Mike sported piercings here and there. Chris was the only one whose mask didn't fit. Although it was cold, they were all in tee shirts and jeans, their Statement: We are above petty influences, weather, and season.

They breasted the outgoing crowd, not without looks from those kids, and went through the big doors and to the principal's outer office, where he motioned them to chairs. There, he laid out his facts. They had been seen and identified and the car they were driving had been identified. He watched Angela, who seemed to be the brains of the trio, and it was to her that he found himself talking, quietly, reasonably. They would come with him back to the Gold Flume town hall and there, call their folks, and then wait until their folks came and signed them out.

Silence, and then, Angela said, "The turkeys at the dump will really be pissed."

Of the three, Angela's mask fit her best. She was small and dark, modern—skinny, none of the curves his generation thought were sexy. She was pert and painted; hard-looking, quick. No one looking at her would think, 'Rich-kid, doctor's daughter, big house.' And for the boys—she was giving it to both, caring for neither. Turkeys at the dump? He swallowed another smile.

"I'll take that into consideration," he said, and then, "If you want to talk to your parents yourselves, you can. They'll come and get you, and later, I'll go to your houses to see them there. I'll want to talk about your options with you and them." He had repeated himself because he thought that with all their posing, they might not have been paying attention. They sat like stone and then Angela got up, and the two boys followed her.

Jay said, "Just a minute. I can understand theft. Somebody has something you want and you don't have the immediate means of getting it yourselves. Vandalism is something else—just destroying—is something I don't understand. Why did you do that?"

3

The boys shrugged, still consciously in their versions of inner-city savages. Angela gave one of those heavenward eye-rolls that Jay remembered from his own daughter years before.

"Excitement," she said. "There's nothing to do in this fuckin' town."

Before he could stop himself, Jay said, "Aren't there clubs after school or groups—sports—band—things like that?"

They looked at him blankly with no change of expression. He thought their parents brought them up to question authority. They had raised themselves to have no respect for authority.

They went out to the squad car, waiting for him to press down on their heads as the cops did on TV, surprised when he didn't. In silence, Jay drove them the three miles back to Gold Flume. The road followed the river, all but stopped with ice and well below its banks. He drove them to his office in the basement of the town hall.

Gold Flume tended to darken early in this season, shielded by mountains in the west, but there was still some light left. There would be paperwork and the calls to the parents. By the time he was cleared to go home, it would be well after eight. The truth was that he didn't want to be at home. He had stopped wanting to be home for some time.

As they pulled up at the town hall, the mayor, Edwina Dixon, was just leaving for the afternoon. Jay saw Edwina's eyes widen at the sight of the three kids, obviously in custody. She knew their parents, all of them the town's richer people. They saw her surprise and hardened against it.

"Cunt," Mike murmured. Angela was looking as though the situation were happening to someone else.

Inside, they went down the newly remodeled staircase to Jay's office. For a moment he thought he would put the three in the single two-cot cell, but realized that such a setup would add a romantic note, something they could brag about to school friends later on. He motioned the three to straight chairs and began his calls.

Mike Ansel's father was an engineer up at the ski area and would probably be at his office, Jay thought. Ansel was blunt and brief, displaying no surprise at Jay's call.

"Be right down."

Jay had encountered Ansel before at various times for problems up at the area and didn't look forward to this one.

Angela's father was Dr. Bruno, an orthopedic surgeon who was making a good living treating ski area accidents. The family lived across the river in a mansion the size of a school, in a gated community of like mansions. He had a clinic just out of town where the ambulance was housed. The secretary there told him that Dr. Bruno was away at a convention in Denver. He got Mrs. Bruno at home. She would come, she said after a long moment of silence. Her tone suggested that his request was an imposition.

Ron Pantea, Chris' father, had just come in and was breathless on the phone. Jay had served on town committees with him. He was a geologist—extractive minerals, he had once told Jay, who thought him a bit of a snob. His response was as curt as Ansel's had been, but the shock behind it was unmistakable.

He and his wife were the first ones down. They looked like the dazed passengers at an auto wreck, standing white and motionless while Jay described the break-in, the theft, the vandalism. He saw them wondering if perhaps Chris had been mistakenly identified for another tall, athletic-looking blond boy. When had it been—Monday afternoon?

"But that was a school day. Chris must have been in class." Ron Pantea looked at his wife.

"He was home when I got there," she said, and to Chris, "Did you cut class and break in there?"

"I was there," Chris said.

Jay sighed.

"You're not denying this, then?" from his father.

"No," Chris said.

His parents' eyes fixed on him. Jay saw them trying to find a way to change the "*no*" into "*No, I wasn't there.*" The fit couldn't be made.

They were standing in the front office, Mike and Angela lounging on the wooden chairs. Into the silent balance, Patricia Bruno burst.

"You're arresting my daughter! Where is she? What have you done with her?"

Jay watched the acting. He had once seen a nature program featuring the frilled lizard, a forest creature that when menaced raised fanlike membranes that displayed two circles looking like gigantic eyes. It began to scream in a manic display of hysteria and ran shrieking away through the forest.

"Mrs. Bruno—"

She noticed Angela and screamed.

"Mrs. Bruno—"

From her chair, Angela, the second part of the act, rose in full street-whore pout. The Frilled Lizard ran at the girl, but Jay noticed that the two didn't embrace. Mrs. Bruno might have been backing her daughter, but the moves were not maternal.

Jay had thought to visit with the parents privately, but changed his mind. He wasn't about to be part of the Brunos' act. As he made his decision, the Ansels arrived. Roman Ansel was direct and directing, his wife all but cowering in the blast.

"What are the charges?" He barked like a sports coach.

When Jay told him, he demanded proof. Who exactly had identified his son? Where was the evidence? Was this some kind of small town vendetta?

Jay's compassion, which had been aroused at the high school door, evaporated. "You can all go home," he said. "Tomorrow morning at eight-thirty I'll be here in my car. Your youngsters will get in my car and we will go to Aureole where they will face the charges of theft and vandalism which they committed on Monday at a condominium between Gold Flume and Callan. Identification will be made by a witness. All three of them appeared on the monitor at the condo. You can get legal representation when they are charged. I have nothing to do with that. I'll see you all here at eight-thirty."

Silence.

They left, Angela's mother not closing the outer door, a cold exit. He smelled her perfume, too heavy an announcement on the air. She and her daughter did look like sisters—dark hair, light skin, starved-looking women who might be fat but for constant rigorous care and a minute concern for every slight change in their bodies. Ansel raged as he went by. The Panteas were silent.

Jay liked to think of himself as fair, uniform in his treatment, but his mood had darkened. He had been willing, even eager, to work with them on easing the situation—recompense, no record. Mrs. Bruno and the Ansels had swept away his good will and his generosity in thirty seconds. The realization saddened him. He went back to his very ordinary day.

It was fully dark when he got home. With the rising wealth of the town, land prices had soared. Back in the seventies, the county commissioners had passed a statute protecting the houses of settler families and taxed them at a lower rate. Jay's house—AnneMarie's parents' home—was on Second Street, uphill on a block with five newer ones. Jay drove up past their evening lights, TV, and computers on in all the houses but his. Paving stopped a foot from his property line, next to the Klimeks. There were no houses on the other side of the street. The ground there was scree and unstable, fracturing rock that often fell into the road, making auto travel hazardous. Every year land speculators came before the Council with some plan to build on that side, and every year the Council turned the plan down. People on Second Street felt lucky—they had an open view of the downtown, balanced by the slight feeling of anxiety that such conditions couldn't last.

He used his key—people locked their doors, now. The house was silent. AnneMarie must have been upstairs, probably in bed. She slept badly, compensating with naps. He went into the kitchen. The table hadn't been cleared from breakfast; plates and cups, cereal, milk and juice were still out, but a light was on in the oven—his dinner being kept warm. He opened the oven door—lasagna, not her old specialty, home-made from her family recipe, but a frozen one. Jay went to the fridge and took out the salad she had made. He put back the juice and milk from the morning, ate quickly and without relish, and went upstairs.

AnneMarie was sitting on his side of the bed, with the reading light on. She was holding a sock in her hand, as though wondering whether she had just taken it off or was just putting it on. Around her hung the aura of her meds, a metallic odor almost like ether.

"Hi, Honey."

She looked up at him. "Oh, hi. Did you eat?"

"Yah, I did. Can you come down?"

"Sure." She smiled, looked at the sock, looked down at her feet, sighed, and put on the other sock. She moved slowly to follow Jay back downstairs and into the kitchen.

"Have you had dinner?" he asked her.

"No; I don't think so. I'll make eggs."

She did, working as though through water, and came and sat down with him, eating them after he had made coffee. She ate little, but the meds had made her bloated and heavy. He began to tell her about what had happened. He still did this, as he had always done; now watching her desperate attempt to listen, truly listen and absorb what he was saying. With her coffee, she took her evening doses.

"So," he concluded, "tomorrow I leave here at 8:25 and drive three kids to Aureole with their parents in procession behind me."

"What did they do?"

"B. and E., theft, and vandalism."

"New people or old?"

"New—two new, one not so new."

He thought for a moment about the families' treatment of him. Jay wasn't physically imposing—5'9" and lightly built. From this body, a deep voice, ripe and resonant, emerged that often surprised people. It was this voice that established his command. When it was soft, he saw people relax. His mother had wanted him to be a doctor, because of that voice.

They watched TV for a while, news from the world outside Gold Flume and the three valley towns. The news was about places far removed. Tourists said that was a blessing. They were coming to the valley to get away from the world's confusions, but Jay knew that this town and all the valley towns were intimately connected to what went on beyond the mountain and over the pass. A stock market slide and tourist dollars diminished. A spell of weather and reservations dried up. The previous year was a case in point. Warm weather and a late winter had kept the lifts and lodges closed until mid-November. The businesses in town also fluctuated, depending on fashions and foreign matters—a war, and trade slowed or stopped. Tourism was sometimes as chancy as farming or ranching, Jay thought, and the whole town knew it, although it was best to further the illusion that here all was timeless and that the people, like the mountains, were complete in themselves, settled, serene.

Later, as they watched the ten o'clock news, Jay saw that AnneMarie was working at understanding the quick, slick presentations that moved before them in as many minutes—here a famine, there a protest, no back-story, no context. He couldn't remember in the morning what had come over the news the night before. Weather came on. Sports. The football was as incomprehensible to her as the famine, but she kept trying to hear it all, to compass it with her wounded mind. They went to bed. The wind had come up, and snow.

CHAPTER 2

THE WIND AND SNOW INCREASED, SIGNALING A LONG storm that hit just before midnight. The few vacationers in the town itself, clubbing at local places, got the early edge of warning and left for their condos two miles south of town, or the lodges in Callan. By one a.m., light sleepers were jarred awake by screaming winds to gape at the vertically blinding snow outside their windows.

Jay's sleep was interrupted by something he couldn't put a name to. First, he thought a tree had fallen against the house, shaking the structure through every beam and joist. He turned, listening. There was nothing but the storm. He decided he had been dreaming and had created the nightmare in response to the eruption of anger in the parents of the delinquents he had seen yesterday. He turned again and fell back into a dream about his daughter, aged ten, then seven, then four, romping with him in the ocean, which she wouldn't see until she left home.

AnneMarie dreamed fragments, bits of her clothing stared at by people moving away from her.

Up at the Community Church, Pastor Elbert Fearing dreamed of a persistent congregant asking him theological questions he couldn't answer. Mike Ansel dreamed of being in prison, a prison out of a very old movie—thick bars and a persistent clanging sound. He woke himself with the dream all but shaken from his body, terrified by that clanging, feeling shut in, wound as he was in his bedclothes. Chris Pantea struggled with his dream in which a shapeless fog enveloped him, ready to eat him alive. He woke shaking and became aware that the storm was booming outside. His body was warm under the comforter, but his face was cold. *The power must be off, the lines broken by the storm—not uncommon, fixed by tomor...* he fell back into sleep.

In his house, by the river walk, Doctor Winograd had one of his holocaust dreams, bombings from low-flying planes raining fire on his house. He woke up on the intake of air in a gasp and lay staring into the night, his bed vibrating. The wind was shrieking down the canyons and pulling at the houses. He muttered in an almost forgotten Yiddish: "Let thunder's wife drag him home to sleep," and rolled over, sleepless, but unaware that the power had gone off and there would be no alarm to wake him in the morning.

In the foredawn, Jay woke up, freezing. There must be lines down. There was a preternatural quiet; no appliances whispered or throbbed. There were no little red lights monitoring electronic life. The snow had stopped. Jay got up, groaning. He took the flashlight in his bedside drawer to see his way to the bathroom utility closet for one of the three heaters, still fueled from the last power outage. He set it up and lit it, not without anxiety when he carried it into the bedroom. In AnneMarie's state, she might walk into it. He had just gotten her a cell phone, which he saw was also dead. She turned in bed and came out of sleep as he was leaving.

"Power's off," he said. "I'll call you from the road."

He made coffee on the small white gas stove he kept in the kitchen, then went back upstairs with a cup and told AnneMarie to stay in bed until the power company men came and fixed the lines. Back in the kitchen, he cut a piece of bread and brought out the jam. The jar was sticky, the top stuck. As he wrestled with it, he thought again of his decision, long overdue, to get someone here to help. He would have to swallow his pride and admit that AnneMarie was incapable of doing housework, of being the woman she had been. On the way back home from Aureole, he thought he would stop at the Molinos'. They had a girl who might come. He would have to be careful to get someone intelligent and pleasant. The family was old Gold Flume, baking bread here for a generation. With the gentrification of the town, they were now making varied and excellent loaves, artisanal, they were called. Good food hadn't been part of Jay's life for some time. It had once been a point of pride to AnneMarie, the baking and cooking she had done, all gone now. It was time he faced it and got some help.

His clothes were shiver-making as he got into them and his sheriff's winter jacket was icy. The power must have been off for hours. He had garaged his car the night before and was glad for the forethought, because he wouldn't have to scrape ice from the windows. He was able to drive it through the heavy haze to the town hall where he was to meet Chris, Mike, and Angela and their parents, who would be even more sour and impatient. Outages always made people surly.

The streets were full of windblown gritty dust deposited by last night's storm. There were the parents and the kids, Bruno and Ansel in second cars. No one wanted to show up in a car that cost more than Jay earned in a year. Pantea was in a hybrid. Motors were running for warmth, the smoke from their exhausts strangely brown.

"We'll drive them," Ansel cried as Jay pulled up and stopped.

He got out. It was his time to assert himself.

"They are, technically, in my charge," Jay said. "The three will fit comfortably in the back of the patrol car." The words "patrol car" made his point. Grumbling, the three kids came. Angela, beyond belief, was in a skirt that ended mid-thigh. She had on a down jacket, though, and boots. The boys were hunched in their jackets but disdained hats. They clambered into the back of the car. Jay was amused. Had they wished to make high drama of their arrest, the cold and the strange weather had taken the stage from them. It dampened the mood. The heat was on high in the car. He turned south on to the road to Callan.

The road followed the river, and as they drove, they saw swirls and patterns in a gray-brown material covering the ground. Jay remembered a similar universal fall and a haze for a week after the eruption of Mount St. Helen. Perhaps that volcano had become active again. Was it likely? The event would have been on the news and days would had passed before the gritty dust traveled as far as central Colorado. For a moment, he thought he might speak of it to the kids, but the mood in the car was so sullen and defiant that his impulse was dampened. He concentrated on driving. The storm had blown snow into wind-slab hills and bands across the road, but he noticed that the grit provided nice traction.

They were a mile from town, and although it was early, Jay was wondering why there was no traffic coming the other way. The power outage must be general. An outage would slow commuters, but certainly not stop them. He looked in his rearview mirror and saw the Ansel car hugging his bumper. Up ahead he saw a truck stopped, lights off. He pulled up behind it, got out, and locked the car. The man was now standing up in the truck bed, looking ahead. There were cars ahead of them, all stopped.

"Can you see anything?" Jay called up to the man.

"Cars, eight, maybe nine, and then there's the bend in the river and I can't see around it."

"I can't leave the car," Jay said. "Could you scout out what's going on? My radio's down."

"Oh, yeah, Sheriff Isaacs, sure."

Jay tried to remember the man's name—Constantine?—no, Considine. Considine looked back at the car, and Jay saw him trying to take a peek inside. Unable to see, Considine hopped lightly off the bed of the truck and moved up the road. Jay saw him hunch up against the morning chill and then disappear among the cars and around the bend. They waited. Behind them, Jay heard a few restless horns and people calling out. Ansel left his car. Inside the patrol car, Jay heard the kids playing Convict Going Mad In Solitary. Considine came back at a trot as Jay stood stamping for warmth. Behind him, cars were coming.

"Avalanche," Considine said. "A big one. These here are cars coming back. There's a turn-around up the road, but we've got to try to get people up to it instead of them trying to turn here and choking up everything."

The two of them went back to Ansel, who was busily trying to work his car out into the road. Cars were coming back. Pantea was in the car behind Ansel's. By that time, horns were blaring. When Jay explained, two men went up the line, while he and Considine worked their way back, telling the news and explaining the plan. On its way back, one of the cars stopped and Jay went over.

The man said, "It's like a wall. A rockslide, you'd see over it. This—it's huge, like a mountain in the road."

Ansel and Pantea came back. "Well, Sheriff."

"Well, no one's going to Aureole today. I'll take the kids back to the town hall and get a statement. Then, we can all go home."

"Not without a lawyer," Ansel said. "Next time I come with a lawyer."

"Bring six," Jay said. "Your kid has committed theft and vandalism. I think we're at a place where a lot more serious things will be happening."

Pantea went to talk to Angela's mother in the third car.

When they got to the turn-around they could see part of the situation. Jay thought it looked as though the mountain had moved and the whole geography had changed; the view they were used to at this spot was no longer here.

Back at the patrol car, Jay flicked on the radio. He heard the air-sound of the open mike, but silence and bits of static were all he got. He made his turn and they all rode back toward town. As they rode, the wind came up a little. The day would be colder. People were thinking of the wind chill when a sound enveloped them, sudden and building, a huge groan like the agony of a giant, otherworldly monster, made louder by the compression of the valley.

Gold Flume lay at the end of the Ute Valley, backed up against the mountain and sharing its narrow geography with the now frozen Ute River. Echoes multiplied. The sound became a roar and Jay all but lost control of the car, his passengers, at last, shocked into silence. The sound rose again, created and faded. Angela began to scream.

CHAPTER 3

EVEN IN THE COLD, THE STREET IN FRONT OF THE town hall was full of people. There had been outages before, some for as long as three days, but this was something worse. From what Jay had seen there might be a wait as long as a week or two before the roads could be cleared and the power restored. Edwina Dixon, Gold Flume's mayor, was standing in front of the building on the steps, talking to two town council members who had shown up. Jay went up the steps and told her what he had seen.

"I think that's what's causing this brown mist we're in. It's an avalanche, a huge one."

"I've tried calling out," she said, "but nothing seems to work. We'll have to wait for some contact with the outside. I'm sure there'll be planes flying over. I think we should calm people down right now."

"But we don't know what the situation is." Brad Unger was a council member and the fire chief. "Are there people in town who depend on oxygen machines—asthmatics, anyone needing special help to breathe? I can hardly pull in a lungful myself."

"Doc Winograd must know," Jay said.

"I'm going to ring the fire bell," Brad said. "We need to get the people together, but I think people with lung conditions will know to stay inside. What was that awful sound? Is there more avalanche coming?"

"I don't know," Jay said.

Brad went down the steps and into the now sizeable crowd. Jay saw him begin to run, check himself, and move through the group, nodding to people, a word here and there, as he went up River Street toward the firehouse. Gold Flume's one-time warning system had been put out of service in 1918 after it had rung the end of World War I. The town had kept it for the tourists, rung ceremonially every July Fourth. There was a pause and then the bell rang, muffled by the strange dust, sounding strange in the ear. Once, twice, three times.

People began to call up to Mayor Dixon, Jay, and Harbison, another council member.

"Sheriff—" Edwina tried speaking but her voice didn't carry. The haze seemed to eat sound.

"Your Honor—" Jay had known Edwina for years, but they were both aware at the same moment that it was important to remind everyone of their official selves.

"Go ahead, Sheriff," she said.

Jay took a breath and, in a voice loud enough to be heard by everyone standing below, told them please to wait for everyone who could come to be present, so he and the mayor needn't repeat themselves. There had been an avalanche. The dust was caused by the fall. News was coming in. Everyone would know about it as soon as possible.

The group was standing below, moving from foot to foot in the chill air, their voices competing, demanding information. What about the loss of all the electricity, computer services, and telephones? When would service be restored? There was no phone operating, landline or cell. No e-mail. Who was in charge? Jay realized that on the other side of the avalanche there would be another line of cars and trucks which would have been bringing people and services into Gold Flume, workers from Callan and Bluebank, maids, teachers, handymen, clerks, tellers, garbage collectors. From what he had seen, it would take some time to get the road open. There would be more pressing problems than those milling, complaining townspeople had in mind. All the services they depended on would be shut down. And the food—all of it. Gold Flume's food came daily on trucks, big trucks that carried everything from flour and coffee to gourmet specialties for the skiers and vacationers. Restaurants would close. These restless people were in for something far worse than a loss of phone service.

People were coming, bundled against the cold. They coughed. Some wore masks or held scarves over their faces against the gritty air. Jay and Mayor Dixon took turns explaining what had happened. They had to keep repeating what they knew. The questions persisted. Mayor Dixon was telling everyone that the information would come in when the extent of the problem was known. The thing might be temporary. Avalanches had happened before, many times. They were always a temporary inconvenience. Then, she caught Jay's eye and put both hands up.

"I've heard you and I need to tell you that when we know the extent of the avalanche and what has happened, we will let you know, all of you. It's time for everyone to go home, get out your emergency stoves and gas heaters. Keep warm. Use your freezers and refrigerators as little as possible and store things in the snow. We will organize a program for dealing with this, and I'll know more, soon." She thought, *Be glad this didn't happen in the summer when all those freezer-fulls would rot.*

Jay had let the smirking kids off and saw them go to their parents, who were standing at the edge of the crowd. The new situation had taken their attention from their children's problems. Ansel came forward, pushing through the crowd. He looked past Edwina as though she didn't exist and went straight to the councilman.

"We have a generator up at the ski area—power for the ventilators for people who need them. Only for them." He left before he could be thanked.

Slowly, muttering, people began drifting off. Edwina came over to Jay and when Jay had told her what he and Considine had seen, she blew through her lips. "I don't even know how to call for help."

Jay was blowing on his hands, colorless with the cold. "People know," he said. "I expect there will be a fly-over before too long with some kind of contact. We'll need fuel and water as well as food, and a way of keeping the sewer lines open."

They stood and stared at each other and then the mayor seemed to come alive. "Drive to the gas stations. Tell Ed Thaxter and Min not to sell gas to anyone, no matter who it is. We'll need to ration it for essential services. There's going to be hoarding and fighting. Fuel, oil, whatever they have up there that can burn, all the ammo—hunting season's not over. They'd still have lots of that."

Jay drove quickly to Ed's Garage and Min's Quick-Stop just in time. Even in the haze, cars were moving up the hill. Ed and Min agreed to shut down. By the time he got back to Main Street, the hardware store was crowded with people buying camp stoves, butane, white gas, candles, and whatever else they could think of for the siege. The store sold all they had, and the ammunition, one box per person.

At three o'clock a helicopter flew over the town and at four, another. Jay, Mayor Dixon, and Fire Chief Unger thought it wise to stay in front of the town hall, providing a presence. Over them the evening clouds went from gold to orange to red, the air scintillating with the billions of tiny chips of granite and quartz from the fall, all illuminated by the slant-shaft of sun. Even the loudest complainer stopped for a moment to watch the radiance passing into gloaming. Jay wondered if there was a relationship between beauty and hope. He felt a lift in himself, even as he dreaded what was coming.

Unger's wife had brought a chiminea over and kept it going with wood and charcoal briquets. Jay had put a spare set of gloves in the patrol car back in September, and now he was glad he had. The men warmed stones at the edges of the chiminea and put them into their gloves as they watched people coming back from the hardware store with whatever they could carry.

"That guy, Considine, he was out at the avalanche, wasn't he? Did he say it was on the far side of the mall?"

Someone said, "No—it's a mile and some from here. All we have is what's in town."

"God, not even a drugstore..."

"This isn't gonna be a three-day problem, is it?" Unger, a glove off, was biting a nail.

"Not from what I saw," Jay said. "The flyover—the helicopters— people know we're here, and they know we're in trouble, but how long we'll be in this shape is— " and he shrugged.

"It's getting dark," Unger said. "I'm heading home." A wind had come up and the mist had parted in places, the heavier part depositing itself on the town, an equal coating on every flat place, large and small. A geometry lesson, Jay thought. The lighter mist pulled its glittering veil away.

"Thank Siri for the chiminea, will you? It was a godsend."

"Sure will."

Jay left the patrol car behind the town hall and walked the two blocks by the river and then turned east and began to go up the hill to home. Full dark had come, but it wasn't the dark he had experienced here for years—my God, he thought, the stars—the valley narrowed where the town nestled in the narrow end, backed up against the rampart of mountains to the north, sharing space with the river. Even with the town's lesser allowance of sky, what it presented now was breathtaking. Starlight made the way easy to see and he went deftly over the mounds of slabbed snow at the sides of the streets. There were clouds of stars, spills of them, big, small, some winking, some still, a sight that blurred his eyes with awe, which made him know how tired he was, how tired and cold. The town was utterly still, and that, too, added to the magic. There were things they had to think about, he, Edwina, Doc Winograd down the street, Brad Unger. They would need to come up with lists of essentials. The mall, with the big grocery and drug stores, was on the other side of the avalanche, unavailable to them. When the skiers had come, Gold Flume had lost most of its essential purposes. It was a boutique town, now. In the magic of the night's stillness and the reign of the stars, he realized that town's isolation gave him many things to think of and plan for. He was at his dark house and looking down the hill at darkness. Then, he left it all and for a long moment, leaned against a tree and peered up at the gorgeous display and savored the grand silence, and the spread-out miracle of the universe.

CHAPTER 4

PEOPLE HAD GONE TO BED CERTAIN THAT ELECTRIC power would be restored in the morning. Outages had happened before, sometimes seven or eight hours. Through the night, moans, the creaking of immense doors, a sound like the screams of children being burnt alive, bangs and whines, cut the silence and reverberated down the river. Ron Pantea, the geologist, told anyone who would listen that the sounds were natural, to be expected, the rocks and trees and all the trapped debris and the earth itself were shifting to the angle of repose, the way a sleeper turns, pulling the covers with him. Anyone still asleep awoke surprised at the continuing cold and near-dark. The coffee makers and radios that had always wakened them to city, nation, and world were dark and silent. Houses were bone-cold where fuel had been burned away during the night. Feet touching bare floors went white with cold. Fires had to be made in pellet stoves, wood stoves, and in some houses, borrowed camp stoves. Most people had food on hand, but coffee was difficult to make in saucepans on the tops of camp stoves. Everyone went to dead phones, TVs, toaster ovens, iPads, light switches, clicking them uselessly and feeling betrayed. The emergency radios, working on batteries, returned static, like an obscene wave-off. Children clicked on lights, surprised again and again, feeling foolish again for trying what obviously wouldn't work. Those who put their Pyrex brewers on wood-stoves saw them shatter.

At nine, Fire Chief Brad Unger, Mayor Dixon, and four others who made up the Town Council drove out to the site of the avalanche and came back with set faces. Dixon told Jay what they had seen.

"It's not an avalanche, man, it's a fall. Half the mountain's gone. It's a wall, like another mountain put there overnight. I have no idea how big the thing is—I mean how wide, but it'll be work to get through it. It's too much to figure."

"Is there no way to get through to anyone outside?"

"No, and there's something else: the condos. I mean the condos on both sides of the river and all those big houses up Breaker Road and Vista Road. Those have all been covered and no way to tell who was in them. We don't know but there must have been at least fifty people in them and they're all gone, buried, and no way to count the victims or even find them."

"Is it like a rockslide?"

"Rocks and earth and sticks and parts of trees and things not to be identified and paving sticking out far up as anyone can see."

They were silent, looking away. If they had faced one another, they might have seen their own panic mirrored in familiar faces.

"We might ask people in town if they knew anyone there at home, or in the condos. Maybe the ski area has some kind of record of reservations or names of people—restaurants in town, anyone we can find who has a list..." the Mayor's voice trailed off.

"Those people are gone," Unger said. "I'm worried about what will happen in town when people find out we're marooned."

"It can't be for long," Jay said. "They'll drop lines and cables and generators. Some government agency does that—and they'll blast a way through in a couple of days."

"You didn't see the mountain," Dixon said. "Get ready for a siege."

"None of my electronic equipment works—" a man yelled. "The satellite should—"

"The avalanche must have narrowed the canyon even more," Jay said. "It was always narrow here. The towers got our signal to where it would get to the satellite. The town's at the end of the canyon. Where it widened is where the fall is."

That afternoon, a helicopter landed on the grade school playground. Its coming brought out everyone who could make a way through the soiled snow to the landing spot. The man who emerged carried two briefcases, which he gave to the mayor, locking the door of the machine carefully, an eye on the teenagers whose schools were now on the other side of the fall, in Callan. A crowd, shouting, followed him up to the town hall where the council, four besides Mayor Dixon, Jay, and Pastor El Fearing were waiting. They called Doc Winograd in and then closed and locked the door of the mayor's office. They were there for an hour, the pilot wanting to leave before dark. The crowd waited, alternately surly and frightened. Rumors settled between the houses like the dust of the fall, universal. People went home and came back. Some, who tried to clean off their cars, found that the dust was gritty and scratched the paint. Nine people were driven up to the ski area with their oxygen equipment. Ansel had told them there was a generator there.

The sun had gone when Edwina Dixon came to the steps to talk to those who hadn't been driven back to their houses by the cold. "This mountain-fall," she said, "is the entire front face of the Hungry Mother.

It's 500 feet high and more than half a mile long. It covers the river and goes almost as far up the other side."

People began to shout. The cries and questions seemed to go on and on, people venting all their fears and frustrations.

"I'll have to go soon," the pilot said, "can't we get these folks to shut up and listen?"

Edwina tried, but had to wait for them to quiet. They were panicking. She took a breath and spoke as loudly as she could. Her voice barely carried, and those at the back of the group stamped their feet in frustration.

"The authorities have been informed. They know how bad it is and will help, I assure you. However—" a roar—"however, this fall is only a small part of earth movements that have taken place on faults near here and also in Oregon. There is a very severe storm moving inland on the east coast that has shut down New York City. We will have food. We will have fuel. We have questionnaires to give out to all the households in town and lists for everyone in town to fill out to ascertain what your needs are. The 'copter will be back day after tomorrow with emergency rations. Everyone take a questionnaire, go home, and fill it out. Anyone with neighbors not here, or people you know not here, take a questionnaire for them and get it to them as soon as you can. You'll have a full day to fill out the lists and bring them here for the helicopter to pick up."

"I swear," Jay told AnneMarie later. "The people wouldn't let us go. I must have answered thirty of them with the same question, and so did Edwina. Everyone wants promises no one can make. When will the mountain be moved? When will the road be cleared? When will the power come on? When will these awful noises stop? People can't sleep. Everyone's nerves are frazzled and it all echoes up the canyon. Everyone's in a haunted house. El Fearing said he'd keep the church open for anyone who needed food or extra blankets. Doc doesn't know all the sick people in town and what they need. People have been going to Aureole for things he can't do, laser treatments and advanced tech stuff."

He looked at her huddled in a quilt in the rocking chair where she had nursed their three children. She had on a muumuu that allowed for the extra weight she had gained from the drugs. She had put on some heavy socks under her slippers. Jay had carried the heater down to the kitchen and she sat stolidly, not sleepy but dull. Where had that competent and compassionate, that tart-witted woman gone? He knew he had to face their own shortages: "Those pills you take—how many do you have on hand?"

"I take so many," she said vaguely.

"Half this town's on something," Jay said, "but until we know how long this will last, we need to ration what you've got."

They had lit a single oil lamp for a glowing, small circle of light. Outside the circle, the ugliness of the squalor was lost, dishes in the sink, crumbs and bits of food that stuck to the countertops, things put down but not put away, all forgiven for the moment in this new darkness.

She did take all kinds of drugs—Haldol, on which she had started, and then Ativan, Halcyon, Cogentin, and now Abilify, adding, subtracting, mixing. The Haldol had been replaced by Seroquel, then by Zyprexa, and Prozac, and several sleeping pills. There were other pills to control side effects. The diagnoses had changed with the changes in medication.

They got the pills from the kitchen cabinet and brought them to the table. Back in the cabinet were bottles of pills half or quarter full when the prescriptions were changed. He thought they might use them if the need arose, but was frightened of interactions. A week's supply of anti-depressants, two weeks' of the others, lay spilled and counted out before them. She took sleeping pills because although she was groggy all day, her sleeps were short and yielded no rest. How many people in Gold Flume used sleeping pills, or were on meds like these?

"Eighteen sleeping pills," she said.

"I think we should ration them, and the others, too. Of course, we'll ask for all of them on the list we fill out," he said, and then saw that her attention had flagged, as it often did, her concentration focused out into the dark.

"There are mice here," she said.

Someone was knocking at their kitchen door. Jay went to it and saw their next-door neighbor, John Klimek. Jay opened the door, noticing that the air felt no colder outside than in.

"Cold," John said. He was tall and thin. Jay thought the cold would be worse for him, but he was lightly dressed, just a jacket. Jay suppressed a shiver. "You guys got enough fuel and wood?"

"For now," Jay said. "I've been thinking about the lists."

"I've been wondering about those, too. Who's to make sure they are picked up once they've been made? Some people aren't able to get out, especially where the snow is deep. There are people up on the ridge who need help. I think we ought to talk to Doc."

"There are probably some records of everyone in town," Jay said, "but you're right about getting the lists filled out and collected."

"I've been up to see Pastor El, too," John said. "He wants to do a memorial for all the people killed in the fall." As he spoke, he noticed AnneMarie, who had been sitting out of the light. "Oh, hi, AnneMarie."

"Hi, John."

"Do you know any of the people who might have been caught in— who live outside of town?"

She shook her head.

"Some of the people up there have kids in my class," Klimek said, "but I don't know which kids live up on those mountainsides, and I don't know exactly where the fall begins. Did some get stuck in Callan by the storm, or were their houses on the other side of the fall? People are making up lists now. I've been here and there getting kids in my classes and in the junior high to write up the names and addresses of families they know in the area between the edge of town and Callan. Whiskey Gulch may have been spared and I think Chinaman's Gulch is clear, but I'm not sure. The bus drivers live in Bluebank, most of the staff of our school lives in Callan, Bluebank, or even in Granite City. I've never felt so cut off in my life."

In the ring of light, just barely, they saw the gleam of tears in AnneMarie's eyes. They stopped speaking for a moment, and then Klimek said to Jay, "You must know people up there. So many of those houses are vacation places for people who live somewhere else. Some are part-time homes with full-time staff. I wouldn't know those. Early tomorrow, I'll start working on the lists with Edwina and the others on the council. El Fearing thinks a memorial will get people's minds off their troubles for a bit—put things in perspective." John stood up and Jay saw him to the door. "This figures to be a long siege, doesn't it?"

Jay nodded. "The pilot told us not to set a date, but people are people and I've been fielding that question all day. I'd like to tell them two months, and surprise them with good news sooner than that."

"Does El have enough food and fuel at the parsonage? Since the Catholics built that new church in Callan and the Lutherans and Kingdom Hall are there, Mountain Community seems to be the only game in town. How about you and Doc?"

"We have to go to Aureole and both of us are pretty much Solstice Jews—twice a year."

29

When Klimek left, Jay went over to the rocker and took AnneMarie's hand. "I've been thinking—those people in the fall—"

She looked at him through tears. Her face was doughy, paler in the lamplight. "Oh, hell—that's the worst part of this thing I've got, whatever it is. How long ago was it that I stopped caring about anything but my deadness and anyone but myself? When John said that about feeling cut off and helpless, all I could think of was how cut off and helpless I feel. What would it take to make me feel anything—babies frozen? Why am I still alive?"

After dinner, Jay went back down to the town hall where Edwina and the council were checking off the names of people and families. There were more than 300 people in town, twice that number of ski vacationers being taken note of up at the ski area's three lodges, which would be their problem. Private services could chopper them out in a few days. Many of the workers and managers with no lives in Gold Flume would be taken away as well. Until this happened, they might be a drain on the town's resources for food and fuel.

"They have more than we do," Edwina said. "Let's get to these lists, in-town people, and people out of town."

They worked until four a.m., checking and cross-checking lists of all kinds, families, singles, people in town and on the outskirts, people who might not be alive. They filled out questions about the water and septic systems. Were there spare generators? Where were they located? Did they have wood available for heating and cooking fuel? Rick Harbison, a council member and the city engineer, said that he had been at a party on the mountain with three families and that he had left early, just as the light snow had started. The party had been on the north side of the mountain and if the people were from that development, living on that road, they might have been spared. If so, they would have to move into town. Were there places for them to go?

"Hell, we don't even know how high up the shear-off was. Maybe those houses high on the ridge of that mountain are gone. The storm kept people in," Harbison said.

"My deputies are away," Jay said, "one with a sick mother in Callan and one in Denver at a trappers' convention. I suppose we should be thankful. If the fall had taken place any closer, we'd all be dead." No one spoke because everyone had thought of that.

A crack of thunder from the fall caromed over them. "These sounds are driving me out of my mind," Harbison said.

Edwina looked at him, and breathed a little breath of relief. As a woman and a mayor, she wasn't free to confess fear, weakness or frustration. Jay knew that to AnneMarie, the sounds were only a reflection of her own despair. She didn't seem to start at them or cry out as others did. He, himself, had moments of extreme reactions. He found himself drumming on the table when he ate. He slammed doors and sometimes tried to out-shout the clamor.

The next morning, four of the board members came to urge Jay to back a recall of Edwina. This wasn't normal life, they said. A woman mayor was good enough in normal times, but now— This idea struck Jay as no more than the sudden need of restless, worried town leaders to do something, to show some kind of action.

"Why would anyone else be better?"

"We need someone who's decisive – strong." Brad Unger's look was intense.

"I hope we don't do it," Jay said. "I'm for going on as close to normal as possible."

"I can understand why you would talk about trying for normal." Harbison said.

"What does that mean?" Jay felt his body tighten.

"Hey —" El Fearing moved to hold Jay back. "Let's simmer down. We're all suffering here from the noise and uncertainty."

"I think Edwina is a good mayor. Problems of the town were as easily faced by Edwina as by anyone else you propose."

"Okay for now," Unger said, "we need to calm people."

Edwina, Jay and Fearing spent the early part of the day at the town hall. The sounds were upsetting, they told everyone who came, but to be expected. The noises would go on for a week or so, grinding, groaning, clicking, cosmic gunshots. All of it would become less frequent. They would stop. Endure. Endure.

"Tomorrow—no, today—El, I don't think it's time to do any memorial yet. There might be some sixty people at home when the mountain fell, perhaps more. There is no way of knowing who had stayed, who left, who had been visiting, who was being visited."

"When is the chopper due?" Harbison asked.

"Tomorrow. The one yesterday landed in the schoolyard. That seems to be okay. The snow there isn't too deep."

Jay lost some more of the conversation. His eyelids were beginning to weigh.

"Jay—" He barely heard until Edwina spoke again. "Jay—go home. Get a nap."

Jay rose and left, counting on the chill of the coldest part of the morning to shock him awake, which it did. He barely remembered Edwina's telling him that they would be counting and collating the questionnaires and requests the next day, and that his neighbor, John Klimek, was organizing the high school kids to do the collection and delivering of the lists. They had divided the town into six areas and the developments up the gulches and counted the huge houses on Jackass Mountain—"Beg pardon," Jay had said, "Aspen Hills Estates." He didn't remember getting home or falling into bed beside the wakeful AnneMarie.

CHAPTER 5

CHRIS PANTEA HAD BEEN SURPRISED WHEN MR. Klimek came to his house and asked him for help in setting out a plan for the chopper drops. Mr. Klimek knew what Chris had done, what he and Mike and Angela had done—the whole town knew by now, yet here he was asking Chris to be part of a group that would meet in the morning to prepare for urgent work. Their jobs would be to see that everyone in town got the questionnaires, filled them in, and returned them. Most people, Mr. Klimek told him, would be at the school yard where the helicopter was to land, but there were old people, sick people, homebound mothers who couldn't get to the delivery point. These were the people Chris and the group would serve. They would, after collecting the papers, be delivering food, fuel, and maybe water to those who needed them. The groups would be serving until the road opened. For a second, Chris was on the point of asking "Why not e-mail everyone to get..." and caught himself in time. The towers were gone and all that was left were batteries in phones and apps saying, "No Signal." Soon, the batteries would dim and die.

Klimek saw Chris' momentary dislocation. Communication now would be entirely face-to-face. This idea was new to him. "You're one of the first three I've contacted," Klimek said. "I'll need each of you to get four others and each of them, four. Not everyone will want to be part of this effort—some won't be able to, but we should end up with about twenty of you guys to do what we need." Chris took a breath. Klimek raised a hand. "No, you don't need to answer all the questions about the details, just get them to agree to come to the town hall at eight tomorrow morning. I'll do the explaining." He told Chris about the six divisions.

When his teacher left, Chris began to think of kids to visit. He realized it would be more difficult to say no to him when he stood at someone's door. What was it like before e-mail and texting made the tactful wiggle easy? Neither Mike nor Angela would be interested in anything like helping. He realized then, with some surprise, that his friendship with the two of them had put him at a distance from kids he had hung out with before. It was new knowledge and it stung. Mike and Angela's style had kept him excited; their friendship was a dare. They seemed to be independent of the opinions of adults, other kids, teachers, and preachers, and their scorn was universal. Chris had admired that, but the fall had changed everything, and would keep changing everything.

Klimek was a good teacher; Chris liked him, and there was a need. People needed what Klimek wanted to do, but Chris wondered what kids would listen to him now. Who would follow his lead? He decided to start on the block south of Sheriff Isaacs' house. Three kids were on that block, one high school and two junior high. His being a senior would help.

All three of them were at home, troubled and restless. The meaning of the fall was beginning to be made real to them. Food in their freezers was softening. Milk would soon begin to sour. At his house the half-gallon cartons were being kept in snowbanks at the north side of the house. In chilly rooms, his neighbors looked out their windows and studied their woodpiles, weighing their cans of kerosene and butane for camp stoves. Smokers counted their cigarettes, drinkers, what was in their liquor cabinets. There had been annoyance at first, now there was a slow, constant anxiety.

Chris had less trouble than he expected. The kids he talked to were eager for action. They all but fell out the doors of their houses, following him like the kids from Hamelin after the Pied Piper. He went to five more houses. Most of them wouldn't stay, he thought, but that was Mr. Klimek's headache.

They did surprise Klimek, who opened his door to twelve of them, some far too young.

"All I want you to do," he told them, "is to deliver these questionnaires. Later, we'll organize the deliveries the chopper will bring. We want all the questionnaires delivered before noon tomorrow, okay?"

<hr/>

Melody Reimer, president of the Garden Club, mainstay of the town's book club, opened her door to someone's granddaughter who was holding a plastic bag with papers in it. On her jacket she had a nametag with her name written in pencil and under it the word "official."

"You're on my grid," the girl announced, "for when the chopper comes. You're supposed to fill this out and it has a list you can make like what you want the chopper to bring you. I'm supposed to pick it up early tomorrow."

Melody took the pages and stood in the doorway, following the girl's slow progress around the filthy piles of old snow that looked like laundry left in the street. Then, taking the pages with her, she pulled on her boots, grabbed her coat and wool hat, and went quickly down the hill, careful of the ice, to the town hall.

As young people fanned out all over town with the questionnaires and lists to be filled out, the reality of the situation became plainer. Most of the skiers who had been staying in town had disappeared up into the lodges at the ski area where they had been told that food and heat were to be found. The townspeople were no longer eager to provide these and the goodbyes were formal.

It was a chilly, breezy afternoon when the chopper landed. Mayor Dixon had already realized that her plan had been overly optimistic. The questionnaires were nowhere near ready, and it wouldn't be until the next day at the earliest when they could be checked against the council's lists, then collated. Half the town was already at the landing spot, burdening the air with the same questions, frustration and anger in the stomping chill. There was no order. People were rushing and cursing, all but mobbing the chopper.

Dixon fought her way over to where Jay, already near the chopper's door, was trying to maintain order, telling everyone that the pilot wouldn't open it until they quieted down. If they didn't, he might just decide to take off again. Jay blew his police whistle. No one listened. Again and again. The crowd, agitated, moved, foot to foot, and then, slowly, quieted to mutterings. Jay made a way for Dixon to come up to the chopper. The pilot stepped out. He was an older man, fifty perhaps, which both Jay and the mayor found comforting. He stood on the step, a little hunched, but still above the crowd, and spoke loudly so that his words wouldn't be taken by the wind. Jay knew that the man must have done this before. The crowd sensed it too and went still.

"What can you tell us?" Dixon asked.

"The mountain has split and a good part of it has slid down and is blocking access to this town. Its north edge is approximately two miles from Callan and half a mile from the shopping mall. The top of the mountain is untouched and is gauged below 600 feet. The houses above the fall are all still standing and the roads, all of that, but the people up there have been evacuated because we don't know how stable the area is. Anything below that is gone and unrecoverable."

A groan came up at him from the crowd. Many people had walked to where the huge wall of avalanche had pulled half the mountain away, but they had allowed themselves to imagine a fleet of earthmovers clearing the highway into town. Mayor Dixon had been scribbling notes but stopped, stunned by what the possibilities might be. Voices came up from the crowd.

"How much time will rescue take?"

"Where will water come from?"

"People have wells, some of them—will we have the right to use their water?"

An argument broke out between people living on First Street where the houses had wells, and those opposite on Second, where city water had been piped in. Bystanders shouted the arguers down.

"What's the difference? The pumps run electrically and there's no way to get the water up."

More questions—"What about there being a tunnel through the mountain?"

"Never mind about the tunnel," a man yelled. "Where will we get food, water, the medicine we need?"

"What about the water—talk about the water!"

"How much time will it take to get through the fall?"

"When will a new road be made?"

The questions got louder, shriller. People were shouting, some accusing. Who had authority? Someone had to have known about the mountain being dangerous. Shouldn't Pantea, that geologist, have known? Why hadn't warnings been issued, plans made? And mustn't there be a way of getting through? The pilot tried to wait for silence, but after a minute or two, realized that the panic was building on itself. He shouted into his speaker and let the sound act like force against them.

"You asked about a way out—not unless you want to climb the thing," the pilot said. He was speaking into a handheld mic, "—which we don't recommend. It's completely unstable, full of holes and ruins." The amplified sound hit feedback and blared. "The other way, of course, is over Jackass Mountain, which, as you know, is a rated mountain climb." He turned his gaze around at the crowd. "You people look okay—any injuries?"

"No, but all our food, fuel, medicines—it all comes from outside— we're cut off here and for how long?"

"Listen to the pilot!" Edwina Dixon was shouting, her voice strained to breaking.

The pilot took a breath. "No way of knowing. The fall of this mountain is just a part of what's happened. There have been earthquakes and tremors over the area. Geologists are studying it all. Other places are ruined. People are homeless—towns are gone. You're all healthy and in no immediate danger. The civil authority is concentrating on other areas where there's been serious damage, deaths, buildings ready to fall, the threat of disease. Until the relief agencies can get to you with earth-moving equipment, there will be weekly drops of food, medicines, water, and fuel. You did get the questionnaires, and request lists, didn't you?"

"They're being worked on now," the mayor said, "but there's been no time to get them picked up and collated."

"I was supposed to deliver them to the office in Denver, today."

"But we just got them—"

"Hey!" came from two or three voices at the edge of the crowd. "What about us?"

"Who is **us**?"

"We're here on ski vacations. We're stuck up in the lodges, and the people there say they're running out of fuel."

"You'll be taken out by a private service. I can take your requests now. How many of you are there?"

"Wait your turn!" others cried.

"He's talking about us, now."

There were shouts and catcalls and the pilot shouted, and Jay put his whistle to his lips and blew, waited, then shouted.

"If this doesn't stop, this 'copter is out of here," he took a breath, "with all your supplies. Everyone will be heard. Take a minute, cool off." People stilled slowly.

"What I have here," the pilot said, "is an emergency supply of food packets and some heating fuel, pellets, and some medical supplies. The next delivery will include a list of what will and will not be delivered. I may not be your regular pilot. You are on the list for immediate aid. The civilian aid services are stretched to the limit and we're dipping deep into our stored supplies."

Rick Harbison had pushed through the crowd and come up to the chopper. "I'm the city engineer," he said, "and I need to talk about the river. It's winter, now, and a dry year, and the river is all but stopped. When the thaw comes and the snow melts, we'll need to have the fall opened or the town will be flooded. We'll be a lake."

"I'm sure the relief agencies know that," the pilot was showing his impatience, "and they'll get to you in time."

"So how long will it be?"

"I have no idea. The Drops will last as long as they're needed. I'll schedule a special one to pick up the information with your requirements and to let you know what will or will not be supplied."

With that, he left the step and went around to the far side of the chopper and opened a door. People began to press forward. Jay stepped ahead of them quickly and held up a hand.

"Stop right there. We want some order here. Ten people to unload." He counted them off. "Ten to stack. Four piles. We'll take it all to the town hall and distribute it there."

The men selected began to unload boxes wrapped in plastic and marked with a combination of acronym and code. When the boxes had been unloaded, the pilot got in, closed the door, and turned on his engine. People stood staring at the chopper as its rotors turned and its propellers began to move. The people were seeing their only contact to the outside cutting the air as it rose to leave them. The propeller whipped the snow on the ground into a whiteout. By the time the snow had settled on them all, the sound of the chopper was receding into the chill air.

❖

Jay looked out of his window. The streets were empty. From his house, he could see over the vacant lot on the other side of the road, down into town. Inside the houses, lanterns, kerosene lamps, candles, here and there an LED flashlight, were warming in the windows. They would be lighting faces poised over the papers on kitchen or dining room tables. From here, the town looked serene, lofty, almost spiritual. He knew that people were asking one another to imagine their bathrooms. What would we need there? Imagine the medicine cabinet, the toilet, the shower. Imagine the kitchen. Imagine the fridge, the freezer.

Imagine the pantry and the cabinets. What do we need? What do we think we must have, should have? What do we want?

Since his kids had gone, the freezer at Jay and AnneMarie's was only half full. People had begun to empty their dead freezers, burying food during the day and at night spraying the mounds with water that froze and stayed frozen. They made chunks of ice and turned their refrigerators into what their grandmothers and great grandmothers had used. People ate all they could. The Panteas ate a once-frozen birthday cake, all of it, it having thawed before they could get it to the ice. Roman Ansel's venison haunch began to get a grayish look, so Janeen cooked it on the camp stove, and they ate more than they wanted of it and froze the rest. As people hoarded, they now ate, hating to throw all that food away.

Add antacids to the list, and charcoal briquettes and pellets and matches and lighter fuel and camp stove fuel and butane and propane and sterno and kerosene and paraffin candles and all the batteries they will allow us and don't forget dish soap and cleanser and Tampax and Trojans and Depends and panty liners. What have we forgotten? What have we taken for granted?

In the morning, the Klimek kids made rounds of the people who couldn't get out to the town hall to drop off their papers. Chris Pantea's grid was up on the ridge, a colder, harder part of town, once company houses for railroad workers. Over the years, people had remodeled some and repaired others, three and four room cabins that got running water in the '80s with many keeping hand pumps in their front yards.

"They all have wells and they all have woodstoves, but they're all old and can't come down for things," Chris told John Klimek later, when he checked in. "I can't get over how much easier all this would have been online, all this counting and listing."

"Sometimes I got nervous," Klimek said. "Everything being so dependent on one idea. For a while, we'll all have to think, to plan—maybe even to remember."

CHAPTER 6

MELODY REIMER HAD GONE TO THE TOWN HALL AND been told that Mayor Dixon was busy and couldn't see her just then. "Sherry, tell Heronner that Garden Club isn't all I can do. Before I retired out here, I was ops manager for a Caribbean cruise line. I can oversee the lists and organize the Drops. I can do that with the ladies of the Garden Club or with any seven people he assigns to me. Seven will be all I'll need."

Later, she explained her plan to Dixon who listened, surprised. "I was doing that before the computers and it took seven of us. Three hundred people aren't a problem when you're used to doing three thousand on the biggest cruises. Whom would you like to give me?"

To the mayor, the woman came like something in a children's story— the unrecognized, queen in the guise of a godmother. Melody—Ms. Reimer, retiree, widow—was in the category of sweet old thing, hat and gloves, and telling the council each year what the hanging plant decorations would be for the summer festival. She had paid Melody little attention. The events Melody oversaw with the ladies went well, the work behind them silent. A woman underestimating another woman, Edwina thought, and not for the last time. She turned away for a moment so that Melody wouldn't see her embarrassment. This morning a deputation had come to the mayor's office with a request for her to step down for the duration of this time of challenge — challenges, really, and "wouldn't it take a man to exercise the...leadership?" (Brad Unger) and "to project the necessary authority..." (Rick Harbison). Edwina had told them that if they wanted to waste vital time getting the town to hold a recall election, she would certainly follow the dictates of the electorate. They had left.

Melody was drawing boxes on a piece of scratch paper. "Actually," she said, "we can get the grade school children to color in the four shapes and to make enough of those shapes that will tell everyone on which line to go. We match up the shapes and the colors with what the deliveries are. There's where numbers of people will be needed. John Klimek already has a cadre of volunteers; one showed up at my house."

"And you say you can do this?"

"Seven with me here, now, twenty on the field. I'll need to talk to them and make sure they understand what to do. It will be a practice at first—not smooth, but by the second Drop, we should be working well. I think you should use the council to recruit the kids we'll need. By the way, I think you should get some fleet young people to be your runners."

Mike Ansel hadn't been as much affected by the fall as others in town. He had just turned seventeen and was wondering why he had to think about a future beyond an hour ahead. He was spending most of his time up at the ski area where his father was chief engineer. In anticipation of a full season, the area had laid in stocks of food and fuel. The great fireplaces were all in use, people clustering around them with drinks. People even went out skiing and sledding. With the area's generator, Roman Ansel was able to get one of the lifts running. The vacationers who had been staying in town were easily accommodated in the big lodges, having been driven up in the area's vans. While the town was dark at night, the area itself had heat and light. Roman had Mike come up with him. Mike brought Angela Bruno. Every night they drove down to Mike's house to guard it from the looters he feared would soon be at their door.

Angela's mother was home alone, Ray Bruno was away at his orthopedic convention in Denver, and Angela spent most of her time warm and dry up at the area with Mike. Leatrice Bruno knew that Angela was sleeping with him—sleeping? They were at it like rabbits. Mike was nobody you said no to. She had questioned him once and the next day had found a dead rat draped over the steering wheel of her car. With Bruno gone, she knew she had to be very careful. Angela didn't care what people thought. Unfortunately, Gold Flume was an echo chamber. Leatrice handled the gossip by pretending she didn't hear it. She had long since lost all control over Angela's comings and goings. Now, she wanted Angela home with her at night. She was nervous and unsure of how she could function in this new non-electric world. On infrequent visits home, Angela regaled her with news of the life going on up the mountain. The girls there were sophisticated, select, trim, and athletic, and Mike was trolling. In a day or so, though, the choppers would come and take the tourists away and the area would close. Angela would come home. She might bring Mike with her. Mike made Leatrice fearful, but with him there, they would have protection and safety from the outside. They would have someone who could fix things and work the fireplace and the camp stove and the propane torches Ray had used to light barbecues. Leatrice Bruno had always been alert to danger. Fear of danger had hooked her to her husband. With a man around, she wouldn't be distressed at Ray's absence.

There had always been town and ski area, Leatrice had been told. Mayor Dixon had warned Ansel and his staff not to allow any light to show from the lodges up the mountain. With the town dark and the people cold, it wasn't past believing that there might be trouble, even people coming up for fuel and extra food.

By the end of the week, privately commissioned choppers had come and taken all the vacationers and the very rich away. With the area closed, its local workers and management decided to stay up at the lodges as long as there was still fuel and electricity. By the time they were out of either, the road would re-open and communication would be re-established. Ansel locked his house in town and moved his family up to a suite.

The move pleased Mike. He could keep an eye on Angela, who spent more time with him than she did at home. Leatrice Bruno was too self-involved to do more than utter vague protests and she would be silenced by gifts of party food. Mike and Angela went snowmobiling at the area, careful not to go into town but not careful of the sound the engines made. People would be angry at the waste of fuel, Ansel told him. That his father made him stop angered him and he kicked a hole in the wall where they were staying. Everyone's temper was short; Mike saw anger, jealousy, even envy flaring over a word or gesture. He saw people raging as they walked, people weeping on the street out of simple frustrated exhaustion. He watched them open packs of cigarettes with nervous fingers. Supplies of candy and liquor were assessed. His mother counted sleeping pills.

Roman Ansel defended the separation of area and town to anyone who would listen. The people down in town were going crazy, he said. Hoarders were stripping the shelves of what actual stores remained for food and fuel, for cigarettes and booze. The liquor store was bare. "Even the goddamn crème de menthe," he told them. The pumps at the gas station were locked and only Doc Winograd's car, Sheriff Isaacs' patrol vehicle, and Brad Unger's trucks in the firehouse were able to use any of it.

Unless relief came soon, people would go ape. Roving bands would commandeer what they could of food and fuel; theft and murder would be common run. How many guns were down there? Any mobs would have to come halfway up the mountain before the area was in danger, and they would be seen and headed off. There were guns up here, and Snowcats to run down anyone trying to take over. Mike heard his father's warnings and alarms and tuned them out. It might be fun to go with a gang from house to house. The vacationers were gone, so some of the fun was, too, but he and Angela got it on twice a day at every suite in Eagle Lodge, the top of the high-end accommodations at the area. The hot tubs and Jacuzzis still worked, and there were still movies being run with old-fashioned technology.

On the day of the Drop, everyone turned up at the schoolyard. They were relieved to see that lines had been marked out with string and colored cards given—singles, couples, families—one, two, three children, families with other dependents. The items were standard, with no choice within the categories. Boxes were already packed with assorted items in each.

"Don't open packages here." Mayor Dixon's high voice had developed a tremor with the strain. "Wait 'till you get home. Your requests are being delivered to the authorities that supply the rescue items. Be patient, cooperate, and everything will go more smoothly."

The supplies were unloaded, the pilot—without farewell—ducked back into the chopper, signaled his leaving, and motioned the crowd back. He started his engine, rose, and, covering them all with snow, disappeared in a complaint of crows that had been scattered by his rising.

The food rations were distributed quickly. Most people had come in cars and trucks to pick it up. The next Drop would be in seven days, the mayor said, weather permitting.

"Complaints will be heard at the mayor's office," she said. Trucks and cars began to disperse to the homes.

The first complaints came just as she and Jay had finished unloading fuel for the town hall's heaters. Five men and three women, bulky with winter jackets and attitude, stopped them as they hoisted the last of the jerry cans.

"There's no fuel allotment for cars!" That was Considine, big in a down jacket and pants.

"Gasoline isn't on the list," Jay said.

Up in the houses on both sides of the river, people were opening boxes and staring at the food packets, fuel, and water containers.

"I'm running out of my medications," Tess Klimek told AnneMarie. She had come to complain to Jay. AnneMarie told her that Jay was at his office. Tess repeated herself as though to make sure AnneMarie could understand her. She spoke loudly, separating the words. AnneMarie suppressed a curse word and told Tess to go down to see the mayor. "And there are no cigarettes, no fresh milk or butter or fresh eggs."

Down at the town hall, people had begun to gather in protest. "I'm not going to talk to every malcontent in town," Mayor Dixon muttered to Jay. "I'm writing up a response and I'll post it on the door. I have to get home myself to unload."

By late afternoon, the notice had been posted. To the crowd gathered in front of the town hall, Dixon had to make a speech. "No, there's no gas for cars. Where would you be driving anyway? If I were you, I would take your cars home, drain the gas and oil and put them up on blocks until all this is over. You won't get cigarettes or coffee or beer or soda, either. Doctor Winograd's been informed that he won't get any medications for psychological problems unless the person is a diagnosed psychotic, or is a danger to self or others. No sleeping pills and no vitamins or supplements. There will be Tylenol, as you can see on your lists, and for other pain medication, see Dr. Winograd. There will be some sanitary supplies, but no cosmetics. There will be some soap. Ask Dr. Winograd about meds for your specific needs—inhalers, oxygen, etcetera. I've told the agency that we don't have a druggist out here anymore, that the pharmacy moved to the Mall two years ago. That means that Dr. Winograd is the man you see. From now on, each week's Drop will feature a specific thing—water, fuel, food, medications, and miscellaneous."

"There is no water for washing," Siri Unger shouted.

"Most of my medications—it just says <u>rejected</u>." Tess Klimek's voice, among others.

"Where's the line for cigarettes?" Andy McNeil was yelling.

"There's no fresh milk or butter or fresh eggs." That, from the crowd.

"We can't live on this! When will the fall be cleared away? Where's the army or whoever can get through? We need food and fuel. We need electricity. Why don't they drop generators and the fuel to run them!"

Jay and Edwina felt hysteria being raised voice by voice, from what had been the beginning of a grim acceptance.

"Without cars, how do we even pick up our stuff from the Drop?"—a voice from the crowd.

"Water will be delivered by the fire department, starting next Drop. Chief Unger will have fuel for his fire trucks and he will deliver drinking water. While there's snow on the streets and in the fields around here and clean ice on the river, we'll be using snowmelt and river water settled out for washing."

There was a cry from the crowd and individual shouts and curses, louder and louder, protesting.

"Listen!" Edwina shouted. "This is the way it is. I didn't cause the fall and I can't cure it. Go home. You'll get nothing here, because I have nothing to give you but hard facts. The fall is an emergency. We have emergency rations only—nothing extra. What we do with those rations will allow us to survive."

The crowd slowly trickled away after a while, people angry and unbelieving, to face shortages they had never, even in past poverty, conceived of.

In her house, Lowayne LeDoux, eighty, contemplated the contents of the boxes and bags that a hulking, huge-handed boy had delivered to her with an encouraging smile. She had lived so far beyond her own prediction that his words to her, urgent from his mouth, lost their meaning even as she heard them.

"The slip's in the box, and you get the next boxes without asking." Most of what she unloaded she didn't need. What she needed, she had in her root cellar, a hole, really, that she and Charlie had mined under the house years ago. In that hole were her supplies of gin and vodka, enough to keep her in a simple, steady, slow absorption of it for the rest of her life. The binging was long over, gone with Charlie. She ate little and was in clothing she had worn and piled on her slab-like body for decades. She had three layers now and could always add more. She began to unpack what the boy had delivered. There was enough fuel for the Coleman stove that she dragged from room to room. At night there were quilts. There was an outhouse, unused for years that might still be usable for her and her next-door neighbors. She hadn't spoken to them or been spoken to by them for years. They were new people, which was to say, not born in Gold Flume as she had been. It was time to get up and go over and offer the use of that amenity. She sighed. They might not even open the door to her. Perhaps she might go over with a bottle of something. There were enough to make that gift. There were also, in the hole, bottles of popskull, homemade, that Charlie had bought as a joke.

Down at the Drop, Jay was loading his supplies in a wagon, not wanting to flaunt his use of a patrol car except on police business. Soon, everyone would be walking. When he checked back six hours later, AnneMarie hadn't unloaded; the boxes and bags were on the table where he had left them. She had heated water for the powdered coffee and filled the six snow buckets that would yield one bucket of water for washing.

"I put it near the fire," she said. "At first, I put it too close and almost burned the plastic, but I got it in time."

"Honey," he took both her hands over the table, "you won't have your pills."

She looked at him blankly. "What will I do? The doctors say I need them, and I don't see how I can quit."

"We'll keep up the requests and meantime, we'll count them out and ration them and I'll ask Doc what he has—you won't have to stop cold. How many of each kind are left?"

They counted her meds out again, and there were pills left over in three bottles of others they hadn't thrown away when their effect had diminished.

"You've been good to me, Jay," she said. "You've put up with so much."

"I see you trying," he said. "I wish I could help. We're in for some hard days, you and I and the whole town. The Drop won't have beer or cigarettes or candy. We won't have TV and the kids will soon see life without their electronic games and their claims to being so much smarter than we are."

"So, their maturity will come this year instead of twenty years from now, when their own kids pass them by. That's a plus in all this." And they laughed. Jay had the feeling that AnneMarie was arming herself, piece by piece, in the armor she needed for the long war, at which her spirit was overmatched by her body and her brain.

CHAPTER 7

THEY WENT DOWN TO SEE DOC THE NEXT DAY, BUT there were so many people waiting in front of his house that they decided to wait. A man in the crowd—it was Considine—noticed Jay and came over. "I wanted to get to you last night—of course there was no phone..." Jay looked at AnneMarie, who was staring out at the river.

"Honey, could you — "

"I'll be over there," she said, and moved away.

Jay turned to Considine. "I'll be working things out with Brad at home and the fire house and Doc," he said. "Where do you live?"

"Chinaman's Gulch."

"I guess we'll have to work something out, a signal, flares or something. What's up?"

"My brother—he lives up there with us since his wife died—and he's out of cigarettes and coffee—he kinda went nuts last night, in a rage at us. We knew what it was, but the kids were terrified and he was banging around like a madman, breaking dishes and cursing us. We had no idea he was an addict—not to booze, but depending on cigarettes and coffee and now there's no relief for him. I'm on edge, too. I never realized how much TV means to me to calm me down when things get on my nerves. Go look at a show, laugh a little, and I'm okay."

"Do you have enough wood for heat and cooking?"

"What's that got to do—oh, I get it. The south side of the gulch is mostly dry. Of course, the north side is where the trees are, but yes, I could get him to go—both of us to get the wood—wear ourselves out with it. I always planned to build the kids a playhouse, fix the porch, work around the house now that the truck's out of commission."

"Do you guys hunt?"

"I've done some, but I'm not good at it, and now our ammo will be rationed. I know what you're saying — anything to get us up and doing and too tired at the end of the day to care whether we smoke tobacco or pieces of rope." Jay was about to ask why Considine would come to him. They stood silent for a moment and Considine must have picked up on Jay's thought. "I heard that pilot say that there wouldn't be tranquilizers or any of those meds unless the person was outright psychotic. Our part-time loonies won't get anything." He didn't see Jay's wince. They had moved away from the group in front of Doc's house and stood side by side, backs toward the river where there was a light but icy wind moving from it. "I guess I kind of wanted to warn you in case things get worse — I mean if my brother loses it and if we have to call you."

Jay nodded. "I'll see that we can communicate some way — flares, maybe. I'll take it up with Unger and ask whoever is in charge of supplying us what we can do."

Considine nodded and looked at the group still clustered at Winograd's door. "I always thought I was pretty stable — salt of the earth — independent. And my big brother was a model to me, a god when I was a kid." He shrugged, nodded at Jay and moved away.

Jay and AnneMarie started for home, walking slowly up the hill. She was panting with the effort. "This will get easier," he said. "I mean walking places. We'll get healthier, too, all the exercise."

"I won't," she said, "I'll just do less." He didn't argue.

That evening, he came back up the hill from the town hall. It was five o'clock, and already dark and night-silent. The day had been lowering and there was a tang of snow in the air. People would be snowed in, he thought, unless all the neighbors worked together to keep the streets open. They could get by with just the places where people walked but a good deal extra would have to be done to allow for the ambulance and fire trucks. John Klimek, their next-door neighbor, was standing outside his door, waiting as Jay came closer. "I want to show you something. Come around back here."

Old snow, gray and rotted-looking from the last week's fall, mounded the back yard. "Look at my wood pile," Klimek said, and he shined a flashlight on the woodpile. Two cords worth, Jay guessed. "Someone's been stealing wood," Klimek said. He shone the light at the base of the pile. Jay could see that the snow had been roiled by many footprints and boot impressions outside of John's cleared path from his back door. There was a hole in the pile that wouldn't have been made by him.

"It's not an animal living in there," John said. "It's someone stealing wood. I've heard other people talking about it, woodpiles shrinking."

Jay said, "This isn't petty theft anymore, it's our heating. I'm going to tell Edwina about this, and I think we can get her to issue a temporary law making it more than a misdemeanor. Wood is now as valuable as anything people might be stealing." Jay had a quick flash of the three kids in his patrol car, Mike, Chris, and Angela, a week ago but in another dimension.

"I can't let it go on," John said. "I'll rig traps first."

"Be careful. If they hurt someone, even a thief, you'll be liable."

"I won't be taken advantage of." John's voice was hard.

Jay thought, *My neighbor, a mild, modest, kind-hearted history teacher.*

The next day, Jay was down at the town hall with a changed council. Edwina had a sour look. "How many of your requests were denied?"

The council members muttered.

"Some," Jay said, "and I can't figure out what the reasoning was. Yes on some batteries, no on others. No on toilet paper, yes on paper towels, no on Kleenex."

"Before too long," Edwina said, "Pastor Fearing wants that memorial service. Since Our Lady's moved and the Baptists took over that church near the Mall, Gold Flume Community is it, and will be it for worship in town, except if people want to set up other congregations, Fearing says they can use the church when there are no regular services there. He and Considine are asking around and think there might have been as many as eighty people in the fall, many known to people here. He's drawing up lists and he wants to get us to pay attention to their loss and not dwell on our own shortages."

Harbison, the city engineer, shook his head. "It's true about how lucky we are. We've been spared because the fall could have taken all of us and the town, too. What if the mountain had fallen in on its north side? I've had nightmares about that. By the way, are you sure that we are the council, now that Elster and Johns have quit?"

"Right," Edwina said. "It looks like the four of us are what's left and I say we elect Melody to serve until we can vote her in. Let's make it unanimous." They made it unanimous.

"I vote we get Doc in here, too, and Pastor Fearing. Doc is the only one in town who could take charge of public health, and Pastor, the general need. It'll mean getting a fuel ration for him," Jay said, "and they may nix it."

"I'll try," Edwina said.

When Jay came out of the meeting, he saw that there were still some people driving. He supposed they would continue until their cars ran out of gas, but the streets were mostly empty, the cars garaged or covered, up on blocks. When he drove home for lunch, he noticed that the street was full of kids on sleds and he saw them riding tires, and one kid on cardboard cut like a boat down to the level road. They were stopped by the banked snow before the river walk. On the slick, snow-covered street, thinking that at any moment his car might lose its traction, he crept up the road to his house, the car thumping with the snowballs they threw. He had always parked the patrol car at his house in case of a call.

On his way back to do a sweep of the town, he saw Mrs. Bandimere at the bottom of the block, standing outside her house in the freezing afternoon. She was wearing only a tee shirt and jeans and her manner woke anxiety in him. He pulled over to her and got out of the car. She and Mr. must have been having an argument, he thought, seeing rage on her face.

"Something I can do?"

She turned a look of fury on him. "I haven't had a cigarette in two days. I been chewing gum, plastic, leather—I'm goin' nuts. I thought I'd stand out here till I got pneumonia and then I wouldn't want to smoke no more. My nails are gone. I want to kill someone. The kids are in the house and I'm scared I'll hurt them. I knew I wanted to smoke. I didn't know I had to smoke."

Jay's own fight hadn't been a desperate battle and was years back, but he had seen friends go through awful times in withdrawal and he knew what AnneMarie might soon be facing with her drugs. "You won't get pneumonia," he said, "but you will get hypothermic and your judgment will go and your kids might end up orphans. Where's Ed?"

"Out looking for wood. He's in as bad a shape as I am. Sheriff—we're not fit for the kids right now. Can't you get someone to take them?"

"Do you have a babysitter, someone they know?"

"Over on Pine—I..."

"Suppose I drive on over there and see if she can come or if the kids can go over there for a few days?"

On his way back from Pine Street, he saw a man calmly pissing into a snowbank. People were using snow water to flush their toilets and those lucky enough to have old outhouses were using them again. Others were mining holes in frozen earth and making tents serve as protection. When he came back from Pine Street, a man and a woman were standing in front of his house.

"Sheriff—we need to talk to you."

Jay waited. The pair was uncomfortable and he sensed that the discomfort came not from a revelation of something they had done. He knew them by sight but not their names.

"Our neighbors," the woman said, "they're fighting. They've been fighting and we're afraid they're going to—someone's going to be hurt or..."

"It's been bad before," the man said, "yelling, banging. You can hear it all the way to our house, but this—this—there are others there, and it's gone on for—two days, and the night."

"Where do you live?"

"Quarry and Eighth."

"And you walked all the way over here—."

"We've been very upset. We can't sleep."

"Get in the car. I'll take you back."

"You won't say who..."

"No, of course not."

Their name was Radek, husband and wife, early sixties, he thought. The mister was, or had been, the manager of one of the upscale restaurants on Main Street. She worked for a real estate company, she told him. Their house was modest. The Radeks were new; there was no homestead exemption.

The noise could be heard from the corner as Jay edged the car around a snowbank on to Eighth. The road went up with houses, three on each side of the street. The street ended abruptly at the lip of a crater on the upland of the hill, where an abandoned quarry had once yielded fine quartz. Listening, Jay could hear more than two voices—more than three. It sounded like a wild party but with no hint of fun or laughter. He now wished for his deputies. Separated from him by the fall, both were living out of town.

Jay brought the patrol car to a stop in front of the house and got his gun and holster, regulating his breathing as he had learned. He was anxious and could feel all that went along with it, a need to clench down, cold feet and hands, an unpleasant light-headedness, while his heart pumped away. He knocked on the door with his baton. The sound stopped. He knocked again. Someone yelled that the door wasn't locked.

There were two dim kerosene lanterns, barely enough light, but Jay had a flashlight, and moving into the living room, turned it ahead of him and saw what looked like the contents of a liquor store stacked on the floor. There must have been fifty bottles. He knew that the two stores in town had been cleaned out as soon as the reality of the fall had been made plain, but no one had taken all of this. Two women were there, and two men. They had been drinking and fighting for so long that their words were slurred beyond their control and some of the blows they continued to level at each other, men and women, were feet from connecting. One of the women fell and sat leg-splayed against a couch. The air in the place, in spite of the cold, was rank as a burrow. Jay sat down beside her, getting a three-day breath.

"Where did all that good booze come from? Maybe I could buy some off of you."

She grinned. "Ms. LeDoux. Eager to give it to us." And she laughed.

Old Mrs. LeDoux lived up near the big Beausoleil house—the one that had burned down years ago. She was a lifetime alcoholic and apparently a lifetime hoarder. In an hour of sympathy and threat, Jay reconstructed the story of how a couple of these people had learned about Ms. LeDoux and her stash. With no source of their own, and needs no less urgent than hers, two of these sages had raided her home and picked her clean. After getting their prize from the house, the woman told Jay, they were faced with the struggle of loading the bottles. Then they had to struggle with the loaded wagons, finally switching to sleds whose covers kept slipping. They had made their way back here. Once here, they had begun to drink in two-handed earnest. Six were involved—the two who had done the work and the four others who had shares in the stash. The host had let them into this house as a good place to set up. Everything would have gone smoothly except for the drinking, which had started the moment they had finished unloading. Then, fights had broken out over the apportioning of the haul and who had the right to decide. They had portioned the haul again and again, fighting over all their decisions, but too drunk to do much damage. And Ms. LeDoux?

"She was alive when they left her, I heard."

Jay got the housebreaking two handcuffed and into the patrol car. He took them to the lockup at the town hall, registered them, and went back up to the LeDoux house.

There, he found the door open, splintered. The woman was lying asleep in a chair, sprawled as though she had been broken. At first, he thought she was dead, but she began to snore as he stood there, and then her eyes opened to stare at him.

"I've been robbed," she said.

He went home and got AnneMarie, coat over her nightgown and wearing boots, to come back with him. "Just to be there," he said, "and when she wakes up, try to convince her to keep her treasures in a safer place. Every one of those bottles has ramped up in value."

"Two addicts in the moonlight," AnneMarie said. "My pills will soon be gone. I'm already feeling jittery and weird."

Jay and the mayor had been expecting a rise in domestic violence and complaints to the mayor's office. More troublesome was a general surliness and annoyance as the reality of their situation was made clear to the town. Gold Flume had been cut off from its comforts. He thought that people were becoming more and more aware of how dependent they had become for amusement and entertainment from sources far beyond themselves and the Ute Valley. They felt caught out, shown up as unable to provide even their own pleasure.

After a night in the lockup and a day sobering up, Jay let the two go with a strong warning. One more such violation and they would be choppered out to jail — in Aureole. All the stash was returned — minus six or seven.

CHAPTER 8

ON SUNDAY, A WEEK AND A HALF AFTER THE FALL, everyone but the very old and the sick gathered at the church for the memorial service to mourn those lost under the fall's mountain of rock and earth. There was a list of those who might have been victims, and Mayor Dixon read it to the congregation. People cried out now and then as friends were named or families whose children had gone to school with theirs. The church was cold; even though there was fuel, there was no electricity to run the system. Some few people had thought to bring small heaters and camp stoves with them. There was a reek of kerosene and white gas emerging from clothing and skin, an oily smell, mingled with the smell of sweat, and male feet. People didn't want to wash in freezing water.

They sang *Amazing Grace*, of course, now the traditional music for mass deaths. They recited the Twenty-third Psalm responsively, and Pastor Fearing began to speak.

The sermon was no surprise. Fearing, the congregation knew, was a steady man, a good man, but a man with no slightest bit of charisma or eloquence. He looked stronger than he had turned out to be. Six-foot-three, thin, deep-voiced and with a shock of black hair beginning its graying, but with no loss of body. It was longer now, sweeping his collar. He expressed the town's consternation over the fall, the deaths, the loss of power, he said, "Power in every sense, power over the environment, over much of their daily lives, and over their own addictions and demons. These demons, these wishes we think of as needs, these..."

He stopped dead and stood there, with his mouth open to speak, his hands in mid-gesture. He seemed hung in the air the way a building could be before it fell. The choke-up couldn't have lasted for any length of time, but it was long enough to make people nervous, thinking the pastor might be suffering some kind of seizure. Suddenly, he gave a shake and then said quickly, "Let us pray."

To Fearing, his moment of removal had been a moment of sudden, blinding revelation. He had been standing before the congregation in a mood of aridity, almost of boredom. He had all but ordered this service, his attempt to move people to stop thinking about their molehills of frustration and petty annoyance and see the mountain in front of them as a symbol of what their gratitude should be. Their lives had been saved from sure extinction under the Hungry Mother. What if the fall had been a mere few degrees to the north of where it was?

Standing before them, he had begun his carefully worded message. He had no wish to anger them; angry people stop thinking, and he wanted them to take his words with their full, open-hearted attention. He was moving into his prepared plea to them when he seemed suddenly to be enveloped in a great, thrumming river of light that opened his eyes wide and caused his body to disappear from his consciousness of it.

The words he would use to himself later to embody the revelation were cliché. Now, before the people, he saw himself stripped of the protection of body and will as they had been stripped of the protections of modern conveniences. From this place of common weakness they, all of them, might rise to a place undreamed of, a minor Eden, if only they might work to realize this chance being held out before them. Their needs were being taken care of, food and warmth and water. The work they had to do now could be deeper into spiritual life and that would open them to the work of the soul, the very ground of human contact with God. The differences between people, men and women, parents and children, friends and enemies could fade until they disappeared. Then, each person could see into his own heart and into the hearts of his neighbors, no shields of class or race or gender or personality.

The vision faded and left him standing, rooted in the message it had given him. He had signaled the end of the sermon, but he had forgotten the part of the memorial he had most wanted to give, a blessing for the souls of those whom no one knew to count, unknown servants, unknown vacationers. Then, he thought that he would say that blessing later. He would live the message that the revelation had given him. It had come personally, and he would send it forth person by person, bit by bit, in his future sermons, and in the life they lived together day by day.

Parishioners whom he greeted at the church door made no mention of his lapse. People were eating, sleeping, living differently than they had before the fall. Many of them had found themselves holding dead telephones in their hands or had turned on dead TV sets ready for the comfort of favorite shows. More than one had come into an upstairs bedroom and found his wife weeping, the vacuum cleaner trailing its useless cord.

Jay and AnneMarie left the church, noting that there were no groups standing outside to chat and joke as at other Sundays, even those commemorating sad events.

Jay, the occasional Jew, was often at churches in Gold Flume and Callan, for the events of friends or co-workers. He felt he understood the discomfort of these people. They hadn't given the dead their deserved attention, not then, not now. As they left, he noticed how differently they were dressed for this occasion, a century away from what they would have worn a week ago. They had thick padded jackets and hats pulled low over their ears. Pretension had given way to necessity.

As the two stepped carefully over the slabbed upthrusts of decaying snow, Jay put out a hand to help AnneMarie. As he looked up, his eye caught Chris Pantea, walking with his parents. Their glances met. There was a moment where Jay could have put his arm up in salute, continuing the gesture, but he thought of it too late and saw the boy's face register shame. Then, Della Pantea saw what was happening and chirped, "Hi, Sheriff," and Jay nodded a greeting. Her "Hi" was completely reflexive, and she suddenly remembered that her son had been in Jay's patrol car, going to Aureole and the courthouse there.

POSTED BY THE MAYOR:
ANYONE FOUND STEALING WOOD WILL BE
ARRESTED AND FINED. TWO OFFENSES WILL
RESULT IN THE OFFENDER'S NAME BEING
READ OUT IN CHURCH.
PLEASE SAVE THE PLASTIC FROM PACKETS FOR
RECYCLING. DO NOT THROW WRAPPINGS WHERE
THEY WILL BE BLOWN AROUND BY THE WIND.

CHAPTER 9

CHRIS PANTEA HAD BEEN SHARING ANGELA WITH
Mike Ansel since they were all sixteen. Now, at eighteen, he was realizing the problems of the situation. He didn't like either of them very much, but he seemed to need them and in his thoughtful moments, he wondered why. Part of it was TV. On TV, guys had buddies they hung around with, and girlfriends, and they were smarter than their parents, newer, more exciting. The Chris-Mike-Angela trio made a great picture. Angela had a great body and she was okay looking, or could be, under all the crap she slathered on her face. She would also do pretty much whatever he wanted for sex. Sometimes he found himself wondering if either of them satisfied Angela.

They had been bored that day, with themselves and each other, and had gone to the condos near Callan to see who might be there. Sometimes celebrities came. Mike had once helped carry Kip Wingate's sound equipment into the Event Center and been given a ticket, which he had sold for $80. The ski season had begun, but there had been little snow and the place was dead. Chris had forgotten, if he ever knew, whose idea it was to see what was in one of those fancy, upscale getaways.

Most of the units had been locked up and Chris had noticed that they were protected by alarms. The three had spent almost an hour before they'd found one where a window was slightly ajar.

They were frustrated and let down. The place was ordinary, like a motel. The kitchen was stocked with food and had been furnished well enough, but downstairs, the doors to the pool and sauna and gym and spa had all been locked. They'd gone back to the suite and by that time they were hungry. Why they'd decided to trash the place after they had eaten, he didn't know, but it was stupid to trash the computers and a neat little TV in one of the bedrooms, so why not take them? It had seemed fun at the time, a way of getting back at... his mind failed him.

He had seen the man and his dog when they came out with things in their hands, but the sight hadn't registered and they had been genuinely surprised when the next day, Sheriff Isaacs arrested them and told them they were going to Aureole, to be arraigned.

Chris had seen the jumpsuit-wearing, handcuffed men on the TV news or the cop shows. They looked special, examples of the loner-outsider. All eyes were on them, but the experience of being cramped together in back of the police car had been nothing like the perp. walks he had seen. They were in the lockup and then, at home, in shame and silence, then on the way to Aureole, stopped by the mountain fallen on the highway.

Couldn't everyone understand that it had been boredom and meant nothing, what they had done? Anybody with a sponge and some soap could clean things up. The condo had insurance, the window could be fixed, and all the stuff they had taken would be taken back. It wasn't like it was murder or something. When he thought like that, he knew his thoughts were worm-like defenses, wiggling things, slimy and self-justifying.

At the time of the fall, their salvation had seemed like the best joke he could imagine. "I was going to jail but a mountain fell." The thing was, though, that people had died. The town was walled in. On one hand, it was like God saying, "Thou shall not take these kids to jail," but on the other, the whole town was suffering and would suffer, and people had died. Mike and Angela seemed to forget the second part of the thing.

So now, there was no high school, no Callan, no cars, no going anywhere, no TV, no cell phones or tablets. Any power lines brought in would be for urgent things, if that. There were shared baths and buckets of water needed to flush the toilet. The house was dark at six, and they had to be careful with the fuel they used to cook and heat. Mike and Angela had disappeared and he felt lonely and miserable.

He was surprised when Mr. Klimek came to his house with two kids and asked him to go with one of them to hunt up five others. Each would get five to meet at the town hall and work delivering food and fuel to people who couldn't get to the fuel drop that was coming. There were other ways to help, also, and there would be a signup sheet for that.

He'd been afraid, not of going hungry, or simply of being cut off. Gold Flume was now an island with no way out and no way in. He was afraid of being shut up with his dad and mom, and all their disappointed expectations of him. Mr. Klimek changed all that. The mood lightened. There would be something to do and some leeway, and Mr. Klimek was okay. Chris knew him as a teacher only, and it surprised him, ridiculous as that was, to understand that he existed with a fully realized life of his own outside of school. At the meeting, Klimek explained what would happen on the Drop. It had all been organized and everyone's job and location were being explained. Chris was impressed with what had been done while he had been moping. Klimek gave out lists and signup sheets. There would be two volunteers with a wagon, delivering packages of food and supplies to people who couldn't get to the Drop—old people, sick people. The work was necessary, important. Chris was surprised that it seemed no word had been given about the fact that he had been in on robbing and trashing a condo and was technically a criminal. Wouldn't they think he might steal some of that stuff they would be carrying up with them? Klimek was talking about there being a sector for each group.

The girl with him on the Drop list was younger than he was, plain and shy. His initial introductions were uncomfortable. Without the message and the signup sheets and Klimek's instructions, Chris would have gone surly and cold.

"The Drop will be made on the day after tomorrow. It would be smart to go to your sectors and locate your assigned homes before that. Introduce yourselves. Tell your people what will happen. Collect their request sheets and leave a new request sheet for each household." Mr. Klimek said a few more things, cheerleading stuff, and answered the same dumb questions everyone was asking—how long would this last? When would the bulldozers come and free them? How much mountain had fallen? Would there be more?

At home, Chris found his father busy in the garage. He called Chris to come and help. "Back in here someplace is an old lawnmower someone sent me. We take the blades off and fit it up for a wagon. I've also got the creeper I use to get under the car. We can put a frame on that and make something."

He knew his father did repairs, minor repairs on his cars, but had never seen him in this mode and tried not to show he was impressed. His mother had been sobbing and moaning ever since the fall at the prospect of hand-washing all their clothes and using the woodstove and fireplace to do their major cooking.

They found the lawnmower behind stacked cartons of geological field supplies. The mower was all but locked up with age and old oil. It had come from a time long gone when Ron and Della had first moved to Gold Flume and before they had learned the hard way that there wasn't enough rainfall to nurture grass, and certainly no lawns.

"Dad, how can half a mountain fall?"

His father looked at him in genuine surprise. Years before, when Chris was little and could barely say the words that geologists use to describe the shifts and heaves of mountains and the architecture of the earth, they had had such discussions. Chris had grown away from it all when his friends had taken over his interests and outlook. It had been years since they had talked geology. His father drew breath to begin to speak of the complexity of the fall, then, thought again and spoke simply. He told Chris that the land had been laid down in layers, and then up-thrust, creating these mountains. The layers had been separated, probably by water, over millennia and had slid apart.

"Get a five-layer cake with icing between the layers and put it on an inclined plane. Pressure may fuse the layers or cause them to fracture. Differences in the nature of the layers may cause breaks, fractures, the fall.... It may take time before one or two of the top layers begin to slide, but at a certain point they will slide, lubricated by the water, or simply overcoming inertia from something a mile away—say the movement of another mountain, a cave-in deep inside, maybe."

"And mining?" Chris was remembering when the new houses had gone up, on the Hungry Mother, huge ones for two billionaires. He had always wanted to go up there and see them. Now, they might be gone, torn away and broken apart.

"Probably," his father said. "We've been studying it all."

"Are you sorry we live here in town, and not in Callan or Bluebank so we'd be outside, free?" Chris and his friends had been talking dreamily of making a hot air balloon and flying away.

"I guess I hadn't thought about it. There's no doubt it's going to be tough—a year, maybe more, but our situation isn't unique. From what I hear, the people outside are suffering, too. We've learned that many earth changes aren't slow at all. We used to think the dance was a pavane. Now we see that sometimes it's hip-hop. This was once an inland sea."

"I know. You told me."

"I'm repeating myself—a sign of age. Have you started your trips to the people on the ridge, yet? There's some interesting geology up there."

"I'm going now, Megan and me."

"Megan and I."

The people on the ridge were people Chris had heard about, but didn't know, and it surprised him that in so small a town, a town that he had cursed as having no secrets, nothing more to learn, there were still strangers.

He and Megan climbed the hill on its south side, and from where they stood they could see across the river to Jackass Mountain, on the rich people's side, and see its huge-windowed houses glaring back at them in the morning light. The people in them had gone, choppered out and away. His father expressed relief. Here the land rose up dry and rocky, keeping its snows later, but too eroded to hold the water when they melted.

Megan was sniffling beside him. She was small and skinny and half running to keep up in the sudden slabs and holes where old snows had been covered by new ones. She was one of those girls who were invisible in high school, shadow-people, forgotten before being noticed.

Out here the view was one Chris had never seen before—the river, curving slightly in a way he had never thought it did, always seeming to come straight through town, only curving later at Whiskey Gulch. Looking down, he saw the town's main streets and features seeming much closer than at any other place in town. Gold Flume looked snug and neat with new smoke drifting from the houses.

Beside him, Megan said, "It looks like a Christmas card."

He nodded, surprised.

There were five houses on this road — track, really, their structures all the same. They had been company-built when the railroad had a depot in Gold Flume over a hundred years ago, and a roundhouse where the school was now, and where the Drop would come. The houses had been simple, small, one-and-a-half stories, the bedrooms laid out under peaked roofs so that standing up in them had to be done carefully. Over the years, they had been remodeled and adapted to other needs. Two had porches, but all had weathered, repair over repair, shingled roofs of varying colors and sizes, chimneys in the middle.

They both took a breath, and Chris said, "Let's go."

He noticed her clothing, then, two hats, a layered mélange against the cold. They all wore sweaters sticking out from under other sweaters, ends of scarves. Megan was so small she looked like one of those little kids in snow suits, cruciform with the pile of clothing they wore.

Frame, Moritz, Denton, Sher. The other houses were derelict. Chris and Megan plowed through the unshoveled snow to the first house. After some time they heard sounds and the door was opened and they were asked what they wanted by the woman they identified as Mrs. Frame. They saw her as infinitely old and fragile, humped and diminished. They explained their mission and here were the lists and the questionnaire to be filled out, and did she have any questions now? She seemed too puzzled to be able to form any. Was she out of food or fuel? Would she need emergency supplies to tide her over? No.

"We didn't have no electricity up here until nineteen and fifty-nine," the woman told them through random teeth. "We did all right before then."

Chris explained that he and Megan would be bringing up the things they needed and that they were here simply to introduce themselves. Chris wasn't sure she understood. Mrs. Frame looked at them carefully, quietly, as one would look at an alien from outer space. She said the neighbors would help. She told them what she wanted, and they wrote it down.

The Moritzes wanted to talk. They wanted to ask about the fall, about the Drop, just to talk, to tell about a fall that had happened in 1967, and an avalanche after that, a big avalanche that took a slab of The Hungry Mother. Their house smelled of age and forgotten chores and human chemistry. Mrs. Moritz had answered their knock and had led them back through beetling aisles of papers, magazines, boxes of string and rope, boxes of canning jars, bags of empty pickle bottles, mayonnaise jars, and wine bottles. In the back bedroom, they sat on chairs they had to clear of cartons of old clothes. Chris listened to the old man's stertorous breathing. He was in the rumpled bed. Mrs. Moritz told Chris and Megan that an agency had been sending caregivers from Aureole, but days had passed.

"We saw what happened. You get a good view from our door, of how the front of the mountain sheared right off. That morning after the storm, we went out and saw how the mountain fell. You'll see it when you go. Just like town's in a cup, mountains, all around. No way to get anyone from outside to help us."

"From the sky," Chris said, "from up. There'll be food and fuel and medicines."

Mrs. Moritz had found ways to help her husband move and to keep him relatively clean, she told them, but supplies were running out. Chris and Megan left the questionnaires. The Moritzes wanted them to stay, offering them cookies and tea, which they had to refuse politely again and again.

The Dentons were frightened and seemed to think the rations the kids would deliver were all that there were to be. Chris referred to the questionnaires. They would pick them up next day. Mr. Denton said yes, yes, but Chris had the idea that the couple didn't believe them.

"That house, there – the Shers?"

"Lynn Sher – she went to visit her grandkids in Tucson. I hope she gets along with them."

Klimek praised them when they reported with the needs of the people on the ridge. "It would be good if you went back steadily – being the ones delivering supplies. Can I put you down for that?"

"Sure," Chris said. Megan looked pinched but finally agreed. She was beginning to like Chris.

"I'll talk to Pastor and see if we can't get some people up there to look after them. You'll be delivering, that's all, unless you'd want to take on more." He saw their expressions. "It's all right. You won't have to adopt them."

On Chris' way home, he saw Mike and Angela on the other side of the street. When they spotted him they spoke to each other, came to some decision and kept on walking. Chris did the same.

Things at home had been difficult. His parents' disapproval over the vandalism charge hadn't been fire, but ice. They didn't mention the crime at all, as though what he had done was too shameful for speech.

He felt a warmth that had been in his father's eyes, die. They spoke, evenly enough, but in a general way, working at it. Since the fall, though, there were too many things to do for the topic to be at the front of their attention. Part of the reason he had volunteered was to get away from the shame he felt surrounding him at home. When his mother asked him about his volunteering, he shrugged. He had pledged secretly to help her as much as he could, stamping out the wash in their bathtub, knowing that they would have sung before, or joked. His throat ached with the loss. His sister and brother, who might have helped, were away at college.

"I was down at the river, today," Ron Pantea said, stirring the contents of a can of soup, "with Ms. Dixon, Harbison, and Ansel." The name of Mike's father made Chris look up. "We're looking at a potential disaster there."

There was a noise at the back door. Ron went to open it for his wife, who had a basket she had found in the garage. She had been hanging clothes in the icy back yard, where Chris had set up a line. The polish was gone from her nails, two of which were broken, Chris noticed. Her hands looked red.

"What's up?" she said.

"It's hard mid-winter, now," his dad said, "and the river is frozen, but the fall has walled it off. It has no way through. When the ice melts, the town will be flooded. We're working on a plan."

"For the three of you to do? For some men?" Chris wondered why he hadn't realized so obvious a thing.

"For the whole town to do, and soon."

76

POSTED BY THE MAYOR: PLEASE PARK CARS AND OTHER VEHICLES OFF THE STREETS. USE GARAGES OR DRIVEWAYS. SKIING MUST BE LIMITED TO THE CENTERS OF STREETS. PEDESTRIANS **ALWAYS** HAVE THE RIGHT-OF-WAY.

CHAPTER 10

PEOPLE HAD COME TO THE FIRST DROP IN TRUCKS or cars that still had gas in their tanks. On the unplowed streets the vehicles were no longer practical and there had been accidents and tires grinding away uselessly on the ice. The Council had ruled the cars out until further notice. People began to show up for the Drop with wagons, shopping carts from the gourmet food store, and all kinds of wheeled contraptions created from bicycles, snow blowers, motorcycles, creepers, vacuum cleaners. At the first Drop, the group Melody Reimer had organized had stood at the head of five lines holding up cards, alphabetized, with five letters to a group. This time, they went to their lines automatically. When the chopper had been unloaded, Mayor Dixon came forward with the sheaf of requests.

The pilot waved her away. "You people are not on schedule two or three—you are on schedule one. That's just the basics, food packets, fuel, water, some medicine, no frills, no extras, no requests."

"But we were given these questionnaires, asked to add—"

"That was a mistake," the pilot said. "Sorry, no extras. You people are small potatoes to what's going on in California and Maine and in bigger mountain towns than this one. Be grateful for what you get." He shook his head at the box of request forms that had been collected and sorted. People shielded their eyes from his rising and he was gone in moments.

The distributions began. Things went fairly well as everyone saw the logic of the numbers and colors on the cards they had been given. This day was cold and people stamped and slapped their sides and realized that talking helped. They hadn't seen what had taken place between Mayor Dixon and the pilot. They began to chat up and back through their lines. The distribution took two hours, and by that time, the snow was packed solid, making an easy way for the loaded carts.

Someone had come up with a name for Mr. Klimek's teenage group delivering supplies from the Drop. The kids used the name and thought up a logo and made badges. They were The Wheeler Dealers. They would have priority on use of the wagons. According to color-coded cutouts exchanged for the needed items, they went through the piles of food packets, fuel cans, and extra supplies quickly and efficiently. The organization gave a feeling of order. There was no shoving. Everyone had examples from dozens of TV news reports in the past showing crowds of starving people thronging a relief drop, fighting for scant, limited supplies, shoving bags and cans at workers who poured out the rations frantically, in the overwhelming forest of arms and hands.

The second Drop was completed this day in bright sunlight, a blue-sky morning whose stillness echoed the calls of crows. Chris had gone out to the fall with his father and seen, high above them, crows massing and disappearing over the new hill's rise. He had shivered at what carrion the birds might have found on its far side.

There were rations of gas for the fire trucks, the sheriff's car, and Doc Winograd's old Buick. There were gallon plastic bottles of drinking water and a greater supply of water that the fire trucks would deliver house to house.

Chris and Megan had a wagon made by Ron Pantea, using the wheels from the lawn mower and one of the family's bicycles. It was ingeniously made, with a deep bed. They had tried it out in the back yard, where Chris had slid around in the soft snow. Ron had had to bite back a caustic comment at his son's gracelessness. Chris seemed unformed to him, without any special focus or purpose. He was a well-made boy, but uncoordinated, especially in adolescence. Edges bit him; he sometimes looked as though he had been in a fight. To Chris, his father had seemed lofty, removed from ordinary life. Now, they were both looking again, and sharing worry about Della and the work she had to do with no equipment to help her. The house was dirty, she, exhausted.

The wagon had been finished, but there hadn't been a convenient way to pull it. "I wish I had some welding equipment," Ron had said. "We could get a pipe and handle—"

Chris' mother had been watching their exertions from the back porch. She had gone down to them, smiled at them, and said, "Rope."

"Do we have any that thick?"

"Not thick or strong enough to pull a loaded wagon, I mean, I'd get some clothesline and bind it with strips of rag, or even braid it, and then bind the whole thing like bandaging a limb. The whole thing should be about as thick as a thumb and very strong. I'll make it long enough for a knot at one end and a handle at the other."

They stared at her. This was a woman they hadn't seen before.

After fiddling and adjustments, they had knots, two at each side of the front of the wagon and two in the middle, bound, easing the pull. It balanced well. Chris and Megan wheeled it smoothly over the melting snow up the hill from the Drop site. Now and then, they turned, looking back down the hill to where they could see people moving away from the

Drop to their houses with their rations. Some had rigged pack-frames with ropes and were carrying the bags and canisters on their backs.

Megan was sniffling with an allergy of some kind, but even without her ailment, she seemed wilted to Chris—little body, little voice that fell off at the end of her sentences. If only Angela, the lovely, vibrant, exciting Angela would be walking up this road with him. He knew that she had no interest in helping anyone but herself. She would give him sex for food or favors, and when he thought that there was a name for such a woman, he told himself that those women demanded the favors first. Angela accepted the idea of future advantage. He hadn't had sex with her since the fall and he missed it.

There were two bags of compressed wood for burning, heating and cooking, cans of kerosene, packets of freeze-dried food, some medicines and sundries. The day was cold and breezy, Megan moaning with the loss of the music which had always accompanied her on her device like a secret fanfare.

Mrs. Frame seemed not to remember their having been there before. They left a standard set of rations. The Dentons kept asking if the two would return. Yes and yes. No one wanted a repetition of the scandal that had happened in 1994, Mr. Denton said, when the Poindexters, in that house up the draw, had died in their bedroom and weren't discovered for two months. They asked about the paper they had filled out about requests—pipe tobacco and bag balm, a liniment he used, mouthwash, toothpaste. Chris had to tell them that no requests would be considered for the present. Later, perhaps — The Drop did supply baking soda. Chris unloaded while Megan held the cart. Where Mrs. Frame was bone-thin, Mrs. Denton was mounded, and it occurred to Chris that old people seemed either to blow up or dry up.

"Are you sure we can't get what was on our list?"

"Not now—not yet," he said, "but food and fuel and drinking water and medicine—" He didn't tell her that the news of no more than that was causing fear and anger in town.

"Could I make you some tea?" She seemed to surprise herself with the offer. "Could you eat a little cake?"

Chris explained that they had another delivery to make at the Moritzes and then they had to get back to town and report to Mr. Klimek. Mrs. Denton stared at the packets in incomprehension. "I thought it would be cans of beans, like they did before. I thought maybe a bag or two of onions or potatoes. Kerosene—we can always use that, but this here food—I don't know if we could eat that ..." Megan explained how they should follow the directions on the package.

"Could you read letters that small? I sure can't."

Megan read the instructions. "Reconstitute...."

Mrs. Denton murmured, "Reconstitute...."

Megan read the instructions again, going slowly and watching for signs of incomprehension. Herb Denton came out from the bedroom again in a coat over long underwear and sat for a while, doomed to ending his day without tobacco. He clenched a cold pipe in his teeth.

After they had unloaded, the Moritzes sat them down. The couple sighed over the rejected items on their list but said that the fire truck had been up with water, which they hadn't needed, being the posses-sors of a good artesian well. It was wood they needed, and fuel for a heater. Chris assured them that fuel and food would continue. Leaving after the delivery was difficult. The couple was achingly eager to tell, to hear, to give, to take, to pass on such wisdom as they had before it soured in them or spilled away. They wanted to tell how it was to grow old here, other avalanches, strange sights, funny, sad losses, revelations. Martin Moritz spoke of sons dead in wars, daughters gone, hating these mountains, of old neighbors: "Ensor"—his voice carrying all the scorn it could hold, "mean old bastard. He'd shoot you, but he got too old to aim a gun. He shot his wife, you know. She almost got better, but died anyway."

Mrs. Moritz said, "I always wondered about that."

Megan rounded on Chris as they walked down the hill. "Why did you keep egging them on?"

Chris shrugged. He had liked hearing them talk. "I'll come up here and check on them in a couple of days, and see how they are. I think I'll go and clear the snow out to their privy—and the snow between their houses..."

That evening, Chris sat at home with his parents, a thing he would never have done before the fall. They ate in the kerosene lamp's mellow glow, kept low to save on fuel. Della had worked hard to make the packet freeze-dried food appetizing. She had heard women talk about the sometimes fortunate combinations they might get to improve on the meals in the packets they were getting. They cut the reconstituted dinners, freeze-dried, with cans of things they still had.

"How are those classes coming?" his father asked. "The ones Mr. Klimek is holding?"

"Okay. We have only three teachers here for the whole thing. Mr. and Mrs. Klimek do the science for all the classes and Mrs. Schindler does math for everyone, and Mrs. Unger does English. They go from the younger kids to the middle and then up to us, and they rotate the hours. Mr. Klimek set the whole thing up. We read a lot. There aren't many textbooks so we use the library a lot. Something I never knew—or at least, never thought about—"

"What's that?"

"Well, in reading, uh... different styles of saying a thing—like in music—you listen to one group and it has one style, and another group a different one. Some you like more than others—the songs may be sort of the same, but the style is different. Our history and English textbooks, the style is all the same, but now I'm getting things from different points of view. They have the book that Darwin wrote, the one on the Beagle— Mr. Klimek has that one. You get to see him finding those animals and getting his ideas. We're reading—well, acting out, *Romeo and Juliet*."

"Angela's Juliet, I guess," Della said.

"She didn't want to. Actually, Megan is Juliet. You know how quiet she is—well, maybe you don't, but she hardly talks at all and when she does, it's tiny, in a little toy voice. When she reads Juliet, though, the whole thing changes. She really gets into it. Mr. Klimek says that she should go to acting school. He says we should put the play on for the town, later on."

"Who is Romeo?"

"Mark Harbison."

"And you?"

"Tybalt."

"I would have thought you'd make a good Romeo," Della said.

"Mr. Klimek says I read like I'm asleep."

"Did I tell you?" Ron said. "I talked to Pete Shively. Council has set up a system of ringing the bell at the firehouse. First ring is for the fire department, and second is for the fire department and Doc Winograd. Third ring is for everyone to meet in front of town hall. Doc, Brad Unger, the Sheriff, and Ms. Dixon have battery operated walkie-talkies. We're setting up systems that will help us get through this. Gold Flume is going to get through this."

"Have you heard about plans to get rid of Edwina?" Della was clearing the table.

"Sure," Ron said. "Considine talks about it all the time. Ansel wants a recall election. The thing's ridiculous. The office is about organization, not muscle. Considine stopped thinking in high school. Ansel thinks women are purely ornamental."

"Do I look ornamental to you?" and Della held up her chapped hands.

"Ornamental, no. Vital, yes."

Chris waited half an hour after the temporary school let out the next day, before starting up the ridge. He wanted to wait until the kids had dispersed and gone home. He was unable to explain this to himself, because whose business was it, anyway? But he didn't want to be seen as doing more than he had been assigned. Why not? Would they think he was a suck-up or waiting for a reward from those old people? Or—the thought hit him and made his face burn—rob them? He had helped Mike rob the condo. Nothing had been returned there because it was on the other side of the fall—if it hadn't been swallowed up in the fall. He had thought to take a shovel up to the ridge, which he would have to find an excuse to be carrying, even though he realized that everyone up there must have one. Old as those people were— He'd seen a shotgun at the Dentons' door. He didn't want to use their equipment. He shouldered his own, not a snow shovel, but a barn shovel, almost new.

He walked up Miner Street, through an alley and back over to the weed-grown depot and so, across and up to the ridge without being seen, he thought. Most of the two recent snows had evaporated, which snow did at this altitude in the arid inter-mountain climate, especially now, with the river stopped and frozen. He saw the brown layer of dirt that had been laid down by the fall. Someone at a meeting of the Wheeler Dealers had remarked that the dirt blown over Gold Flume must carry molecules of the dead—people killed in the fall. The thought had made the girls squeal and the boys laugh with embarrassment and Mr. Klimek had said that was unlikely. Still, the idea remained and people gathering snow for melt water were careful not to reach down to that layer.

Up on the ridge, he saw the Frame house was abandoned—no tracks, the snow lying as neatly as over a grave. He went up to it. The house was empty—he sensed that it had been left. Mrs. Frame might have moved in to stay with the Moritzes or the Dentons. At the Dentons he began to open a way to their privy. As he worked, he murmured songs to himself. Like Megan, he had been used to having music backing what he did. After digging a way between the Dentons' house and privy, he went from the Dentons' back to the Moritz's and cleared the way to their woodpile and privy. The Moritzes wouldn't let him go without some of the powdered coffee from the Drop, fixed up with evaporated milk Mrs. Moritz had in her cupboard and some cognac Mr. Moritz had in his root cellar, newly uncovered. The job had taken him two hours.

The Moritzes had come from East Germany just as Russia was closing its fist on it, bride and groom. He had worked at the molybdenum refinery and then had retired here, living on savings in the very careful old age of a life of heroism and change.

By the time Chris made his way home in star-darkness, it was time for dinner. Reluctantly he told his parents where he had been.

"Before you started going up there, I didn't know there were people still living in those houses," Ron Pantea said. "With land around here going for what it is these days, they could sell their pieces for a small fortune."

"They're too old to move," his mother said, "unless it would be to a nursing home or in with kids."

"Did Mr. Klimek assign you to go between Drops?"

Chris felt an obscure discomfort at the question, an anxiety he couldn't identify. He didn't want to lie and he didn't want to reveal his feelings. He sought a middle way. "We have to make the deliveries up there. Megan's this toy girl. Some of those drifts are bigger than she is, and we have trouble with the wagon. I just cleared some stuff so we can get in there and Mrs. Moritz thought she had to give me something to eat." His manner suggested a faint impatience. Nothing more was said about it.

Why couldn't he have said he was happy with what he had done, interested in the Moritzes and the Dentons, wanting to hear their stories, imagining their lives, years long, their changes, the world's changes around them? Kids his age were supposed to be interested only in other kids—tribal, insular. If he told his mother, she would blab it all over town—how fine he was, what a good soul he had. He couldn't let that happen. He would have to add the secret to the others he had collected over the years.

On Drop days, people living on the east side of the Ute passed the town hall on their way home. Next to the fluttering notes posted on the board at the bottom of the town hall steps, someone had added silly verses and headed them 'The Fall Fantom.'

POSTING FROM THE FALL FANTOM

Freeze-dried food for freeze-dried folks,
Freeze-dried water, freeze-dried jokes.
Everybody's life's now open—
Who does drinkin' who does dopin'.
Secret passions large and small—
Nothing's hid, we know it all.

POSTED BY THE MAYOR:

WILL DOG-WALKING OWNERS PLEASE PICK UP THEIR
DOGS' SOLID DROPPINGS? CAT LITTER HAS BEEN
REJECTED BY THE DROP. USE WOOD SHAVINGS OR
PINE NEEDLES.

People began to wait for the poet to give his identity away. People said
it was a kid. Some women were sure it was someone on a Drop delivery
list. The gossip settled on one person, then another. It must be someone
older than a kid.

FROM THE FALL FANTOM
Using this week's mystery meat
To line my shoes and warm my feet;
The coffee powder tastes like gall
But strips the paper off the wall.

CHAPTER 11

ANNEMARIE WAS HANGING WASH IN THE BACK YARD on lines Jay had strung for her. The two of them had used the bathtub, dancing the sheets and underwear, not caring about whether the things were colorfast, nylon, cotton or polyester. The house was old. None of the newer houses had space outside in which to grow vegetables, keep a sheep or goat or a coop of chickens. Zoning laws had taken all of that away. AnneMarie's father had told her about the Morning Concert — at least a dozen roosters and five or six jackasses calling, each in his native language, reveille, all those years ago.

She thought about the endurance of those people—the pneumonia years—just go up on the little rise that began Croom Mountain on the other side of the river where the cemetery is and see all those children. There were waves of them from the pneumonia years, the polio years, the flu years, the measles years—how awful it must have been to wash the burial clothes for all those children, grieving as the clothes were readied.

It came to her that she hadn't thought of anyone else's pain in a long time. Her eye went up from the pile of wrung out sheets in her basket. Jay's uniform couldn't be ironed. She remembered her mother telling her about sad irons, the ones heated on the stove or filled with red embers.

She thought of the Drop, the one yesterday. There was enough room at the side of the house to give her a good view of what went on down the hill. As she had gotten ready to go herself, she had seen a parade of makeshift vehicles, two with platforms set on rollers, two-wheeled carts, an old baby carriage, stripped of its hood, shopping carts with built up sides, skateboards held together and built up to carry loads. The sight made her smile, and she marveled at how creative people could be when the need was there. Her own symptoms were shifting. The feeling she had had, of things crawling under her skin, seemed not to be so constant. The psychiatrist had said that was part of her illness, for which she had already been given three different diagnoses, but she realized that the awful feeling had been an effect of the medication—or the combination of medications. She was more groggy in the mornings and sleepless at night, but the odorous sweat she had exuded was diminishing, and also an indefinable sense of selfness had begun at odd times, now and then, but present, wavering before her. She had been forced to ration her pills, tapering them down, skipping days. Sometimes her fingers and hands shook. She had headaches. She felt sudden rages, blown up and blown away, but not before a moan or a string of curses broke out of her like an eruption, something foul that had been buried deep in her. Rage and fear came and went.

She was aware of her cold fingers—you couldn't hang wash wearing gloves, and she knew the sheets would freeze the minute they were hung. When the sheets and towels thawed and dried, they would be softer than they had been without the freezing, and they would smell of sun and wind.

She missed fresh food. The freeze-dried stuff was carefully measured in its packets with listings of all its many nutrients, and it tasted reasonably good, but reconstituting wasn't cooking. *When this is over*, she thought, *I'll get back to the recipes I made in the years before the cloud came down.*

Later that week, a group of men and boys went up the mountain behind the town to get wood. They had chainsaws and took the dead trees from ten acres or so and rolled them down the hill, then pulled them into town. The plan was to pile the wood in front of the town hall and let anyone who needed it come and take some. The local trees were all conifer, quick burning softwood. There were some aspen, too, no better than the pine and spruce. Jay had laid in a good supply of wood before the fall, but they were burning almost every day now, and their pile was shrinking.

Standing in the cold of the short January day, AnneMarie took in a long breath full of the wood smoke of fires burning in neighbors' hearths. Some people cooked with kerosene indoors, which was dangerous, and the mayor had posted a warning against leaving candles unattended in rooms for convenience. Doc had treated people for burns and some children for severe burns from stoves and heaters. The fire department had dealt with a dozen or so kitchen and chimney fires. They would all have to re-learn the care to be taken with fire. She said aloud what Jay had told her, "We will adjust. We will all adjust. We might even get some fun out of it. People have lived this way for longer than they lived the lives we had last year, and now, teenagers won't be dying in auto wrecks or from overdoses."

What about the other addicts, though—tobacco? Alcohol? She herself was in the throes of some kind of habituation. Her dullness had been joined by those rages, and now and then by hallucinations that she had hidden from Jay, struggling to make rational the sight of cobras wound around the legs of the bed and table, knives in the air, fingers aflame like candles. There were night sweats—he knew about those, of course, damp sheets in the chill of the morning, chills, a limpness and apathy that she forced away with everything she had. Her trying, straining to look sane, was, above all, exhausting, draining and defeating. Terrors assailed her, rooted her in her tracks, and she clenched her teeth and cried aloud, "Endure!"

And she was enduring, and after it had its moments with her, the terror pulled slowly away before her eyes, leaving her limp. Endure.

She thought this endurance was less isolating, now that others shared some of its edges. Part of her depression had been the loneliness of a person adrift and rootless in a penumbra of half-light while a world she saw but couldn't enter spoke of light and pleasure, of work that had worth and lives that had meaning. The people from that life had gestured to her: join us; all you have to do is... and the answer: take this drug, do this exercise, drink this supplement, pray this prayer. It seemed to her that while the earthquake was turning her room in a crazy sway and dishes and furniture were ricocheting off the four walls, people were telling her that her hair was a mess and her outfit unflattering. "If only you would...."

Now, women were talking about saving soap. The Drop included it and detergent, also, but those items were, in some sense, rationed. They were all facing a harder world, a world a little closer to the one she still lived in, but one she could reach out from if she only had the energy.

She crossed the yard with the empty wash basket she had adapted from a wicker magazine caddy. Of course, the house was cold. These weeks had made her accustomed to wearing long underwear and sweaters, a hat, and often gloves, inside. The camp stove was meant to be used outside—there were warnings about that all over it, but Jay had decided to leave it turned low and it gave just enough heat to make the kitchen bearable. They had to be careful of the firewood. The Drop delivered pellets—a 'product' like wood but which burned slower and hotter than the local conifers. Many people went foraging for dead wood up Kinchloe Hill. They used the branches of trees downed by snow load or wind. Against advice, they burned paper and cardboard and old furniture and scrap wood from past projects. The town streets and roads were neater than they had been in years.

Jay came home late from yet another meeting of the council. She heard him clumping up the steps and on to the porch, pausing for a moment before he opened the door. She knew that in these later years, the pause had been to nerve himself to face what she had become. Endure. That he hadn't left her still amazed her.

Over a reconstituted meal, he told her what Harbison, the town engineer, had reported "concerning," he said, "the diversion of the Ute around the fall." There would have to be blasting of part of Croom and Cascom mountains to allow for the channel redirecting the river. The work had to be first priority so as not to flood the town when the thaw came, and all the run-off from the mountains.

People wondered if there would be blasting material delivered in the Drop. Was there anyone in town with the skills to do a job like that, and where would they get the heavy equipment—the backhoes and dump trucks—to carry the material away? The army moved equipment like that in huge copters. Would those be available?

There were two Drops and more complaints. Why couldn't they include more? There was sunscreen but no toilet paper. There was Clorox but no ammonia. There were batteries for Jay's car radio and his hand-held but none for general use. He had deputized Bud Considine and Rick Harbison. Mayor Dixon had hired six high school kids as runners, delivering messages, two for Jay. One showed up, breathless, at

11:30 at night, pounding on the front door until Jay opened the upstairs window and shouted for her to stop.

"Sheriff, neighbors of Ms. LeDoux ran over to my house. There was a break-in. They said four or five people were there."

AnneMarie could hear the girl's voice from the front door. She shook awake. Jay was going for his clothes. In a long box under the dresser were socks and boots, underwear, pants, shirt, and jacket. The gun-belt and badge he kept ready on the dresser. Car keys, kept ready, were swept into his pocket. His coat and hat were on hooks by the door. He was gone for the rest of the night.

He came home in time for breakfast. "Just a couple of eggs and a piece of toast," he said, joking. She opened a packet. He was pulling off his coat in a way that showed how tired he was. "I'll get an hour or two on the couch and then get back to work."

"What happened?"

"Four idiots broke into Ms. LeDoux's again, thinking that she must still have booze. They ransacked the place."

"Was she hurt?"

"I told her to put that stuff in the vault at the bank. I guess she couldn't stand not to have it with her."

"I remember people talking about them years ago— the LeDoux couple, Charlie and Lowayne, that they were both alcoholics."

"God—how they had stocked up! The woman had cases of the stuff— enough to keep her quietly blotto for the rest of her life."

"Isn't this the second time she's been through this?"

"I'm going back over there tomorrow and get her to move that booze."

"What did you do with the thieves?"

"Took them to the lockup."

"What happened to Mrs. LeDoux?"

"I went back there and got her out of the room where they had locked her. She was in a screaming rage."

"They must have been teenagers, kids."

"No, men. Addicts, I guess. There's a need."

"What will happen?"

"Mrs. LeDoux will file a complaint, I imagine. I'll keep them in the lockup for a few days. You'll have to feed them. I'll file a report, and when we get opened up, they'll have to answer the charge."

"So you'll let them go..."

"Looks like it."

"But—"

"Reporting would mean getting the State Patrol's chopper to come and pull them out of here. They'd be held pending investigation or let out on bail while I filled out all kinds of communication about the special circumstances surrounding why neither Ms. LeDoux nor I could be present. The State Patrol doesn't run a taxi service. Once out, they wouldn't be able to get back. I don't think any of them could charter a helicopter to get them back here."

"Are people stealing more?"

"They're stealing different things. The fall seems to have booted up the crime rate."

AnneMarie said, "What are they stealing now?"

"Wood. People mostly sneak. Water—drinking water. A comforter off a clothesline. Boots off porches. People are diverting snow water from other people's roofs. Nothing like Ms. LeDoux's problems—those cases of booze must be worth thousands of dollars, even though she wasn't buying Glenfiddich or Moet. People are brewing and distilling alcohol, stealing to do it."

"I thought sin would stop, there being so little to steal. Jay?" She looked at him, helplessly. "Aren't these the good old days?"

"Except for Ms. LeDoux," Jay was saying, "lots of drunks are sobering up; lots of smokers are putting anything to their lips and smoking it. I see people eating toothpicks, bits of wood, swizzle sticks, and their dwindling stocks of gum. Gum chewers are sucking little stones. People who gave up nail biting years ago are back at it with a vengeance. I wonder whether life was like that back in the 1880s, or whether denial has built up our frustrations to this level. There was always something, I guess, to put up against—against—" Jay looked at her, disordered hair, the harried, stunned look of her, as though she had just escaped a horror she couldn't name. "What did the guy say, 'the secret pain of living.'"

"My pain is no secret," AnneMarie said. "I wish it were."

POSTING FROM THE FALL FANTOM
Hidden faces in the puzzle,
Those who stuff and those who guzzle,
Those who turned out to be wiser,
Mrs. Reimer, organizer.
Pastor Fearing, Town ecstatic,
Mr. Klimek charismatic.
Sheriff Jay, we thought was dull,
Slow of wit and thick of skull,
What an amiable surprise—
Who would guess he was so wise.
Doc, our healer, now our vet,
Hasn't lost too many yet.
Lost his smarmy little nurse—
One small blessing from our curse.

POSTED BY THE MAYOR:
DO NOT LEAVE ANY HEATER UNATTENDED.
CONGRATULATIONS TO OUR FIRE FIGHTERS
WHO PUT OUT THE THREE FIRES WE HAD
THIS WEEK. THE JESPERSON BOY WILL HAVE A
COMPLETE RECOVERY FROM THE BURNS HE
SUFFERED LAST TUESDAY. DO NOT USE LIQUID
FUEL TO START A FIRE.

CHAPTER 12

DOC WINOGRAD LIVED IN AN OLD HOUSE FACING
the road from Callan, the river walk, and the Ute. He had come to
Gold Flume in 1967, when the government was paying new doctors
to move to underserved rural places. His move allowed him to pay off
his medical school debts, but he had liked the area and the people and
had decided to stay. His affection for the locals had been a surprise to
him. These were boom-and-bust people, mostly in the bust phase then,

the four towns dying since the end of World War II. There had been a boomlet that came with the uranium-molybdenum need, then that bust laid everyone low, causing the greatest migration of their young out of the valley since the thirties. Then the skiers had come and turned the towns around again. With the sport came ski shops and clothing shops and orthopedic men and a sports physician, all moved into mega-mansions up on the Hungry Mother or Kinchloe Mountain. One became a gentleman rancher with a spread in the valley. The fall had left Doc as he had been at first, the only family doctor in Gold Flume. He and the sheriff had been the only Jews in town until the nineties, when the ski area extended itself and became a complete destination spot, with an airport in Callan and a full four-season tourist location.

When he had told his fiancé all those years ago that he loved this place and wanted to stay, she had looked at him with complete incredulity. This dying town? This nowhere? She had felt overwhelmed by the mountains that loomed over it, keeping the sun from it morning and evening. She left. Doc married the town, cared for it, nursed it, and was grateful for every sunrise in it. He went to medical conferences twice a year and so had been to many cities in the world, never yearning to spend more time in any of them.

He hadn't felt old until last year, when his few ills appeared together: muscle aches, touches of arthritis, a less than perfect control of his various sphincters, high blood pressure, and some difficulties retrieving the word he needed from the thousands he used.

The fall had ruined his plans for retirement. There were the two orthopedic specialists and the sports medicine guy who had lightened his load, and there was a good enough man in Callan, and two others just moved to Bluebank. Gold Flume was now prosperous enough to attract good medical care. The emergencies were regularly choppered out to Denver's top drawer trauma hospitals. Now, he was back where he had started in the mid-sixties, the only doctor. He still had the chopper if needed. He could send up a flare for help, and the Drop supplied many medicines along with the food and fuel, but his first fear, when he learned about the fall, was now a constant, low-running anxiety.

He had calmed himself at first, thinking that he would be dealing with only a quarter of the former population, only those who lived in town and within a mile of The Hungry Mother. Counting those in the development at the base of Jackass Mountain, there were about two hundred people left in his care.

The early surprises were the presence of injuries caused by people unused to working with woodstoves and camp stoves—burns. The Emmett baby had first and second degree burns from an overturned kerosene lamp. Arms and hands touched the hot woodstoves or were scalded by a dozen kitchen fires put out with water buckets waiting close by. Six chimney fires had shot their sparks up into suppertime skies. Cannon sounds of their million trapped molecules roared along with them, and only the updrafts of the last rising from the valley kept the fire from the town itself.

Hunters went out full of the fear-joy of breaking a long-standing rule: the mayor had overridden state law limiting hunts to arbitrary seasons and to license holders. Everyone was desperate for food that wasn't freeze-dried or powdered. Twice they shot one another. Once a man shot himself. None of the wounds were serious.

There were unexpected medical problems: a rise in wife-beating, child beating, rage, despair at the loss of the massaging balms of addictions—to booze, to TV, to the Internet, to cigarettes, to uppers, downers, levelers. He watched AnneMarie Isaacs go from dull vacuity to anguished restlessness.

Doc, himself, had had his own before and after experience with smoking. Even now, he was surprised and a little ashamed at the memory of what he had said and thought and done in the two years of his recovery from the habit after the initial high had worn off. He liked to think that his experience might be helpful now, counseling people.

Fire Chief Brad Unger sat facing him, fidgeting, passing his watch-cap around and around in his hands, pull-release, pull-release, until Doc wanted to reach over and take the thing away from him.

"I can't sleep at night," Brad said, "and because of that, I get to where around three or four in the afternoon, I can't stay awake. Bein' chief, with what there is to do, now, I can't be asleep. And I yell, and people can't take that. Tommy Bergstrom and his pal left a hose on the floor at the firehouse instead of racking it to drain. Bad? Sure, but I all but took their heads off. They're not firemen. They've come on the force out of boredom and Tommy's wife being a nag, and because there's no work in town. I'm afraid I'm going crazy."

"What's caused all this?" Doc asked the question, but he had a strong idea, and needed to hear the words from Brad.

"It's cigarettes. I'm no addict—I don't smoke no more than a half a pack a day, but I smoke to get me started on the john in the morning and now, I'm bound up like to die. I smoke after I eat and now I can't stop eating. I find I'm eating and don't even know I'm doing it. I'm hard to get along with and I get angry and yell. I'm not like that—yelling at people."

"The Drop doesn't include cigarettes," Doc said, "but have you thought of chewing on something—a willow twig, maybe?"

"It's not only that. I want to sit down and watch TV. I can't even do that. I try to read, but I can't concentrate. I'm a mess. I'm falling apart."

Doc caught himself on a thought-nail: This was Brad Unger, level-headed, no nonsense, not some neurotic woman with nothing better to do. Then he thought—*Am I still thinking this way about older women, even after seeing Edwina and Melody at work?* The thought stopped him for a moment, and he lost the thread of what Brad was telling him. To cover his misconnection, he asked, "What are you doing to help yourself?"

Brad looked puzzled and then half-smiled. "I guess I never thought about it that way. Do you think people can change the way they feel about something? I mean without faking, lying to themselves?"

Doc felt himself at a loss, out of his depth. "Well," he said, "there are ten libraries of self-help books that say you can."

"The thing is, I'm stopped by force, not by choice," Brad said. "Nobody voted. I've tried to stop lots of times, and I can't. It's too much a part of my life. I've been smoking since I was thirteen. Things seem so dark. Dan and Lisha go around looking and acting like I had caused the mountain to fall. They have to help Siri do laundry and hang wash. They went on the wood-walk, and they know they'll be going farther and farther up the mountains to get at the dead trees and brush up there. The place is going to look like a park by the time all this is over. And, of course, their grandmother laughs at it all. She says she started her marriage out here that way, up Kinchloe Gulch. It was true, wasn't it, back in those days?"

"Town got electricity back in the thirties, but people up in the homesteads didn't get lines in until the mid-sixties. Now, of course, Sherpa on Everest have cell phones and hikers and skiers and ranchers can call India from a hillside. Lord, I remember when TV came. That was 1968 and we all got to see the cities rioting and people promising to burn down everything. Back then, can you believe it, there were people wishing something like this would happen. Our valley, all four towns, felt shut off from that world outside, with its wars and riots and dope and craziness." Doc looked at Brad. "I know you are suffering," he said. "There are people missing heroin here, right here in town, and crack cocaine and booze and prescription stuff that mail order doctors get for them. I'm not saying your problem is trivial. I'm saying you've got partners in it."

A week before, Doc had treated a broken arm, supposedly caused by a fall, and bad facial swelling, supposedly caused by another fall. The woman fell again, and Doc stared at her husband and said, "If this woman falls again, I'm going to the sheriff and see that she's taken out of the home as being too clumsy to stay there. Who'll do your wash then?"

He wasn't sorry to sit by a fire in the evening, eat out of food packets, and heat water for washing on his woodstove. To deter wood-thieves, he had rigged a series of cowbells and tripwires around the woodpile he had built up three days after the fall and with judicious use, he could heat his rooms through the winter. He wasn't surprised at the response Gold Flume was making to the fall. He had passed rage years ago, at what people did to one another. Now, he sometimes cursed cancer, Parkinson's disease, dementia, and illnesses that ate away at people picked at random the way a sniper does from a tower.

He had a pile of books on his bedside table, saved from the library sale last year at Callan: two histories, a few novels, a biography, and an old William Manchester about the war in the Pacific. Now that there was no phone and no TV, no computer, no e-mail, his reading habits had changed for the better. There were no distractions and he could read for hours, his candle behind a Rotterdam Jar, a round glass globe, formerly a fish bowl, rigged so that the water concentrated a strong, if small, pool of light on his pages. This trick he had learned years ago and had never had the chance to use—until the mountain fell.

He had forgotten about the medical request list until Jay came over for it. He had been enjoying his novel when he saw the sheriff's car pull up and Jay get out. He wondered for a moment what the sheriff wanted until the reason came, and with it, a shock at the passage of time. The list. He went to his desk and began to paw through the papers on it. It was simply a re-stock of what he had used, with another date at the top. Where was the damn thing? Jay was at the door. Murmuring expletives, Doc opened to a blast of cold air. "Come on in—I'm looking for the list now. Sit down. I have a shot of tequila for you if you want one."

Jay put up a hand, demurring. "No, thanks. I haven't just come about the list," he said.

Doc had a sinking feeling: AnneMarie. Without all those meds, she must have been eating the paint off the walls. "Would you mind if I hunted up the list while you tell me about it?"

"No, Doc—it's simple, really. AnneMarie is having an awful time, but—I don't want you to try to get any more medications for her. She has all but run out and what's happened is that I'm seeing glimmers of the real woman, the one she used to be. I know you could make all those medications part of your list and some might be approved, but I want to see if we got AnneMarie off them, what she would be like."

Doc frowned. "Isn't that up to her?"

"It wasn't when we started all this. Neither of us knew what the drugs did. They were meant to lift her depression, give her some breathing room, not turn her into an obese shadow. Her body was changed entirely; her mind was worse, really, blunted, and she had an odor. We cut the drugs way down, because we... thought they would be included in the Drop. She says she hated the things that are crawling under her skin. She wanted the odor gone and she wanted to start to lose some of that weight."

"Quite a few people are on neuroleptics," Doc said. "Those meds made up a sizeable part of my drug order. Most have been rejected. I didn't prescribe all these for AnneMarie and most of the prescriptions people have listed were from other doctors." He saw the sheet, which he had put on the sideboard under his keys. "How many of these folks are really psychotic?" He looked over the list and then turned a questioning glance at Jay. "The psychotropic medicines take up more of this list than anything else except Tylenol and the medicines we use to control blood pressure. I've never looked at a list like this. Out of 268 people—should so many of them be on anti-psychotics? Should kids be on this stuff?" He looked up at Jay, who was standing, getting ready to leave. "Have her come over tomorrow. Oh, and here's my list, the one I made up." He handed Jay his office list—there were splints, fuel for the generator he had had put in last year for emergencies, refills of oxygen, vials of all the injectables he used.

Jay took the list and said goodnight, leaving Doc in a meditative mood. Doc picked up his book— World War II in the Pacific. His mind kept wandering to what he had seen on the list. After a while he realized he hadn't been reading but thinking about what Jay had said. He was old enough to remember some of the medications he prescribed being used for psychotics in hospitals. There were thirty children on daily doses of some of these chemicals. What was withdrawal entailing? It would be a wonder if the whole town didn't dissolve in chaos and violence. He remembered his Aunt Marion, long ago, with her anodyne; they called it soothing syrup, and there was morning gin and later vodka. Hadn't his father's people smoked the harsh, unfiltered cigarettes of World Wars I and II, and spoken of bathtub gin when Prohibition kept them from their regular schnapps? *Is living so hard that it has to be blunted away every day by so many addictions?*

He was suddenly cold and realized that his fire had gone out. He went out the back door for some wood. The night had come on. He smelled the wood fires of his neighbors. He hadn't bothered to put on a jacket and the cold air hit him like a blow. He heard the familiar whistle of the wind announcing itself down mountain and on through the valley. He wondered if the fall would produce a sound when a big wind hit it.

A shape was behind the wood pile—not seen, intuited, somehow, a shadow that should not have been there. He walked very carefully in silence over the tough skin of the snow that had thawed during the day and by sundown clutched into rough ice. One of his cowbells gave a muted sound. He felt, rather than saw, the motion of wood moving, and there was a small sound of its bark catching as it slid. He moved forward quickly and grabbed, and there was a struggle of dropped wood and curses at the noise Doc made, legs kicking, wood knocked away and rolling, and at the rear of the next house, a man's voice — his neighbor.

"What's going on?"

The figure was heavy and strong. Doc landed a punch, his fisted hand blooming with pain. Someone lit a lantern. His neighbor came closer and Doc saw in the light that he was holding on to Mike Ansel, whose nose was bleeding, one arm still cradling a length of aspen log. Around them lay an array of aspen, pine, and spruce that Doc had cut and stacked carefully last summer, and had thought was safe with his precautions.

"Didn't you know that wood theft is not a misdemeanor now?" Doc asked.

The boy was too involved in shock and pain to answer. Doc's neighbor, Ken, came closer, and took the wood from Mike's gripping arm and laid it back on the pile in a solemn, almost reverent way. The pile shifted slightly, telling Doc that the wood had been taken from the bottom so as to leave the pile looking untouched to his casual eye.

"What do you wanna do?" Ken asked Doc.

"Do you have time for a walk?"

Ken called to his wife to come with some coats for them.

"It's not too late; town hall might still be open."

Sheriff Isaacs was downstairs in his office, filling out forms for requests that might never be read. He looked up as the three came in, having heard them clatter down the old staircase. "What have we here?"

"A wood thief," Doc said.

"I'm a witness," Ken said.

"My dad will sue him," Mike said. "Look at me—I can hardly breathe and he broke my nose."

"I think your face hurt his hand," Sheriff Jay said, "and I think your dad won't like the idea of your stealing."

"Well, it's just wood."

"It was just wood two months ago; now it's something else. It's looting. It's a felony. You're already on the books for the vandalism you did back in December. Do you have a clue?"

"What were you planning to do with the wood?" Doc asked.

Jay said, "Your dad wouldn't be fooled into thinking it was his."

"Angela said we could sell it," Mike said.

Jay looked across at Doc and caught his glance. Gallantry—Doc cleared his throat. He was getting cold in the unheated office.

Ken said that if nobody minded, he would go on home. They nodded, and thanked him. "If you need me as a witness, I'm okay with it," and giving them a wave, he left.

FROM THE FALL FANTOM
I asked for red, they gave me blue,
I wrote for rice, they sent me stew.
I said size 6, they sent me 2.
I wanted tea, they sent me glue.

CHAPTER 13

"So, Angela told you what?" Jay asked. The boy
got a righteous look.

"We could sell the wood."

"It'll be a while before money has any meaning around here," Jay said.
"I assume you were planning for your futures, you and Angela?" Deftly,
he moved the boy's arms behind him and motioned to one of the two
cells at the back of the basement room. "We're on a generator, here," he
said, "so you can use the toilet, but we're saving our power, so you won't
have any lights or hot water in the cell. I'll be here for a while, yet, and
then I'll go see your folks and tell them where you are."

It was late when he left. He was sure the Ansels were in bed—
everyone was now, saving fuel. He was angry enough to wake them,
which he did, having driven over the bridge at Orecart Street and up
into the gated world where the Ansels lived. He had beaten on the door
until they heard him and something about Mike.

"Mike's in bed."

"Go look."

They had been asleep and he had them come down, coats over their
night clothes, to the town hall.

The interview was all Jay had predicted, the Ansels defensive and righteous. The boy wasn't stealing a *car*—the woodpile was—what did the law call that, an attractive nuisance? Everyone liked a fire to augment the heaters they were using. It was just wood, after all, and boys—

"Yes, I know, will be boys," Jay said, "but wood theft is a felony, now, because it's not on the same ration plan as camp stove fuel. Some people have no camp stoves, and depend on wood for their heating. I also know that Mike wasn't stealing—" He noted their shocked look at the word, "to bring the wood to you or supply any additional comfort for you this winter. The wood was to be sold, for what, I don't know, since money doesn't mean the same thing these days as it did back in December."

Their attitude annoyed him; Ansel was standing with his arms crossed; his face was rigid. Mrs. seemed to be wishing herself away to a more pleasant place.

"Your son is a vandal, and now a thief," Jay said. "Technically, I could have him picked up by the helicopter as a felon and put in jail in Aureole, where he would then be sent to their juvenile facility, which was where we were going, if you remember, when we were stopped by the fall. He'll be in the lockup here now. My wife will be doing his cooking. I'm sorry that it'll be just the packets because she's a very good cook. The mayor has temporary judicial power. See her tomorrow. Any questions?"

Mike's mouth dropped open. "Do you mean that crazy woman's going to make my dinners?"

Jay felt absolute white rage rising, sudden as fear. He wanted not to be sheriff, older, responsible, professional. He wanted to break the face of the overgrown ox of a boy. He had to put his hands behind him and stand in silence while he continued to feel his heart vibrating behind his eyes. Janeen Ansel moved forward to put her hand on her son's shoulder. For a moment everything was absolutely still; no one moved or breathed.

The moment passed. Mike knew he could get away with saying that because of his father's importance. When his parents left, the underling might want to beat him, but wouldn't because of his father's prestige. His mother was useless, no power at all. The underling might handcuff him to the cot but what else could he do? His wife was crazy; people said so. He went into the cell and sat down on the cot. His parents spoke to the sheriff for a few minutes and then left.

He had seen his parents' surfaces give a little. They were beginning to realize that what they thought of as youthful hijinks was being seen as more than that. His mother would protest. His father would say, "What would it take to make all this go away?" Maybe it would work.

<hr />

AnneMarie was outraged. "He offered you a bribe?"

"Almost. I could have been a rich man," Jay said. "We could have been eating our freeze-dried entrées on porcelain plates."

"We do eat on porcelain plates," AnneMarie said primly. "Twice a year, at least, when we get Mama's good dishes down. It just dawned on me that nobody will be here for either of our birthdays. Do you think July Fourth or the summer holidays? Will we be open for them?" Her voice had a combination of eagerness and dread.

"I don't know," he said. "There's the problem of the river and no one's started taking the mountain off the highway. There are plans to blast through it all and create a tunnel, but that poses problems, too, I gather. From what Edwina says, it'll be a year at least."

AnneMarie sighed and he felt, again, her ambivalence. Her difference seemed to be losing itself in the general distress. The children and grandchildren wouldn't have to see her and suggest things to get her out of her depression, but she would miss them, and still be visited by the ghost of past holidays.

Since the second week, the Drop had been including mail out, but the post office had decided to put Gold Flume in an emergency category, the way areas of fire or flood were treated. Incoming mail was bundled and saved at the Callan post office, pending pickup by the authorities. Letters going out were collected by the pilot at the Drop. Because of that, writing was re-invented; letters flowed out until the supply of stamps at the post office had been exhausted. Diaries were begun or taken up again. Jay had been writing to their sons and daughter, always saying, "Mom sends her love." It was a relief to stop trying to be cheery and give town anecdotes while the unspoken pain grew. AnneMarie's collapse had happened after they had left the town, and until the last two years, she had managed to energize herself in a desperate charade of normality when they and the grandkids visited. In the last year or so, the falsity of her performance had become more evident, but he didn't remember their saying anything, only giving quizzical looks now and then, and the hand up as a child would say, "Why is Grandma so...?" "Why does Grandma walk like...?" "Why does Grandma smell like that...?"

"Will you be telling the kids about all this—the river problems, and how long it's going to be?" AnneMarie asked. "It seems so... pessimistic, so horrible, and really, except for some of it, what we have to do, it sounds worse than it is."

"Do you really feel that way?"

"Walking gives me time to think, and I don't always like that, but I see people to say hello to. Except for me being so—so different, I know it's good for me to do."

"What do you mean, different?" he asked. They had never gone on that ground. He had always pretended that her depressed dullness was a new normal, her way. He felt a ripple of anxiety.

"I know I've changed," she said. "I used to do so much, and there was so much to do. Some of the girls I grew up with—most of them, I think, had big ambitions, big dreams. Perk Adams wanted to go to Hollywood and be a star. She didn't do any of that, and neither did Annie Padget, or Doreen McGuire, but they all left here. I liked it here. I always have, but town's changed, with all the tourists, and skiers, and now there are richer rich people and poorer poor ones—I never minded that before, rich and poor."

"Don't you think I make enough?" The terrain was getting more risky. There were holes to fall into.

"It isn't that—we have the life we wanted. We raised good kids—there's nothing we need that we don't have, only—"

"Only what?"

"Is this all? Mama died, then Papa. Your folks always thought you could have done better than me, as a wife. Friends are moving away, Pastor Fearing replaced Pastor Nichols, and everyone knows that was a step down, but no one seems to care. Once—" She sought the words, "—once I knew where I was and where everything else was, and then, when the kids left, and your dad died, and your mom got so mean—I looked around and I couldn't figure out what I was going to do then."

The kitchen where they were standing seemed to have lost its glow in the lamp light. It looked ugly and shabby. The house was old fashioned with this most important room stuck away in back, isolated from the "social" parlor and sunroom, a glassed-in porch made in the twenties. This room was dirty, too, sticky in the corners. She looked so wan and lost standing there that he felt himself choking up.

Jay liked clear lines. He had gone to police training after the Army partly because the clarity of police work appealed to him; right and wrong were like east and west to him, dividing the world and giving life a line and a direction in which to steer. He was to find that even in his job, the lines often wavered, and sometimes even converged, and that reality had a way of going cold in the hand. It was true, when he thought of it, that his mother felt herself a little higher than her neighbors. She had been disappointed at his choice of career, at his choice of a small town, and even more at his choice of AnneMarie, whose family had been railroad employees, and when the trains had gone from the valley, had run a few cattle and whose sons had hired out to larger ranches at Bluebank and Callan. Although he didn't want to, Jay could remember the look of shock and disbelief on her face when he brought AnneMarie to Denver to introduce her. After the death of his father, Jay's mother had shriveled in on herself and had become demanding and capricious until she died. AnneMarie was talking about what had happened years ago. The stories were like familiar stones, sticking up and being tripped over still, years later. Why couldn't she step over them and be done?

"The ski people, the tourists—you know yourself that without them, Gold Flume would have dried up and died years ago. Gold went, silver went, and there's not enough rain in the valley to farm or support any more than five ranches. We've got to cherish what we have."

"Back before the new people came, nobody would try to bribe anybody," she said.

"Nobody had the money to bribe anybody," he said, and saw a small smile go quickly on her face.

CHAPTER 14

"I SAW TESS KLIMEK TODAY," ANNEMARIE SAID. "SHE was talking about the women up here getting some kind of a big boiler and doing a wash, all of us, outside on good days. We'd get enough water and have a fire under the boiler. She was talking about one of the old coal cars, the smaller ones, that are still up in the weeds near the old railroad siding." And she gestured to a place where some of those works had overlooked the town and had been rusting the years away.

"What do you think about it?" Jay asked. He wasn't sure it was a good idea. Were all of the women to stand spaced apart around the boiler under which a fire was going? Whatever it was, he sensed a social element in it that he felt he should encourage. They had been heating water in kettles and doing the laundry in the bathtub, stamping it like the *I Love Lucy* grape-crushing scene on TV. Being with a bunch of neighbor women would be good for AnneMarie, he thought, but he knew he had to be careful not to show too much enthusiasm that would make his encouragement seem condescending. "How would that work?" he asked, and suddenly he had a thought. "Whose idea is this?"

"I just heard about it from Tess," she said.

"Come on," he said, "we're going over there."

The Klimeks were at the dinner table, a plate of muffins at the side of their entrée packets. Jay's mouth began to water. "How—?" The muffins were sending out their warm, sugary aroma, melting the butter spread in their parted halves.

"I rigged up a sort of bake-oven that goes over the woodstove," Klimek said. "Come on into the living room and I'll show you."

"I wanted to talk to Tess about the idea for washing clothes," Jay said. "The boiler."

Tess Klimek reminded him of an alert, chirping thing, a small bird. She was tiny as a child, dark-haired, and AnneMarie had told him that in school she had been so ebullient that people got nervous around her. John Klimek had been her high school teacher, his first job, and there had been quite a scandal about cradle-robbing, but he wasn't all that much older than she was, and they had waited until she was nineteen before they got engaged. Tess looked up at him, smiling, mouth a little open with her eagerness. He asked after their kids.

The Klimeks had finally had the three they wanted, two now in college. Jay noticed the roots of Tess's hair like the flood-line at the old Callan school. He was surprised that she had been dyeing it. The undyed part was still chestnut brown, but not as bright, and there was some gray here and there. He tried not to look at it. "AnneMarie was telling me about your idea for using one of the old coal cars as wash boiler," he said.

She twinkled up at him. "It may sound silly. Some of us up here could use one of them and it wouldn't be a big one—we were thinking of the thing that's up there on the old tracks—they used it to bring the rocks and things out of the mine up there."

"I wonder," Jay said, "if we could move it to the place north of where it is now, not far, where there's a lot of run-off. You could sluice the water into the thing and out the other end and have running water, without having to cart it in and out in buckets."

"How far is that?" Klimek asked.

"About sixty yards, maybe a little more—you know the place I mean?"

"Have you looked at that cart? It might be rusted through by now. Let's go up tomorrow and check it out," Klimek said.

Early the next day, the Klimeks, Jay, and AnneMarie hiked up the hill, slowly, talking about ordinary things and their remade lives. Klimek said he was happy to have the four-hour-a-day school schedule. It seemed to stimulate the learning; his class was more attentive. As Jay was beginning to say something, he turned, looked around, and saw that AnneMarie had dropped back and was following them, fifty feet or so behind. She had stopped and was bent, hands to knees, pulling for breath. He called to her.

"I can't..."

"We'll wait till you catch up."

"No; I'm going back home." She turned.

He shouted after her. "I'll be back soon." She didn't respond. They had gone no more than thirty yards up the hill. His house was still in sight. He looked up the hill so as not to encounter any look from Klimek.

The ore cart was smaller than Jay had visualized and it was full of brush and forty or so years of wind-blown earth and the pine needles of all those autumns. "What do you think?"

"I think I like the idea," Klimek said. "We'd need to see if it's rusted out and we'd need a way to filter the run-off before it gets to the boiler and a big gutter and downspout to lead the water away—"

"We'd have to make sure of the soap they use, too—something that wouldn't pollute. Doesn't everything we do pollute something? Look at the smoke we see from the chimneys before the wind blows it away."

"You know our sewage system isn't big enough for all these new houses with their heavy use of water," Klimek said. "We've started to feel like unwelcome guests on the planet instead of necessary inhabitants, part of the scene."

Jay shrugged. "Now, we're in the 1860s with a twenty-first century mentality. We've got the blahs. What could be worse?" They laughed.

Jay looked long and hard at the ground, which was just at the snow line. They walked back down by way of the run-off gully, noting how far it was even from the houses at the top of the street. Getting wash up and carrying the wet clothing back would be a hell of a chore.

AnneMarie was sitting in the living room, staring at the blank black rectangle of the TV. "I couldn't even make it up that hill," she said, "and I see all the fake sympathy on Ms. Sparkle-pants' face. I can hear her thinking, 'How can that old, sad exhibit wash clothes when she couldn't even walk ten feet up a hill?'"

"Honey, she knows we're older than they are."

"She knows I've gone crazy; the whole town knows."

"AnneMarie—I'm not going to deny anything—what you're saying is too silly—but I am going to tell you that when half The Hungry Mother fell, nobody had any secrets anymore. We know who drinks and who smokes and who has addictions and who has ulcers and who has hemorrhoids and who has an eating disorder and who has every kind of mental illness known. No secrets anymore. You'd be shocked out of your shoes to learn how much of your problem is common run. Half the town's on something, or was, before the fall."

"She's just so chirpy," AnneMarie said.

"Sometimes she tries too hard, it's true, but they're good people and good neighbors. We could be living next to—well—"

"Name names," she said. "I love it."

"Never mind that. What delicacies have you cooked up for the Ansel boy?"

"Packets. I'm saving my flour for an occasion. How long are you keeping the overgrown little stinker?"

"I can keep him for seventy-two hours, which I will do."

"Just to piss off Roman Ansel?"

"It's the law."

"What about the wash idea?"

"It'll work."

A week after they went up the hill, John Klimek appeared at the town hall with a plan for eight gravity-fed sluices on both sides of the river. They would use run-off, channeled and equipped with filters and settling pools that would then fill basins made from ore carts. The ore carts would be built up to the sluices, water heated by mirrors mounted on poles. Edwina was impressed and took the plans to the council.

At first people seemed shocked, almost angry. The installations would be a message to the town that their situation was long-lasting, months, perhaps. It seemed to some to be an admission of defeat. Klimek went in to plead the case. Then, he brought up the topic of the river's diversion that would be taking up months of time and effort. Months might pass before crews could even begin work on the mountain itself. The whole arrangement, the boilers and ore carts and sluices could easily be broken down and taken away after their usefulness was over. People would no longer need to carry wash water into their homes, while run-off was going to waste. Many were too old to manage lugging that water upstairs to the bathtubs they used for washing clothes.

Roman Ansel had huffed like a moose, but Edwina — whom Jay had always thought of as bland — had said, "I am the chief executive of this district. When the road is open you may sue me." She looked at Jay. "Sheriff —"

"He's no sheriff," Ansel was red-faced, "he's only an under-sheriff."

"I'm technically sheriff in this district. I have the power to deputize, to arrest, to carry weapons. My duties are listed in my contract, which I will show you on request."

Jay was surprised at himself. He was aware of how little anger was rising in him. That strength came from Edwina's complete aplomb.

"If I build it, they will come," Klimek said. "I can get some of the Wheeler Dealers to help. Let's vote." The resolution passed. Wash boilers. 1860.

FROM THE FALL FANTOM
Hailed washdays from the past —
Shouldn't we keep our red hands to show the tourists?

POSTED BY THE MAYOR: 1: MANY ACCIDENTS
ARE BEING CAUSED BY PEOPLE LEAVING SHOVELS,
ETC., OUT. DR. WINOGRAD RECOMMENDS THAT
SHORT STREET CLEARING EQUIPMENT BE TAKEN
HOME AT NIGHT.

2: THE POST OFFICE HAS GIVEN US AN
ADDRESS WHERE LETTERS CAN BE SENT FOR
LATER DISTRIBUTION. GENERAL DELIVERY,
PROVO, UTAH.

CHAPTER 15

MIKE ANSEL HADN'T BEEN A BIG KID IN ELEMENTARY
school, but by his second year in junior high, he had found himself
solidly built with a wrestler's body and an abundance of energy, for
which there seemed to be no outlet. Sports were on offer, but he had
no interest in chasing a ball or running down a field. He did have an
interest in pushing people out of his way, and for a while he was on the
wrestling team, until the coaches saw that his principal energy was spent
in doing damage. They tried, unsuccessfully, to channel that aggression,
but finally told him to leave the team. That evening, he cut the brake
line on the coach's car.

His stopping football was a great disappointment to this father.
Roman Ansel had been a high school hero and a college star. He was the
top man at his job, overseeing the smooth running of all the machinery

at the ski area. Mike feared his father, even when he rose to Mike's defense. There would always be an after, when Roman would give him a withering glance. Mike found that he could gain popularity by imitating the powerful figures he saw on TV or in the movies—strong, decisive men. They won admiration from other men and love from women. He was amazed that some guys were able to have friends and girls without bribery or threat.

But he had been happy screwing Angela. She was living out a dream. She wore as few clothes as possible and dropped them without shame. Girls in her class called her a slut, but she and they thought of prostitutes as being freer than ordinary women. Mike knew that she thought of herself as far above the little lies and hypocrisies of the girls around her. He had never argued that idea because although she wasn't his alone (he had heard things, and even seen some), when they were together, they both seemed to themselves to be courageous and powerful.

The break-in at the condo had been done out of idleness, boredom, and his need to be a leader of something. Chris Pantea was a bright kid, attracted to Angela, who let him go just so far. Mike knew that it was important to impress Chris with his leadership. If that man hadn't been coming from the back of the condos, they never would have been spotted and Mike would have had Chris as a follower, one who would bring a brighter group of followers to him.

Mike began to wonder why he had vandalized the condo. He knew that while he was doing it, he had enjoyed it. It felt good to break things, but an hour later, driving home with stuff he didn't want, the reasons for what he had done disappeared. Later, Chris told him that the condo break-in had been stupid, that their haul was junk. Angela had been content to draw pictures on the mirrors with lipstick.

The fall had given Mike his get-out-of-jail card, but he still had to put up with his father's curses and his mother's tears. He intuited that it was shame that hit his father hardest. If his mess hadn't come out, his father would have been content to yell at him for fifteen minutes and blame his mother for not having raised him with enough discipline. His triumph quickly turned downward. Chris had signed up with old man Klimek's team of do-gooders. Angela was sharing her time with a guy she had latched on to—"someone who won't get me busted."

Then came the worst: the March snows kept everyone at home for days at a time. The first storm lasted for three. The second was less than a week later, and there was nothing to do but stare out the window or have his nerves jangled by one or the other of his parents and whining sister. He had heard about brother-sister incest from someone's reading about it, and had thought it revolting, but now he thought he understood it as a thing someone might do out of pure, soul-cracking boredom. After a day's lifting, there was another snow, and another three feet. This time, he knew he couldn't stand being inside with this family one more minute and he bulled out the door as soon as the snow stopped. He battled through the drifts by main force, pushing against the wall of them, making a way through with his body until, exhausted, he reached the river and could go no further. Town was on the other side. The two bridges, equidistant from him, were too far. The snow itself was a barrier, heavy and wet, a true spring snow. Why hadn't he taken his skis?

Since his being caught at Doc's woodpile, Angela had dropped him like he was a dog turd. "Not what you did, stupid, but getting caught. I'm going to Saint Anne's in the fall—I _was_ going to Saint Anne's in the fall. If they found out about me being with someone with a record, juvi or not, I'd be finished, and you're not that good a lay, either." He had hit her, hard, but still felt the sting.

He was at the river bank, looking at the water running sluggishly under a pane of ice, and thought that if he went in, he could walk—the river wasn't deep here—to the lower bridge, but he realized that with the flow not given its full channeling, there was no way to tell how deep it was, and his boots weren't very high, anyway. God damn the river, the snow, the town, and everyone in it. God damn Angela and Chris Pantea, one-time friend and, it turned out, loyal as an Irish setter. Pantea, no doubt, was doing some damn good deed with his cow-like herd. Mike knew he had been asked to join them. Pantea had made a special visit, sent, no doubt, by Klimek, to get him interested.

For an instant, he saw that he might have been inspired to attack Klimek's wood pile because Klimek headed that group of ass-kissers. He put the idea away. Before the mountain fell, he had never had ideas like the ones he was getting now. There had always been music, talk on his cell phones, or a CD playing in his ear, to make the days okay. Before the fall, he had everything there for him. Now, he was standing in a snow pile, bits of which had found their way into his right boot and lay melting and running down to his foot. He felt like crying, an emotion he hadn't experienced for years. The tightening of his throat horrified and shamed him.

He was wet, cold, angry, and at a loss. He didn't want to go back up the hill to *them,* and he couldn't stay standing in the aisle he had made in the walls of snow, hip-high on both sides. Above him, sky; down river, trees; standing, burdened by heaped snow, which at the touch of wind, unloaded with sporadic thumps.

And nothing else, no diversion of any kind. There was nothing in his hand, nothing in his coat pocket to provide a respite from the weight of the sky. His rage exploded. He threw himself down in the snow, kicking, screaming, fighting, punching at the places where his body was compacting it.

When the fit was done, and he was exhausted and dry-mouthed from his howling, he stopped abruptly. He took a handful of snow and put it in his mouth. He had left the house in his terrible unrest without hat or gloves, and was now aware of the chattering cold.

There was the road back up the hill. Slowly, and slipping on the packed snow, he made his way back to the house.

With the ski area closed, his father was concentrating on home repairs and on the rearrangement of his mother's kitchen in a more efficient manner. He was there now, showing her which of the kitchen drawers should hold the serving cutlery and which the silverware. Mike saw how his mother resented the advice but how she swallowed the anger she had about it. His father was now explaining to her why it was better to keep the dishes on this shelf and the cups there, to move the pots and pans from the places she had kept them for the nine years they had lived here, to where they should logically belong. The spices should be moved from where they were too close to the range top where the heat was harmful to them. This shelf was better, only ten steps or so away. Mike knew that his father was a powerful man and everyone knew it. His mother knew it, too. Mike thought that his father's appreciation of his gifts tended to spread wider than their limits. That was all right in normal times when his energies were expended on his job at the ski area, where Mike knew he was regarded as a mastermind. Since the fall, he had been home, unable to give his creativity its full play.

His mother caught his eye. Mike looked away. He noticed that she had been scratching at a rash that had appeared at her neck. It had become worse during the snow. She had mentioned the rash to Melody Reimer, who had diagnosed cabin fever. She and Mike had laughed at this storybook ailment, but Janeen knew that cabin fever was real. She had sworn Mike to secrecy. His father would never stand for a weakness like that. Secretly, Mike thought his mother was ridiculous.

FROM THE FALL FANTOM
Get heartburn from the zombie meat
Get ulcers from their brew;
What's good enough for Gandhi
Is good enough for you.

CHAPTER 16

WHILE MIKE WAS A BOY, ROMAN HAD BEEN PROUD OF him. Mike was sturdy and unafraid, and Roman had called his willfulness "high spirits." He had often shown Mike off at the ski area, the nine-year-old breaking through a mogul field, doing double black runs without a hint of nerves. Roman told Janeen that Mike might go into racing or extreme skiing, an Olympic contender, perhaps. Janeen had been surprised that a man as brilliant as her husband wouldn't want their son to be more interested in academics. There was nothing wrong with his intellect, but off the slopes the boy was lazy and unmotivated, and her husband didn't seem to mind. In odd moments, Janeen wondered if Roman were helping to shape Mike toward sports in order to avoid competition between them.

"A boy should have fun growing up," Roman declared. "These kid-years'll never come back."

And then Mike was fourteen, and fifteen, and the skiing became reckless and the driving became more reckless, done without a license in the cars of upper-classmates bullied into giving him their keys. Mike was a bully. Roman turned bully in his defense. The first time Mike totaled a classmate's car, Roman refused to pay for it on the ground that the boy had consented to Mike's driving it. The incident hadn't happened on a state road so there was no police involvement. The second accident had been a draw, both boys swearing that another car had forced him off the road.

Roman was so sure that Mike would get an athletic scholarship that he didn't press the issue of his mediocre grades. Janeen was silent, only listening, looking, and noting the things that saddened her.

The vandalism shocked but didn't surprise her. Her son wasn't a pleasant or respectful boy. She knew he was a bully and couldn't understand where that had come from. They weren't poor or divorced or drunks or dopers, the conditions supposedly the breeding grounds for aggression. Mike hadn't been abused—quite the contrary. He had been loved and petted and forgiven through a comfortable and lucky childhood. Roman pooh-poohed the vandalism—"He's all boy." The fall had done more than save them the embarrassment of a problem with the law; it had seemed to be a validation, a divine vindication of Mike's luck.

The offer by the Pantea boy and the teacher up at the high school that Mike join their group came to Janeen as a gift, a wild hope, too soon dashed when Mike rejected it flatly. Roman got him to help in some home repairs, but Janeen never saw her son put himself out for anyone, except, perhaps, for the Bruno girl, Angela. What would happen to Angela when the gum ran out? There was none on the Drop. Janeen had met Angela, milling away on her Juicy Fruit, and had seen her four or five times since, at high school events or on the street, chewing, slackjawed in the street-whore pose that was her teen persona. Even in winter, Angela was half-dressed. Janeen knew it was a pose, overdone to the point of parody, but without the charm that should have gone with it. Angela could have been a beauty except for the bad make-up and her expression of vacant scorn. They were sleeping together, she and Mike. Sometimes Janeen wondered what kind of introduction to love-making

Angela was giving her son. Roman was good enough, she thought—nothing special. She had adapted to his sexual needs as she had adapted to his genius and his impatience.

Mike came back home in the near dark and took off his wet boots, cursing. Since her most recent disappointment, Janeen had ceased to bustle and fuss at his discomforts, to question him or to try to alleviate any of his complaints. If he missed these signs of her concern, he made no mention of it.

At dinner, Roman declared that this was the weekend when the clocks were to have been turned ahead. Janeen wanted to say that ideas about time had changed radically since the fall, but she knew that unless she formed that thought and spoke with absolute precision and logic, he would demand to know what she was talking about. He would hunt that idea down because time was scientific, and science was a kingdom belonging to and run by himself, and in this house, by himself alone. So she asked, "Will people change their clocks?"

He said, "You know how foolish that move has always been. Noon has meaning. Noon means that the sun is at the meridian. Having winter and summer hours should be what makes sense," and he gave her a look that included her in the vast assortment of human beings less intelligent than himself.

Mike was barely listening. Now that he was warm and dry, he was glad he had made that trip today, created that road through the snow all the way down the hill to the river. The exercise had calmed him and given him an appetite for the boring packet-rations. Some of the snow had been chest high in places. Tomorrow, he would go back and reconnoiter the spot by the river and maybe get to the bridge and over into town. Or, he might go up river to the Prospector development where Angela lived. She might be glad to see him. She, too, must be going crazy, stuck at home. Her father was a bone doctor, fixing up the broken legs and dislocated shoulders of ski-accident victims. He had once told Mike that his work was easier than that of most doctors. The patients were almost all young and were all in excellent health otherwise. There was less left to chance or accident, such as you got in obstetrics and unlike neurology or oncology, your patients weren't dying on you all the time.

"Have you ever thought about med school?" Dr. Bruno had asked. Mike had said no; his grades were too low and school bored him. "What do you think you'd like to do?"

He didn't answer the thought that came to his mind: fuck Angela's brains out every day for the rest of my life and drive a Mercedes and get free of this dead town. Vegas, maybe.

This conversation had happened just after he had begun seeing Angela and before she had revealed her sexual gifts. He was also relieved that the doctor was gone, leaving her beyond his control. With no need to share in the care of ordinary townspeople, Dr. Bruno was now free, free on the other side of the fall, with money to spend, and things to spend it on. Having Angela had slowed Mike's hunt for other willing girls. Maybe some were not as willing as she, but available all the same. His mind returned to her again and again. She hadn't really dumped him. No one would do that.

If he got there, where could they go? The snow had stopped falling. By tomorrow people could dig out. The two of them had always used Angela's house when her parents were away, his house when his were gone. They had made it in Mike's car, and in the cars of forced friends, and five or six times in school cloak rooms or faculty bathrooms. She seemed to want it as much as he did, but sometimes he wasn't sure. He was a bully, but he wasn't stupid. Now and then, when there was light enough and time for him to look at her while he dove and pulled, he saw a look of vacuous remove on her face. She might have been watching a dull program on TV, or a dull class at school. When he was done, she sometimes sighed, getting up, practical and practiced and workman-like, to fix her shirt or put her panties on, no wasted motion. Lipstick was refreshed in a flash of her little mirror and she redrew her eyeliner and heavy eye shadow that gave her the look of illness she took for sophistication.

Mike wasn't sure he liked Angela, and he was almost certain that she didn't like him. Their talk was random and the only time there was passion or feeling in it was in sharing their hatred of this town and the people who lived in it. He got the pot she smoked and the coke she sniffed, and the occasional hit of whatever else there was to change what they saw as unlivable lives. Her ordinary talk bored him. She was a diary of the couplings and decouplings of their classmates: who had missed a period and was afraid, who was in this week and who out.

Now, she was all that was left of the larger life they had known before the fall: no more pot or coke or drugs with stranger names. He always had money. Mom and Dad were easy touches and there was occasional work up at the ski area for tips. Money meant nothing now and whatever drugs there had been had long since been used up. There were lots of rumors of cellar-grown pot or roadside weed; none of these stories had proved out.

Up in his room, cold even with a camp stove, Mike worked himself and started for sleep until a thought, one of those connections that can never be traced, rose up and pulled him up in bed. There were five or six abandoned mines on his side of the river. Most of them had fallen in, their shorings rotted or gone to dust with the action of insects. There were also caves, some created by wind and water, some by undermining. Why not find the best one and get up some supplies? He would have a perfect place to go with no fear of discovery. Angela would yell, for sure. Climbing a snowy hillside to a cave would hardly appeal, and she had a whine when she was balked, like a chainsaw felling an oak. Still, if there were a cave close enough and big enough for parties, she would like that. Rumors were also going around that the Maki twins were brewing booze. If they came up and brought some of their stuff... and he was asleep.

FROM THE FALL FANTOM
Here's a world turned upside down
In the poorer parts of town.
Privies give the needy ease
From the snow and icy breeze,
While in rich parts, tiny lots
Mandate use of chamber pots,
And wealthy drop clandestine loads
On the sides of public roads.

POSTED BY THE MAYOR: SUPPLIES OF WOOD ARE
SHRINKING. I AM REQUESTING MORE FUEL FOR
HOME HEATING, BUT PLEASE TRY TO ECONOMIZE.
THE DROP IS FOR BARE NECESSITIES ONLY AND
WE ARE SHARING SCARCE SUPPLIES WITH AT
LEAST SIX OTHER TOWNS.

CHAPTER 17

PASTOR FEARING HAD BEEN HOPING TO SEE SIGNS OF
what his vision had held before him at the memorial for the dead of
the fall. He had led the services with his list of names, pitifully incomplete. The uncertainty had caused his wife Cheryl to call the service, "For
Whom It May Concern."

To the most pious of his flock, Fearing spoke of the possibility of
redemption, the way his vision had shown him. There would be evidence; all they need do was to see it being made plain day by day. God
had told him so. Day by day, he tried to find these proofs. Were people
less selfish? Were they less materialistic? He saw the Wheeler Dealers
pulling wagons up to the houses of people in need, the ill, and the
old. The sight moved him, but he didn't see the spirit expanding to

the population of the town. There was no lift in spirit that virtue was supposed to bring. People complained; tempers were short. His congregation whined like those Israelites in the desert so despaired of by Moses. Ancient sulks were replaced by modern ones, even less defensible. He saw shock give way to a fast-moving relief, replaced all too soon by anxiety and impatience. At times, his congregation reminded him of patients in a halfway house, coming off addictions. Why was it given him to be a sandlot Isaiah preaching joy in a madhouse? If only they could see the glory that lay before them, ready to be used as a stairway to higher, better selves.

After the memorial service he had gone home to Cheryl, who hadn't been at the church, saying that she was nursing an attack of chills. "What will happen to us?" Her shock had worn off, but so had any gratitude at being spared. She had refused to see the fall as anything but a catastrophe, one more disappointment to which Elbert Fearing had subjected her. Almost everyone in town had walked to where the mountain stood sheared away and had seen what they knew was only a small part of its extent. A wall of earth and stone and broken-off trees towered over them. Cheryl had stayed at the parsonage, a clear message of her separation. The rescue helicopters had come, the food Drop had been set up, but she had done none of the writing of requests, no counting the cans of food still on their shelves, no eyeing how low the flour was whitening in the bin, no eyeing what they had on hand, figuring for their or for anyone else's possible need. Fearing sighed and did it all.

During his prayers, night and morning, he tried to revisit the moment of light, the sense of encompassing in this small community, sheltered by The Hand of God, each person as a radiant shard of the material of the original creation.

Surely, the fall was God's direct intervention. To what place, so much as to this place, where quiet and simple town life had been sold away to tourism and luxury. Had anyone seen the fall as a message? All the real stores had moved away from town to the mall, leaving only boutiques selling tourist mementos, high priced non-essentials, and status artifacts. Even the churches had moved down valley, toward Callan. His church remained, thanks to a land purchase three generations past. The donor had been a railroad magnate who had had the foresight to buy up all the land necessary for the church's later expansion.

All around us, he thought, *was plan, meaning, glory, design, the dance of mountains thrown up, islands being formed in seas that eons ago had risen and fallen here.* He had always felt that the first feeling mankind had wasn't fear of God, but awe. From this awe came ethics, the desire to be worthy of that great awe. If his calling was to make his congregation see this, to feel and know it, he had failed and failed miserably. There was left to him only to be an example, to be good and helpful. Where was the thunder in that?

The afternoon of the most recent Drop, Fearing went to the church and began to clean the floor, digging in the corners the generations of build-up, the castings of rubber-soled shoes, crushed mouse droppings, and general filth. He would be doing more of this work in the future. Life was making things harder for the Altar Guild ladies who customarily did little more than re-arrange the dust in the sanctuary.

The floor was linoleum laid over worn wood. He had been hoping for money that would get carpeting. The pews themselves should be seen to. They creaked like old bones whenever the congregation sat back after the Doxology and the Eucharist. The church had been full, and with standees, this past Sunday. He knew that most people weren't coming to services for certainties or with hard questions, or with religious doubt, but for purely social reasons. No one wanted explanations of God's saving one child and letting another die. When he was first ordained, nine years ago, he had been embarrassed by a woman, the only one saved from a burning townhouse, who told the reporter that God had chosen her to save. The reporter had smirked. Fearing could all but hear his thoughts.

With few other forms of entertainment and a need to hear and spread rumors, all of the town bundled up and gathered in the barely heated sanctuary under the altered light of stained glass, armed by singing, and—lately—clapping and swaying. No one was complaining of the church going Pentecostal. The need was to keep warm.

And Cheryl had begun coming, too. She had married him with other dreams, something about being his inspiration and walking in a rosy glow. She had had no idea that a pastor's earnings were related to the wealth of his congregation. This she had learned in his first three placements. When they had been posted to Gold Flume, her ambitions had soared, but while the pastor's wealth had risen with the town's success, his congregation members were not the wealthy people in the gated communities, but town people, the relentlessly middle class: bookstore owners, caterers, retirees. Her will had been tightened. She had been very pretty when El Fearing had fallen in love with her. She had glowed with excitement to think of their starting in parishes where people were friendly. She had seen lovely manses next to great churches. Her earliest years with him had been spent in Kearney, Nebraska, in a church full of retirees. El had officiated at more funerals than weddings. Then had come a small church in Bags, Wyoming, and finally, Gold Flume, Colorado.

She had been fooled by the wealth of the town, but little grew here. Her flowers died, the parsonage was old and inconvenient, the elders always promising a remodel when there was money enough. Two pregnancies had miscarried like the frost-killed rosebushes she had planted for each one.

The people of the town were the usual mix of humanity, but Cheryl learned early that their acceptance, the thing she had counted on as an expected benefit, was tinged with feelings that bore no relation to her as a person. She and El were symbols, meant to represent Christian virtues. They were niche figures. People who swore seven days a week, stopped when they saw the Fearings. People who told jokes, or talked sex, pushed the words back into their mouths at sight of Pastor or his wife. El didn't mind—he had been called. Cheryl was expected to be Garden Club, Altar Guild, Church Choir. When she proved to be none of these, there came to be a silence around her name.

Melody Reimer, Garden Club lady turned executive genius, had come to Cheryl a week or so after the mountain fell. "We need to organize something for the older people here," she declared. "We've got people helping with the food Drops, but who's to help with washing and sanitation and carrying things—water, fuel..."

Cheryl had shrugged. "I'm not very good at organizing," she told Melody, in a way that made the message clear. When El praised Melody's skills in an attempt to enlist Cheryl's participation, he got a cold stare.

Some of the town men had set up wash basins here and there in town, using ore carts and runoff from the mountains. Even when these big washbasins were set up around town, Cheryl didn't join the women who gathered at the places closest to them. As time went on, the ones washing, mostly women, made habitual days at the ore carts. Fires were lit under the basins on Mondays, Wednesdays, and Fridays to save fuel. Ansel and Harbison mounted glass on frames to warm the area the women worked in. Cheryl could look out her front and back windows on those days and see women, and some men, moving with carts and wagons or carrying laundry bags, chatting as they went. In back yards, wash lines pulled from tree to post, festooned with dignified sheets and undignified underwear. Everything froze, sometimes, then thawed to dry, softer for their freezing. Neighbors' judgments long dead were reanimated—who was late getting her laundry in and who let her sheets drag.

It was the end of March, three months after the fall, when Mayor Dixon addressed the people gathered in the field to wait for the Drop. "We are doing okay, here—we've pulled together, our kids have come through with deliveries and we've been assured that we're on the list for help, but that won't come for at least six months." A groan went up. The early panic at news from outside had given way to dread and then, anger. The panic could be re-awakened at any sudden change, even at a Drop delivery held up by bad weather. The mayor raised her voice. "That creates a problem—you, there—don't leave yet. What I have to say is important. If the help would be coming this month, or even next, we wouldn't be faced with what will most certainly happen if we don't go into action now." She paused. People were hugging themselves and stamping their feet, chilled at their wait and impatient for the chopper and the distribution. "I mean, the river," she said, giving the words time to sink in. "It'll be thaw soon and when the thaw comes, there'll be no place for that water to go. Roman Ansel, here, and the Council have been working on this for some time, and we've come up with a plan. We've got to divert the river, move it west to where the fall is lightest, and we've got to dig out a channel, and we've got to do it now, because if we don't, the thaw will make a lake with us at the bottom."

"We'd need heavy equipment to do that!" someone yelled from the crowd.

"That's not gonna happen." The mayor threw her voice against the growl coming from people just confronted with a new, sharper edge of reality. She wanted the sound as male as possible, feeling that a voice that lacked authority wouldn't be listened to. She envied Sheriff Isaacs his deep, rich sound. She took a breath and went on. "We do this the way it was done in the mining days not so long ago: pick and shovel, and we haul the dirt out in buckets."

"Where do we put the damn dirt?" another voice called.

"It's a problem, but we're handling that. There's a space here, where we're standing, that will handle a good deal of it. We build up the banks of the river all through town and up to the fall itself. We work in shifts and we use everyone who wants to live here. Roman Ansel, Ron Pantea, and Rick Harbison have calculated the amount of earth and rock that will have to be removed. They say it's a hell of a big job—a hell of a job, but it's one we can do. The chopper is coming. Take your distribution home and then we'd like to see everyone at the fall site so you can see what there is to do. See you there."

Voices erupted with objections and refusals, but objections to reality were soon reduced to whining and bluster. The chopper came. The distribution's impressive order spoke to the people more convincingly than the mayor had done. The crowd dispersed. The loudest sound was the squeaking of the wheels of carts and wagons pulled up from the Drop landing to cold houses.

When they stood at the border of the fall, they realized slowly, a widening revelation, open-mouthed, what their disaster would be. A mountain, earth, rock, tree-trunks, limbs and broken branches rose in front of them. Behind the fall, if someone went back far enough to see the whole of it, the shear could be seen, the mountain's bone—rock straight up and down, all the dressing of tree and earth pulled away down. Where they stood, the river, ice-locked but not low in its banks, was stopped under mounds of snow. Harbison, the city engineer, spoke first, saying what they all could see. The snow would melt, the ice would thaw, the river's flow would open and with no outlet, would come back on the town, first flooding it and then drowning it. Pantea, the geologist, spoke. He said that he and Ansel had walked out to the far end of the fall, climbed it, and saw a way they thought might be cleared into a trench made there, so the water might be diverted.

Ansel spoke. There would be no heavy equipment available, but the railroad had come through here, had laid its silver lines over all these mountains, had gone through them, pick and shovel only. He, Pantea, and Harbison had planned a strategy that they were confident would open a way for the river to go. Once an opening had been made, the pressure of the water itself would widen the gap.

"This dig has to be our first priority," Pantea said. "We'll need everyone at the job, as many taking the dirt and detritus away as digging. That, or we lose the town. We have twelve lists of two-hour shifts, one shift digging, one moving the earth, four hours a day, total. It would be good if we could get people to sign for more than two shifts."

"Dixon told us the dirt should go on the Drop site—that's a mile away!" someone yelled.

"We have a plan for that, too. The rocks we can't break will go on either side of the river—here. Trees, we'll cut with chainsaws—we'll get fuel for those. We'll use that wood we get in our fireplaces. We can slide the buckets up on the ice of the river, and with all of us working, we can also have a bucket brigade that will work without everyone's having to walk a mile."

"Men? Just men?" A voice came from the crowd.

"Men and women, kids, everyone. Please sign up now and go back home and get your shovels and buckets, pails, picks, hatchets, chainsaws—whatever will help. We won't just be a mob poking earth; we'll be an organized work force, saving our town. You've seen what this is and what we have to do."

Growling, angry, resolute, wavering, they came forward for the sign-up sheets. "What about the people who stayed home?"

"Everyone will be asked. Everyone will have work to do."

For the fifty people working at the face of the fall, the work had to be coordinated, and Ansel and Harbison began a soft-spoken, intense argument over who was to command the scene. Mayor Dixon and Klimek gave them fifteen minutes to work it out and then moved in.

"This is too big a job for one man," Edwina Dixon said, addressing the crowd, "As Mayor, I'll coordinate. Dr. Pantea here heads the geology, what gets moved. Mr. Klimek does the workforce, who goes where. Mr. Ansel works at the fall, Mr. Harbison heads disposal, and Miz Reimer works with Mr. Klimek because we've got the Drop to do, too. I get reports from all of you."

They stared at her in wonder. Edwina Dixon had never been a take-charge mayor. She seemed to have grown taller, stouter since the fall. Jay, who had been standing a little away from the group, had seen what had gone on and was as amazed as they were. He had noted their tight faces and body language and had moved slowly to be on hand in case of trouble. He had always considered Dixon as a friendly, modest woman— good hearted, good tempered, but no one to take charge of anything more daunting than the Solstice Festival they held for the tourists and the Fourth of July celebration. Their shock put the men off stride and when the moment passed, it was too late for argument. Ansel called to Mike, berating him for having brought only one shovel, and the day progressed, fifty diggers, fifty dispersers, people strung out over the mile between the fall and the edge of the field.

FROM THE FALL FANTOM
HAIKU: Lawyer to teacher
Teacher to geologist
Passing the buckets.

POSTED BY THE MAYOR: WILL WHOEVER TOOK
THE TWO SHOVELS LEFT AT THIS NOTICE BOARD
PLEASE RETURN THEM.
WOOD THEFT CONTINUES. THE PUNISHMENT
FOR ANYONE CAUGHT STEALING WOOD WILL BE
PUBLIC SHAMING.

CHAPTER 18

PANTEA AND HARBISON SOON REALIZED THAT THERE would have to be double the number of people needed for the dispersal of the rocks and earth than there were at the dig face. The dispersal work was more difficult and demanding and would be until they could get some kind of a pulley system for those working at the side of the river and a more dependable method of sliding the buckets of earth on the ice or in the water when the ice melted. Mechanically minded men from all over town brought ideas for the easing of the job of dispersal. Some were harebrained, others could be considered. Edwina took them to the chiefs, who added Brad Unger to discuss their feasibility.

Pastor El Fearing spent a shift digging and a shift moving dirt. He realized that his self-evaluation, years ago, had been overly optimistic. He had seen himself as steady and dependable, comparing himself to the charismatic firebrands of faith, evangelists of mega churches. Yes, God's shock troops were necessary, he said, flagging spirits needed to be re-energized, but after the fire and fury of revival, the calm, consistent, patient work of bringing Christianity to life had to be in the hands of people like him. For his work at the dig, he found that he was giving the minimum required to keep gossip quiet. He was surprised at the number of people who committed all but full days to working at the fall. Most of the young put in time, but many others were working the way he did, enthusiastically for an hour or so, but not faithfully; showing up here and there, now and then, like the spring beauties that would soon make their appearance among the pines and firs on the hillsides.

He had prayed often for self-revelation, but when it came, it was no pleasure. He confronted his mediocrity, realizing that he had written off his lack of preaching skills by telling himself that his gifts lay in comforting troubled parishioners, and then that he lacked the will to do parish visits because his true gifts lay in prayer and study. But he did not study, and seldom prayed beyond the minimum ritual prescribed. Gold Flume liked him because he was cheerful, accepting, and didn't get in anyone's way.

Looking down street through the parsonage's front window, he would see Chris Pantea and his father leave every morning, good weather or bad, on their way to the fall and come home every evening after sundown. They were shaming him without their even guessing it as they passed below the parsonage.

He began to exhort Cheryl to go down with food, to join the women who were helping by moving rocks or tree branches. She had signed up for half-duty, pleading separate status as Pastor's wife. Older people, the ill, and those with special responsibilities had been exempted. She might be exempted also. The threat was real; the need was great, he told her.

She answered sharply, "And who has to wash your clothes and hang them out, cook the pouches, and clean the floors without a vacuum cleaner? I've got lamps to clean, and what about all the work I do at the church?"

"Hasn't AnneMarie Isaacs volunteered to help in all the work at the church? I thought all the older people..."

"I wasn't meant for this. How am I supposed to carry all that stuff down there?"

"There are women up here who wouldn't mind taking food down in the picnic boxes, making extra cocoa from the Drop—we could—"

She shut him up with a look.

Later, she said, "No one should have to go so long without good food and clean clothes and electricity. Where's the government? Where's the power company? Why don't they open up the mountain or take us all out of here!"

"We do this work or the town drowns."

"And so? The town goes to Bluebank and sets up again there."

Fearing knew that Cheryl's unhappiness wasn't about wash she did in her bathtub or water she had to bring to the house in buckets. Her loss went much deeper than present inconvenience. Cheryl was like a tree whose living parts were all on the surface. Her core had hardened years before, though when it had started, he didn't know. Perhaps it was when she realized that he really was second-rate and always would be that she had pulled her heartwood tighter.

He asked her about her requests for the Drop. There had been lists of what was and was not to be part of what the helicopter delivered ever since January, modified only slightly over the months, but like teenagers with rigid parents, people had begun to wheedle, dicker, indulge in special pleading to get the mayor to beg for increases in food or medicine, to expand what the Drop allowed. Edwina submitted their requests. Word came back. Their situation was being considered. Their level of need had been assessed. Their designation had been 2A - Basic supplies only. They could file for a change in designation if their situation materially altered. Some people claimed pregnancies and diseases. They demanded special medication. They woke up at night from dreams of the Drop stopping, leaving them to starve. These night fears stayed into their daytime lives, darkening them. Suspicion grew. Rumors grew.

The attitude of the rescuers had become cynical over the months. They missed the gratitude shown in the early days. The people manning the helicopter sensed the manipulation and were increasingly impatient. The last Drop had featured an angry confrontation between the pilot and men in the group assigned to unloading.

"We need bicycles and we wrote in bicycles and carts for hauling things."

"Carts? I think not," the pilot said, "and it's not my decision. What we deliver comes from decisions made by higher-ups, but I won't ask for it. You're thinking Army convoy bringing tanks, but this ain't that kind of operation. You don't like us, call the Army. We're Red Cross and FEMA. FEMA trucks housing components. You don't need those. Food, medicine, fuel, water, that's it," and he turned his back, growling, and took his seat. The helicopter, when it rose, blew snow into a storm around those waiting to distribute the materials it had brought, and nearly blowing those waiting off their feet.

Fearing heard about it all the rest of the day. He knew that part of the problem was ethical and that the ethical part should be his to own. There were 314 citizens of Gold Flume. The Drop supplied camp stove fuel and gasoline by the gallon. Doc drove to see sick people, but only if they were incapable of getting out of bed or moving. His car was almost never seen. An in-town system had been set up for emergency use, a town-wide party line connected the sheriff's home and office, Doc's, the mayor's, and Brad Unger's, as fire chief. All the bicycles in town had been commandeered for official use.

This tangle should be a topic of his Sunday sermon—even now, the need at the river was causing rumors and divisiveness. Who was slacking? Who was pleading sickness? Again and again he had preached the sure knowledge that in seven or eight months, or a year at the outside, the mountain would be moved or tunneled through and normal life would be restored. On every street some houses were bare of winter debris, their walks shoveled and cleared every time it snowed, woodpiles cared for, tools stowed, lines hung with wash cleared in a day, steps swept. Others bore uncared for rags flying from sagging lines, heaps of pine needles choking the corners of the doorways, unused tools decorating the house fronts, old snow decaying in mounds on the walkways. It was all but impossible to hear compassion preached for the feckless neighbor.

These differences in management had announced themselves in Gold Flume, high and low, from the upscale developments on the far side of the river to the town streets. Everyone saw these differences, but Fearing knew he couldn't touch them in church. Cheryl had drawn up her list. Everyone now made them with a certain bitterness—from the beginning questionnaire to the weekly Drop. Individual lists were gathered to be accepted or denied in offices far away, but the list, like the Drop, had become a matter of great importance. In January, income tax forms had been delivered along with the meal packets, flour, sugar, coffee, powdered milk, and dried eggs. People joked that even while they were writing checks for this year's taxes, next year's would be zero. As pastor, Fearing and Cheryl got extra supplies for the church—grape juice for communion, cocoa for meetings. He had, once or twice, taken a wagon with the cocoa down to the people working on the dig, and was cheered for his efforts. Cheryl would do none of that work.

"I think I'll go over to the church," he said. "Melody Reimer has an idea about some decorations."

Cheryl nodded and bit her lip against another sting. The Christmas poinsettias had not done well in the cold of their rooms. She had always taken the garden club arrangements home after the Sunday service, where the flowers would last for as long as two weeks before they died, and after that, the leaves would continue for months brightening the kitchen and bedroom. Since Christmas, of course, there had been no flowers. Melody had also left Cheryl the potted plants from weddings and funerals. Those, too, were gone.

"I'll say hello from you," he said as he left. No answer.

Fearing walked over the sodden back yard to the church. Sometimes in dreams he saw a covered walkway between the two buildings, allowing him to go without—what had Jay Isaacs said once, "wetting or sweating."

The church was old—1874—and had been renovated and repaired many times by men of widely varying talents. He went in through the back door, noticing its warp. Why was his eye always drawn to the faults, the cracks, this ill-fitting door, the tired pews, the creaking parts of the floor? His annoyance was weighing on him, too, so why blame Cheryl for hers?

Melody had said she would be at the church at 2:30 and he had come early to see if the big room downstairs had been cleaned up after the children's service. As he went down the stairs—a notice at the top implored people to walk softly—he heard sounds coming from below and a grunting, which he took to be animal. There had been bears now and then at other people's houses and in their garages this early, famished from their quasi-hibernation. Sometimes coyotes came in out of the cold and he had heard of mountain lions moving in for leftover food.

He went slowly, cautiously to the bottom of the stairs and looked around. They were there on the faded and sagging couch, deep in the act, which, except for certain moments in films, looked ridiculous. They didn't notice him.

He stood wondering what to do. The room was dim. They were hard at it, the boy—it was a boy, naked from the waist down—puffing and groaning in the fierce athleticism of his need, the girl all but lost beneath him. Fearing stood staring, and suddenly met the eye of the girl whose head had turned slightly. He saw a vacuity there, as though she were waiting through a TV show someone else had turned on.

Her look unnerved him. Before he went back upstairs, he locked the back door. They would have to come up the stairs and he would be sitting in the room that fronted the sanctuary. He went up the way he had come, automatically avoiding the creaking places, and sat in a chair near the vestment closet.

They weren't from his regular congregation, but he had noticed her at the Drop. She was that Dr. Bruno's kid, he thought. The boy had been facing away from him. He prided himself on his sympathy with young people, their clumsiness and the half-mad look he remembered from his own anguish at the mirror years ago. These kids were different. For one thing, they had money. Their parents' wealth meant that they had no need to get jobs to help support the family. Their potential for drug use and violence kept their parents paralyzed. Their parents' partisanship kept their teachers passive. This power allowed them to become tribal—not all of them, he thought, not all, he hoped.

Up they came. He had smiled when he heard them rattling the back door, the boy's curses, words from the girl, and both clumping up the stairs. *It takes it out of you,* he thought sourly, *all that puffing and heaving.* They would go for the side door and be in full sight for only a few seconds. He had been sitting in a little pool of light from a narrow window. Outside were three small pine trees and they sifted the light, softening it. He noticed that the days were lengthening; thank God for the long, sweet afternoons to come.

"Stop a minute," he said. The girl had known he was there and had seen them; the boy was caught. She hadn't told him—a chilly little miss. He said, "Please take your activity somewhere else. The congregation shouldn't have to pay for your cleaning bills and we have people in and out of here all the time."

"Where else do you want us to go?" The boy was posing tough. "This town is tighter than a nun's cunt." It was the Ansel boy, Roman Ansel's kid—uh—Mike.

Fearing fought a desire to laugh. "Find another place. If I see you back here, I call the sheriff and everybody's folks get to come down to his office. Now, go." They left, muttering.

While he was thinking, Melody Reimer came in, greeted him in her perky way, and went into the sanctuary. She had always struck him as a generic Sweet Old Lady until the fall and her emergence as an organizational genius. He was further moved by the fact that she seemed to take no special pride in her accomplishment. She had coordinated the Drop and was working her gifts at the dig. She was still fiddling with the logistics to make both even more efficient.

Now, though, she was in flower-lady mode. "We won't have anything blooming until July, from our own gardens," she told him, "but I think we've let down our energy on this. We can get the Garden Club to go up near Jackass Pass—excuse me—Prospector Pass—and get cedar boughs, pine, fir, spruce—the way we do at Christmas. We'll make wreaths for Sunday. Pasque flowers will be up soon, but they're too fragile to last a day out of the ground. We'll have to..."

She went on while Fearing lost the thread of it; nodding now and then in an agreement he wasn't part of. He was thinking of that boy and girl, of her utter self-possession, her sang-froid, in a moment that would rattle anyone else. She was beautiful. He smiled: brash, brazen, and beautiful. Melody, seeing the smile, was cheered by his approval of her plans.

"I saw Mike Ansel outside," she said at last, "with the Bruno girl. Such a shame, Dr. Bruno away at that convention. Some of the people who were out of town were brought back in that private helicopter they hired. You would think..." She was gossiping. Fearing took a breath.

"Mike Ansel—" he said.

"Yes," Melody nodded. "His father is a brilliant man."

Fearing, on the council since the fall, liked serving with Melody, but wondered if she had noticed the combination of impatience and condescension Ansel routinely practiced on them both. He yearned to gossip himself. He bit back the words and said, "Oh, yes, he is that."

FROM THE FALL FANTOM
Waiting at the Drop, I hope
We'll get chicken, aspirin, soap.

POSTED BY THE MAYOR: TO THOSE WITH
SYMPTOMS OF SICKNESS AND AGE, IS THERE SOME
LESS TAXING WORK YOU COULD DO? THE NEED IS
URGENT. SEE THE MAYOR.

CHAPTER 19

THE FALL AND ITS NEEDS HAD WAKENED AN ENERGY in Chris Pantea. Mr. Klimek had never mentioned Chris' part in the condo break-in and his saving by the fall. He had taken up the teacher's offer and gone to work immediately. Helping house-bound people who weren't able to get to the Drop themselves meant that for the first time in his life, Chris had become a necessary part of someone else's day, eagerly awaited, cheered by his appearance. He had been given Megan, his first partner, who had later changed her route, wanting to work with the women who had cute babies. Other partners had followed, but none was willing to plow walkways or stay and chat with the old people. Work on the dig took up many hours of his day, but on Drop days he was up at the Ridge, shoveling the paths between houses or between houses and privies, eating floury cookies, drinking watery cocoa, and hearing their wisdoms. With this work, he came to know the people on what he thought of as his route.

The March snows had been heavy. The first week's Drop had been postponed due to weather, but Chris got out the sledge he and his dad had made and got ready to go up the hill. He hadn't told anyone about the extra things he did. He used the equipment the Moritzes, Dentons, Frames and Ms. Sher had up there, but on the last visit the handle had come off Denton's shovel.

"Can I get your other shovel?" Chris asked his father that evening, "I need to clear a little of the road up to the Ridge."

Ron stopped and looked at him. "Don't the neighbors take care of that?"

"The neighbors are all old up there. They don't use the road." The conversation was making him uncomfortable. He didn't want to admit to his father that he liked the visits he made.

"Well, fine, then," Ron said, "here—take this one."

Chris took the shovel, put it on his shoulder, and began his walk through town. The shops were all closed, the walkways uncleared, and snow filled the streets. Shopkeepers had been told to keep their spaces clear, even if their shops were closed. Packing by the feet of pedestrians had made the job almost impossible. People worked their way along as best they could.

He was almost at the end of the three-block heart of town when he saw Mike and Angela coming toward him, pulling a sled that had been modified with built-up rails. He felt caught out, exposed. Why hadn't he gone around the back streets where he wouldn't be seen? It was longer, but he would have escaped this. "Hi," he greeted them without enthusiasm.

Angela sparkled at him. "Hi, Chris-to-pher," and a giggle.

"Yo," Mike said.

Chris was stopped. "What's up?" he said, in a level voice.

They took his tone as pose. Everyone tried for uncaring cool, bored and indifferent outsiders playing against the "healthy" vigor and enthusiasm of conformists and the popular kids. This custom limited the wardrobe of expression severely. Angela, being a girl, had somewhat more play.

"We've got a place," she said, "and we're going there, now. Why don't you come with us?"

"Aren't you supposed to be out at the dig?"

"Do we care if the town is a lake? Come on."

Mike shot her a look. He knew he needed a group, but he wasn't sure he wanted Chris to be part of it. Ever since the break-in, he saw how different Chris' reactions were. The kiss-ass had signed up with those Wheeler Dealers, the kids providing help for the Drop and people too old and stupid to get the packets for themselves. Angela could be annoying when she twinkled at every guy. She was twinkling now. As soon as the guy responded, she would sink away into her little pout and stare.

Chris had often dreamed of Angela, but she wasn't one of his recent hungers. Her little act had swallowed him the year before but no longer had its effect. He was, in fact, dreaming now about Cheryl Fearing, riper, fuller, more frankly open than Angela, or girls her age.

Chris shifted his weight. He wanted to be away.

"We got a place," Angela said, again. "It's a cave. Mike found it and we all go up there. We got everything you want up there."

"Like what?" Chris was pretty sure that any weed or coke or even cigarettes had long since been used up. Booze was a rarity. Most people, his parents, too, had locked up their supply because there had been break-ins over booze.

"We've got stuff," Mike said, "while you've been kissing little old ladies' asses up the hill, I've been figuring how to keep ourselves nice and warm inside and out. That means booze and chicks."

Chris saw that Mike couldn't wait to impart his big idea: "They're bored, man, they have to wash clothes and dishes, the chicks, then what? They come up to our cave and when they get there, it's party time. We worked on the potato stuff in all our packets and that stuff brews up real strong. The Maki twins rigged up a still and the stuff you get out of it is awesome. It's all up in the cave. Why not come up and see?"

Angela was surprised. She hadn't thought of Mike as being able to fit his approach to his mark. Rah-rah eager or toned-down disengaged. He was as unsophisticated as any of these boy-men, but that didn't mean he was stupid. She began to pay attention.

The invitation was half scorn. Chris knew that if he didn't go with them, Mike would tell everyone that the wimp had turned down a chance at a willing girl and the adventure of the booze they had made, for a dusty cookie in a wrinkled widow's kitchen. Who but a pussy would choose that? Angela twinkled at him.

The cave was on the other side of the river, and it took them almost an hour to get to it. The entrance was hidden by trees, but Mike pointed out its location as they crossed the bridge. Chris noticed the snake of a trail into the grove of trees, tracks made by feet and the lines of sledges, but he also saw that unless someone pointed it out, few people would notice. The cave itself was around the north side of the hill and looked difficult to get to, being high on its flank.

"That's the secret," Mike said, "there's an easy way up."

He guided Chris to an old logging trail that switch-backed two or three times and led up past the cave. There, too, the snow had been packed down with the passage of feet and drag-marks of sledges. People had even skied there.

He found good use for the shovel he was carrying and which he dug into the packed snow now and then when the road's rise got more acute. He heard sounds from the cave well before the three of them reached it.

Kids were having an argument of some kind, voices raised, male, female, and single words were skidding past them, most of the sounds lost among the trees. Chris didn't want to be in the noise of the cave. He didn't want to be with Mike, either, or be part of the argument with the unseen antagonists. He thought he might stay for half an hour or so, establish his normality, and get out and down the hill in time for one visit before the light left and he was due home for dinner. People were eating earlier than they had before the fall, and going to sleep shortly after dark.

The three of them moved around the last loop of the switchback and into the grove of spruce trees. A girl came out of the cave, clutching part of a torn jacket to her body, and rushed past them, sobbing and gasping. Behind her they heard a male voice, cursing. Chris knew the girl faintly— Tim's youngest sister, he thought. They went in.

Threadbare rugs had been brought up, things from basements, bent tube-chairs from summer patios. The cave reeked of sweat-damp wool, urine, and an odor from the distillate they had made and vomit from a body's reasonable resistance to it.

The kids were enjoying this or seemed to be. Chris had the feeling that the event wasn't what delighted them so much as the idea of the event as they were telling it to themselves or would, later. If all of this was Mike's finding and organizing and Mike's idea of a good time, what had he and Angela been doing downtown while it was all going on? Someone put a plastic glass in his hand half full of a cloudy, grayish substance. He looked up. The boy stood there, waiting for him to drink and give back the glass. The smell was booze, all right, but with an undersmell of a gas pump and a whiff, under that, like licking the white crust on a dead battery.

"Come on," the boy said, "I don't have all day."

Chris brought the glass to his mouth and the stuff moved its oily way, burning, to his front teeth. He couldn't. He stopped and handed the glass back. "No, thanks."

"Wuss," the kid said, flat-voiced, "candy-ass."

"How long has this party been going on?" Chris was trying for a tone of interest.

"Since yesterday," the kid said. "Some kids go right on through, some cut out for an hour or so or even go home to keep the folks from going ape and hunting up the place."

"Don't people know you're not out at school or the dig?"

"The dig's perfect. You get out there, sign up, and wave a shovel or bucket around for fifteen minutes and then drift off and everybody thinks you're still on the job. Still, that's funny. Like the still we have up here."

The cave was north-facing, but there was enough light from outside to allow them to see. Chris assumed that after nightfall there would have to be fuel used for lamps, but he saw through the tangle of arms and legs to a fire-pit in the middle of the hard-packed floor. There was no fire, now; the space was heated by their crowding bodies. He was having a difficult time breathing—he wanted to leave. He turned, or half-turned, toward the cave's entrance and stopped.

Two girls, naked, were lying on the floor at the south side of the cave. They looked to be unconscious. They were motionless, legs spread. The group had moved away from them toward something going on deeper inside. Over two other girls, two boys were working feverishly, their sounds lost in the noise of the others. Chris realized that he was the only one paying attention to them. The kids around him were moving further into the cave. He tore his eyes from the sight, understanding that now

153

would be a good moment to get away. He backed out of the cave into the chill, pure air of the outside.

CHAPTER 20

HE WANTED TO BE QUICKLY AWAY BEFORE HIS absence was noticed, but he didn't remember how hard-packed the snow was at the cave's entrance. Turning to go, he slid, his feet going out from under him and their force catapulting him over the bank and into the trees. He was falling fast, down the side of the hill. He had skied enough to remember to let the fall take him, relaxing his body while trying to work his legs downhill of his fall. It had never worked on skis, and it didn't work now. Eventually, a tree stopped him, and he found himself head first, all but buried in the deep, soft snow that banked it.

Turning, shifting, and struggling, he got himself moved to his side and from there, around to vertical, resting now and then, and when he could, looking up the hill, hoping no one had seen him or noticed him there, like a wounded elk in the snow. He was relieved and grateful when he realized that no bones had been broken, nothing requiring cries for help. None of any noise he made would be heard through the din of the cave anyway, and he wanted nothing less than to draw attention to himself.

At last, fighting, panting, and struggling in waist-deep snow, Chris freed himself and began to work his way around to a lower part of the logging road, then down, with the twilight, to home. He had forgotten all about the shovel until he was at his door.

The mistake meant that he would have to go back up to the cave. When he told his father, the assumption was that Chris had left the shovel up at the last house on his route. His father was annoyed. "Go up there tomorrow. We may need it."

His mother was waiting for the two of them to remark on the dinner she had taken pains with. She had turned the boredom of the packets into a challenge. The proud announcement printed on the foil-sided packets was that the food it contained was nutritionally balanced. It was Della's mission to bring variety and flavor to their nutritionally balanced nutriment. Her brother and his kids had begun trapping and hunting and Della was creative, blending the packet food with what they brought. Some of the meat was not identifiable to her and she asked no questions. Sometimes there was a cut of deer or elk. She made stews of the freeze-dried vegetables and used the meat from the packets as background flavoring for the wild-caught meat. Ron told them that he had heard that a neighbor had trapped some quail near the river and was breeding them, sacrificing some of his fuel to keep them warm. She spent the remainder of the meal discussing recipes and plans and the packets, which spared Chris the need to create a story about his afternoon.

He went to his class the next day, noticing that Mike and Angela weren't there. The need for people at the dig was an excuse for school absence. What had started as mandatory attendance had degenerated into a sketchy now-and-then school appearance, minds on anything but the curriculum. No one knew if the plans and studies with three teachers and volunteers would be counted toward graduation, which, in any case, would happen in Callan in the first week of June. The high school was on the other side of the fall and might as well be in China. Classes met at the church social hall and there were rumors that summer vacation would be canceled and the four-hour lessons continued through the summer break.

The growing absence of so many of the junior high and high school students alerted John Klimek, who sent a girl down to the town hall and then over to one or two of the homes of the missing teenagers. One of the teachers said she thought it might be an epidemic. The fear of illness was a constant undertone. There could be typhus from bad water, pneumonia—all the diseases rampant at the time in which they were now living. There had been talk of viruses or bacteria or other pollutants in the river water some people used for washing. "What if it's something serious?" Klimek remarked that if this were the case, the victims would cover a greater range of ages. "This is educational cholera," he said, "teen-age typhus."

After the session, Chris took off for the cave. March sun, warm and long lasting, had begun to melt the snow, making his way treacherous. He fell several times on the logging road where there were long patches of glare-ice in the melt-and-freeze weather of the mountain pre-spring. When he could, he walked the ridge beside the road on crusts that gave and crusts that held, taking almost an hour to make the trip that in summer he could have done in half that time.

He had expected to find the cave empty, but there were a few kids lying inside or sitting at the dead fire ring. He wasn't sure whether they had come back or stayed over, but the rhythm and energy of the party were long gone. The smell was revolting. Urine, fecal, and vomit smells had the acetic odor of many bodies' attempts to flush the chemicals they had ingested, smoked, or injected the day before. Chris began to laugh. No need to fear bears or mountain lions, wolves or dogs, he thought; one sniff of this miasma and they would take off across the mountain as if they had been scalded.

He wondered why the kids' absences hadn't been noticed at home, why no one had become alarmed. He went further into the cave, all but gagging, and began to look for his shovel. The floor was matted with clothing, rugs, food packets, fuel pouches, and broken pieces of unidentifiable equipment—he remembered the still they had brought up there. He realized he would have to make a complete search—the shovel wasn't in sight. Someone might have taken it away. He began a careful circle around the perimeter.

The kids still in the cave's back gloom seemed to be sleeping or dulled with hangover. Most of them barely stirred as he passed. Stopping at them seemed a waste of time, but he did ask a boy whose eyes turned to him for a moment. "I ain't seen it." Mike had gone, and so had Angela, and the boy said he didn't remember when they had left. He didn't seem to know that half the day had gone also.

Chris thought that wherever their kids had disappeared to, the parents must have decided they were safe. There were no drugs left in town. The liquor store and the bars were closed. Those working on the dig would sometimes go to houses closer than their own to bed down on friends' floors. Bad influences had always been assumed to come from the outside, and now that there was no such influence, parents had relaxed their guard. As he thought of this, Chris saw the shovel propped neatly against the north wall of the cave. It had been picked out by a shaft of sunlight that had moved since he had come in. Near it lay a boy, younger than most—somebody's kid brother. The boy didn't stir. Chris had to step over him to get the shovel and when he did he saw how *other* the boy was. There wasn't even in sleep such a removal. Nothing stirred. Chris bent closer, not able to smell anything special in the overwhelming stench, but he saw vomit at the boy's gray lips, and that the boy didn't seem to care that what he had fallen on had pulled his lower eyelid down. The pulling made Chris wince reflexively.

He straightened. "Hey!" The half-alive didn't move. "Hey, I think this kid is dead." One or two sets of eyes turned to him, blearily. "This kid, here—he's dead. Somebody needs to go get the sheriff and stuff." The gazes turned, annoyed, uninterested. He heard their thoughts as though they had spoken. *This kid? There was a whole rave of kids up here last night—how would I know the kid? It's cold here. I've pissed myself and tossed a couple of times—how could I go down there? Later, maybe, yes, later.*

Chris took the shovel. He felt rage rising in him. Why had he been chosen? He had never wanted to come up here at all, and he had left as soon as he could without sampling any more than a sip of the garbage that was being passed from one of them to another; filthy pipes, used needles, some homemade like what prisoners would make.

"This isn't my job!" he yelled at them. "Not my idea!" and he left the cave, muttering, out into the clean blue smell of the hillside. He was about to start down. He'd decided to fade away, to let someone else, a survivor up there, explain it all, when an idea struck him. If he traversed the face of the hill, he would be able to see the fall and also the river and where the bore-hole would be. The hell with the cave and the kids in it.

CHAPTER 21

THE WALK WAS PLEASANT, THE SUN WARM, BUT THE snow was hazardous. He used the shovel to stabilize his weight and break some of the treacherous wind-slab. He came around the bend of the hill and saw the world laid out before him.

He couldn't see beyond the fallen mountain, but he did see how monumental the fall had been. The town was in a bowl, now surrounded on all sides, dwelling in its little pocket, and unless its people dug that borehole to relieve the river as the snow melted, there would be a lake in which an entire town would be at the bottom. What his dad and the other men had said was absolutely true. He could see them all working away at the edge of the fall. How inconsequential it all looked; how doomed and useless. He suddenly wanted to cry, overwhelmed with what he was seeing.

He looked at the shovel. Tiny people were down there shoveling, carrying the earth away bucket by bucket or on sledges. Against such a picture, its complete, inevitable clarity of doom spread before him. What was the death of some kid? His father had been meeting with the people in town who knew about earth falls, hydrology, physics. Chris hadn't really listened much or given the problem much thought. Here was what they would be facing—he stood, taking in the sight and measuring possibilities and outcomes until the sun went behind the mountain. He turned, then, and headed back the way he had come, easier because of his footprints in the snow. When he passed the cave again, he looked in. The light was dim with the sun gone, and he saw no one. He didn't go in to see if anything had changed.

Down the mountainside, the going was quicker, and with the shovel for support, his trip took only a little over half an hour. He was in town among people he knew and had known all his life: kids, parents, Mr. Engel, two of the Unger kids, Mrs. Harbison—"Hi, Mrs. Harbison," Mr. Brown, the bank manager—-"Hi, Mr. Brown." He had never sensed the comfort of normality before. Normal was the wallpaper of a day. Now, he treasured it. All these people knew him and there were other people whom he hadn't known before the fall: the Moritzes, the Dentons, the Frames, Ms. Sher—whom he had visited and helped, up on the ridge.

He passed the place where Mike and Angela had stopped him only a day before. He had never yearned, hungered as he did now, to reverse the rotation of the earth, detaching it from its tether to spin backwards and stop at that minute so that he might unmake it. If he had come out of the house fifteen minutes earlier or fifteen minutes later, how different everything would have been. The truth of that, he saw, was a complete defense. There had been no motivation on his part, only coincidence. It wasn't fair that he should have to be responsible for something he had not initiated. His trouble at the break-in was another matter and he still felt guilty and diminished for the part he had played in it. He had gone up to the cave on his own, that was true, but leaving the shovel and going up to find it, and finding the dead boy, wasn't part of his voluntary actions because he hadn't been there when the kid died, or at any time during that night, or even later that day. He wasn't part of all the doping and screwing. He wasn't responsible.

How comforting his house looked now, so much different from the way it had looked yesterday morning. He shivered a little. The evening was chilling—maybe it would go below freezing. At sea level, water froze at 32 degrees Fahrenheit. Where they lived, freezing was about 25 degrees. At sea level, water boiled at 212 degrees, here at about 170. That's why cooking took longer. Boiling water wasn't as hot. What a good thing that was to know. His dad had worked it all out with him years ago. His dad dealt in knowledge like that, knowledge you could trust, knowledge that wouldn't betray you.

———————◆———————

Chris' mother had found some gray hair in November and had gone back and forth about whether or not to let herself go gray. By the time she had decided to use something, the fall had happened and within a month, any of the colors she might have used lay beyond her ability to procure. Here and there throughout the town, dozens were going two-toned, measuring on their heads the days and weeks since the fall. When Chris saw his mother, he was aware of her as being unadorned, but there was something in her plainness that wasn't hiding her character. She seemed more... he thought... herself.

She greeted him, "Big news—the bears are out. One was looking in Mr. Klimek's garbage and he shot it. He's sharing the meat with the Wheeler Dealers. We'll be getting bear meat for stew—not a lot—he'll have to share it out among all the kids, but it'll be enough for a few good meals. Whattaya think of that?" She was all delight and grin. She stopped—"Honey, what is it?"

"I'm just tired, I guess." He started to go to put the shovel back in the garage, and realized how tired he was. He had been hiking up and down difficult terrain, unused to the pace he had set himself and the difficulty of traveling in snow. He tried to project an attitude of interest at the idea of the bear meat stew. "When are we having it?"

"I'm not sure. He has to skin the bear first, and cut it up and sort it all out—a few days, probably." She grinned again.

"Isn't it illegal to kill a bear?" he asked.

"It was. Now — well — no one will come after us about it, and I can't help being glad about getting rid of all that crap about protecting the environment, as if that were even really possible. The environment has just given us a pretty raw deal. Somebody in Washington, D.C., made that law about killing bears. We're in competition with them now, with all the animals, the deer and the elk and the mountain lion and the bears." She caught herself—the Mother template slid back over her. "I don't mean we should stop obeying the law—I don't mean that, that we should—"

"Ma," Chris said, "it's all right, really." At that moment, he felt older than she was, wiser, because of what he had seen and the secret he was keeping and where he had been. There was a new sense of himself that his tiredness increased. He had been somewhere, all right. He had the exhaustion to prove it.

"You do look a little tired," she said, "why don't you go up and rest until dinner?"

The bedrooms were freezing now, and had been all winter, and Chris felt the wet socks icy cold on his feet. He took his boots off and peeled away the socks, grunting with disgust. Water could be wrung from them.

In the months of the fall, people had suffered terribly from cold. Many women went back into floor-length skirts, layered for warmth. Some wore ski clothes all day and hauled out the down quilts from their attics. They heated plates on their woodstoves to take up to beds at night. Chris knew he would have to stay near the heater in the kitchen until his feet stopped hurting and he stopped shaking. That meant he couldn't be alone up in his room to think about things. His mother would rattle on. His dad would come home and there would have to be chatting at dinner. They would ask about his day. He would lie and lie, and he wouldn't be alone until he was in his bed, waiting for his body to warm the icy sheets.

And so it was, and so he lied and the image of the dead boy in the cave lay in his mind, blurred at the edges with their talk and his lies. Here, in their questions, and here and here, were moments where he might have begun to tell them about the dead kid, but the moments passed under rivulets of conversation—a rigged-up oven on the wood-stove, chilblains, plans for tomorrow. His need to tell faded.

The next day was a Drop and Chris and his new partner, Nicole, went up with the cart he and his dad had made and delivered the packets to his people. Chris used his own shovel and cleared the way between houses and privies. Nicole went home.

He knew the Moritzes were glad to see them and mentioned, after Nicole left, that they had liked Megan. "Send her our regards." Housebound, on this ridge, they were lonely in a way only the old can be. Now that all computers, phones, pods, electronic and electrical communication was impossible; the Moritzes were on a more equal footing with town than they had been. There was speech and there was silence. There was the offer of food, drink, and warmth. There was the gift and favor of work done that eased living. There was reading and work during daylight. Privilege sank away.

Mrs. Moritz, tiny and chubby, had shown Chris their wedding pictures and pictures of her youth, slender—cute, but it was impossible for him to imagine her or them as anything but what they were now. He knew that they were squandering their saved sugar, flour, and freeze-dried eggs on him with cakes or cookies baked on their woodstove with the rare and treasured supply of wood, riskily gathered from deadfall on the hillside. Their age and frailty made their sacrifices more moving, their attention more special.

It seemed they wove a spell—it was the stillness, the intent listening they gave him, a peaceful, profound absorption in what he thought and did that made Chris want to stay. Sometimes they would speak of their pasts, not longwinded or ponderously, but with point. Then they sat still. Chris had never been in an environment where silence was part of language.

They had come to America after World War II, tired of "living in rubble," Mr. Moritz said. Mrs. Moritz laughed. "You, a mining engineer. What else was your day, but rubble?

"We're going to tell you something," Herman Moritz said. "We're reposing our trust in you. Some years ago, the Frenches—a big family here then—discovered a flock of wild turkeys up the hill here. They hunted them and killed them, every last one. None came back for years, but last week, we saw a tom and his little harem. We think they live up past the big rock—they came down at first light, picking around the back of the house, for old pine seeds, we think. You can hunt them. Take one or two. Leave the rest—just you and your dad, maybe."

"I'll tell him," Chris said. For no reason that he could think of, Chris said, "There's a cave—it's on the other side of the river. One of the kids discovered it."

"Is it off a logging road?" Moritz asked.

"Yes... "

"... and looks out to the east?"

"Yes."

Both Moritzes smiled, looking at each other with an old warmth, and then at Chris.

"They all used that cave—they went up there afternoons, our kids, when they were in school to get together and later on to smooch—kiss and pet. So you're still using it?" Mrs. Moritz asked.

Chris nodded.

"Tradition," Moritz said. "Nice to know some things don't change."

Chris said no more, but the quiet in the room was easy and the Moritzes were smiling. These were memories they had carried lightly, Chris saw, because the memories were good. He would see the cave in his mind, and how he had gagged at the stench, the racket, and the vacant faces and the dead boy.

"No need to work so hard," Moritz cried out the door at Chris as he went back to finish shoveling.

FROM THE FALL FANTOM
With our work we'll save this town,
Break a smile, forget that frown.
As your tootsies ache like hell —
You'll forget the sweaty smell.

POSTED BY THE MAYOR: WORK AT THE DIG IS
GOING WELL. HERE IS THE LIST OF PEOPLE SIGNED
UP FOR EACH OF THE FOUR-HOUR SHIFTS. IF YOU
ARE UNABLE TO WORK FOR MORE THAN TWO
HOURS, SEE CHIEF UNGER OR SHERIFF ISAACS.

CHAPTER 22

CHRIS SAW ANGELA TWO DAYS LATER AT CHURCH
with her mother. Wakened from his dream of her, he saw her flat against
her background, beautiful enough, but too extreme in pose, so self-
aware that she was unaware of anyone else. He saw the five or six boys,
sharpened with need, staring after her, and he felt safe and superior on
the shore of his new wisdom.

He had also learned that a person could be witness to horrors and
could do horrors and that no one would see it on his face or notice it in
his movements. Lies, evasions—they had read *The Picture of Dorian
Gray* in school—you could do it without the picture. One way only
was open to him—expiation through goodness. He remembered that
Dorian had tried that himself. Dorian had failed because there were too
many temptations. Chris thought that he had fewer of those, and with
no one kindling him like Lord Henry did to Dorian, he might overcome
his weakness.

For a while he practiced this goodness, making himself aware of any need in his family and his people, until his mother asked if he were ill and Mrs. Denton told him in a nice way to stop fussing.

The kid was Billy Shively. For two days after seeing him in the cave, Chris had waited for inquiries. There were some and a few of the kids who knew he had been up there eyed one another, but Chris was amazed that many who must have seen the boy there seemed to have forgotten it—just like that. Then came another surprise. The boy's body had been found by the river—down river from the town, midway between the dig and town.

The boy's death had been a drowning, people said. Kids had been warned not to go near the river, unevenly frozen. It was fun to walk on the lacy ice and feel it crumble and to jump back just before it broke away into and re-froze. Parents of younger children warned them again, using Billy as a new example.

At the dig, people were asking who had seen the boy near the river. It seemed no one had. Everyone was at the funeral; the kid's younger brother looked as shocked and maimed as his parents. They sat, stunned with grief, as the town walked past them, murmuring sorrow. Chris moved in the line as they sat. He had gone, fearing someone's suspicion. The parents looked like wax figures, pale, unmoving, almost robbed of breath. Suddenly, the mother's hand shot out and pulled at his sleeve. She spoke in a soft, flat voice, telling him how much Billy had appreciated his words of encouragement, and valued his mentoring.

Chris gaped. He'd never taken the slightest notice of the kid. Encouragement? When? He swallowed and thanked Mrs. Shively and said something to Billy's father and younger brother and moved on. He realized that he had said that everyone would miss Billy. Behind him in the line there must be kids who had known Billy. Did they care about him at all? Chris was amazed at the ease and smoothness of any of the kids' escape from the whole thing. Who had taken the body down from the mountain and when and how had the body been arranged to make a drowning so obvious a conclusion? It was an accident; people were sure. The death was simple and no one was to blame. The parents' grief was hard, but unambiguous. Who could complain of that?

As they left the church, Chris told his father about the wild turkeys up at the ridge. "Later, when the snow dries off a little more, we'll go up there."

"I'll bring one to the Moritzes," Chris said.

The town breathed out the long, sad day and then took up its task, the re-routing of the river. Ron Pantea had been meeting with Mayor Dixon, Harbison—the city engineer, and the others on the council. When the snowmelt began, the bore hole would have to be there and be big enough to take the spring runoff. There would be sufficient force in the river to blast a way through, carrying rocks and stones and heaped earth with it. The boulders would help to shape the river's new course. Would a town full of people used to bulldozers and dump trucks the size of rooms have enough will to keep picking up hand tools day after day? Mayor Dixon had requested a plane to come over and bomb the way open. The state engineers and the federal geologists had denied the request, saying that the instability of the fall made such actions unwise. Three representatives from three government agencies were flown in and all advised that the entire town citizenry be evacuated and resettled on the other side of the fall. They told the mayor that she should call them when the run-off from the thaw began to edge toward flood. All of them were against the river's diversion, saying it would result in other problems.

There had been digging on the other side of the fall with snow-plows and tractors located in Callan, they said. In Gold Flume, the old problem of where to put the earth that people were digging was becoming as big a problem as the water itself.

Pilots on the Drop were speaking of larger problems outside this ring of mountains—hurricanes and floods on the eastern seaboard. There had been an earthquake on the other side of the divide, a heave all along the plate line, north to south. Some of it had affected towns in Utah. People were saying that it was man-caused by drilling and extraction. Gold Flume's problems were small, the experts said, compared to troubles in other places.

People had asked that newspapers be included in the Drop. The pilot said, "We pick up your packages at a warehouse. They're part of a standard delivery. If you ask for a paper, somebody would have to go to a box somewhere and get the papers on his own. Maybe somebody should keep requesting it — maybe then..."

Chris had heard many rumors about what was going on outside the fall. One of the Wheeler Dealers said it was God's judgment. Another said it was terrorist bombing. Going up with one kid or another to the ridge, Chris and his partner would fantasize about what the world out there was going through. Were people in cities reverting to savages, looting and murdering? Were some becoming cannibals? Chris' dad had heard them talking and reminded them that there was an efficient component of society still functioning, which was providing food and fuel to Gold Flume. What was the kick they got from imagining horrors outside their protecting mountains? The mayor had been assured that even if no other help were then available, the Drop would continue for as long as it was needed. This meant that there was law, planning, and organization out beyond the fall, whatever was happening there.

Still, the wild rumors persisted, festooned with the thousand horror stories that people had read and watched on TV, the gathered mythos of generations.

Gold had drawn the first settlers here. A walk up to the Gold Flume cemetery, only a few yards from the edges of the fall, testified to the hunger that called people to this secluded valley. Joachim and Hulde Schmidt had come in 1866 and left a son Peter, six, and a daughter Annie, four, in the ground before moving on. The Ingmars and Janosches, the Gilles and the Gustaves, had sons and daughters who were transmuted into the Bobbys and Marys and Jackies and Annies, and lay beside them, or were left behind when gold was discovered in the Black Hills.

A few stayed after the easy gold had been taken. Some even outlasted the silver booms and those of molybdenum, uranium, and strontium. The heirs of the gold mountains opened stores or ran cattle. Some few of the cemetery names still appeared on the plaques of the war dead of World War I and World War II, Korea, Vietnam. Some were on trophies at the new high school.

There was interest in what Ron Pantea talked about when he mentioned that it might be wise to look again at possible exploration of veins and pockets of gold and silver and rarer elements now that half the mountain had been sheared away. The fall might provide benefits after all. He advised that the heaps of earth being moved be gathered into mounds and sifted for possible wealth when the river ran once more. "There just might be a payoff in all this digging."

The April snows hadn't come yet, nor the May, which were notoriously wet and heavy, but under the dead weight of the winter's grip, the earth was unlocking and the river was reawakening, moving up in its bed, turning over, under the ice.

CHAPTER 23

THERE HAD BEEN TALK OF TEAMS—MAKING A GAME of the digging. They had already upped the hours for the younger men, cut them for men over sixty. The young ones shoveled furiously until the more experienced told them about rhythm and pace. Someone thought there should be a keeper of the rhythm—with a drum, perhaps; until another said that was too reminiscent of galley slaves they had seen in the old Bible western dramas.

"We see that every Easter on TV."

"TV? What's that?" and a sour laugh.

Adaptations and increased numbers had made the dumping easier. Jay hadn't wanted AnneMarie to take part. Only those women who were young and in good health had to go, he said, and he could surely get an exception for her. She waved him away.

"I can carry two buckets half-full," she said, "and besides, how would it look—you and Edwina and the council putting all this together and now you're asking for a special exemption? They'll have your head on a plate like John the Baptist."

Surprise. In her old haze, AnneMarie would never have made that simile. Jay was beginning to see here and there, now and then, lights, little breakings for moments at a time, moving through her, behind her eyes. Sometimes they would be in her voice or in a graceful, unforced movement—just for a moment. "Are you—will you be able to do that, take buckets for two hours at a time?"

"If that's where the action is, I guess so."

"Get out your boots—"

"I haven't worn them in so long, I wonder if they'll still fit."

"Why shouldn't they?"

"Feet get bigger when you keep standing on them," she said. "I used to be a neat size six—no more, not since the girls were coming up. I wouldn't be surprised if I've splayed out to an eight or eight and a-half."

"Paddle boats," he said, "canal barges. If your boots don't fit..."

"We can't send for new ones," she said. "I'll have to wear something of yours and heavy socks."

"You're set on doing this?"

She nodded.

"Because of what people will say if you don't?"

"More than that—dim as I am, I want to be part of something necessary, something normal people are doing. The river will rise and flood the town, if I, AnneMarie Melaragno Isaacs don't get up off my big fat ass and start bailing. I used to be strong—maybe I still am." She sighed heavily. "Where are those plastic buckets?"

Her gaze dropped. He had been doing the wash with those buckets, work that should have been hers, work he had had to do at night and at odd times when he wasn't being called out on the increased family violence or wood theft.

"I've let you down," she said.

He weighed that. There was no use denying what she said, but he hadn't thought of their lives that way. He loved her and when the cloud had come down, he had missed her and sometimes thought he must have betrayed her in a way he didn't know. Had she had expectations of better things after the work and her involvement in the kids' growing up? Now that they were gone, had she dreamt of ease, travel, some hobby or interest that living in a small, isolated place was denied to her?

"If I took over the wash—"

"Let's wait on that and see how you feel on the bucket brigade."

"You're the only man up there at the 'laundromat' you and John Klimek made—"

"Not so," he said. "It's true that most are women, but John comes up, and other guys, too, now and then."

"I want to be normal," she said, "regular. I want to be ordinary, to do ordinary work and fill my place." She gave him a look that made him want to weep.

A terrific snow fell that day and night, two feet in some places, but the town came out and cleared the dig and women carried the frozen mud up from the river to one of the three bucket brigades going to three different dump sites, passing the buckets full and empty back and forth.

When people exhausted themselves, they left the line and were replaced or those still on the line made it reach a little farther, so to arrange and rearrange itself to adjust to those moving in and out of it.

AnneMarie took her place and fell into the rhythm. The buckets weren't standardized and some had clumsy bails. Some were over-full and very heavy. It made the rhythm difficult, and in less than half an hour she was exhausted and stepped back, letting Siri Harbison move into her place. She thought she might go back home but resting—the men had put up a makeshift bench of bricks and a board—she watched and half-dozed for a while. The resting women sat and talked around her. Their talk sounded comforting, like bees in summer. When she came out of her doze, Melody was beside her, huffing a little. The urgency of the situation, the threat of the complete destruction of the town, had given all of them—almost all—resources they hadn't known they had. The threat of a flood like Noah's made the town's separation from the world more poignant and its salvation more urgent. They were saving a dear and cherished place—a unique place, infinitely worthy of their sacrifices. They complained about their strained arms, blisters, chilblains, of cracked lips and roughened hands, of wet feet that dried to cracks in the skin of their heels, of coughs and headaches, and they heaved themselves up after short rests to work again.

AnneMarie stretched and began to listen to the talk around her. Melody was wondering how much effort would be available during the summer for garden club activities. That would be after Gold Flume had been saved, of course, after the abnormal-normal had been restored. Melody had always struck AnneMarie as being a busybody, engineering projects and people. That feeling had been made when Melody first came to town and had continued without any thoughtful reappraisal until now. She must have been a hectoring little body in school: "Come on! Let's go!" There was always someone like that in a class—female, usually, athletic, although Melody had spread a little and her curls were gray. AnneMarie had been quiet in school, happily in the background watching. She knew she wasn't stupid, only that she felt most secure when she was settled into herself attending to everything, separated from no one.

Even though she hadn't seen Melody grow, marry, and lose the terrible responsibility of her own rightness, she knew that Melody had come to Gold Flume after marrying a mean drunk who, on a vicious tear, had thrown her through a window. The glass had shattered, and a piece had flown off by the force of his rage and severed one of his arteries. Melody had been too badly injured herself to attend to his bleeding. He had been unaware of his wound until he noticed an inability to stand up anymore. He had fallen to his knees and died. All of Melody's wit and skill had been spent in keeping the secret of her husband's drinking, but someone had known someone and had brought the word to town somehow—a vacationer, maybe, someone's cousin—AnneMarie didn't remember where she had heard all this.

Melody had made a good widow, useful and obliging. In the garden club, to which AnneMarie had contributed time now and then, she organized as she had in her job on cruises, and everyone was in awe of her work during the fall. She was just now beginning to look her age. "Quite a workout," she said to no one in particular. "If we'd done that all our lives, do you think we wouldn't have that flabbiness in our upper arms?"

Margo Larson, sitting next to AnneMarie, said, "I'm not sure—I think it's just what happens when you get old."

Down the bench there was laughter at someone's joke. The women relaxed into silence and watched the buckets move along the line.

"I'm giving myself twenty minutes more," Melody said, "and then, I'll go back."

"Work long enough," AnneMarie said, "and they'll have to take us home in wheelbarrows."

"Or in body bags," Margo said.

"This job will be hell in summer," AnneMarie said.

"Summer? You don't expect it will take that long, do you?"

"We don't know how big the fall is, how much there is to move."

"We don't have to move the whole mountain," Melody said. "We just have to relieve the pressure on the river. People are even talking about making a tunnel, like a long, huge culvert. I think we might get the Drop to deliver pipe in sections. Does anyone know how big this job is?"

"People have asked the pilot on the Drop where the edges are. Apparently, it's almost to the edge of the Mall."

"This conversation is scaring me," AnneMarie said. "I've got to get back to work."

The women all rose and joined the line.

By the time AnneMarie got home, she could barely walk. She hadn't seen Jay, who was on the digging part of things and had stayed on. She had been too tired to eat and had gone to the house, pulled herself up the stairs, clinging to the banister and leaving her muddy outer clothes on the floor, pulling the wet boots off with the last of her strength, and flopping on the unmade bed.

Jay came home two hours later and found her asleep. He reconstituted two food packets and warmed them using their insulated camp stove that could be fueled with a handful of twigs. He woke her, and they ate.

"Back tomorrow," he told her. "We've been hitting boulders, but the water's helping and will help us more if we can only break through before the town is flooded."

"I wish I was young," AnneMarie said. "It's frustrating not to be able to move any more than ten or fifteen buckets before feeling it. An hour and my hands feel like claws."

He couldn't see her in the almost complete darkness, but her voice, though tired, didn't have the drugged quality that had become her way since her illness. She was tired—he could tell that, but, he thought, not hopeless. "How are you doing?"

"I'm worried about the fall," she said, "that we won't get done in time and that the water will defeat all we tried to do."

"Listen, there are more than 200 people working on clearing it—not all at once, and not for twelve hours a day, but think the pyramids—think the Great Wall of China. They weren't built with sophisticated tools. We have lots of human labor. We've moved boulders and any new highway will have to be placed somewhere else, but whatever is going on outside will be eased and help will come. In the meanwhile, we will rescue this town, all of us, bucket by bucket. Brad Unger discovered a bunch of old axes, McLeods, and shovels in the back room of the fire house, and for a wonder, hand pumps. We can't use the fire truck to draft out of the river because the water's too full of detritus, but the work is going forward."

The thought opened to Jay that he wouldn't have been talking with AnneMarie in this way last year, or even last month.

"I'll be a wreck tomorrow," she said.

The next day, she lasted only half the time, leaving early and having to stop seven or eight times to rest on the way home. Women who had been on the lines longer than she had told her that she would toughen; only keep on at work. How could she believe that? She felt as though she had been systematically beaten or been in an auto wreck. She wanted no more than to lie down and fall away from herself into sleep or coma. Jay came back later, too exhausted himself to eat, so they both collapsed into bed, sleeping and waking twice during the night and rising early and ravenous. AnneMarie felt a little better.

Jay's work was doubling. There were wood thieves and wife beatings. He had to bring burn victims and fall victims to Doc, to break up fights and set out after missing children and two confused elders who had wandered away from home. He listened to dozens of rumors of all kinds—that this man or that kid has sloughed off and stayed away from work they had been assigned, that kids were breaking into houses while everyone was away at the river, that the drowned boy had been murdered, that drugs and booze were being made up in old mine-workings, that the ghosts of the buried inhabitants under the fall were coming out at night to frustrate the designs of those who wanted to save the town. Marcy Day was saying that God had sent the trouble outside and the peril inside to destroy a mankind that no longer worshipped Him.

People had asked Jay about some of these possibilities. "When the river has a place to go, I'll look into it," he said, "ghosts and all."

The diggers had come upon the broken materials of houses and the corpses of cars, a bathtub, a hot tub, but as yet, no human remains. Most of the houses on that side of The Hungry Mother were vacation places, second homes for summer-winter two-weekers. Luckily, Christmas had passed and maybe there had been skeleton staff or no staff up at the mansions. Were any of those servants or cooks there when the mountain fell? No one knew. Some houses had been huge, meant for entertaining, but had any of them been anything but waiting?

Lower on the mountain and a little to the south was Al Franklin's cabin, taken away, and it was for him and for Arlette and Tim Engstrom that people had mourned. The diggers hoped they wouldn't come upon parts they could identify of people they had known, any clothing or possessions that were familiar. Now and then the diggers comforted one another—after all, they weren't clearing the mountain away; they were working on a minute portion of it, at the end of its slide. There was only a small chance of having to find anything more than they already had, things randomly picked up into the air as the mountain gave and the storm poured water, sluicing things down to come to rest on the far side of what had been the bed of the river.

FROM THE FALL FANTOM
In a fairer world
Reimer pretty, Fearing wise,
Dixon tall and bold.

POSTED BY THE MAYOR: A MAP SHOWING THE
EXTENT OF THE FALL IS COMING ON THE NEXT
DROP. IT WILL BE POSTED HERE.

CHAPTER 24

"WHO IN THE HELL WRITES THESE?" JAY ASKED
Edwina Dixon. "Have you ever seen anyone putting them up?"

"They're posted at night. People read them with more interest than
they read mine."

❖

AnneMarie's hands were beginning to blister, even under her gloves.
At home, she looked about for something that would help, thought
about potholders, and sewed herself a pair like oven mitts, which she
wore over her gloves. They worked so well that other women and some
men came to see them.

"You sew these edges together so the pad won't slip," she told them.
Later, she sewed three more pairs for women and heard praise for
'AnneMarie's Mitts' as the buckets were passed.

More snow fell, melting into the river and mounding on the places
where the women were trying to dump their buckets. People would have
lost heart and quit but for the desperate necessity of clearing the river.

Mayor Dixon sent long letters to the administrators of the Drop to bring any small plows or tractors the people could rig to help. It seemed that nothing could be spared from whatever was happening on the other side of the pass. The relief was Category Three. Gold Flume was on a list, she was told. As soon as equipment was available, clearance would begin on the Callan side of the fall. In the meantime, the Drops would continue: water, food, fuel, and only those medicines for life-threatening conditions, mail in and out.

Roman Ansel told people to pace themselves, but some of the younger ones still dug furiously for half an hour, then became exhausted and had to step aside for older men working with the slow, steady intent that the young would learn to respect. The men didn't overfill their shovels, either. Ahead of the diggers, a group had formed to clear rocks, cut the bodies of uprooted trees, and wedge up boulders, some of which needed to be broken before they could be moved. The work was slow and made harder because much of it was done in the mud of melting snow. Brad, as fire chief, called the rest periods. They all thought of the two months before them when the snow, high on the shoulders of the mountains, would begin to slip away into dripping water, then into running water, then into pouring water, in its hundred ribbons, down on them.

Snow fell again and the town came out to the dig in the morning, murmuring about how hopeless the whole thing was. All the earth and rocks they had moved seemed negligible compared to what was still there, even where they were working, at the far side at the edge of the fall. What they had to move was daunting, and where could it be carried away? John Klimek said he had nightmares about it; others dreamed, also, of false victories over the mountain.

On the third week of heavy work, someone started singing. It was "Old Man River," and people laughed, but some joined him, self-consciously at first, and made jokes about the chain gang and Ole Capt'n with the whip, but they didn't stop. At the end, someone shouted a title and a ragged tune began, gaining as people harmonized it with the work they were doing.

Jay had been digging at the east side of the wall of earth next to Chris Pantea. He took up the song, which Chris didn't know, feeling the lift of it as though someone had loosened a binding that opened his lungs and freed his muscles. The song was simple, and Chris learned it quickly. Some people knew the words; some went along humming, piecing the sounds together. They sang "Dixie," they sang "The Battle Hymn of the Republic." They sang spirituals and "When the Saints" and "The Rising of the Moon." They sang rhythmic pop music, and the young ones learned that the rhythms they had loved racing through their hands and feet had to be slowed and made as heavy as the work they were doing. They took the simple, strong beat that moved the work. Sometimes there were fifty people singing as they dug, and fifty women singing as they passed the buckets down the line, each woman now having to walk farther to make it to the dump sites as the nearer ones filled and the lines stretched out.

On Drop days, people didn't want to take time off to do the distributions, so Jay and Melody arranged for the pickup to be done by the kids in junior high who were too young to do much digging and people too old for loading or carrying. The idea worked reasonably well, although there were some complaints about confusion and incorrect apportionment as people collected their deliveries on their way home, lengthening the day.

The big rift came at the end of the third week, and it was about working on Sunday. Roman Ansel and Rick Harbison met with the town council to present a report on their estimate of the time required to clear their part of the fall and divert the river. If the weather stayed cold, they might get as many as three weeks of grace. If spring came early, they might lose the fight. Would a Sunday rest make that much difference? To everyone's surprise, Pastor Fearing declared himself on the side of the seven-day week.

"Surely work can be seen as a form of prayer. We can make it be so. We aren't so spiritually advanced as to turn our minds away from a looming crisis to pray with sufficient concentration and focus. If there should be a flood, I don't want our religious observance to get the blame. Maybe, we could get up an hour earlier for a short service before we go to work. The ancient Hebrews had a law..." He trailed off into thought.

Rick Harbison said, "Maybe, being a Sunday, we could sing hymns and work." Jay laughed.

"I know that may sound silly," Fearing said. "Only half the town ever came to church, any church, until now. We've filled every pew since the fall."

Jay was surprised. AnneMarie had always gone to church; Jay had never gone with her until the fall.

Fearing said, "People want to have contact with one another. They want to trade packets and gossip and listen to the awful rumors circulating, in spite of the four sermons I made on the subject." He looked wistful. "Church has never been solely or even mostly about worshiping God—didn't you know?" He took a breath, his big hands taking up the habitual rubbing of a button on his coat. "I like the idea of hymns at Sunday work. It would mean teaching many of the kids words and music they would never have heard. What do you think, Edwina?"

Edwina was smiling at the idea. "I must know ten hymns about rivers," she said, then laughed. "You can preach Noah's flood while we dig."

The women knew more hymns than the men did. They led the singing, in high, sometimes quavering voices, the songs now and then taken away on the breeze that pushed the music up against the fall. They taught line by line, often about the Old Testament river, the Jordan—"Shall We Gather At The River." One woman sang old shape-note songs: "Rivers Of Delight" and "Wondrous Love," making the teenagers laugh because of their doom-ridden words, but the modal sounds made a hook in the mind, calling forth something that the new music didn't compass, some feeling new to them. At one point, another woman joined her song for a harmony of fourths and fifths that made Jay stop for a minute in awe, only to see others stop also to listen to the strange, hollow sound.

When Jay came off the line to rest, he looked at the group, seeing some people and noting the absence of others. On Sunday, no one had to sign in or be questioned about absence. Fearing had convinced the mayor that on Sunday, people's freedom should be displayed – "Let people be good without reward, freely."

"You mean good for nothing?"

"Yes, absolutely—" Then he caught Edwina's joke.

People came early, people came late. Some left early, some stayed. Jay noted that neither Mike nor Angela had been at the fall for several days.

Their absence made a touchy situation. A spirit had been kindled in people through the work, which, as Jay saw it, was a perfect challenge. The task was urgent; everyone understood it. The work took no great training or intellect, he thought, but it did call forth creative solutions and action, and best of all, it was time-bound. People could see a goal. They would also, in time, notice the absence of neighbors young and strong enough for the work.

Leatrice Bruno was on the line most days. Lack of a number of beauty products and no access to a hair stylist had leveled her to the general female look—drawn, wirier, the thinness stretched and sinewy. She talked with few of the other women except Janeen Ansel, and Della only now and then. Roman Ansel had been involved in the engineering plans for the dig and worked with Rick Harbison to find ways of attacking the problems of excess water and the disposal and collapse of earth at the dig site. He didn't seem interested in doing much digging, but neither was he sloughing off. Now and then his eye fell on Leatrice and when their glances met there was a moment that burdened the air between them before they looked away.

Jay had gone back and forth several times on errands and had not seen Mike or Angela. He found Chris Pantea loading buckets on line four and thought to ask him about his friends, but decided to wait until Chris stepped back for a rest, away from others. Jay looked up and down the six lines radiating from the dig. The edges of the fall were taking loads of dirt on what had been the highway and people were moving up Kinchloe and Chinaman's Gulches with earth. There would be run-off from rain and snow-melt on both of those places, but that problem would have to be dealt with later.

As he stood, waiting, he watched AnneMarie covertly, every so often. She was working hard and coming home exhausted. She set herself to the work as though to prove herself to everyone—that she was sane, in contact, aware. She had been away for a long time, and the announcement that she wanted to return could be made in no form but action.

Jay asked Rick Harbison, "How are we doing?"

"We'd be doing well if we could get water to run uphill. I think we'll make it if the weather cooperates. The fall happened after the November freeze and what part of it that's loose earth is workable. We've dealt with that well and the rocks here fracture easily, but we'll need a steady temperature, cold, but without too much snow and no big warm-up. If it stays steady and not warm into June, we'll be all right. If we open enough of a way, we can release the river before the snow up there..." and he looked up at the rimming peaks heavy with their load. "The river will push its way through, if we give it an opening, and all we'll have to do then is to help it along and sandbag the banks up near town to keep the flooding manageable. I expect the west side of the river will be flooded, but most of the new houses are a good way up the hillside." He turned. "Hey," to a man leaving at the edge of the dig. "What's up?"

"Big tree. We used the saws."

Rick nodded.

"Oh..." Jay remembered. "Have you seen the Ansel kid around anywhere?"

"The dad was here this morning with Heronner, talking about requests for the Drop." He moved closer. "Uh—my boy got an elk, a big one, over on the upland near Chinaman's Gulch. Why don't you and the wife come on over tonight? Klimeks're coming, Panteas."

"What time?"

"Say, seven."

"We...thanks; we'll be there."

Rick went over to where men were sawing up the tree, part of which had been uncovered and was sticking out of the side of the dig. The town council had passed an act that said that all the wood from the dig had to be given to families with babies and to the old people. Wood had become an informal medium of exchange.

AnneMarie tried to beg off the dinner. "I'm tired—why don't you go yourself?"

"I know you're tired," he said. "We're all tired, but don't you want to eat something that hasn't been reconstituted? Something that does more than remind you of real food? Besides, we've been invited—it's a privilege. It's something special—it would be insulting to beg off."

"I don't mean to stop you—you go."

"I won't insist," he said. "I know you're shy with people these days, but look how great you've been on this—" and he gestured at the line she had just left.

"I like being part of what's going on. All I have to do is work. I don't need to talk or be sociable, and when we sit down, we're all the same then, resting."

"Are you thinking that people are judging you?"

"They know I've been depressed. I'm no better and no worse than lots of other people. My pain is no worse than other peoples'. People get terrible illnesses; they get widowed; their kids die; they get divorced—I know all that, but..."

"But what?"

"When I'm not working, I start to think—especially when I'm walking—my mind goes to places that I shouldn't be visiting. When I have to talk to people, it's hard not to pull away. I know these are people I'm supposed to be comfortable with."

"Suicide?"

"Ways and means."

He had once read a poem called *The Panic Vine*.

"And you want to—"

"No, but I dwell on it—it's like the pine beetle. It invades me."

"The tree can protect itself. Its sap drowns those beetles."

"If the tree is healthy enough. Who knows how strong this big old tree really is?" It was a comfort to her that he could hear her metaphor and not think her mad for speaking it that way.

FROM THE FALL FANTOM
The man who makes our city run
Is six-foot Richard Harbison.
His manner is direct and bold,
You'd better do as you are told.
He has a soft side, it is true;
I haven't seen it yet, have you?

POSTED BY THE MAYOR: WILL THE PERSON
WHOSE FOOD PACKET POUCHES BLEW THROUGH
TOWN IN THE LAST WIND PLEASE COLLECT
THEM? ALL PACKET POUCHES SHOULD BE
KEPT SECURED.

CHAPTER 25

THE HARBISONS LIVED ACROSS THE RIVER IN A HOUSE
that had been surrounded by a new development, one of two that had
come in before the seventies, built for people involved with the running
and maintenance of the ski area. The houses, huge as they were, had
some of the look of a company town—carefully covenanted and controlled by a homeowners association, rigid as any overseers set up by the
robber barons of the 1880s. The modest Harbison house stood out—it
had land around it. People in the development said stuck out—some
gave the family frosty stares.

Amber Harbison was not a neat housekeeper and the outside walls
always had, according to the season, an assortment of snow shovels,
brooms, spades, ice-breakers, wood-slash, pine-needle waste, empty
flower pots, cast off paving stones, and bags meant for recycling. Inside,
the house was clean, but cluttered. Amber, herself, a large woman in

capacious layers of flowing clothing, greeted Jay and AnneMarie at the door. She was carrying a cat and a drink.

Years before, when their boys were in the first grade, Stevie had come home from an afternoon playing with Peter Harbison and told AnneMarie how beautiful Peter's mother was. The Harbisons had just moved to Gold Flume and AnneMarie hadn't met her yet, but had had phone conversations with Amber, whose voice she had thought was very pleasant.

"She's so beautiful, Mom, you should see her. Peter told me she was, but she really is."

AnneMarie thought that most children don't objectify the looks of their parents. Familiarity rendered them special. She thought that if Stevie, six years old, had been asked whether his mother was beautiful, he would have said he didn't know. Peter Harbison came over to play with Stevie once or twice and was picked up by Rick, so it wasn't until a month later that AnneMarie had had the opportunity to cross the river and go up to the Harbison house.

AnneMarie had been a perfectionist as a housekeeper. As she had approached Mrs. Harbison's door, she couldn't help glancing around at the shovels, piled pinecones, dead leaves, bits of blown plastic, and a dance of Styrofoam peanuts caught in the untrimmed weeds. She had made a mind-picture of an elaborately painted and coiffed Amber Harbison, too self-regarding to bend down and pick up a blown plastic bag. From inside, she heard the sounds of the two boys. She knocked.

The woman was so different from Stevie's picture of her that for a moment AnneMarie had stared at Amber, who was overweight, in a caftan like a piñata explosion, with hair of different lengths escaping the band she had put on to contain it.

"Oh," Amber said, "you're Stevie's mom. Come on in."

The woman's eyes had lit with pleasure. Her smile was wide, opening to white teeth, her whole ample body generous, welcoming. The kids had been right. Later, when Stevie had asked her if she thought Amber Harbison was beautiful, AnneMarie had said, "Yes—I think it's an inside job."

She had never forgotten that first impression, even as the women had aged together, kids grown and gone. Perhaps that was one reason why she hadn't wanted to spend an evening at the Harbisons'. The sense of how far behind she had fallen in the years of her change would pervade the space between her and the laughing people, all at ease. Jay would never understand an emotion like that.

"It'll be all right," Jay told her at the door. "Good eats, good talk."

The March night was cold. AnneMarie fantasized that even with the door closed, the smell of meat would rise and there would soon be a crowd. The aroma, wafting over the river to town, would be a message louder than the fire bell.

Inside, the room was crowded with people, and at first no one noticed them as they unwound scarves and took off their coats. Most people were standing, talking in small groups. Many were holding glasses of lemon water, the lemon dissolved from a powder that had been included as an extra in the last Drop. The taste was cherished as any flavoring was. People were using dried rose hips that developed their flavor as they reddened after the first frost of the year. A few women and girls had gone almost all the way up Kinchloe Gulch and gathered them in late November before the fall. The rose hip jelly they had made was now a delicacy that was rationed by the teaspoonful.

AnneMarie found a chair in the corner of the living room and sat in it, trying for a look of friendly interest. There were the Panteas with their boy Chris, Mr. Klimek in a ruffled shirt as though this was a wedding, town people she had known growing up, and some new—new perhaps being here for only twenty years or so. As she sat and watched them, she began to think of all the things she knew about each of them—childhood squabbles, moments of cowardice, cruelty, lying, theft, moments of courage or awe, moments when she had envied them their looks of grace or wealth, or confidence. Some of the memories were treasured— acts of their generosity or shared wonder. Some she wished she could eradicate from her mind. Why wasn't that knowledge healing to her, strengthening? Other people felt despair, others shook out memories of pain and even horror. Why was her own anguish separating her from these people who were talking away about the next Drop or the rate of the dig, or even what someone had made to stretch out a fuel ration?

Here came Amber, smiling at her to include her and bearing a platter piled high with slices of the elk. People had brought their own salt and pepper, cayenne, or chili mix saved from before the fall. The elk had been seasoned with wild sage and cooked for hours. People had also brought cans of fuel to make up the Harbisons' spent rations.

They feasted on the meat. AnneMarie knew that she had eaten elk before, that it had been prepared in more or less the same way every time, but this was the most delicious food she could imagine. The elk was like the food of childhood that would be remembered years from the tasting. There were potatoes—reconstituted from the packets of the Drop, and people, out of politeness and with a rigorous self-control, used them to fill up on so as not to leave only gnawed bones behind.

The guests had brought their guitars, accordions, violins, and trumpets to the evening and two dulcimers were being played, their small sounds overtaken and drowned in the blare. Everyone sang rousing songs, but as the diners settled and people sat back and fell half-asleep with activity, excitement, eating, and group warmth, Brad Unger, to everyone's complete surprise, began to sing Irish songs, half sentimental-phony, half truly wistful, the love-and-death combination of generations past. They knew he had the rare voice that was a true tenor, but they had only heard it in church, carefully controlled in harmony with the choir. Now, he uncorked it and let it go and the sound sailed up over their heads: "The Green Green Hills of Home," "Danny Boy," "Glocca Morra"—people found themselves weeping for a loss they had never sustained and a country they had never seen and the long, lost love.

Sated with food and feeling, by one and two, they began to leave. AnneMarie had eaten her fill and noticed that these tears were different in some way from the tears she had been weeping day and night, in her depression. She thought she might want to talk about that difference to somebody, but she couldn't think of anyone who could take her discussion seriously.

Not Jay; Jay liked solutions. If she ever raised a problem to him, he would pause, then with quiet kindness, give a solution. Jay wasn't cold—he was patient and loving, compassionate and long-suffering—surely she knew that, but he saw the world as a series of problems that could be alleviated or even conquered by the application of intelligence and perseverance, hard work and a rational outlook. Life could always be made manageable.

As they were leaving, Ron Pantea came over, shepherding his son Chris, to stop them at the door. "Jay, would you, for a minute..."

"Sure, what's up?" Jay had seen something in the two, a position, a gesture that alerted him. AnneMarie saw it, too, and left them to speak to Melody Reimer, who was getting her coat.

"Chris came to me, today—he's been mulling over something and decided to talk to me about it." Ron looked at Chris, whose face was turned away. "Tell him."

Chris took a breath. "There's a cave up past the logging road on the other side of the river." His voice was almost too soft to hear.

Ron said, "He means Mercedes' Twat. That's what we called that cave when I was a kid. We all went up there." Chris looked surprised. Ron added, "There's more."

"They drink some stuff—"

"I didn't know there was any liquor left in this town," Jay said.

Chris went on. "It's something someone made. They go up and drink it."

"And?" Jay had heard it all before, the homemade popskull of his own mid-adolescence. He had heard that half the men and a quarter of the women in town had thrown up on this version of it at one time or another.

Chris went on. "And I saw the kid, up there, uh—Shively. People say he was drowned, but I know he wasn't. He died in the cave."

Their faces changed. "How do you know?"

The boy looked down at his hands, then at his father's boots—anywhere but at the men. "He looked dead when I saw him."

Jay looked up. "And this was when?"

"Two days before they found him."

"Why didn't you come and tell us then?"

"It seemed like snitching." A kindergarten word.

Jay stood very still for a long moment, weighing options. One victim; how many perpetrators? Which of the kids up there at the time had known what was happening? Who had given the stuff they were using to the kid? On the other hand, the boy had been buried; the Shiveleys were in mourning. Jay hadn't seen them since the funeral. "Okay," he said, "who was up there?"

Chris immediately pulled back. "Lots of kids."

"How did you learn about it?"

"Kids told me."

"Which kids?" Jay realized that this was no conversation to be having at the door at Harbisons' house. "Come in tomorrow, to my office," he said.

"Do you want me there, too?" Ron asked. "When?"

"I'm early on the dig tomorrow. Come at noon. There are things to figure out."

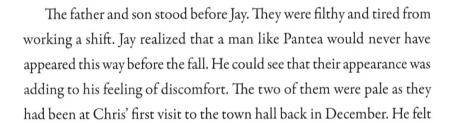

The father and son stood before Jay. They were filthy and tired from working a shift. Jay realized that a man like Pantea would never have appeared this way before the fall. He could see that their appearance was adding to his feeling of discomfort. The two of them were pale as they had been at Chris' first visit to the town hall back in December. He felt the need to brace them a little.

"I understand that cave has been used by teens as long as teens have been in Gold Flume. Cigarettes and booze and weed have been a part of that for as long as anyone can remember. Whenever some new chemical garbage got popular, they did that, too. The only reason the cave hasn't been re-discovered by your friends until now is that all of you were at home, nursing your computers. This boy's death is serious. I'll need to find out the details, and I'll need to know who was there, and exactly how the boy died. It's the law. And, I'll need to know how you came to be there. Sit down. This will take some time."

Chris began, as though the words were something memorized, and he was having to bring them forward one by one as memory bereft of meaning. "I was downtown on my way to the Moritzes to shovel their walk…" and the story, pulled out word by word.

Jay came in on him with quiet persistence, stilling Ron, who kept taking breaths to begin to speak. By the time the telling was all over, it was noon and Jay had a list of names that was almost a roster of the youth of the town.

There would be no way to ascertain how the boy had died. Everyone involved, some twenty of them, would defend each other and themselves with ignorance. Who had taken the body down to the river and staged the drowning? No one would admit to that, but he suspected that it was Mike Ansel, or someone working under his direction. The Shiveleys were grieving about an accident, a slip on ice and a drowning, not a drug overdose at an orgy. The truth would be doing them no favors. Jay would also need to see Doc Winograd. Doc had seen the body, of course, but hadn't done an autopsy—he had had no reason to, and had no sophisticated equipment for drug testing or suspicious signs. Jay felt the urge to discuss the moral issues with someone—Doc, yes; Klimek? Pastor Fearing? No—with AnneMarie.

The thought surprised him. He had been thinking of her as an invalid for so long that he had allowed himself to forget that she had been as astute a reader of people and their ways as anyone in town. First, he would have to make sure of his facts. Perhaps the Shively boy hadn't been dead as Chris had supposed. He might have wakened from his stupor and gone down to the river to cross to his home. He had told his parents that he was staying with friends—a party. Since the fall, and the unavailability of transportation, drugs and even alcohol, parents had relaxed their guard. One of the few but pervasive benefits of the fall had been the change in focus of their fears, away from the problems of delinquency to the less coruscating ones about accidents at the dig, or an illness that Doc couldn't handle. The town's dependence on the Drop was the cause of the greatest anxiety. Superimposed on those things was now the looming disaster of flood. The Shivelys had assumed Bobby's safety long after they would have, back in November.

Later that afternoon, Jay went home, and not finding AnneMarie there, went up to the wash hut that was now roofed and with a good fire under the ore-cart. He greeted the women.

"Fun's over," he said to her. "I need you at home." He helped her with the wash basket.

"What's going on?"

"Police business," he said. "I need your help, yours and Doc's."

CHAPTER 26

Doc had been invited to the elk feast, but he had had an emergency and didn't appear. When Siri, passing by, heard his name mentioned, she saw AnneMarie leave Jay and the Panteas, who were talking intently. She asked AnneMarie to deliver a portion of elk meat to Doc. "Tell him to return the freezer box when he can."

Jay cached the box in the snow that night. By the time Chris and Ron left his office, it was mid-afternoon. Jay decided to wait until early evening to see Doc. He helped AnneMarie hang the clothes on the wash line, learning to appreciate how her fingers ached with the icy job of hanging them.

"Why are you helping me? Don't I do a good job?"

"I have things to tell you. In a while, we dig up Doc's elk and bring it down to him."

In the early dusk, Jay and AnneMarie walked down the street to Doc's. As they went, he sketched out the picture Chris Pantea had made.

A kerosene lamp was burning at the house. As a town official, Doc had an extra fuel allowance, letting him use the lamp into the night. As they went up the walk, they thought they saw shadows behind his drawn blinds. Most people now used only a few rooms to save heat. Doc saw his patients in his parlor. Jay knocked.

At the door, Doc looked down at the freezer box AnneMarie was holding and smiled. "If you'd wait a minute, we're just finishing up." Someone behind him turned and left to go out the back way.

"I know it's late," Jay said, realizing that they had all adopted a new idea of what late meant. Artificial light had been the great determiner.

"Is this something that needs examination?" Doc lifted the cover from the box and smelled the contents. "Food for the gods," he said. "Do you mind if I eat while we talk?"

"Not at all."

Doc was white-haired and white-bearded, a small, compact man, now, with a little paunch sitting on him like an afterthought. Jay could remember when Doc had begun to grow that beard and that paunch. The beard had given him a pleasing look of vigor and benignity. With his weight, people thought Santa, not Jeremiah. Doc had gone through several hair styles and lengths as the rich black had grayed and then whitened.

"I've been too busy," Doc said, "not only with my regular folks, but with the accidents and problems from the dig and accidents by people who aren't used to the work they have to do. It's kept me jumping, and then there are the pregnancies, and—" and he sighed, "the home abortions. I'm going to demand that they include the Pill in those Drops." He blew his breath—"Well, what can I do for you?"

Jay told as fully as he could what Chris Pantea had said. For a moment he could see a look of defensive annoyance on Doc's face, clear even in the muted view available from the kerosene lamp. The look passed, overmastered.

"There was water in the lungs," Doc said, "or I might say fluid in the lungs, the bronchi, anyway. Whoever took him down to the river, if it did happen that way, might have held him under and pushed hard on his diaphragm, hard enough to get water into him. In our day, that would have indicated a great degree of sophistication, but now, everyone watches hundreds of police procedurals and detective stories and knows all about blood spatter and water in the lungs."

"Did you have any suspicion at all, any sense that something wasn't right about what you were seeing?"

Jay could see Doc thinking back. "He wasn't wearing a coat—I assumed that it had come off in the water as he struggled. It might be in the river, washed further down or snagged on a rock somewhere. You may want to look for that. Some of these kids do go out in very cold weather with next to nothing on. I don't think a crime could have been proved with the equipment we have here. This business makes me think that people must have gotten away with a lot more in the old days than they do now. Without proof, and with the body buried and with the family already beginning to move through agony into grief—I don't know if leaving things as they are isn't best for everyone. The kid was, what, ten?"

"Eleven."

"What was an eleven-year-old boy doing up there with high school kids?"

"My—uh—informant said that practically every kid in town over the age of ten was there at one time or another. The younger ones would leave earlier, and the older ones would get on to the serious stuff of the party—popskull and sex."

Doc made the medical 'humm.' "No single story. No way to prove. I saw bruises. I figured they were from ice and rocks." They were silent until Doc turned to AnneMarie. "How are you getting on?"

"It's been a nightmare," she said, "but in some ways, it's been better—I did cut down gradually—"

"I've been campaigning to get these psychotropics put on the Drop, but so far—"

"I don't know that I'd take them if they were approved. I'm still sleepless a lot, and my feelings come and go, but I never had suicidal thoughts before I started on the meds. That awful feeling of creeping things moving under my skin is gone. I remember that the meds did work in the beginning, but—"

"And the depression itself?"

"Still there, but different, less—" She strained for the word. "—damp."

They stared at her.

It was late; the three of them felt it suddenly, the evening letdown, a welcome relinquishing of the day.

"I'd like to talk more about what you're feeling," Doc said, "say, early next week?"

"Sure."

"That kind of medication is prescribed more commonly than any other, except for aspirin. Back to the boy—what do you think?"

Jay shrugged. "I don't see exhumation, and unless someone comes forward—I don't mean someone like Chris Pantea, who isn't sure what actually did happen. What I will do is to have a little talk with some of the participants; Mike Ansel and Angela come to mind. The little saps thought they had discovered that cave."

"I don't like feeling helpless," Doc said. "I'm sure you don't either. Isn't there something?"

"Not unless someone other than the Pantea boy gets to feeling guilty and comes to us. The Pantea kid didn't check pulse or respiration. I've seen people who were clinically dead to eye and touch with drug overdoses suddenly come back, sit up, and ask for a headache pill."

"Were you ever in that cave, AnneMarie?"

"We all were. I didn't do orgies up there. We roasted hot dogs. We escaped from family fights there. It was more clubhouse than whorehouse."

"We didn't have any caves where I grew up," Doc said. "I'm sure the loss is mine."

"There are more than we need here," Jay said, "Old mine workings, caves created by wind and water, by shifts in the earth. Some are hot, others stink. Brad Unger told me that the Indians used some of them as they came through the valley after antelope, deer, and elk. There never were any permanent settlers until people fetched up here after the gold fever, too poor to leave. AnneMarie's folks made pittances placer mining the dregs and running a few cows, getting by. Who could have imagined this valley becoming a playground, all those mansions between here and Bluebank?"

"The fall seems to have returned this place to the way it was before all that," Doc said, "with one doctor and limited equipment. I wonder why Bruno chose not to get air-lifted back in here—he would have been a big help."

"And they say women are the gossips." AnneMarie shook her head.

"We are duly chastened," Doc said, piously. "So what do you think?"

"I think we wait for a break, someone's conscience."

"Thanks for the elk," Doc said.

That Monday, Jay encountered Mike Ansel making a rare appearance at the dig site. The Sunday problem had been solved. Those who wanted to spend the day as a day of rest signed up for extra hours during the week. The boy was helping his father take measurements. Levels of the water had risen, and the labor would have to increase or the water would rise above the dig and they would find themselves having to dredge, wasting time and increasing the difficulty of the work. The diversion now had to be directed around several huge boulders that were too heavy to move without blasting equipment. Jay greeted Mike pleasantly when he stopped for lunch, with an easy wave.

"How's it going?"

Mike looked back at him, suspicious and truculent. "If you're asking why I haven't been digging, there's no law that says I have to. If this fucking town disappeared in a flood tomorrow, I wouldn't miss it. I hate the place."

Jay suppressed a desire to strike the overgrown delinquent. "Well," he said, pleasantly, "many of us like it here and want to see it survive. I hear that you and some of the kids have been going up to Mercedes' Twat, now and then."

"What?"

"That cave. Kids used to go up there all the time, I understand, and for generations. I never heard of anyone who knew who Mercedes was. They smoked up there and made out." He relished the look of surprise he saw on Mike's face. The guarded look followed it quickly. "The thing is," he continued, "there's talk going around that a bunch of you were up there drinking this and that, and that Bobby Shively was there and got sick from it and died. I imagine there are some who saw it happen and can tell me how and when and who else was there, and who gave Bobby the stuff in the first place. The kid was eleven, too young to be up there at all, drinking homemade popskull."

"I don't know anything about it. I wasn't even there."

"Then you have nothing to worry about," Jay said blandly, "I always figured you as some kind of leader, someone with the say-so in the group. I guess I got it wrong, that you counted for something up there."

It was a rich moment, passing quickly, but worth the time. Mike's self-definition as a clever leader was razor sharp but razor thin. Mike looked over to his father yards away, silently invoking his help. This sheriff was someone Roman Ansel could put in his place. For that to happen, it would mean his telling about the events in the cave and listening to his father call him stupid. Jay had seen all of this on parade across Mike's face.

"I gotta go," Mike said, and Jay took a breath.

"Perhaps it would be better if you took some more time out here and spent some of it digging or carrying."

"I gotta go." Clumsy with emotions too big for him, Mike stumbled off.

Jay had, that morning, checked in at the town hall and heard laughter coming from Edwina Dixon's office. "Life on the farm is full of hazards," the mayor was saying to someone Jay couldn't see behind the door. "The farmer's frustrations are many. Shed a tear."

"What's this?" Jay came in. Farm? There wasn't one in fifty miles.

"My granddaughter told me this one," Edwina said. "A bunch of kids were in on a deal to grow marijuana. There were some plants they had before the fall and an enterprising agriculturalist figured that he and his fellow farmers could grow product from the seeds. They had a neat thing going, three seeds each, in twelve to fifteen pots. The trouble was that the stuff was hybrid and the plants had been bred for their leaves. Most of the seeds were sterile and those that did sprout died within days. Where go the hopes and dreams of youth?"

"We still have tobacco smokers pounding the floors."

"And drunks drinking mouthwash and vanilla extract."

"Something I need to discuss with you," Jay said.

The man Dixon had been joking with nodded to them and left.

"What's up?" Edwina went to her desk where requests for the Drop, progress reports on the dig, and the various committees on fuel, water, and snow removal were stacked.

"You've heard the rumors about the Shively boy by now."

"Yes, I have," Edwina said, "and I hope they are just that. I remember about the doings up at the cave, too."

"I'm pretty sure that the boy did die up there, and that fifteen or twenty of them are ready to lie about being there, or if they confess to having been there themselves, about seeing the boy there or giving him anything."

"Any real evidence?" Edwina asked. She had the politician's desire to make no enemies.

"Doc said there was water in his lungs, but he also said that chest compressions given under water could have forced water into the kid, and without sophisticated equipment and a complete autopsy, we don't have any proof."

"And you think you know who masterminded it all?"

"I have a good idea, yes. I think two or three of them were in on it, but I don't know who the others are. Grilling the kids in town would, I suspect, produce nothing. I want to talk to one or two of them, but even if we get some strong suspicion of who actually gave the boy whatever it was that killed him, we wouldn't be able to link it to the boy or boys who moved the body. That, in itself, is not a crime."

"Impeding the police?"

"Yes, that, impeding an investigation of a crime, but it's a misdemeanor. The Shivelys have buried their boy—will they want to see all the hypocrisy in the flowery praise the kids heaped on him at the funeral when there's nothing we could do about what we found out?"

Edwina tapped her finger on the stack of papers. "My real worry is the dig. The weather is warming up, and the April snows will be melting, giving us more water and still more as the mountains melt. Already our dump areas are filling up. We're having to move the earth farther and farther upriver, and that takes time. Worrying about your delinquents is far down on my list. Today, Harbison and Ansel and a couple of other men showed up with plans for a kind of cable thing they've been making that will—is supposed to—move the buckets along. It would run all the way up to Blair's ranch. I'm going out there now to see if it will work. Apparently, they've been messing with the idea for months and have just now perfected it on paper."

"Mmmm—" Jay was thinking that Ansel would be in no mood to discuss his son's possible role in the death of the Shively boy. If the truth came out about the boy's death, the family might go into vendetta mode in response to the justice they had been given. "I'm riding a tiger," Jay said. But Edwina had turned back to the pile on her desk and only nodded. Jay went home in the twilight chill.

"AnneMarie," she was at the table smoothing out the used food packets, "I need to talk some more about the Shively kid."

She stopped her work, put aside the pile, and sat down. "People have been gossiping. I've heard things."

"The problem is that they're not seeing anything being done about it. What's your advice about, say, closing the cave, or posting someone up there?"

"We're about to get lots more to gossip about."

"What would that be?" he asked.

"When the river gets diverted, we'll find things lying in the old bed, lots of secrets. I think there are some people even now who aren't sleeping all that deeply, even after working hard at the dig. And there will be corpses and parts of corpses from the avalanche, lots to talk about."

"One thing does bother me," he said, "not tied down."

"What's that?"

"The kids, maybe more often than we know about – the Pantea boy for one, feel guilty about the Shively boy. What does Mike Ansel feel? How many others know something? Who will wonder why nothing is being done? The Ansel boy will get the idea that he's invincible."

"That must be killing you," AnneMarie said, and Jay nodded. "Kids' ethics are pretty rigid, though," she gave a little laugh. "Remember how ours were. The Pantea boy deserves a talk. Maybe Big Chief Ansel has to realize that while he isn't scared of you, he'd better watch out for his Indians."

"You think we're doing the right thing?"

"No, but I don't see any other choice, and there's the dig. Anything bad for morale on the dig is bad news."

Jay nodded. "I will talk to Chris, and I think I can see a way to ruffle our peacock's feathers."

"How bad is it, with the dig, I mean?"

"We're running neck and neck with the calendar," Jay said. He could see AnneMarie shiver.

"I have nightmares about it," she said.

"I do, too. Find anyone with good sense in this town who doesn't. Ansel, Pantea, and Harbison have been given information about the size of the thing. They've done the math and they say we can dig through if the weather holds, and the snows stay small. Just. We have to try."

"Every day I see so much progress," she said. "I measure it against Kinchloe. And there's something else." She had turned her face away. "I've needed to talk to someone. I can't go to Winograd. He's too interested in my brain chemistry and not enough in my spirit, which his boxes can't measure."

"And you've found someone?"

"Pastor Fearing."

Jay was genuinely surprised. "He's on his mystical salvation wagon."

"Yes, but that's not all he is. He has an idea about us as an experiment in mankind, but I think he also sees me as a person in trouble. He's known enough sick souls to recognize another one." She looked up at him. "You can't do this, Jay. You're too close to it. I don't need brilliant analysis, just an ear. You want to solve things; he doesn't. He wants to heal, not cure. And he really believes in divine aid."

"I'm at a loss."

"Me, too," she said.

In her dream that night, a tremor in the earth pulled the mountain away from the river and just as the water began to flow, two avalanches from Croom and Kinchloe broke away and closed the gap forever. The water was waist high when she woke up, gasping.

Doc Winograd turned in his bed and found himself standing on a rock surrounded by people drowned or drowning. Who was dead and who could be saved? Decide. Hurry up and decide.

Mike Ansel was deep in Angela's sweet cunt, rising for another push when he heard a sound, or felt a sound, and had himself impaled by rows of metal teeth, looked down, and saw the blood.

Edwina Dixon was up on Croom, which she didn't recognize. There were fields and fields of wild iris. She threw her arms up at the glory of it. Below her was a lake, shining in the sun. She ran down to it, seeing her long dead father standing by its edge. No more than three feet below its wind-patterned surface was the town, all of it, and in it nothing moved.

FROM THE FALL FANTOM
It's early morning, hit the bucket,
And not the rhyme you did expect —
So, if a boulder falls, please duck it,
To get the Gold Flume Dig's respect.

POSTED BY THE MAYOR: THE UPPER GRADES OF
THE TUTORED CLASSES WILL BE SUSPENDED SO
THAT THE STUDENTS CAN WORK AT THE DIG.

STUDENTS: PLEASE USE THE FREE TIME TO HELP
US SAVE THE TOWN.

CHAPTER 27

MIKE ANSEL HAD NEVER FELT HE BELONGED IN THIS
anthill. He had seen enough TV to know that there was a big world
beyond these mountains that were squeezing his life. He envied the
skiers and rafters and vacationers who came to enjoy the mountains
and then went out over the pass and got money and fame. With money
you could get anything you wanted and anyone to obey you. Very rich
people had built houses on the slopes where celebrities joined them, and
they gave parties that had security men stationed at all the doors so only
the favored could go in. He had questioned people who had actually
been in those places and who had seen the hot tubs that held dozens
and had eaten and drunk things he had never tasted. They all had other
houses in other places, three or four, even in other countries. Was the
snow better in Gstaad or Cortina, or Alta, or here? If they wanted to, it
would be Gold Flume this year and the Alps next. He had a pass because
his father worked at the area, but he had been all over the place fifty

times and knew it all and he could only ski when he was out of school. He couldn't ditch school to go because everyone knew him and would rat on him, and now, there wasn't even weed or booze for chilling out or coke for climbing out of this place, lift-off to the dream nearly in sight.

Angela helped. She would let him do anything, even things she thought of before he did. Once, just as he was coming, she shoved an icicle up his ass—double-shock—and she was laughing while he came and screamed.

It wasn't love—he didn't even like her. She didn't lie, in that she didn't pretend, like everyone else, that there were all those emotions people talked about when they got serious or when they wanted something. But Angela didn't like danger and risk and he knew he needed both so that he didn't die inside. Sometimes Angela sulked, but it was to get something. She laughed to look pretty. She smiled to show her perfect teeth and to get things from people or to impress them.

There were people—he had seen them—that the fall had helped in some way he couldn't understand. Look at that Chris Pantea, and all the kids Klimek had in his little troop, delivering the stuff from the Drop, digging, getting praise from everybody. He knew they were dreaming, in their bundled beds, of being heroes of the flood, opening the way for the water to free itself, and if some of it backed up, they would be in boats, saving everybody and being praised. He'd seen it, how Klimek smiled at them, how the town greeted them when they passed, stopping them to chat, treating them like neighbors and friends, not like kids. His own dreams were of the flood that would come and drown him or sweep him away through the hole they had made and cut into the world outside, naked and without friends or money. These dreams would please him as he woke naked. In his dreams he was often naked. He would dream of getting clothes, taking them from someone. Friends were to be made anywhere. Money was there to be taken, freely or not. The doing was all of it. The cloud to be avoided, the cloud to be feared was the cloud of boredom. He already had a handful of fantasies he could use in the times he was forced to keep his will from expressing itself.

The sheriff had corralled him on the afternoon he had gone with the old man to work at the dig, and he had zeroed in on what they were doing in the cave and all about that fucking kid who hadn't been invited up there anyway, but found out about it somehow and had gone up and then started nagging and threatening everyone to tell if they didn't give him some of what they were drinking. Then the kid had started puking. Lots of kids did that—the stuff was pretty bad, he had to admit. The little creep started crying but there was so much noise and people moving around—he must have choked on something, but anyway, he was dead and it was his own fault, because no one wanted him up there. Most of the others didn't notice him falling. They didn't know what to do after that, so they left him in a corner by an outcropping and forgot about him. Chris Pantea must have seen the kid after most of them had gone home. Mike had found out that Chris had been there. Chris was the kind of asshole who would rat them out. Mike had told two kids who had been there to go up again and help get the body. The three of them had taken it down river almost to the dig at night. Mike had forced water into the kid and left his body there, with his shoes in a little tangle of willows upstream.

Now, the sheriff was asking him about it and it was just like TV, cat and mouse, good cop, first friendly, asking a few questions, and the dumbest viewer could see the net hanging over the killer's head waiting to fall over him. Mike had watched a thousand of these moments, including all the reruns, watching intently, even when he knew, having seen the show two or three times before. So, seeing all those shows had made him an expert, he figured, on how to deal with this piss-ant sheriff. He had been in big city interrogation rooms, hundreds of them. What could happen in a nothing town like this, that didn't even have one of those soundproof rooms, two-way mirrors, a light over the table, and the two chairs facing each other?

Still, it might be a smart thing to show up at the dig and put in a little work. Mike knew intuitively that the sheriff hadn't told his father about any of it. Roman Ansel was too important a man to be messed with.

There was his dad's cable, too, the one he and the others had worked on so long, sitting up nights at the kitchen table with papers and things they had put away years ago, protractors, slide rules and hand computers, using cherished batteries. The cable was really five cables like the ski-tows, stopping off midway to take on or let off skiers going to other parts of the hill. They had dismantled the tows to use those cables and pulleys, dirt buckets being pulled full going up and empty going down to the dig. People could now rotate easier and harder jobs and so, work more efficiently. He saw that at once and couldn't help but give a grudging credit to the old man. The next problem would be to pick a place to work that would give him a maximum presence for a minimum of effort. He was strong enough to be at the dig-face, breaking rock, shoveling the stones and earth, sawing away fallen trees whose trunks, roots and branches, amalgamated with the packed earth and rock holding them all together. Chainsaws blunted continually with the rock and stones and could have only limited use.

He chose a place where the beginning of the first cable line would be and spent an hour there. Some woman came by with a clipboard and paper that listed the assignments of times and places and approached him. He put her off, saying that his dad had special work for him. Her eyebrows went up, but she didn't say anything and went away. He was almost ready to slip out when here came Sheriff Isaacs, who brought someone from Klimek's troop to take his place.

"Let's go over to the rest spot—the one over there. No one is using that, and we can talk a little."

Mike had heard that the sheriff's wife was crazy, but there she was at the buckets, and the sheriff flipped a quick hi-five at her, smiling. They went to the cinderblock-and-board bench up from the works and sat. The day was crisp but warm in the sun. The light had begun to last but was shadowed in this narrowest section of the valley, and cool. Before the fall, you could look down river to where the valley widened and see the later light glowing there.

"I'm here to give you a little warning, a heads-up," the sheriff said, "which is only fair."

He was going to threaten, to say that as soon as the town was freed, he was going to the authorities with the story about the cave and the kid. That was bullshit. No one could prove anything. The ones who had helped wouldn't risk going to jail. Mike faced up to the sheriff with a grin that told that junior patrol cop what he thought of him and his threats.

"The warning," Jay said, "is that some of the partiers who were up there with you are feeling pretty guilty, now. You may notice a falling off of visitors to the cave. There was the funeral, and the mom, crying, hearing all the nice things everyone said, showing the pictures she had of her son as a baby. Some of that gets through to sensitive kids. You may have to start watching what you say and how you act toward weaker members of your group. A bully can go just so far. If I hear of anyone getting hurt or being bullied, I will investigate."

"You can't do shit."

"I can tell your parents in detail about your activities and I can declare you a safety risk and lock you up until you are taken in shackles to the jail in Aureole. I won't hesitate to pump your friends for information, either. Hard."

"I didn't make any of that stuff he drank—"

"Can you prove you didn't? Can you prove you didn't force it on the boy? Can you prove you didn't kidnap him and bring him to the cave in the first place? Your folks may have defended you in that vandalism you did. They gave me the old 'boys will be boys' routine, but kidnapping and murder—I don't think they will defend you on that. Be careful, that's all." He got up. "I think your dad's invention will work well. He seems to want to save this town. I'm not sure he knows how much you would like to see him fail." The sheriff turned and went back down to the dig.

Where was Angela? While she had never come to the house, she had always managed to come around where he was, to be there as if by accident. Was she seeing someone else? Mike knew that she went with other guys and that she let them do what they wanted to her. Sharing her had never meant much to him until now. He went up to the staging area where the men were setting up the first cable, got on the line, and began the rhythmic motion of taking and carrying the buckets, his mind removed from the work. Was Angela ready to rat on him? He and Angela had been so drunk that they were barely conscious of what happened around them. Lift, carry, hand-off. Lift, carry, hand-off.

If Isaacs told his father, there would be hell to pay. It was one thing to be separated from your parents at your wish, sneering at them, dissing them to friends. It was another thing to be separated by their choice. And there was that guilt thing. Some people felt or acted like they felt bad about what they said or did. Sometimes he got a sudden sense that other people saw reality in a different way than he did. He thought some things were very important to them, things he could only guess at. This difference was one reason for his attraction to Angela, that she had none of those funny ideas about what should be and shouldn't be. A person's mind-tangle could tangle his feet and screw him up. He had thought to get water into the kid and leave the shoes upstream because his mind was clear and concentrated on what he was doing, but it was Angela who had suggested the drowning scenario. Yet, both he and Angela had been at the memorial service. That had been organized by the pastor and seemed to him to be something they should go to or they would be missed, and questions asked. He knew that all that weeping and gargling about what a great angel the Shively kid had been was put on and hypocritical. The kid was a little pest, but Mike couldn't figure out why people would want to get in one place all together and moan and cry over someone else's dead pest.

He had been amazed when Angela had broken away and gone up to the platform and spoke, teary-eyed, lip trembling, her few words of love and loss. The disparity hit him like a blow. People who cry aren't pretty. They are puffy-eyed and they make weird faces and their noses run. Angela was beautiful. The tear hung on her lashes and she pulled a little sob into her lungs that made her breasts rise and her hips move forward a little. Every boy and man in that audience would spend time—minutes to hours to long nights—thinking about Angela and her ripeness and her juiciness and the little tear. Afterwards, she had laughed.

Mike began to listen, as Sheriff Isaacs had said, and to think about losing his power. Kids had been so sick on the stuff they had drunk in the cave that they didn't go back. The reek of piss and vomit didn't leave the cave for weeks after the bash. Angela said it would be a month before she would let him take her up there again. They broke into stores downtown and went up to second floors where merchandise was stored, waiting for the end of the town's isolation.

Most of the town was working at the dig, now. The mountains above them were still locked in snow, but there was a definite hint of spring in the air, and the river was well above its normal channels, gathered in some places into ponds. Even on Drop days the needs at the dig site trumped everything else. Why did people, even his folks, want to save this place? Money. 'Remind me,' he heard himself say to the self waiting in his head, 'not to spend my dough on land or a house, anything stuck anywhere.' He heaved up off the plank bench and went back to the dig.

His dad told Mike about the Town Council's meeting with the dig's engineers to talk about sandbagging the vulnerable places along the river and shoring sections of the banks. For years, the valley's problems had been the effects of drought, not flood, although people still spoke of the awful torrents of 1956 and 1982. During those emergencies, help had come from outside, but there had still been commandeered labor at sandbagging and dike building, and the town had been saved. The council had also taken up the problem of slackers on the dig. The same people signed up for shifts but didn't appear. Excuses proliferated. Some came out to the dig, carried three or four buckets, and disappeared or sat on the side benches for the rest of their shifts. Should requirements be enforced? How, and by whom? Should there be some kind of punishment for slacking off? Mike heard news of the probability of this and realized that if he waited to show up until force was instituted, he would lose any power he still had with the kids he commanded as followers. The finding and use of the cave had been a huge coup for him and, until the little creep's death, his reputation's crown. He had convinced ten or twelve of his crew that slave labor on the dig or at the Drop was demeaning and a job for Klimek's boy scouts. But, as the thaw approached, he and the kids who followed him could see everyone's increasing anxiety, including his own father's. If the thaw came quickly, in May or early June, tons of water would thunder down-mountain, and with no place to go, would flood the town. The fact was that if the way weren't opened from the outside, there would be no escape. It broke on him like a revelation. There would be no place to land the Drop and everyone would be dispersed on higher ground with what they could carry and no more. That eventuality was months from now, but his reputation was leaking away as hard facts percolated through people's defenses.

He also realized that his buddies had stopped wondering about what was going on outside the Ute Valley, even happening outside the town. The daily needs, cooking, washing, warming, keeping dry and fed and healthy were taking up the full day, shoveling snow, melting it for water, and of course the dig, had narrowed everyone's interest to the dimensions of town and a mile west northwest and east southeast. He had better join the working crew and be seen. His work should be somewhere that didn't involve receiving orders from anyone. Where was Angela?

FROM THE FALL FANTOM
The hand
With the callus
Shakes the friend's callused hand.
Last winter's grasp had been smoother;
We smile.

POSTED BY THE MAYOR: GOLD FLUME MUST BE
SAVED. MANY OF US ARE DOING DOUBLE SHIFTS
WHILE OTHERS STAY AWAY AND MAKE EXCUSES.
WORK WILL SAVE THIS TOWN. ALL MUST HELP.

CHAPTER 28

AT THIRTEEN, ANGELA HAD BECOME RESIGNED TO
what men really were. She had thought them to be powerful and smart,
smarter than the women she knew. They ran things; they knew things.
She had allied herself with them, using her dream-evoking body in all
the ways they wanted. But that gift, as she used it, made her understand
how vulnerable they were. Some of them, she thought, must be superior
to the rest. She had imagined that Mike, young as he was, to be one of
these, but she had soon understood that his bragging and strut covered
something darker. He had been shaped by the town and, as she saw it,
his condition was the town's fault. Growing up in Gold Flume, people
thought it was the world. They thought their stupid, pinched little lives
were reality and their poverty, wealth enough. The fall had only pointed
out what Angela had known for years. Gold Flume was the petering out
end of the world. The outsiders, those in the million-dollar vacation
homes outside of town, *they* were the people who knew what real life
should be like. No wonder her father had chosen to stay outside when

he could have been choppered back the way the tourists had been choppered out. The blow was why he hadn't taken her with him, but had left her to stay with her mother flapping and dithering after her.

People had marveled at Angela since her childhood. Her father was a dark, gnome-like man with an orthopedic surgeon's powerful upper body and a rugged prognathous jaw. In a Greek story, he would have been Hephaestus, the crippled fashioner of things necessary and frivolous, who went around seducing earth's women. Her mother must have been a beauty, but now, she was skinny and morose, with stringy, sparse, darkish hair, and a fretful expression, martyred by his infidelities. These mismatched people had produced a girl so beautiful that people had stared at her on the street ever since she could remember.

What good was it all in this sandbox of a town? She had been planning her escape for years, and now it was all to be put off by the fall. The mountain's action had been a slap in the face to her, personally. Granted, they had been on their way to the Aureole police station when the fall saved them, but Angela was sure that she could have beaten the charges. Her father would have bailed her out. The idea for the vandalism had been Mike's. The cave parties were her idea; he had jumped at it. No one could know that she was the reason Mike had started them in his desire to impress her.

Since that kid had died in the cave, Mike had been crowding her more urgently than ever. Would she talk? Would any of the kids talk? His pressure was weighing on her, and he was demanding sex with her at odd times and with a compulsive need that deadened her desire. She was forced into hiding at home, at other girls' houses, on parts of the dig where he wouldn't see her. She had never tried for popularity with other girls, but some were glad enough for her company now.

The week after the sheriff's questioning, Angela was up at her mother's, grumbling at the pile of laundry to be taken to the washhouse on this side of the river. Her mother, a fastidious woman, now left their sheets on the beds for three weeks at a time. The washhouse's primitive arrangements had been improved on week by week, a little structure over the ore carts helping the fire-heated water stay warm. A board floor had been put in. Angela hated the work and usually left it to her mother, but Leatrice Bruno, in sudden, unprecedented indignation, had demanded a fifty-fifty split in the work they did. Now, they were both there, wringing out the sheets and piling them in their supermarket cart.

The fire-bell was ringing. Angela wondered why. Today wasn't a Drop day; there didn't seem to be anything visibly wrong as the women looked up from their work.

They saw people moving down from houses below them toward the town hall.

"Let's go," Leatrice said, moving in close, "everyone else is." The women were putting their wrung-out laundry into baskets and buckets.

"Why? Let them tell us when they get back," Angela said. Her mother's very presence annoyed her.

"Why don't you want to go?"

"You go and tell me what they said." The women were looking at them as they moved past.

"You'd better come. People notice." Leatrice was showing her impatience.

Angela shrugged and the two walked down the street with the others.

The town square was full, and Angela saw that people were coming from the dig to be there. Mike's father and Rick Harbison and Mr. Unger, the fire chief, and the sheriff were standing to one side, facing the people. The mayor had a megaphone and began to speak. She thanked them for coming. Angela made a huffing sound. Summoned, she wanted no thanks. She told them that work on the dig was now urgent. The water was backing up and had already gone over its banks at the Drop site, which would soon be flooded. The runoff from the winter snow hadn't even begun yet, and no amount of sandbagging would save the town when that happened. The cables had been set up and were beginning to make the work easier, but not every available man and woman showed up at the dig. The mayor kept urging everyone to get the river moved before it was too late. The engineers were unable to calculate exactly how much more would have to be cleared before the river was freed, but everyone could see in their faces and gestures that they were frightened. Mayor Dixon looked as though she had been beaten. Sleeplessness made dark swellings under her eyes. Brad Unger talked too much. Rick Harbison all but stopped speaking. Jay Isaacs kept checking lists he had made, over and over, fearful of having missed something, a detail that would doom the project.

"Once we're through, the river will help us," the Mayor said. "The force of the water will open the way and the backed-up power will slow the silting downstream. We'll have the help of the people from Callan and Bluebank then, too. We've set up a system and we need everyone who can to sign up on one of the three work lists. The shifts will take advantage of all the light there is—six to ten a.m., ten to two, two to six. There will be rest periods within these four-hour blocks. The work won't be killing, but it should be steady. There are two additional sign-up sheets for people who can't do the job because of physical limitations. We'll have other work available. Get lots of rest; we have to clear the opening before the Drop site is unusable. That's first."

People were moving toward the sign-up sheets, and Angela saw Mike ahead of her, moving forward as people paused, deciding on the times they would work. She knew he had no more desire to save the damn town than she did, and she knew that if things got too bad, all of them would be choppered out as the town became a lake. She also knew that status meant a lot to him, as much as to any of the men in this dead-end place. If Mike didn't lead in this effort, he wouldn't be able to lead anywhere else. His all but hysterical behavior in the cave when he discovered the Shively kid had cost him whatever shred of admiration she had felt for him, but she also knew that if he found this out, his violent streak might cause trouble for her. She couldn't diss him. Any insult, spoken or shown, would get back to him. She decided to fake a reason to be on another time sheet. ("I wanted to be with you but my idiot mother...") That might not work. He knew her mother had no more power over her than a leaf over a raindrop.

———————◆———————

The work was heavy, but people moved off the line to rest. With so many doing the labor of digging and moving the fallen mountain, there were logistical problems of keeping workers out of one another's way. They worked in lines, up at the dig face, and then moving away to the cable areas and then to the dump sites for dispersal. People moved their buckets along the ski-tow cables so they didn't have to carry for any distance. The Drop site was 450 yards from the dig and Mike's dad and the other planners had decided that all the earth dumped there and leveled would raise the Drop site above the reach of the river. This site was twice as far as they had been dumping, but once the decision was made and the cables strung and the supports shored, dispersal began to pick up speed.

"We've been used to derricks and backhoes—big and big," Angela heard the mayor say. "We've got to do this with a lot of little."

In spite of herself and contrary to all her desires, Angela found herself engaged. She caught the rhythm of the work and eased into it. Now and then, people would sing. She had no desire to save the town and no loyalty or love driving her, only the exertion of muscles and the taking in of air, the swing up and swing down, push of shovel, guide of bucket on the cable. Swing up. Swing down. The days were cold. The days were warm. They worked in snow. Need seized them, but for Angela it was only the force of so many people moving in the grand dance.

Over them, Jackass and Croom, Barrel Stave, San Pietro, Cardiff, and the fall and the rest of the Hungry Mother loomed, holding the winter and the water one day at a time. But the enemy was there, waiting in the gulches and the gullies for the first two or three words to be uttered: spring beauty, pasque flower, aspen bud. Those words, which were uttered at their first sight, would free the terrible force from the mountaintops, leaving only that ancient ice that never melted. And every day, the sun shone on those mountain faces for a few minutes more.

Angela was keeping Mike placated without letting him in any further than she wanted. He was tired much of the time, having made the big gesture—double shift, carrying it out in the sight of his followers.

Social lines were blurring. The good kids—Klimek's group—were no longer shown in such stark relief against the bad ones—the ones who stayed away from the Drop except to pick up their own family packages and leave, who spent no time with anything more than what their families demanded, and sometimes, not even that.

Particularity was fading, like and dislike being shadowed over, muted under the clatter of shovel against rock, bucket against bucket, snatches of singing, grunts of labor as rocks were moved. Chisel sheared, pick rang, hand saw and bow saw, back and forth of voices calling to help or warn, and the cowbell sounding the shift changes. Someone had resurrected it from uselessness in a barn.

Angela fell in with it all, even against her will. Working as she did, the flat look of her make-up, which she had applied with a slather, wore away and her lip gloss was licked away in effort. Her teased hair was too difficult to keep up. People who had seen her and had thought of French street whores now stared in wonder and gaped at a brimming beauty. Pastor Fearing, who was standing as bucket man when she came to take her bucket to the first cable station, murmured as she turned away, "How beautiful is she among the maidens." During the rest periods she noticed people moving away from her, standing back to look at her. At first she thought it was anger or disapproval, but their expressions had none of that pursing of the lips, no closing of eyes. They were agape, rapt. Suddenly the world went quiet to her as she realized that the stares were because of her beauty. The caking on of make-up, the low-cut blouses and high cut skirts had been costume, a disguise. She hadn't been ready to handle the real problems of beauty. Men had stared at her before, but this was as different as fish from flower. The moment passed and she hefted her bucket and raised it to the cable.

FROM THE FALL FANTOM
Gray shirts that once were white,
Loose pants that once were tight,
Gourmet tastes that made us mutter
Are now content with peanut butter.

POSTED BY THE MAYOR: PLEASE PICK UP
YOUR LITTER. STOP LEAVING IT AROUND THE
DUMPSTERS, WHICH ARE FULL. THE WIND
REDISTRIBUTES IT ALL OVER TOWN.

CHAPTER 29

PEOPLE WERE BECOMING MUSCULAR. PASTOR
Fearing looked out at his congregation on Sunday (one service instead
of the usual two) and saw that each pew held more people, even though
they were wearing coats and had layers of underwear and sweaters. The
church had been given its ration of fuel, but Fearing couldn't keep it
solely for Sunday. Weekly activities had proliferated with the darkening
of TV, computer screens, and video games. People came to evening talks
and recitations, bingo, Bible contests, and trivia bowls. They wore gloves
in which heated stones had been placed as they laid dried beans on
handmade bingo cards. Attendance at these events had slowed as work
on the dig took its toll of energy. Those who did come, young and old
people, formed acquaintances they wouldn't have had before the fall,
each meeting the other for the quizzes and contests dreamed up by the
women at the library.

The pastor saw this change as part of his vision of the Peaceable
Kingdom. In that Kingdom, all would be fed but none would be fat. All

would be equal; all would be strong. When that happened, as it seemed to him to be happening now, gossip and scandal, ridicule and rumor, envy and greed would come to an end, shrugged off like filthy garments. The creature God had intended when He heaped up and molded the metaphoric clay that was man would, at last, deserve the titles he granted himself. This lifting of the soul had been the meaning of his vision, the revelation that day in the middle of his sermon. In his later sermons he acknowledged what was happening, the perfecting of Gold Flume's people through work and prayer. They were getting closer, in their isolated, unique place, to the Golden Mean. Soon envy would go, meanness, and miserliness. Generosity and tolerance would take the place of social class and personal vanity. They were at a door that was beginning to open. On the other side the radiance was waiting.

Fearing was doing the mid-day shift out at the dig. He had wanted Cheryl to come with him, but she had argued and shouted and made the issue so important that he had put up his hands at last and said, "I'm not an adversary, Cheryl, honestly. Go in peace." She had signed up for shifts staggered by weeks, early and late, so they were seldom together until the evening. There was peace in that, he realized, as there hadn't been in years.

AnneMarie Isaacs had been coming up to his study for their talks. Fearing was a good listener and he found her problems neither trivial nor self-indulgent. Her true darkness, he thought, unfortunately showed up Cheryl's shallower concerns with looks and status. He had tried to turn his mind toward her reality, but against AnneMarie's simple, quiet authenticity Cheryl's concerns seemed flimsy and trivial. He wasn't counseling so much as hearing AnneMarie, and through her, seeing all the human undertones—regret, remorse, aging, loss. AnneMarie's father and mother had each died away from Gold Flume—father, hunting;

mother, visiting relatives. There had always been arguments, anger between AnneMarie and her parents. The two had died six months apart, with no reconciliation or goodbye from her. The anguish ate at her. And, there was the present...

AnneMarie had been raised in Callan and had gone to Gold Flume and Callan schools, and but for yearly trips to Denver for the stock show and once to Disneyland, she hadn't been out of the county. She had always wanted to visit Matera, where her people had come from.

"I want a look backward," she had told him, "even though I can't look forward. We have three kids and four grandkids, and yes, we've visited them, and had them come here a few times, but I don't know them, not the way I would if they lived here. We get the cards and the calls, the Christmas letters and E-mail, but that's not the same as knowing someone the way I knew my grandparents. Jay says we should visit more, but the grandkids' lives are lived with their tribes, not with their families. I've gotten that message. The last visits they made they spent texting their classmates and playing video games on their computers."

"Does Jay feel separated, too?"

"He has less investment in the grandkids and he doesn't seem to need the sense of lines of lives braided in, before and after. Can you see that this pain I'm in isn't helped by altering my brain chemistry?"

Fearing didn't know how to answer. He was a pastor, not a medical man. He had felt, in a wavering way that something in the new definitions of mental illness was incomplete and was obscurely insulting. He knew that the soul has no physical location in any of the places ancient people placed it, and modern medicine had done away with the term altogether. His religion used the term all the time and everyone knew what was meant: "Be still, my soul; I wait upon the Lord." One couldn't define either soul or the Lord and yet, here was this woman who knew both, as he did, and whose soul was sore and who was crying out before God. He smiled at her.

"What?" Her voice was unsteady.

"I was thinking," he said, "that I am grateful for your visits. Pastors seldom get to share the inner lives of their congregants. Our time is taken up with soliciting funds, worrying about mice in the robing room, performing rituals, few of which may actually be believed in. It's been a while since I've used the word *soul* outside of sermons. You're heart-sick; soul-sick; and if I may say so, I know it hurts like hell."

She began to cry. Fearing squirmed. He had never gotten used to people sobbing. He didn't try to make her stop. Uncomfortable as he was, he sat it out, and when the apologies came, he sat those out, too, handing her a rare Kleenex. Handkerchiefs had come back to Gold Flume. She shook her head at his offering and took out a square cut from an old sheet and blew her nose into it.

"I have a picture in my head," he said, "because we pastors are brought up on biblical stories and scenes—we make our comparisons to those pictures. Women in those stories weep a great deal. Sara, Hannah, the three Marys at the cross—all had good reasons, and so do you."

"Pastor..."

"You'd better call me El—my friends call me El."

"Do you think we'll be done in time, that we can open the fall?" AnneMarie knew the question was meaningless. The words established a comfortable distance, the new currency in Gold Flume.

"If not, it won't be for lack of trying. Where are your children and grandchildren?"

"California, Chicago, and Kansas. We get letters, but people aren't used to writing long letters anymore. We know they are well, but it's like seeing a skeleton standing in for a body. I have to admit—my longhand letters are nothing to rave about. Where are your people?"

"Two sisters and their families—in San Diego and near Chicago. My brother is in Alaska. There's been no mention of anything in Chicago, and the trouble in California seems not to be as bad as they had first thought it was."

"People are saying it's the End Times," AnneMarie said.

"I don't think God will let us off that easily." Fearing rose. "My shift is beginning soon. I'd better go."

"I'm working this shift, too," she said.

They walked through town and out to the dig together, chatting. A few of the morning crew were beginning to drift away. They passed the stacking of shovels and picks. There had been complaints about care of tools and some hard words exchanged. Jay had stopped a fight two days before over a supposed misuse of a shovel owned by one of the men. Petty arguments broke out all the time about the way the work was being done or who was supposed to be doing it. Fearing, himself, had felt abused now and then. People on the lines were taking more authority than was theirs or being generally pig-headed. It was only his position as pastor that stopped him from giving as good as he got. There were mornings when they had to work in the ice-whistle cold, freezing to the knees, and knowing that there would be only the rationed warmth of their houses when they got home and no hot bath or shower, only the possible help of a dishpan of water heated on a woodstove or camping setup. Everyone knew that grandparents had done these things and thought nothing of the doing. The people at the dig knew they would, eventually, be dry enough and warm enough to sleep well, but their lack was that of a rich man suddenly poor, or a person long accustomed to a soft, warm bed, suddenly made to sleep on bare boards with a scratchy blanket. Tempers exploded and charity shrank. The helicopter pilots from the outside world, their only strangers, spoke of droughts and fires in other places, which were causing massive flooding and destruction. These conditions added to the problems of distribution of aid. Perhaps the pilots were offering the examples to show the townspeople that their situation was not unique, but what the people heard was that help might be stopped abruptly at any time in other overwhelming need.

Fearing felt all these things. Close as evening, close as memory was the glimmering promise of all these souls growing into a higher spirituality. He had seen this future of grace, dignity, and virtue opening out of their forced privation. What was standing in the way, blotting out the light, but the daily inconveniences like hangnails, tearing at patience and forgiveness, the odorous bodies and loose dentures, the loss of all but the simplest forms of entertainment and escape. Sometimes it took him huge labor of mind to bring back the vision he had had, to hold on to it, to keep the promise he had made to it.

His sermons, once standard admonitions about charity and love, however, now had the bite of real urgency. People were taking out their frustrations on their families. Rages broke, patience and forbearance strained and frayed and came apart in curses, slaps, black eyes, and broken noses. Two men had been seriously sickened by home-brewed popskull distilled from kinnikinnick berries and willow root and whatever could be spared from the food packets. One had almost died.

The buoyant moments of challenge at the dig had given way to a slog as March imperceptibly slid into April. In these mountains April kept its winter face—cold, snows, sudden warmings for a day or two, then freezes as sudden as the warming had been. High winds blew howling down the gulches, beating snow ahead of them. The only hint of spring was the lengthening of the days and the angle of the sun toward its solstice position. The snows went thick and stubborn and clung to their shovels, "on purpose," Brad Unger's little grandson said.

The pastor had married Cheryl while they were still in college, and their wedding had been the glamour moment of a college spring. Maryland had been glorious with cherry blossoms, dogwood, the lazy earth stretching in the sun for the spring wind to lose itself in their petals. Meadows had moved with wine-mad bees—and she was going to be his helpmeet and he was going to proclaim the Word of God, which was as sweet as that springtime perfume. Shadows were only there to encourage the light.

The mistake had made itself obvious by his second year in Kearney, Nebraska. Cheryl hadn't included work in her idea of what a helpmeet should be, and because they'd stayed at a rooming house there was no "home" for her to make. She had been thinking of a parsonage to manage. In the sweetness and enthusiasm of their courtship, he hadn't known that when she was thwarted, she sulked.

When he was offered Gold Flume after the two dying parishes, the placement seemed like heaven. The community was a vibrant one, growing, fascinating in its diversity, with upscale condos and long-timers, families whose patriarchs had been prospectors and railroad men. Recently, celebrities had built palatial houses off private roads. The town itself was an 1870s railroad stop for a narrow gauge that went across the valley and up over Prospector Pass, carrying cattle from the valley ranches and ores from the mines. There was a special siding for the turn-around where the line ended against the all but impassable mountains enclosing the valley. There were still some carefully preserved mansions from those days of mine and railroad owners. Much of the town was replica, but the town council had put in good systems of sanitation and lights and the volunteer fire department had been state trained and was well equipped. Most of the houses in town had wells and the water was excellent.

Fearing felt happy and at ease. Cheryl hated Gold Flume. She had once said in anger that the shops were now so high priced that she could barely afford to walk past one. She felt poor. She kept the house in compulsive perfection, but without enthusiasm. Two miscarriages had ended her desire for children, and she had no wish to adopt. When he thought about it, Fearing knew that he had none, either.

He liked being a pastor. He wasn't a great preacher, and to Cheryl's disappointment he was no scholar. He felt he fit in well in Gold Flume. The fall had reinforced that feeling. He would have been happier, he thought, had he not married. Only once had he discussed their mistake with Cheryl, but when he mentioned divorce, she had raged, wept, threatened, called him names. Who was the woman? Was it Bruno's trophy wife? Was it Sharon at the library? She would let the whole town know. He calmed her and changed course. Her response freed him. He now felt a quiet sympathy for her, but no more. He was courteous to her, withstood her anger, and tuned out her vitriolic comments about Gold Flume and its people.

But he had underestimated her response to the fall. Anger had given her vigor. She and Melody, never friends before, worked out the logistics of the Drops, managed the distributions of non-food items correlated to the handwritten requests filled out by the residents.

He noted that there was one advantage to Cheryl's being a pastor's wife in this small place. She loved to listen to gossip. She collected it, treasured it, stored it like a miser. In her rages she gave him reports of weaknesses, sins, peccadilloes, large and small, that proved to her what the people in Gold Flume actually were. Fearing used this information as a means of helping the targets of the town's arrows. People coming to him, like AnneMarie, were often unable to discuss their deeper wounds. What he knew allowed him to ask the right questions.

After their session, he and AnneMarie went out to the dig. The new snowfall had been cleared away. Had there been a ski season, a day like this would have been its crown. The sun was warm, but the faint breeze came fresh and lively. The sky was rich and clear. Snow still resting on the mountains was blessed with its reflected blue. The day seemed bright enough to ring. Crews working at the dig face soon shed their heavy jackets, and by afternoon the workers were in their shirts, and hatless.

A man, well down the line to the west of Fearing, began to shout. Fearing thought there must have been an accident. They had them, now and then—people being struck on the legs by others shoveling beside them, fingers pinched, an arm broken by a boy driving a pick into solid rock and not letting up on it in time. The cry came again and then another. Fearing toed in his shovel and went over.

Two or three men were pointing at the ground. "What is it?"

"Look—see—the water isn't rising like it was yesterday, and it isn't still. The snow's melted into it and it isn't rising. Why ain't it rising?"

Harbison went over. "Keep digging," he said. "Move that rock away."

Fearing began to follow the water as the men dug. The earthwork formed by the fall was still over their heads, the branches of trees, the trunks themselves and their roots forming a vast sieve. Fearing looked down at his feet. The backed-up water would have been up to his calves, but he noticed a little fold in the water, not even strong enough to be a rill or an eddy, but as they dug, the fold began to move. He saw another.

He had imagined that the opening would be a sudden vast push, like the plug being taken out of a bathtub, but this was almost too subtle to notice. People had begun to go at the surface with picks and saws to cut the tree parts away, branches and roots and the shattered bodies of their trunks. By noon, it was obvious that small as the area was, somewhere along the line of the dig, the water was making it through.

The afternoon crew came on, but the morning crew didn't want to leave. There was a feeling of pure exaltation as the water began to move along as it hadn't moved since January. The town was far from safe, Harbison warned them. There was a lot more water coming along than the opening would handle. Low places would still have to be sandbagged and the opening widened as soon as possible. The river was being rerouted, and that would mean significant back-up, even when the earth was moved by its force. A damming downstream would be as bad as one here.

But nothing Harbison said could dampen the spirits of the workers or their triumph at what they had done. Two hundred people, in shifts, had been able to move part of a mountain and stop the death of their town. All afternoon, song broke out. People all but danced with exaltation and exhaustion. By afternoon, the word had gotten back to the town and the workers were greeted by those too young and too old with cheers. Fearing declared the following Sunday as a thanksgiving with a special service. Brush carried from the dig had been piled up at the grade school play area. Someone suggested a bonfire in the town square and people would walk around that evening giving the news again and again to people who already knew it.

"We're through!"

CHAPTER 30

AT THE DIG SOMEONE GRABBED ANNEMARIE AND kissed her and began to hand her around to other people who kissed her, and old and young were being kissed or pounded on the back and shoulders.

A secret made itself plain to AnneMarie, then. She could see it in glances and the expressions on the men's faces. The secret was about the feelings they had kept closed away regarding the Drop. The town depended on the Drop. The people here weren't farmers or ranchers anymore, but hosts, providers to skiers and vacationers. They raised no food, cut no timber, mined no coal for warmth. All the food and fuel on which they depended came from outside. The Drop had brought that home to them in the most unequivocal way possible as they stood in the field and watched the helicopter settle itself every week with items that would be allowed them.

How much they hated this dependency was brought home to AnneMarie in that moment. *Women*, she thought, *aren't as frustrated by it as men are. Women are freer to ask for help and to accept it gratefully.* Now, in the uproar, the stamping and clapping and kissing, she saw the pride the men had in having done this impossible thing. For the women, breaking through called forth sighs of relief. The town would be spared. For the men, the opening was a validation, a return of their self-respect. Half an hour passed before Harbison and Roman Ansel could shout hard enough to get the clamor to stop so that Ron could, with his booming voice, remind everyone that in one month, two if they were lucky, the heavy overcoats of snow would be melting away, pouring down all the gulches and canyons and runnels into their valley with the force that had carved it in the first place.

They were in for more struggle, much more. The water would help, washing soil and gravel down and away, but all the trees that were making nets to hold the water and all the boulders impeding it would have to be wrangled and broken up and pulled away and moved and carried. And there was detritus, too—fine houses had been crushed and sent under the fall, hot tubs and bathroom and kitchen fixtures, washers and driers and stoves and refrigerators, bedsteads and bodies and parts of bodies—all that would have to be moved and dealt with.

"Enjoy today," Ron told them, "and be back at work tomorrow. The clock is running."

AnneMarie was walking home with Jay, not saying much. She had been visiting Pastor Fearing for a month, now, and she knew that Jay harbored, guiltily, some resentment. Why couldn't she talk to him instead of to Fearing, a good man, but not all that bright? What did they talk about? What did she say about him? Was it about how he left his clothes hung over chairs or looped over doorknobs, how he chewed toothpicks and then left them where they fell? Did she talk about his habits in bed? Jay knew that Fearing must have many of Gold Flume's secrets and wouldn't let them go, but what would Jay see behind Fearing's eyes as the two men shook hands after the service or stood talking to him at the dig? Usually these thoughts of his could be made to lie down, their teeth hidden. The two of them had been married so long that they had the same ideas at the same time. She wasn't surprised when he said, "When's the next time you see Fearing?"

"I hate to take up too much of his time." She looked down at the snow banking the road. "He doesn't say much, but just me talking, I come up out of myself, like coming up from under water." He said nothing. "It's been hard on you, I know," she said, "my being like this for so long."

"I might have been more understanding if I knew what you were thinking. You seemed only to pull away, where I couldn't follow."

"I know; I couldn't follow myself there, either."

"Have you seen Doc Winograd lately?"

"He's a good enough doctor for most things," she said, "but not for this. For him it's all about the brain and brain chemistry. Isn't everything? Isn't love? Still, no one tries to give people drugs to make them love Bob and not Bill."

"AnneMarie... I..."

Coming toward them were five teenagers who stopped about thirty feet away. "They shall not pass," a boy cried, unaware of an old allusion. He was hefting snowballs, one in each hand. They were all smiling. They had heard the news.

"Don't toy with us," Jay said. "We're savages."

A girl—Jay identified her in his mind, hurled a snowball that fell short. "You throw like a girl," he said.

"Why not? I am a girl."

"Even a girl should do better than that."

"Come closer and say that to my face."

People had come up behind Jay and AnneMarie—Ken Blair and his three kids. "You've insulted my wife," Blair said, "and I demand satisfaction."

"These arms are registered," Jay said, "with the Bureau of Alcohol, Tobacco and Firearms. They are lethal weapons."

The woman's next snowball hit one of the Blair boys who had come up to Jay's side. The fight was soon joined by a young couple, other teenagers who were going toward the dig, and by three coming off the dig. The air was soon full of snowballs, shouts, taunts, and laughter. They fought with great energy and mediocre accuracy, until one of the combatants declared that if he and his friends were late at the dig, people would notice. By then, everyone was wet with the spring snow and beginning to be tired from exaltation.

AnneMarie and Jay walked on. "You know," Jay said, "I've been wondering why you give me foot massages when I come home from my shift, and I never give you any."

"I just work the cable," she said. She brushed snow off his shoulders. "I haul buckets and drag wood up to be cut. My feet aren't wet all the time, like yours."

"I'll get my massage — I'm addicted — and then I'll do yours."

"My neck," she said. "That's where all the tension goes."

The road was busy with people going and coming, to and from the dig. AnneMarie waved at several and greeted others, Jay raising his hand as people passed. Their walk had been slow, and by the time they got to town they stopped before going up the hill to their house. On the left was the Ute, already risen further than they had ever seen it, level with the road.

"Will we get it in time?" AnneMarie asked, knowing that the question was rhetorical.

He shook his head and shrugged. "I meant to ask you," he said, "has anyone been at the house, begging?"

"More than one," she said.

"Do you give them anything?"

"What else can I do?"

"AnneMarie—everyone gets the same packets—the food, the fuel allotment, medicines, all the same. Why would you want to give them our things?"

"They seem to need them."

"Who is it?"

"People are sending their kids—I can't turn down kids."

"Which kids?"

"It makes me feel like I'm squealing."

"I want to know. Melody Reimer tells me she gets visitors every day for hand-outs."

"I'm not approached every day." AnneMarie sounded defensive.

"Who is it?"

"Jacksons—they're the biggest, Sugie French—she comes to the door herself, the Lamborn kid, Ambrosier—"

"Regular bridge club. Why didn't you tell me?"

"It isn't a secret—most of those people have kids and you know how much kids can eat, and sometimes people try to make something new with the packets and it doesn't turn out, or... and we're not starving. I don't see why we shouldn't give to people who need it."

"That's just the point—they don't need it. The Drop takes care of all of it."

He couldn't fault her—AnneMarie had always been charitable, but that the ludicrousness of this situation didn't dawn on her made him impatient. How could there possibly be beggars when everyone got the same rations? Wouldn't that shame the beggar and shock the one who answered the door?

"Never mind," he said, "just let me know who it is, or who they are, and what they are asking for."

"Fuel," she said, "and food."

"What kind of food?"

"Fruit, then, the brown rice..."

"Fruit and brown rice..."

"What's the problem with that?"

"Dear, they're not eating those things; they're making rotgut out of them. How much have you been giving them?"

"Of the rice, maybe two or three cups—we had some saved from the last Drop, and the dried cherries, two packages."

"And water?"

"Am I the only idiot?"

"That, I have to find out," he said.

"I know Melody gives food—we talked about it after church on Sunday."

"Anyone else?"

She named several women, all older, all heirs of the traditional teaching about charity. Jay felt himself beginning to seethe. He knew he could have laughed with equal honesty. The Drop included no cocaine, no nicotine, no vodka or Scotch or even beer. What to do? Scam old ladies and middle-aged depressed matrons. And they must be kids, doing this—teenagers unused to a single hour between wish and fulfillment. They send their little brothers or neighbor kids to do the begging.

"Melody, you said?"

"I think I heard Lettie Shively say she gave to the Brown twins... and one of Min West's kids, and one of the Bergstroms, a younger kid."

"Quite a little group to draw from."

"Others, too."

Melody Reimer was up earlier than usual and wondered why she was excited. Oh, yes, they had dug through – a hole, a small hole had been made. She got up slowly, expecting but always surprised by the pain in her shoulders and knees. She stood, swaying before being able to go along to the bathroom.

She was dressed and down at the Drop field waiting for the chopper, when she saw Sheriff Isaacs catch her eye. A light snow was falling. He came over, and she asked him if he thought the Drop would be canceled for the day. Everyone knew that if there were much snow, or high winds, the 'copter wouldn't appear. When it didn't, there was tension. The question: what if they stop coming? What then? Jay asked Melody if she had had beggars at her door.

"Not beggars," she said, "kids asking for food and fuel." Even when they had been given everything on the lists, she told him, most people knew enough not to use all their rations for the week—most people did save up. At first, the young ones requesting her extras embarrassed her, because they seemed embarrassed. They had—their moms had had an accident, a cooking mishap, a friend or son or husband or dog eating more than the Drop had given them. Mice got into their storage places, a rat took to raiding their cabinets. The children coming back seemed always to be the same ones, and after the fourth or fifth excuse, became unable, or unwilling, to mint a new one.

"They've been getting brazen," she said. "I always considered myself a good Christian, charitable, generous. Maybe the fall has eroded some of that, people so passive and dependent. Once, I lost my temper at Jen— at someone who said, 'You wouldn't let us starve, would you?' I had to stop myself from saying, 'Why not?'"

"It's not about food," he said, "or water. People will give up necessities for luxuries every time. It's for booze—sugar, fruit, water? What do you think that makes? Fuel? Wine isn't wine anymore when it's distilled. Potatoes? Corn? Wheat? Rice? Starch in any form? What does that make? They're fermenting it somewhere. They need heat—warmth, to bring on fermentation. The **where** is my problem. Get the word out. No one is starving." He left.

She felt stupid, unprotected. She had expected that there would be a slackening in the work now that a breach had been made in the fallen mountain and some water was flowing away. If that slackening went on into April and May, when the whole clothing of snow that was on the mountains melted and poured from the arms of the rock, the Frenches and the Bergstroms of the town would be amazed and horrified at all the water flooding their streets and homes. Where would their drinking take them then?

The fact of that let-down was causing restless sleep, a condition she hadn't suffered for years, not since the loss of her nightmare of a husband. Her guilt over her inability to mourn him had been worse than any grief she might have felt at the loss of someone loved and missed.

Now and then, when she was tired or dispirited, she would be overwhelmed for long moments with a brutal, searing envy for couples like Sheriff Isaacs and his wife, who seemed to love each other fully, without weighing or measuring. Melody had known AnneMarie when she was vigorous and happy and when the pall had fallen on her, Melody had expected some alteration in the relationship between her and Jay—a divorce or separation. Neither had happened. Now that the fall had forced AnneMarie to come out a little, Jay Isaacs seemed to be happy, never, at least to Melody's knowledge, holding before AnneMarie the pain she had caused him.

In Melody's worse moments, she railed in her mind against the Isaacs and other old couples—the Moritzes, the Klimeks—whom she had once dreamed of as pairs skaters holding hands across their bodies as they circled the ice together, smiling.

All the more reason to rise early and put her mind and her gifts to the service of the town. She could shut off that part of her mind and forget its demands and the envy it woke in her.

The breakthrough was dimming the fervor of some of the people working the fall. The number showing up each day sank by almost half, and Mayor Dixon and the two engineers began to look at the mountains, measuring. Their figures weren't encouraging. Unless the work was put forward intensely, unless the number of workers picked up again, and the length of the workday stayed at a high level, the breach they had made wouldn't mean a thing.

Melody watched them as they pondered the problem. They had approached Pastor Fearing with the idea that he give a strong sermon about continuing the work and being faithful to the promises they had made. The town council members had suggestions for postings declaring the problem and raising enthusiasm.

A week after the first breach in the fall, Melody went to Dixon's office as soon as it opened for the day. "We're no longer running on enthusiasm," she told Edwina. She saw Edwina's shoulders move slightly and there was a flicker of impatience on her face. Melody knew Edwina had to listen to her because she had become very important in the organization of the Drop, but Melody was still an older woman, and shreds of her garden club identity still clung to her. "The Book of Luke says, 'The laborer is worthy of his hire,'" Melody said.

"And you're suggesting we pay people?"

"In a way, yes."

"Money—"

She could see Edwina was keeping herself in check with an effort. Money had almost no value in Gold Flume, now. One of the few advantages of the fall had been the all but disappearance of a class system in town. Big houses were hard to heat, gourmet foods were unavailable, and fashion had long since died in the need for warmth and protection from the snow and wind.

"I don't mean money," Melody said, "but don't you think we could get the Drop authorities to go along with a plan that rewarded workers with—say—one extra request for every week worked full time, some small thing—beer, cigarettes, ice cream? We could even have a lottery available only to people making full hours."

"It might work," Edwina said. "I'll frame a letter—or do you want to do it?"

"It's better coming from the mayor," Melody said.

"Write the letter," Edwina said, "and I'll sign it."

Melody worked on the letter for the rest of the day, but she couldn't get it succinct enough, and still describe the slacking off, normal enough in normal circumstances, perilous in these, or why the bringing of beer or cigars or a piece of real fresh meat to the Drop was vital to Gold Flume's existence.

Unable to sleep, she walked the freezing floors of her living room, where the dead telephone, TV, and all the electronics whose guardian lights had announced themselves in red, were now dark. At a time no longer announced by her oven, she had the thought to go to John Klimek with her letter. He was a good writer. Eased by the good idea, Melody went to bed and slept well.

The next day, she walked past the church and through the snow to John Klimek's house, passing the Isaacs' place, where AnneMarie was shoveling their walk and filling buckets with snow. She was just early enough to catch John as he left for his shift. The day was gray and smelled of snow. He stopped, looking up, his face showing pleasure. He was one of the people in town surprised at the blossoming of this orderly garden club president into an organization dynamo. She explained her plan and showed him the letter. She saw him smile a little and hoped the smile wasn't for her writing style.

"I've been wondering myself," he said, "what to do about my kids beginning to lose their edge. Enthusiasm will make kids scale mountains and swim rivers, but staying power is a harder sell. Do you mind if I fiddle with this letter?"

"That's what I hoped you would say."

"I think it's worth a try," he said.

Later, they met at the town hall for their daily hour. Melody told them her idea. Harbison pointed out that a lottery would be counterproductive. Luck would rule and luck was the opposite of work. The point was to praise attendance, easily verified by the sign-up sheets, initialed on the job.

Reward. What would the prize be? Food, Harbison said; service of some kind, Edwina Dixon said, imagining a candle-light dinner with the person or persons of the winner's choice. Someone hunting and giving the best part of the elk or deer to the winner, Jay said. Only Jay's suggestion wasn't dependent on the Drop and protocols made by agencies and people many miles away. Brad Unger had been hunting in the mountains here all along, but the scarcity of ammunition meant that no one would hunt without a sizeable share of the animal. Jay realized this as soon as he voiced the idea. A house-cleaning? That was Melody's idea, but who could be drafted to provide such a service with money having lost its value? What incentive would there be for one person to work for another? Apart from the altruists, the leveling had leveled away the need to work at anything but the private good.

John Klimek said that he had hoped the Wheeler Dealers would be continued and go into areas beyond bare need. Pastor Fearing said that he had had hope of peoples' souls expanding in the simplicity and authenticity of life here. Gold Flume had all the advantages of modern life and the cessation of need to work at unrewarding jobs. Simple lives, simple rewards—a dinner—yes, from packets, but a dinner made by the best cook in town and a memento, a plaque, maybe, memorializing the fall itself, and the winner's role in saving the town.

Melody asked who knew who the best cook was. Harbison tried to clarify a nagging doubt. Surely their showing favor in any way would compromise their idea of fairness. Envy would be the result. Jay asked if the Agency might not be appealed to. Edwina reminded them that envy was the outcome when rewards came from outside. Along with reward, she said, there might be punishment as well. Eyebrows went up. Punishment of a sort, Edwina said. She had been frustrated by having no way to confront slackers. She asked Fearing if there might be a shame-reading, names of no-shows at the dig to be read out on Sundays, or posted on the notice board at the town hall. For a time, the council took up this idea, which was simple and, they thought, effective.

Jay spoke against it. "Do we want to divide the town more than it's divided now? Why did the original colonies get rid of stocks and public whipping? Because they didn't work. The same people got whipped and the same people brought them to the posts. Running people out of town isn't an option here."

"Well, what do you suggest we do?" Edwina's voice had an edge of impatience.

"The only thing we can do is talk to everybody; bring the reality to them: dig or drown. If we don't dig, we will be re-located to a clutch of emergency housing set up between Callan and Bluebank, in tents, maybe. We will join the world's dispossessed." For a while they were all quiet, seeing it in their minds.

"Rewards, then," Edwina said. "What can I ask the Drop to send us?"

"I've written a letter," John Klimek said.

His letter was concise and in places, eloquent. Tweaked here and there by the council, it was sent on the next Drop. There was no reply.

CHAPTER 31

"WE NEED TO HUNT," MAYOR DIXON TOLD THE PILOT of the chopper. "Here's a list of the ammunition we need. Many of us have the guns—rifles, pistols. Of course, the weapons are different, and we'll need ammo for each."

The pilot's look was incredulous. "You're not in a war. These rations are strictly civilian, relief rations."

"Can't you try, anyway? This isn't teenaged boys at play. We're people who need protein."

"Your rations are nutritionally balanced. Read the labels."

"We're not passively waiting the way other people in other places are. We're working like prisoners on a chain gang. Your balanced diets are only half of what we need."

"Fill out a formal request."

"I have it — here."

The pilot's expression didn't change. He glanced down at it and put it in his shirt pocket. She hoped he would give it to his superiors — if he didn't forget to or harbor a feeling they were taking advantage of the system.

As she left the Drop site, Edwina was conscious of how remote the town had become, how distanced from the outside world's concerns. Every two weeks a Drop would arrive. Klimek's kids' group would take their carts and wagons down to the Drop site and then up the streets of town to deliver the items to each house on their routes. Every three weeks, mail would come—first class mail only—and the joys and traumas of those outside would intrude briefly on the people receiving the letters. Banks had put special arrangements in place. There were newspapers now and then, a magazine or two, put in at the pilot's whim.

Reading the news, she felt more separated from the events that were being reported. There was a tsunami in Japan, another earthquake in San Francisco. Drought was hurting the east coast. It all seemed interesting to her, but not quite real.

While the outside world sank away, local rumor flared. Gossip blew through the town, settled between the houses and then wafted away, displaced by the next wind: More of the mountain would fall. The water being delivered had been treated with chemicals to render the population sterile/docile/calm, all completely shown up by the facts of their daily lives—pregnancies up and the people neither calm nor docile. Doc was begging the Drop for condoms and the pill, but these were specifically forbidden to the Drop by federal law.

Angela Bruno had used her own, and then her mother's supply of pills. Her vulnerability made her careful and demanding. She and Mike were seldom together. They had been forced to search for new places to meet. The cave was still a possibility, but too often they found it being used by other kids and the place had never quite lost the smells it had taken on, at least to Angela. Now, it had become locked away in the April snows, the way impassable. Outbuildings were cold; attics were cold, too, central heating having disappeared. Their sexual lives were now constricted, limited to quick moments in each other's houses when their parents were gone.

Angela was becoming even more dissatisfied and harder to please than she had been before the fall. Back in December, and last autumn, there had been the car, and they'd gone on shoplifting tours of Callan and Bluebank and now and then, over the Pass into Aureole. Mike got her things. There had been vodka and weed, and even cocaine. Mike, himself, she thought, wasn't a very interesting person. He wanted sex, but he wasn't interested in what would or wouldn't satisfy her. He liked followers, but wasn't interested in what leadership was, beyond the ego massage of command. Now, he had only power to bargain with. Twice he had punched her in frustration. She sensed that the act gave him pleasure. Now and then, someone would talk about the Shively boy's death, about how it was strange that he had been by the river at night.

Mike knew that Angela was fully ready to rat on him, so keeping her sweet was more than his need for sex or show. He had thought he might kill her, but it was too much trouble and too dangerous.

And he knew that she was brighter than he was. That knowledge made him nervous and less stable. He hadn't done anything violent to people, yet. He had learned to control the sudden white rage that came down on him, not to hurt the mope standing by him when he was thwarted or denied. He couldn't offer drugs to her or his followers – his supply had been used up and the rot-gut held no attraction since the Shively brat's death. The cave? The sheriff had said how generations of teenagers had gone up there. The Shively kid had died, who knew how, but Mike had only moved the body. Angela was the one who had figured out about putting water in the lungs.

Because of that damn kid, Mike had to spend time at the dig, acting as innocent as it was in him to act. The sheriff kept an eye on him, and so did Mayor Dixon, the cunt. Angela managed as little work as possible— signing up for two or three jobs at once so she could say at each that she was at another. The dig was complicated enough so that no one had the time to sift through all the excuses and scan the rolls of attendance and the rolls of who was up at the Drop, distributing rations.

Five months after the fall, women were beginning to run out of cosmetics. Lip gloss, lipstick, and blush would last for years, but face creams, moisturizers, shampoos, conditioners, and hair dyes had been used up in the first few months. Many women, some to the surprise of the town, had to endure two-tone hair or cut their hair at the color line. The shades, one bright, one drab, reminded too many people of flood-lines. Considine said, "Out at the ends? Scarlett O'Hara. In at the scalp? Grandma Moses."

Leatrice Bruno, before the fall, had been one of the few stylish residents of Gold Flume. Tourists, passing, took her for a celebrity, and though Angela was critical of her mother on almost every level, she secretly envied the flair and sophistication that had attracted the attention of Raymond Bruno. Angela sensed that her mother had been relieved to have her father on the far side of the fall. The sight of his wife, bundled against the cold and without her usual presentation, would have disturbed him.

These lessons about presentation weren't lost on Angela. Youth and her beauty meant that however she dressed or made up, heads turned at her arrival. She was certain that heads would also turn in New York, London, Paris, and Rome. When she thought of the dig breaking through, she had a picture of herself swimming through the opening, slipping in like a fish and flowing away. She would have to get a man who wasn't tight with money. She had seen her mother reduced to tears of frustration, ticking off the items she had bought at every store under her father's grudging nod and the grudged check, torn off in annoyance.

She and her mother got along better than both had expected, now that Dr. Bruno was away. They both realized that had they fought harder to have him back, he might have come. Bruno, at his medical convention, had surely found low-hanging fruit and wasn't unhappy to stay where he was. The women weren't spending his money. There were no demands to be made.

Two weeks after the fall, Leatrice Bruno had gone to the bank where the doctor had a sizeable amount of money from investments unreported to the IRS. The account was in her name, and this she transferred to cash and put in a new safe-deposit box.

Angela knew none of this, but she did suspect that her mother had freed herself in some way, a freedom that was reflected in Leatrice's every expression, gesture, footfall. They had begun, very slowly, to become friends. Leatrice knew that she would stay with Bruno until she could get a good divorce settlement. Angela would go to a good college and work on an MRS degree. She would make a perfect trophy wife.

When Leatrice spoke of this idea to Angela, praising her for the good grades she got with a minimum of study, Angela looked at her the way someone looks at a two-headed calf preserved in a bottle. "Why would I want to do that?"

"Well, beauty doesn't last forever," Leatrice said.

"It doesn't have to, only long enough to get what it wants."

Angela had received more from her mother than the unwanted comments, and more than Leatrice imagined. She disliked Mike's crude sex practices, but it had never occurred to her that she might talk him into changing them. She abetted him in theft, she encouraged him in building his gang and the cave. She and her mother had always been subservient to powerful men. They never argued or put their own opinions to them, yet they managed to make their preferences the most convenient way for their men to go, day to day. He ruled the roost; she defined what the roost was. Before Ray Bruno's disappearance, the two women had fought like lions. Now, they were at peace. No one liked the lives they were all living now, the hard work, the smells, the cold, the dependence on the Drop, but for some, there were secret advantages in their changed world.

Leatrice had never understood how her daughter could put up with Mike. "Can't you find anyone better? The boy's a loser. Yes, I know his father is a big cheese around here, but that boy will get you into trouble—he already has. I grant you, there's not much here to choose from, but that one?"

"What about what we get?" No one in Gold Flume saw as much fresh meat as Angela and Leatrice Bruno—real soups and stews, when others were eating from their packets of reconstituted meals.

With no other ways to pass the time, Angela and Leatrice found themselves talking to each other. Neither thought much of public opinion unless it went toxic, so neither worked any more than minimally for the town's approval. When they did work, it was with Melody Reimer, whom they savaged when they were alone together. Neither of them had become hard-handed from working the buckets or digging at the face of the fall.

Melody had noticed Leatrice's gift with numbers and also that Angela seemed to have inherited it. She had been amazed at first to see their instant understanding of the spreadsheets she had created, unifying the requests of everyone served by the Drop. Recently, Leatrice had been making suggestions, one of which Melody had instituted immediately. Instead of people needing to go from line to line, food, fuel, medicine, miscellaneous, Leatrice's plan had the unloading changed: one line for the standard delivery, another for special items (the baby care line, the medical line). The plan saved time and confusion. The success of this idea made Melody rethink her assessment of the Bruno women—Leatrice as a useless clothes-horse and Angela as a slut. She knew they laughed at her as dowdy and even ridiculous, hair gone gray, wrinkles in a face uncared for, not even eye makeup.

CHAPTER 32

THE APRIL SNOWS HAD BEEN PARTICULARLY HEAVY, and on May second, a hard freeze destroyed all hopes of the later flowering of lilac blossoms, spring beauty, the fragile looking pasque flower, the wild cherry. There was the usual quick fall and quick disappearance of the snows by evaporation into the dry air, further chilling the day.

Then, high on the south and west faces of Barrel Stave, Croom, The Hungry Mother, and Jackass Mountain there was a scarcely noticeable change in the quality of the snow. As it froze at night and melted during the day, it became coarse and grainy. On one of Kinchloe's watercourses, a tree whose branches the snow had bent and frozen to the ground, shot out of the snow and shook itself off like a laborer ridding his shoulders of his load and standing to take a breath. A rock bastion formed by years of erosion from a vast rampart wore its high cap of snow, but from under the cap a drop, then two or three, formed and rolled away. The blue air took a shimmering vapor from the shining snowfields that covered an arm off the lower crest. This vapor congealed on the rock face in drops.

These drops joined others from other mounds and formed tiny threads of water that carried bits of ore tailings from forgotten mines, dots of alluvial gold and lesser ores.

Nights that had been twenty degrees now were forty and the days' sun warmed the ground. A person walking the crests of these mountains might hear, under the still high gathering of snow, the sound of unseen streams' faint friction. Over the shale, sandstone, limestone, and granite heaved up millions of years past in the great paroxysms of the earth's unrest, the water moved.

The melt was slow at first. There were still freezing nights at the tops of the mountains, and down into the town. Anyone could see the slow rising of the river. People who passed by on their way somewhere or to the dig became anxious as they measured the level of the water against their memories of other years. The way they had argued ball scores, they now argued water levels.

"See that line on the trees—that grayish line? That was the flood level back in '82."

"No, Harbison looked it up, that was the '03 flood."

"Are you crazy? The '03 flood never got that high."

The increased pressure of water in the river was helping them at the dig, cleaning earth and sifting it even as the level rose. In the mornings, the relays of diggers cleared and moved earth, stones, trees—root, trunk and branch—and bits of houses. There was window glass and drywall resisting their shovels, slate from roofs, quarry tile. Chaz Bergstrom, just turned fifteen, on his first day at the dig face itself, felt his shovel turn and, thinking it was a tree root, struck the thing hard and felt it give. In the earth loading his shovel was a something, not earth, not stone, not tree. As soon as he recognized what it was, he threw it off his shovel and screamed. It was the lower part of the leg of a child.

Paper products: books, bills, stamp collections, toilet paper and magazines had all been compressed by water and dirt. Pots and pans were unearthed, smashed barbeque carts and broken tables, couches, dishes broken and whole, silverware, bent but some usable. Melody and Leatrice set up a committee. Body parts would have to be seen to, furniture and possessions assessed and assigned, clothing gathered and decisions made about saving or disposing of it. There had been four houses above this part of the fall. A town man had made repairs and done handyman jobs for three of those families. He knew their names and might have a fair idea of who had been at home on the night of the fall. Another six houses on the south had escaped destruction. Three families had stayed; three had left. School kids were making tasteless references to 9/11 and the clearing and claiming of the bodies, referring to these as 9/11 West, until someone demanded they stop. Their comments were squelched and later Pastor Fearing observed that this work of theirs had given everyone an idea of the immense labor involved in disasters of war and earthquake.

The first priority remained the dig itself. Overnight, the water rose, and the work of widening the breach became as dangerous as it was difficult. Ron Pantea made a harness for himself as he struggled in the water and the idea was quickly adopted for anyone working near the rising river. The big melt of the peaks had not yet come.

They found huge boulders and moved them. A group of men broke them up with picks so they could be taken up to the ground away from the river.

Mike had an idea about raiding the dig at night, for things found, but not yet moved. The shovels were unearthing more than pots and pans and ruined books. There might be things like money boxes and guns, things that could be re-sold after the fall was cleared away and life returned to normal.

"Are you telling me you want us to go down to the dig and root around in the dark, in the mud, for some filthy clogged something?" Angela was incredulous.

"Nobody's there," Mike said. "We'll have light; there's all kinds of stuff they haven't taken to the school gym yet."

"Why don't we go to the gym, then, if you're so set on sifting through garbage."

"Are you nuts? We'd be seen—the light—"

"Go if you want to—just be careful no one sees you."

"You won't come?"

"And get filthy? No, thank you."

"It's a gold mine."

"I never knew you were that big a—" she searched for the word, "—materialist, and why risk your life for a gun or something that will be identified by someone?"

He couldn't explain to her that he needed to be on the edge, excited, alive. He felt the need so desperately sometimes that he took risks even he thought would end in ruin. And they worked. He made them work, laughing afterward with the triumph.

She was going on. "You have the wood thefts, and what about the kid?"

She knew immediately that she shouldn't be talking about the Shively boy. Mike was no lawyer. He didn't know if moving a body and concealing a cause of death might not result in jail time. The break-in and the wood thefts could be tut-tutted away as kid stuff; his father had already done that, having told Mike some of the tricks and pranks he did when he was young. ("The damage—well, they have insurance to take care of things like that—just don't do it again.") Even the drinking and doping in the cave—hadn't the sheriff told him that everyone had done it—but the dead kid—Mike knew what no one else did, that he had seen the kid come up, a kid too young, and that he had been the one to give the kid the stuff. He had given the booze and dope the way you'd give it to a dog or a horse, to see what would happen, and the kid had been fun to watch, because he was dancing around and laughing like crazy. Then, all of a sudden, he had stopped and looked out of eyes wide and shining in the firelight and died, standing up and dead before he fell on his face. Mike had tried to concoct another story, not for any authorities, but for himself, that he had just come upon the kid, not even knowing the kid was there, or what he had taken.

"You're not coming," he said it flat, half-threat.

She laughed. "What gave you your first clue? Cold, wet, dark? Not me." And she walked away, swinging her butt the way she did when she had won an argument or put somebody down.

There was a moon that night and the snow made everything brighter with no competition from lights in town, streetlights, or from the go and come of cars along the highway. Mike saw that he wouldn't need to use the lantern he had brought to make his way to the dig. He walked easily alone on the highway until he came to the loom of the fall.

The working face of the dig, he had heard, was eighty-six yards wide. He had had so little interest in the project that he was surprised at how much earth had been moved. The planners had dug the bed of the river significantly lower so that the water would flow into the diversion out of its former banks. People had to climb up on parts of the wall and move earth down to be picked up by those below to be moved out of the way. The face was terraced like a Chinese hill and there was now a dig going on on top of the wall over the river.

He held up the lantern. It shed a weak light. His father kept the flashlight and batteries locked up, damn him. In the puny glow, he looked for glints of anything shining in the wall, but his first sightings were the peeled branches of trees that shone in the light. The river flowed slowly through the new bed at the far western edge where the fall had been lightest. He saw that the breach—all their work—was far from being wide enough to take the snowmelt coming from the mountains. The problems with the river didn't affect him at all, but the technical part interested him. Angela had said that if the river did flood the town, people would go up hill and be rescued by 'copter on ropes, if necessary.

There, over there, was a gleam, something, just for a second. It was eight feet or so up the wall and ten yards from where he stood. He raised the lantern and looked—a hard gleam, not a soft one, not like the peeled branches had been. He looked around for something to stand on. The boulders he saw were too heavy to move, but he found a plank and used it to lever up and move one boulder out of the water and roll it under the gleaming thing. His perch was precarious and it was a while before he could get his balance, holding the lantern up to see what was there. It was metal, yes, and some cloth—providential, because he could use the cloth to pull out what was there. The metal thing seemed held tight to something, but as he pulled on the cloth, he felt something slowly yielding, coming toward him. He set the lantern down, but the boulder was too irregular and he nearly fell over. He jumped from the rock and moved the lantern beside it, losing most of the light it shed. He climbed up again, got his balance, and found the cloth he had been pulling. He had an idea of silver. His mother kept silver knives and heavy tea things in cloth bags. He saw those bags in his mind, fifteen or so, in gray flannel, each sized for the longer knives and the shorter forks and spoons, and some big ones for tea-servers she saved for holidays.

He pulled. The thing gave a little. He pulled harder; it gave more, and all of a sudden, all of it came free and he was sent backwards off the rock and on to the wet ground, bruising himself on pebbles and detritus, but what he had pulled out was in his hand. It was heavy, as heavy as his mother's tea set.

The breath had been knocked out of him and he had to rest a moment before he could crawl over and get the lantern, bringing it close to his treasure.

It was an arm—a man's arm and hand, and what had gleamed on its wrist was a watch. The arm was clothed. It had been the sleeve he'd been pulling. The shock of discovery stopped everything in his mind for long moments.

The watch—the people up the hill were rich people and wore expensive watches. It might be a Rolex. He had seen ads for those watches. They sold for thousands of dollars. Nothing seemed broken. He'd expect a watch that had been in an avalanche to be destroyed, but the strange thing about working at the dig was learning what could be shattered and what pulled from earth and crushing rocks, undamaged.

He studied the arm, and then the hand. The fingers and nails were caked with dirt. He could imagine the fingers grasping for purchase, trying to pull, to protect. He felt queasy, lifting it and going to the wrist—left wrist. Maybe there was a ring, too. Yes. Brushing the dirt away, a wedding ring was on the third finger. Mike congratulated himself on his courage and on keeping his head.

He tried to slide the ring off, but the fit was tight and the hand swollen. He cursed. How did people get tight rings off—Vaseline—and he had seen it done with soap and once a thin fish-line wound tightly behind and then in front of a tight ring—he had none of those things and no knife to cut the finger off.

The watch. He tried to pull it up, but dirt had choked the band slides, clogging them tight. He tried to tear it off, but it wouldn't come, and all the while, that little gleam around the rim, the gleam that had first caught his notice, continued to glow and dance in the light of his lantern.

For a moment, he thought of taking the arm home, where he could work on it and get the ring and watch off some way, or, going home now and coming back with a hatchet that he might use. He might get caught by either of his parents, roused by his looking for the thing. They had the garage strung with flattened tin cans to keep wood thieves off. His dad might get his plan, but his mother would have a fit, and there would be another screaming fight and maybe she would get a sock or two, and walk around leaking tears for a week.

He realized that the arm was now out of the wall and he wouldn't be able to jam it back into the dig-face—at least not where it had been. The earth was too packed. Perhaps further along, he could find a place where he could hollow out a niche for the arm. He walked along the wall, dragging the arm behind him, holding on to the cloth of the sleeve. So intent was he that he was past a tree ten yards back before he noticed that the arm had come out of the sleeve and that he was now carrying the cloth, empty, in his hand. Cursing, he went back along the way until he found the arm, stepped on the flesh above the elbow, put down the lantern and, using both hands, tore the watch off the wrist. The ring would have to be a loss. He left the arm where it was. There would be no way of proving his presence at the site. Besides, what had the big crime been? The body was already there—he hadn't killed or hurt anyone, and, he had what was probably a Rolex, worth thousands. It was a big watch, heavy in his hand. He picked up the lantern and went home.

CHAPTER 33

THE QUESTION WAS, SHOULD HE TELL ANGELA? HE felt like a hero who had done a great deed in isolation. For years, his father had laughed at newspaper accounts of thieves and even murderers who had been caught after having gone to this or that bar and bragged about the deed. How ridiculous they had seemed, and how deeply he understood that urge now—to tell someone about the challenges he had met, the fears he had suppressed. He ached to share the moment—funny, in a way—the shock, the dark, the struggle, and how he had finally torn the watch free and here it was, worth thousands, and how cleverly it had all worked out.

People would see the sleeve and the arm, separated, and assume that some animal had unearthed the thing, a bear, or a mountain lion. He liked associating his personality with those animals. He spent the next day cleaning the watch, soaking the band in oil. The watch wasn't working, but he was sure it could be repaired. There were three heavy scratches on the glass face, and some smaller ones, but they could be fixed. The watch was wonderful to look at.

Out of curiosity, he decided to revisit the dig. He had done what that dumb sheriff had told him to do, keeping his head down and taking his turn with all the other able-bodied people there, putting in his time, not at the face, but working the buckets, so as to be seen by more people, saving his reputation. He had been faithfully attentive for almost three weeks.

Things weren't so bad the first week. The exercise made him feel healthy and vigorous. People smiled at him, now and then. Sometimes they all sang, and that was when there was a rhythm, shoveling away earth, filling buckets—half-full for women, full for men—over-taxing would only land you in Dr. Winograd's Riverside Emergency Room with muscle strain, tendonitis, or hernia. When they were in that rhythm there was a kind of joy he liked being part of.

During the second week, he began to be annoyed at some of the people trying to boss him around: "Mike—we need you over here." "Mike—you should go all the way to the cable." "Mike, your break is over."

The third week was slog and insult. People were working against time, but he could see no progress—the wall stayed the wall, studded with rocks, boulders, trees, and broken furniture. They were all crazy, ant-like and crazy. He had quit in the middle of the week and then had had his treasure hunt idea. Two days after finding the watch, he had gone to find Angela.

She had tired of the dig herself, and was spending her time at the Drop, helping to unload and distribute the food packets and fuel canisters. Now and then, there was the opportunity to get a little extra. People with one package short weren't likely to complain, especially if they were old and didn't have terrific appetites. The kids doing the house-to-house never seemed to notice how much or how little was being given out, as long as each house had been visited. People were supposed to save up from weekly distributions for emergencies.

With work at the dig increasing, many people had stopped going to the Drop, depending on the kids and the organizers to deliver their rations. John Klimek trusted the Wheeler Dealers and he had set up different contests to keep them interested.

Mayor Dixon was always on hand when the 'copter landed, getting the newspaper, the mail, and any new information the pilot would supply about what was going on beyond the mountains. The pilots on the copters were rarely the same. They said they had no time, did the delivery, and took off. Now and then one did stay for a few moments to give them news. One said that federal help had been held up by continued earthquakes and aftershocks in California, hurricanes in the Midwest, and storms in the East. State help was being hampered by the fires resulting from a dry spring, 97,000 acres in one fire, 90,000 in another, and two small towns wiped out with people homeless. Of course, Gold Flume would continue to be supplied with basic emergency rations, but anything more was, for the foreseeable future, problematic.

This man looked around, his face carrying something like scorn. Edwina read his look. The man saw these people as beggars, clawing away at the heart of compassion, whining, then demanding. They had all but mobbed him with needs that were never satisfied. Their avalanche had spared the town. No one here had lost everything in the mad wind-driven wildfires or floods or had seen their homes disappear in an instant of touchdown twister, streets torn, houses reduced to heaps. When they crowded in with last minute requests, his patience snapped. "Things are tough all over," he said laconically. He waved them away, climbed back into the 'copter, and troubled the air with his leaving. Klimek walked over to Edwina who was standing by the boxes and jerry-cans.

"What did he say about the new requests?"

"It seems," she said, "that we've become suppliants."

265

Pastor Fearing was urging everyone to work at the dig. Every day he studied the tops of the mountains around them. A snow and freeze that week in late May was keeping the water from over-running their work at the dig. In the lower world, weeds and grasses were going green, pasque flowers and spring beauties were being succeeded by harebell and penstemon. The aspen leaves burst their cases. New, lighter green growth appeared on pines and firs, and the air was muzzy with pollen. The Drop was applied to for asthma medicine, Benadryl and Claritin, inhalers, and more bottles of oxygen.

"God works in us," Pastor Fearing declared in his sermon, "to finish our communal work. Mayor Dixon says that people are slacking off the dig. Yes, we've broken through, and yes, we've enlarged the passages where the water will flow, but if we don't widen that passage a great deal more, we are going to get major flooding in this town. Outside these mountains, people are dealing with tragedy they have no power to overcome. How sinful would it be for us to have the means to avert our tragedy and not use those means fully? I beg you... us... to redirect and rededicate ourselves to the work of the town's salvation."

It had been many years since Fearing had used the words sinful, dedication, and salvation. The prayers in the liturgy were heavy with those words, but his sermons had long since done away with them. The word *sin* had been changed for *illness* and then for *issues*. Fearing had heard people talk about a man having boundary issues, and later learned that the man in question had beaten a woman and broken her jaw. "Dedication" sounded prissy in his ears and "salvation" too far to the religious right. But what else was he but a pastor and what was their situation but one of good and evil? Now, there was none of the ambiguity in life that had made people question and ultimately laugh at the words religious people used.

Jay had begun to go to the church, arriving at the close of services in order to hear the announcements and talk to people as they left. AnneMarie had always attended, partly, Jay thought, because in one small part of her soul, she felt the danger attendant on her marriage to a Jew. Her church going, he thought, was a form of insurance, a protection for them both. Had Jay said this, she would have denied it and given him the tired cliché about their God being the same and all religions having the same ethical beliefs and so on.

Even in the haze of her drugged-up illness, when her pores exuded the smell of their chemicals, she dragged herself to the back pew, far left side. When the kids were small, they had gone to Sunday School and then to services, sitting with her in pews toward the middle front and taking communion, gravely. It dawned on Jay that it was a year or so after Alicia, their youngest, had left home that the cloud had slowly settled on AnneMarie who was sitting by herself, then moving to the back and leftward, drawing away, physically and psychically from the heart of things.

Now they sat together, back and leftward. Jay realized that he had given his own practice no attention. He was here in church for updates and to get a feeling for the temper of the town, once an interest, now essential. He went with Doc twice a year to the congregation in Aureole and celebrated Passover there, invited by the members in town. He hadn't wanted any more until now. He would be missing all of his holy days. In missing he felt more loss than he had expected.

He leaned over and whispered, "When did they stop having church bells?"

She gave him a puzzled look. "Why are you asking that?"

"It just dawned on me. When I first came here it was kind of a feature, St. Mary's, Valley Methodist—this church. Before they moved out of town, down valley, there were Sunday mornings, bell Sundays, 9:00 and then again at 10:00."

Tess Klimek in the pew ahead of them turned and gave him a look. He smiled and nodded at her. AnneMarie opened her purse, took out a pen and small notebook and wrote, handing him the torn off page: "Noise pollution. The skiers and tourists didn't want to get up so early, and they complained, and then came Church And State. Church And State took away the bells."

"I liked them," he mouthed.

"Me, too."

"Comforting."

She smiled at him.

Jay looked over the congregation as people got ready to leave. Roman and Janeen Ansel were there, but without their son. He wondered how much they knew about Mike and what had gone on up in the cave. When he had discussed Mike's behavior with them, Ansel had been truculent and defensive, Janeen cowed and apologetic. Were these reactions real or defenses against his authority as sheriff? There were people who, at the sight of a badge, seemed to change their natures. He had once stopped a woman on the highway between Gold Flume and Callan for speeding. When he had asked her if she knew how fast she was going, he realized that her pallor was genuine fear and that she had no way of answering his question. She had opened her mouth to give some kind of response and fainted where she sat. Some people, men mostly, got surly. Everyone addressed him as Sheriff, and he knew that most people thought of him as The Sheriff, even though he was under-sheriff to Sheriff McMasters, who operated out of Aureole. Only Ansel had chosen to remind him of his lower rank. What had gone on after the Ansels had gotten Mike home? He knew that Angela's mother was accomplice, not parent.

Rick Harbison came over to where he and AnneMarie were standing outside the church. "Did you hear? They're finding body parts out at the dig. Yesterday afternoon they dug out a woman's body, and there was a torso, a man's, that was wedged between some rocks over on the east side. Considine was up there early and found an arm and hand close to some boulders. Sleeve was pulled off, but nearby. Coyotes?"

"I don't know? Are they uneaten on?"

"So they say."

"Probably bear, then. A coyote or mountain lion would have gnawed at it."

"Uh."

"Do they have any identification? Have they checked the list?"

"They moved the body and the torso over to the courthouse yesterday afternoon, late. I don't think they know anything, yet."

"I'd like to see the body," AnneMarie said. They looked at her in surprise. "I might know who it is."

"Why would you?"

"You forget that before—a few years ago, I used to do collecting up there, for charities and things for the town. Unless the people have moved, I might remember them. Only a few people up there lived there year round."

Jay wanted to tell her that he was proud of her, but he could see that her face was set in a way to discourage what she could have taken for condescension. Melody went past them with a smile, and Harbison excused himself quickly and went after her about something.

"Sorry," Jay said.

"Why should you be? He's right; I've been away for three—more than three years on my journey to nowhere."

"You've got guts, girl."

"It doesn't take much guts to jump out of the window of a burning building," she said.

They walked home, slowly, grateful for the sweet May breeze.

Mike Ansel had heard about the discovery of the body and its transport to the town hall. What about the torso? Having been unearthed, he wondered why the smell of it and the arm hadn't been stronger. He was afraid to ask.

That evening was one of the rare ones that he and his folks ate together. Janeen was using a soup packet to liven up a stew. Many women enjoyed the challenge of experimenting with the packets, blending or separating their contents in various ways to achieve different flavors and textures. Janeen had tried many food combinations. Some worked, some didn't. When they didn't, Roman would call her stupid and wasteful. She wondered why she kept trying.

Mike came home, but instead of going to the kitchen and getting out a packet, he helped the astonished woman carry the dry clothes into the house and waited while she prepared their meal.

To the surprise of all three, they found themselves together at the table again. Janeen was carefully quiet in her movements and didn't speak. She knew the moment was special and that a word might spoil it. Roman wasn't in a temper, Mike not mulish. She wanted to mention the rumor that Angela Bruno and the Harbison boy had been found making love in the bed of one of the fire trucks. Someone had told her that the two of them were hot at it when a few of the firemen opened the big doors and went in to wash the truck. She was interested when Mike asked, "Anyone know about that body they found?"

"It's up at the town hall," Roman said.

— and a pause. "And the part?"

"That, too."

"They must smell to high heaven," Mike said. Janeen opened her mouth, but closed it, quickly.

"Not much odor left," Roman said. "A lot of the fluids in them were taken up in the what, five, freezes and thaws we've had. The body fluids'd be leached out by the surrounding earth. Maybe down in the tropics you'd get rot like that—" Janeen blanched but they didn't notice, "but up here..."

FROM THE FANTOM
A little hole, a crack, a breach,
Fearing takes the time to preach.
Plaudits to the pastor;
Klimek leaves The Dig to teach,
Reimer's dream exceeds her reach.
Gold Flume waits disaster.
Mrs. Klimek, Praise the Lord
Tells us Angel Flaming Sword
Sent from Christ the Master
Shall with one amazing hack
Give us Gold Flume's future back.
Can't we make it faster?

POSTED BY THE MAYOR: WILL WHOEVER TOOK
THE SHOVELS FROM THE FIREHOUSE PLEASE
RETURN THEM IMMEDIATELY? THEY ARE
NEEDED ON THE TRUCKS.

CHAPTER 34

ON THE SHOULDERS OF THE MOUNTAINS, THE THAW
began its resolution. Water, carrying the glittering contents of its per-
suading way over rocks and spillways and the tailings from defunct
mines, poured downhill, reaching other streams, competing on slope
and slide. When challenged by boulders or narrowings, the torrent shot
over them, sometimes carrying them along, breaking crusted soils into
curds on the sides of its passing. Sometimes, coming to a narrowing, its
force boomed like a cannon heard along the town's edge.

In last summer's late somnolence, the river had contracted from its
bed, leaving sandy spits with spots of water here and there, which in
September had also dried. The line of willows and water-needy green

marked what seemed to be impossibly wide boundaries. Small pools left by the river's drying had gone sour and brackish. But now, it was early summer, and the river remembered itself and took up all its old holdings and beat along.

The people's grueling work had created a new course for the Ute, but one barely sufficient for its demands. The water hit the wall of earth, rock, and debris, trying to find its new way out. It became confused, splashing back on itself. Some of it forced a way wider, some gathered on the banks and settled its mud in the willows.

Now, the diggers could only work at the sides of the dig on the west and south. The water rose and rose again. People went at sandbagging the river walk that had been so lovingly and carefully created and tended by the Garden Club back in the nineties.

The water rose and rose again. The Drop was delivered in ankle-deep water and no one could predict how much deeper it could get. People on Front and Main Streets began to think about leaving their homes. The water rose. A constant low-level anxiety pervaded the town. Gold Flume had seen floods in 1882, 1898, and 1926, and a major one in the spring of 1982 that had floated cars on Main Street, three people dead. Many remembered that there had been a terrible rainstorm soaking everything and keeping people imprisoned in their flooded homes.

The water rose, and then, stopped. Mayor Dixon came out on the morning of June 15, a day of sun and clouds, and saw the river full in its banks and two feet higher, washing over the flagstones of the river walk, but not as far as it had been the day before. Half the town was down at the river, all along its course, measuring, talking, smiling, noting that a hard rain or two could ruin it all, and saying there was still snow melting from the high ridges and saddles of these mountains, but yes, the river itself had been working at the dig, pulling the earth it took through the passage, "stating its case," as Klimek said. He had been standing at the bank viewing the torrent with satisfaction. The cheering and exaltations were calmer, less rambunctious than they had been when the dig had first breached the fall, but they were deeper. People grinned at one another.

Here was June, summer and no cold, no hibernating in the rooms of their houses in fear of the next hard freeze with no fuel drop because of a sudden storm. Some people had seeds and had planted them as soon as they could and were seeing what might come late in August. Wild greens were on the uplands—orache, yampa, pigweed. The shaggy manes and chanterelles were over, but the boletes and the russula mushrooms were coming and the campestris and sylvestris, big and tasty for frying, were profuse in the draws. Soon it would be berry time.

It was pleasant, now, to take clothes to the big washbasins set up where the streams ran. The men had mounted panes of glass to warm the water a little and save on wood, and they had dammed some of the water higher up, opening and closing the wooden shed-piece so as to settle the water some so it wouldn't be as muddy. A few people went higher and panned for gold, having nothing better to do. They took flakes the size of pinheads and thick as the letters on newsprint and pounded them into nuggets the size of gnats.

AnneMarie had been chatting with Melody and Janeen after church about the possibility of brewing some dandelion wine. They were getting a small sugar ration and if they pooled some of it, there should be enough to get a good brewing—seven or eight gallons. People heard them talking and told others and the word got to the kids. Mike saw a way to get back some of the power he had lost with the debacle in the cave. He knew no one would tell him anything about how such wine was made or who would make it, or how to get the sugar to make it, but he might be able to get Angela to find out for him. Since she had been forced to ration her cosmetics, she had stopped painting her mouth vampire red and her eyes like a battered woman's, and the town was a lot more accepting of her. He knew that while the Shively kid had died, many more kids had been sick, some, very sick. Their parents, not knowing the source of this illness, had taken it for flu, blaming the lack of heat in their homes, or some bad packets from the Drop. Any kid disagreeing with these assessments was sure to face trouble from his friends.

Very few people were willing to give up their coffee sugar, sugared cocoa, or cookies for a wine-brewing. The women sautéed young dandelion greens and flavored them with soup from their packets. They studied mushroom books and talked to women who had gone for what wild mushrooms were in season. These they picked and fried, trembling with anxiety, but their inventiveness didn't include wine or anything distilled. A few men had tried it with packets of potatoes and turnips. Older kids had tried it, too. Their product was disgusting.

Mike had heard that hallucinogenic mushrooms grew in these mountains. He had goaded Chris Pantea to talk to John Klimek about them, to find out which ones they were, and where they grew. John went to AnneMarie, who asked him if he wanted to go on a walk with her.

"Chris asked me about gathering wild mushrooms—I'm not particularly interested for myself..."

"I'll take him if he wants to go."

Later, when she saw Chris and asked him, he said, "I don't care much—Mike wanted to know—"

She laughed. "For you, yes—for him, no."

"How can you tell a poisonous mushroom from a good one?"

"You look at it—stalk, bulb, if there is one, veil, if there is one, color—color of gills, color of spores, color of cap. Never eat a mushroom without a formal introduction."

He looked at her and she grinned at him.

He had been told that the sheriff's wife was crazy, that she walked around in a haze and smelled funny and seemed never to see the person she was looking at. This woman just looked like a regular person, grandmother-age, maybe, or a little younger. Her hair was gray; her eyes did see him, gray eyes in smile wrinkles. Going up to the Dentons and the Moritzes and knowing them almost as friends had given him an appreciation of old people he had never had before. He realized that before the fall, had he had any interest in mushrooms, unlikely enough, he would have Googled the request without any need for personal interaction. There would be pictures, too, all there, and the messiness of ask and answer, negotiation and politeness avoided. There was a richness he heard in what she had said, "formal introduction" on a mushroom walk. Soon, the electronics would be back, and the grandmothers gone again.

"Could we do a walk now?"

"Sure—now that the dig isn't life and death," she said, "my social calendar has opened up a bit."

They walked the town side of The Hungry Mother, down Kinchloe, going slowly and stopping often to look or simply to let AnneMarie rest.

"I don't know why this is," she said, "but you won't see mushrooms at first. After a while, you'll spot one and then you'll begin to see lots of them. It's as though they're training you to see them, even though you've been walking the draw for years, looking. Each kind picks its spot—some where there are trees, some on flat ground. I hope you're not coming just to find the ones that get you high. Some of them are worse than booze for the hangover. You get high and then you get sick."

Chris was careful about letting her rest. She seemed grateful for their pace. "It's been years," she said at a stop before climbing higher. She had brought a basket and a small paintbrush. "You can put mushrooms in a paper bag," she told him, "but never in plastic. Remember what it says about not letting babies play with plastic bags."

"But—"

"Mushrooms are alive. It may not seem like a good life to you, but they like it. Give them air."

Was she crazy after all? When he looked at her, he saw she was smiling at him. Chris' father had a sense of humor, his mother didn't. She had a cynical bite, sometimes, but not a sense of delight with the world around her. AnneMarie's humor was about fun.

"Does a mushroom know that it's alive, then?"

"A mushroom is a periscope sent up by the mycelial mat. Mushrooms are the spies of a vast underground empire that wants to take over the world. The empire is stopped by housing developments and lack of water. If you put your ear to the ground, you can hear the mat making its plans. Look over there—"

"Where?"

"A man can't find a can of tuna in a refrigerator; what can I expect in the woods? I'll show you. Here's one conspirator I would take home and fry in butter—if we had butter."

They gathered fifteen, passing by twice that many, that she said were poisonous or maggoty. She had shown him how to look at a mushroom to identify it and told him about making spore prints. "You take eight of these; I'll take seven," she told him.

"No—you take them all."

"You're still scared of eating a mushroom not sold in a store, aren't you?"

"Well, kinda..."

"Where's your pioneer spirit, your sense of adventure?"

"I don't want adventure to be Cause of Death on my autopsy."

"I'll make this deal with you. I get the mushrooms today. I eat them all. If you see me alive tomorrow, you write me a poem of apology—rhyming, too, none of that free-verse crap. You deliver it to me with a sorrowful look, and we go out again after the next rain."

"I don't know..."

"You make this deal or I tell the mycelial mat where you live and it will come and strangle you in the night."

"I wouldn't want that," he said.

Chris sat at home, picking the stickers and seed husks he had found on his socks. He wondered what was wrong with him. He had been completely comfortable and at ease in Mrs. Isaac's company, as he seldom was with kids his own age. She demanded no pose from him; she didn't pose herself. He wanted to be with her again, to relax in her accepting presence. He also knew that, like the Moritzes, she was glad to see him, but where the Moritzes needed him and needed his help, with Mrs. Isaacs—AnneMarie—there was no need, no other motive.

Was such a relationship acceptable? Was **he** all right? Weren't kids his age supposed to go through their teens separated from elders until they were parents themselves? He had heard that gays used to keep their loves deeply, deeply secret—sometimes even from themselves. He knew he wasn't gay. His mind was littered with fantasies of women; a mere whiff of some girl could cause him anguish and embarrassment. He had had the usual struggles in the back seats of cars, but they were more lust than pleasure. There was no information here, no advice that would tell him if he was crazy for wanting to be with a woman in her fifties, for going up into the draws and gulches after mushrooms and berries, comfortable and relaxed and without a need to be anyone but who he was, not wishing to be anywhere but where he was.

People said she was crazy... He didn't really know what the word meant. Crazy seemed to range from a sudden creative hunch to staring madness, from an unexpected plan or idea to the rationale of a serial murderer. Where were the lines drawn?

Let his meetings with her be kept separate, secret even. They could be freer now that the dig's responsibilities had been scaled back. He would see her in town and write a poem. What rhymes with 'mycelium'? Helium. What rhymes with 'mushroom'?

FROM THE FALL FANTOM
The Ute in its banks
The struggle now is deeper—
Our humanity.

POSTED BY THE MAYOR: WORK ON THE DIG
IS STILL VITAL. IT'S NO TIME TO LET UP. THERE
WILL BE A PICNIC – WEATHER PERMITTING –
ON SUNDAY AFTERNOON. PACKET STEW. WILD
ONIONS. IT'S <u>SPRING</u>!

CHAPTER 35

ANNEMARIE STILL HAD TIMES OF DEPRESSION, EVEN of despair, but she knew that she was recovering from what the medicinal cocktails had done. Intense exercise at the dig and the work she was doing were bringing benefits, but she wasn't sure yet what they were. She still rose each morning dreading the hard work of the day. She still had broken sleeps and dreams of opening food packets that were spoiled and foul. She realized, though, that she was recovering a strength she had had years ago. She was able to watch the psychological states of people in Gold Flume with insight. Sometimes, she caught herself responding with feelings that verged on arrogance.

The let down from the fear of flood was natural, to be expected. The people had been congratulating themselves, she thought, proud and full of joy at the job they had done, the frantic work that kept the river in place through town and guided into its new channel. They had relished watching with giddy delight the slow, twisting rope of water being pulled through the opening and over its new bed. The smiles were gone, replaced by looks of gloom and annoyance, even, as the work didn't end. The opening had to be extended, the course not allowed to be slowed by silting up or choking with rocks as it pushed along its burden of mud and pebbles, sticks and leaves to be carried on past Callan, Bluebank, and Granite City. It would swing south and forget itself in the merging of the other rivers into the Gulf of Mexico.

They had done it. They had done it with hand-tools, picks and shovels, and the wonderful creativity of necessity: the cable and the day-by-day harmonizing of strength and skill.

Now, they wanted to rest. Some went back to their private lives and concerns. Tempers woke. Siri Unger and Cheryl Fearing argued about Cheryl's getting extras from the Drop. Siri told Cheryl that she knew Cheryl was using those extras for herself and the pastor, and not for church events. Ron Pantea beat Rick Harbison's Spy away from Queen Esther, who was in heat, telling Rick that if that damn dog jumped the fence again, he would shoot it. Melody Reimer said that Spy had better stay out of her flowerbed or she would poison him. Jay Isaacs got called to three scenes of domestic violence in as many days, one by a wife whose husband was trying to force from their daughter the name of the boy who had caused her pregnancy.

The absence of beer and whiskey, of cigarettes and TV, of VCRs and DVDs had resulted in an upswing in pregnancies. The Pill wasn't included in the Drop. The pilot had shown Mayor Dixon a letter with a statement that the government couldn't be in the business of terminating incipient or even potential life.

Doc had been asked to do abortions. He had done several, to Melody Reimer's seething disgust. She had come out of church one Sunday, gone to his house with a folded paper that said MURDERER, and slipped it under his door. When Melody complained to AnneMarie about all the

281

promiscuity in town, AnneMarie said, "Most of these people are married, some, even, to each other." Melody sniffed. "I'm more worried about the boys up on Kinchloe cutting wood with handsaws," AnneMarie said.

With the work at the dig, which was still going on, and with the climbing and descent, hunting and fishing, there were many more accidents in town, but aside from four more deaths than that of the Shively boy, one a stroke, one a fall, two from old age, life had gone fairly well.

"I'd forgotten how little real medicine I was practicing," Doc told Jay one afternoon as they sat in Doc's front yard and looked down the walkway to the river, now slowing in the hot-dry, late June day. "I used to send all the broken bones and surgeries to Callan, where they have the clinic. Anything really serious could get choppered out to Aureole or even to Denver. Most of those were auto wrecks, and the fires caused by gas leaks, careless campers, and electrocutions that we don't have now."

"But what about the burns from fires in fireplaces and portable heaters?"

"Oh, sure, and falls, and cuts from tools, but manglings? No."

"How does it feel to get all that work back?"

"A little scary, maybe—I've done full surgeries in the office, obstetrics—I guess I never realized how specialized I'd become, how routine my practice was. I like being back in the nineteenth century with twenty-first century drugs. The Drop has kept me in plaster of Paris, and ipecac, but also all kinds of antibiotics and meds for stroke—which reminds me, how's AnneMarie doing?"

"Better—she's a little better. She still has bad times, but she's weepy, not zoned out, and there's her wit back, her smarts. She may be in pain, but she's not an invalid."

"I have to admit I made a mistake, there," Doc said. "I followed along. A quarter of all the drugs on any insurance plan are psychotropics.

Anybody's got depression or sees things or hears voices, anyone with jitters or who can't concentrate or has ants in his pants, we know ten or twelve medications we can shoot to 'em. The Drop doesn't give me any meds except for actual violent psychoses, and clinical, long-term depression. Maybe one person in 10,000 ought to be on any of them long term. I was prescribing for plain grief." He shook his head, "Well..."

"No one wants to suffer if he doesn't have to," Jay said.

"So things are good?"

"Better than they were."

Doc leaned back, smiling. "My clothes are washed, my house is cleaned. I get fresh meat now and then—"

"How's that?"

"My patients can't pay me—money has no value now, and nobody's making any anyway. I get it all in services. I'm living the good life. I haven't filled out a medical form since January. I also do a little dentistry and veterinary medicine on the side."

They watched the water for a while. They were sitting in the shade of Doc's big spruce tree. Beyond its benison, the air rilled in the heat, but Jay knew that in another few minutes, the mountain would swallow the sun and the air would cool quickly.

"Y'know," Doc said, "I just came clean about making a mistake and hurting a good woman. Out there, beyond this Valley, words like that might end up costing me plenty in a lawsuit."

"It won't happen here," Jay said. "You weren't thoughtless or indifferent."

"I didn't know—I simply didn't know. I checked with psychiatrists and they said it was all I could do. The only question was which medication to use. It worked for a while, and I thought it was fine, and then it didn't, and so we added another to bolster the first one, and still another."

"She's losing the weight she put on. It was a side effect, one of many. It helped dull her down."

Doc smiled. "Everyone's losing weight, working like we do and eating the way we all have to, now."

"Have you ever thought about what will happen when all this is over?"

"The mind boggles." Doc hefted himself up and stretched. "Well—Lettie Shively is bringing her boy in. Since what happened, she's been worried about this one. Anxiety clones itself. The kid's caught the fear, too, and no, I won't claim psychosis and put in for the pills." He followed a little rill in the brown river. "When the water clears, what about a little fishing? I don't think we'll get people so greedy for fresh food that they'll have fished it out before we get there."

"I've already broken up three fights over who got what from some seine fishing someone did upstream."

"Why not let 'em fight it out?"

"Too likely to spread. Wives get into it, kids. Before you know it, there's a feud and more work for you."

"I see that," Doc said.

They watched Lettie Shively and the boy, handsomer than his brother and more assured in his movements, come down the street toward the house. It was difficult to see him as a hypochondriac. Jay thought that one of the demons hounding that family was the mystery of it all. They must have assumed the boy had been down at the riverbank, trying to cross in the snow, that he had slipped and hit his head and gone under. But what had he been doing down there alone? Where had he been coming from? There was talk about a group of older kids in some kind of clubhouse, but no one would tell them anything about it, and one boy Lettie had tried to question had run away, run she had told Jay, like he was scared out of his mind. Jay had told her that there had been no way to prove that Billy's death had been anything but an accident, a fall, a drowning. The boy hadn't suffered—the cold would have taken care of that. Gossip had blown through town and settled like fine dust blown from a mine cart. Gossip had gone elsewhere, now. Marguerite Mason, fourteen, was pregnant and votes on who the father was were split three ways, but the Shivelys were stopped where the gossip had left them, marooned on their island.

Jay walked home, wondering if the excitement of the crisis at the dig had become addictive to some people. If so, they would eventually have to go through withdrawal. He himself was feeling the let down, but the rise in other work had kept him too busy to share in the deeper part of the general slump.

And it was hot. Day after day burned with no letup, except after sundown. People who had been used to air conditioners, fans, and swamp coolers felt the heat as they worked. In the past, the summer days had meant less to do, even for those whose jobs were in the tourist part of the town's economy, but the work they had done had mostly been in an environment that was cooled by humming motors they were barely conscious of. Now, people were making sun tea, without ice, and it was only lukewarm. The lemonade packet stuff that had had no acquaintance with a lemon was warm as cough syrup.

News from outside was that the people in the quake had buried their dead, left ruined homes and shattered lives, and gone to other places. The ones who had stayed were rebuilding, but slowly, the extent of the damage slowing everything. At the last Drop, the pilot had told Jay and Edwina that people in the Arizona quake with no electricity to cool their homes or run their refrigerators were leaving.

"Count yourselves lucky," he told them. "In other places, there was looting."

"To get what?"

"They don't seem to care."

Streetlights were out in the city, he told them. The cops and hospitals had generators, but the rich people had left the high rises to the looters, anyone who could walk up and down twenty or thirty flights of stairs, to carry away their treasures.

"Things are coming back slowly. This place, here, is Eden, when you think about it," he said. "When you <u>do</u> think."

"When will we get power back?" Jay asked, trying to keep his voice level.

"Can't tell," the pilot said, making them feel like demanding children of a patiently exasperated parent.

"Summertime in Eden," Edwina said caustically, as they walked away from the 'copter and past the lines of distribution. Jay caught the tone and tried not to smile. Edwina had been elected to be a pleasant face in this tourist town. She was deft and tactful. The fall had brought out her toughness, a necessary quality in the light of chauvinists like Brad Unger and Roman Ansel.

The routing was now efficient, understood by all. People hailed them as they went through the lines. Jay pulled his kids' old wagon, Edwina a grocery cart. Neighbors still asked what the 'copter pilot had said.

"When will we get some relief?"

"What did he say?"

"Not this month or next."

Hot as Egypt, I'm reminded
Of the pyramids they built.
Waves of workers, all sweat-blinded
Moving up the fearsome tilt.
China's wall and Rome's achievements
Now are joined by Gold Flume's pride.
I can hear their disbelievements
As we gain the Callan side.
To the fame of distant nations
Let the name of Gold Flume ring;
We are more in our creations
Than Chuck-E-Cheese and Burger King.

POSTED BY THE MAYOR: PLEAST TAKE CARE
OF YOUR PETS' EXCREMENT. WITH NO STREET
SWEEPERS WORKING THERE IS DANGER FROM
TYPHOID, TYPHUS, AND EVEN PLAGUE. PICK
UP THE POOP.

CHAPTER 36

ON THE DAY AFTER THAT WEEK'S DROP, THREE
strangers who had, impossibly, hiked up and over the still snow-covered Wolf's Head Mountain and over Jackass Pass, came down following the river, and made their way into town. Hikers and townspeople stared at one another as though they were in a sci-fi story being read for the first time.

The hikers had wandered casually onto Main Street, asking where there was a restaurant and some place for an overnight stay. Their hike had been more challenging than they had expected, they said, and they would need a rest, and to re-stock their gear, food, and fuel before they ventured on or went back the way they had come. There was an expectation of welcome and awe at their achievement. Megan Harbison, the city engineer's youngest daughter, encountered them first. She stared and then directed them to the town hall. Edwina Dixon came out of her office at the news of their arrival and stared also, but not with the awed welcome they had anticipated. Their requests died on their lips.

After a long moment of mutual surprise and confusion, Edwina realized that she now had a way to get a clear picture of what was happening outside Gold Flume and the valley. She sent a kid running up to get Pastor Fearing and Sheriff Isaacs and Doc, to come and meet the newcomers. She told the hikers that they would get free lodging at the parsonage.

"Isn't there supposed to be a good hotel here—we thought..."

"Closed."

"Motels?"

"Closed."

Fearing was back before the hikers had time to learn why Main Street looked like a movie set, empty and shuttered in the middle of the day. He greeted them and introduced himself, offering his hand.

With news of the hikers, Gold Flume roused itself. Someone ran to the dig. Jay arrived, saw the three—two men and a woman—and sent someone for John Klimek, who was with a few of the Wheeler Dealers, so that by the time Pastor Fearing arrived there were twenty or so people moving toward the town hall and gathering at the steps leading up to the building.

The hikers, who wanted nothing more than food and sleep, had been taken up to the mayor's office and were being questioned. It was an hour before they were treated to cups of freeze-dried coffee and the promise of some reconstituted stew at the parsonage. They emerged from Mayor

Dixon's office to a silent, staring crowd. The group was twenty or thirty, with faces they couldn't read, more people coming all the time. Suddenly, the murmur erupted in questions. To the town, the hikers represented The Outside, suddenly present and available. To the hikers, they were almost a mob, no welcome, but a demanding set of questions that were all but incomprehensible. The hikers found themselves with the power to give or withhold, but their status was as balanced as rope-dancers in a wind. They were being asked the same questions in twenty different voices. Would the Drop continue? Was there work going on from the Callan side to open the river wider? Was there equipment to take the mountain away and free them? Was the government taking charge? Could the Drop be counted on? The three stood in the rain of shouts for a full five minutes, the crowd not realizing that without its silent attention, there would be no word at all. Dixon had come out behind the three and raised both arms, palms out. The crowd had grown larger, and now stilled itself, some people shifting foot to foot.

"The thing is—" He was big and blond, wearing khaki shorts and a light blue T-shirt. He had shucked his backpack, which probably had some warmer clothes and his bedroll. It lay beside him. In those shorts, he seemed all leg and thigh, his calves bulging with power over his rugged boots. "The thing is," he repeated, "we don't know—" he was going to say "What you are talking about" but the look of them sobered him—"we don't know, like, what's happening here. We're from Boston, and Boston—well, we had bad storms, real bad. I mean you guys got this, I guess—and then, there was, like aftershocks or something, but we..." He couldn't tell this crowd that he had only half heard the accounts— one after another, the background distraction of ten o'clock news, no more, and that was back just after Christmas, six months ago.

The girl behind him, slight, dark, but also obviously athletic, a runner, Jay thought, tapped the young man on the shoulder and stood up on her toes to whisper something into his ear.

"Yeah," he said, "it was like after Christmas, I guess and here and California, oh, and Arizona. People were freaking out because they were blaming some countries for making climate change and causing all this. There were a lot of homeless, so they set up tent camps, and trailer camps, and shelters and shit, and then they were getting food to people and water and everything. I don't know how many, but, like, they have to get all this stuff rebuilt—" He turned to the other, younger boy who seemed less confident but who was also well fed and athletic. He was brown: skin, hair, brown pants and shirt. He spoke from behind the other two.

"We saw this on TV, but it must have been on the other side of the mountain," they said. "There were houses buried. They were digging for a couple of months, just clearing the dirt and rocks away from places. Where the ground—the mountains, like slid off. People are talking about The End Times. It gets really weird."

The girl spoke. "We climbed the fourteeners, most of them, last summer, and this summer, we wanted to go to some lower ones—thirteen, twelve, but harder climbs. I wanted to go on the mountain that slid off, but that's been closed off, posted. At least we wanted to try from this side—you'd have other challenges." She saw their look. "We didn't know where the mountain slid—I mean, like, here."

She could see the sudden change in the crowd, from impatient interest to impatient disapproval. These three spring timers had come to play, taking advantage of a catastrophe they had been too self-involved to think about. Jay felt it, but realized he was being childish. There might be something to be learned here.

"You'd done this hike before—the route over the pass—was it easier or harder this time?"

"Harder," the blond boy said, "much harder."

"Talk about the Drop!" a man said from the crowd.

"What?"

"The Drops, the food and the water—will they still be regular?"

The three looked at one another, shrugged, and the blond said, "Huh?"

Both Jay and Edwina could see the crowd beginning to move. Anger had replaced annoyance. The hikers had come at the wrong moment, one of let-down and uncertainty. Their indifference hinted at a more dangerous indifference outside—an indifference some of the pilots had mirrored, a hint that their supply of the means of life—food, fuel, water, medicine could vanish in a day, that their lives were in the hands of people busy and harried and taken up with their own problems and more recent calamities.

The world was being reflected in these careless campers, who had food choices and liquor and beer, who had iced drinks on hot days and warm houses in winter, whose washing and drying and refrigeration and lighting and the cleaning of rugs were all done by mechanical slaves. A groan came up from the crowd that was moving closer, pushing up from the back. The three hikers, Jay, Edwina, and Pastor Fearing, who were all standing at the top of the town hall steps, felt the almost palpable disturbance of the crowd. One wrong word, one eyebrow lifted, would turn anxiety and annoyance into rage.

"People..." Edwina was speaking with a voice pitched to be heard so it was higher, and seemed shrill to Jay, "these three have come to our town here as guests, our guests, for a day or so. They're not geologists, and they're not folks from FEMA or the Red Cross and they're not responsible for supplying news about any of the places hit by what's happened.

They're going to go with Pastor, here, up to the parsonage and rest and refresh themselves before they go on."

The girl thought to clarify. "I'm an English major."

From somewhere in the crowd there was a laugh—Jay thought it was that sound described as a horselaugh, and he picked out John Klimek with his mouth open and his head tilted back.

"Oh, Miz Fearing!" Klimek was laughing. Everyone had heard the rumor that Pastor's extra food allocation was for just such emergencies and that Cheryl, who was not well liked in town, was using them herself and trading them for privileges and luxuries. The girl's declaration and the idea that Cheryl's store was at last being called upon for its intended purpose veered the mood away from rage. People began to laugh.

The comic aspect of three hikers, dumb as rocks, coming into a town that had known catastrophe and been hardened by seven months of deprivation, broke on the crowd. The more dumb-struck and uncomprehending the three hikers looked, the harder people laughed. The laughter itself caused more, and soon people were weeping with it, holding their sides, borne away with it, clinging to one another, then slowing, until someone said, "Chill the champagne and caviar!" and they were off again.

Slowly, the crowd dispersed, some still carrying the mirth away in little hiccups. Jay led the hikers, Edwina following with Pastor Fearing, up the hill to the church and the parsonage. Later, he saw John Klimek carrying a dishpan of water out the side door of his house to the struggling cedar he was promoting in his side yard.

"Thanks," Jay said.

Klimek looked up and gave him a smile. "Call us any time; sign up for free prizes."

"Did you know you were going to do it?"

"Not until that second. I've made an enemy."

"Cheryl doesn't like many people."

FROM THE FANTOM
Welcome, welcome three galoots,
Fancy shorts and hiking boots.
Eat our rations, ask for beer,
Dumb as bricks; who asked them here?

POSTED BY THE MAYOR: WE ARE COLLECTING
SUGGESTIONS FOR A DIG CELEBRATION. THERE IS
A BOX JUST INSIDE FOR YOUR IDEAS.

CHAPTER 37

THE HIKERS STAYED AT THE PARSONAGE FOR FIVE days. The day after they came, the brown one tripped and strained his ankle. All had been exhausted by the hike. The third day they spent restocking gear as best they could, and washing their clothes. The day after that, a violent thunderstorm broke over the mountains and wind went screaming through the canyons like the trumpets at world's end. Rain pounded the town, the river rose, and torrents streamed down the roads. On the day after the rain, Cheryl Fearing made her way around broken branches and stones sent down from the hill in back of the parsonage and came in at the back door of the church, which Fearing had demanded be kept open in case of need. He was in the church office, preparing the week's homily. Although the church liturgy and order of the service had remained the same as before the fall, the addition of Catholics who used to go to Christ The King and the evangelicals who used to go to Good News—all of whom were now at Gold Flume Community—presented many challenges for the pastor about modifications dealing with communion and other parts of the service not liturgically set.

Cheryl came in, speaking. "How long am I going to be running this hotel?"

Fearing had put it out that youngsters arguing with parents or couples in trouble or anyone in need might come in to the church at any hour and rest or go to the parsonage and spend the night there. Cheryl had let it be known that anyone doing so would be treated to icy stares and not-so-veiled comments. Only the desperate had turned up. There had been only four over the eight months, each staying only one night.

At her voice, Fearing looked up from his work. He saw her in a new way. She had been gorgeous, alive and vibrant when they met, her hopes shining in her eyes—New York, Los Angeles. She had slowed with disappointment and now, with no makeup, she looked washed out. Her hair had a gray band that measured the eight months she had spent without a visit to Glamour Tresses in Aureole. She was out of eye shadow, and the use of the mascara and liner without it gave her a Halloween look.

She had tried to get a parishioner to do their washing. A spiritual leader had to have a clean white shirt that would show at the wide circle of his neck and shoulders when he robed for Sunday. Darlene Tompkins had finally been bribed with the promise of pints of heater fuel. When winter came, the fuel would ease the dread Darlene had of another season of icy cold in the drafty guest room where her father stayed.

The hikers planned their climb and spent some time wandering around town, looking at the means people were using to adjust to the situation. They had expected to recharge their cell phone batteries there and were loath to use them for more than one call out. The mayor implored one call to a FEMA representative. After six minutes on the line, the leader demanded his phone back. Edwina had been on hold for all of those minutes.

Everyone was happy to see the hikers go. They didn't retrace their route up over Jackass Pass, but chose to go up Whiskey Gulch and Croom Mountain, then down the other side and around, making a big circle back to where they had started. The route would take them three extra days, more if the weather went bad. They left in sour moods, annoyed that their phones couldn't be recharged and that their stunning trek over the all-but-impassable Jackass Pass had not been fully appreciated.

AnneMarie had been going regularly to see Pastor Fearing. She talked about children's leaving, hopes turning downward, about sorrows of inadequacy, the loss of beloved family and friends. Now and then they shared readings. Since the fall, four book groups had started up in town, formed mostly along social lines. With the harder lives people were living, reading tended to be comic, or at least light, books of uplift and inspiration. The town library had been left a good many more books than had ever been read before the fall. The pastor's library had Wodehouse and Lawrence Durrell, some of Mark Twain and a book called *Clochemerle,* which, when she read it, astonished AnneMarie that it was part of Fearing's collection. Now and then Cheryl would hear AnneMarie and El laughing through the half-closed door of the study. Cheryl had no interest in reading, except for cookbooks, which, although she never made the more complex recipes in them, gave her the vicarious life of a gourmet without causing her to gain a pound or stand over a stove.

Her battle, besides the one she was losing to age and reality, was the one she fought with the parsonage. This place was old and inconvenient and had to be kept perfectly or it looked derelict. Its loose wallpaper, dust-producing furniture, discolored floors, cracking plaster, crazing linoleum balked all her efforts to bring order. Once shining knobs and fittings had been worn away to base metal that no amount of polish could bring to beauty. Cheryl hated disorder. Even as a child she had kept her room immaculate. She even slept neatly. No mouse whiskered among the crumbs in her corners. Being devoted to the way things looked made her suffer far more when the Drop denied her cosmetics for her face than she did for the denial of cleaning supplies for her house. Part of El's attraction for her all those years ago had been the impressions he gave of cleanliness and self-possession. She had hated the shambling, hairy, rumpled looks that were fashionable during her dating years. El Fearing wasn't prim, but he had the clean look she liked and there was the promise of prestige—on her wall was a picture of Billy Graham.

She was riled by the sight of that overweight madwoman who looked like a bundle of old bedclothes in winter and a ballooning sausage in summer, laughing with her husband and confiding her lunacy, holding his attention.

There were times that El was out when AnneMarie arrived. Cheryl wanted to park her in the dark, antimacassared front parlor and leave her there. El had demanded that she bring the woman back into the kitchen and give her some tea or coffee. "Chat with her—"

"She's a lunatic."

"She's nothing of the kind. She's a bright, sensitive woman with a lot of pain."

"Oh, pain—spare me. Why do churches attract every dependent weakling and hypocrite in sight?"

"Why are hospitals full of the sick and schools of the ignorant?"

"Why couldn't we attract a better class of madwomen?"

"We've gone over this so many times before. I know these days are hard for you."

"The inside of that house—what must her kitchen look like?"

"Have you ever been in it?"

"No—I wouldn't want to be. She spotted my food packets and I saw her eyebrows shoot up and her mouth pop."

"You mean because of so many?"

She hated his look of tolerant humor at her impatience.

"What does she do with her used packets?"

"I don't know...what?" He was grinning, now. "They're plastic and foil, those wrappers, and they shouldn't be thrown away."

"She throws them in a bag, unflattened. They'll never be ready for recycling."

"I know we're aiming toward something here," he said.

Cheryl was furious. "She never thought to open them up flat, wash, dry, and stack them and tie them in bundles. I've been seeing some blown around in the street and snagged in bushes. People should be ashamed."

"True," Fearing said, "but wouldn't it be good if we could do our bit, pick some of them up and not judge our neighbors too harshly."

"Onward Christian Soldiers," Cheryl said sarcastically.

"Good Lord, I haven't heard that hymn since I was a kid."

<hr />

AnneMarie walked home slowly and found herself looking up toward where Kinchloe Creek—dry now that it was July—trailed its green scarf of willow and aspen. With the drying of the creek, the washday setup had been moved to dependable water, but the arrangements, the sluices and gathering pits for basins were still there, waiting reactivation when new snows fell high on the mountain and reawakened the watercourses. She felt good, knowing these things, their purposes and rhythms. She might not have the energy, even this year, to get to the later berries, but she knew where they were ripening. She knew there had been another world that had been created and placed invisibly over the world of her existence, a cyber world that relished change, any change that lived in cycles of months instead of years. For a while, in Gold Flume, those cycles had stopped pushing against her. Longer, more direct rhythms were giving her space to breathe.

The walk wasn't hard. The Isaacs lived up from the river, three streets over and one block down from the church and the parsonage. She thought about Cheryl Fearing. When Cheryl had first come to Gold Flume as a bride, all these upper streets had been dirt: summer dust, winter mud. AnneMarie imagined that first look, the sudden revelation that she and El Fearing were to be town people, not ski area people. AnneMarie began to chuckle and then to laugh and then had to stifle the laugh. If someone saw her at it, they would surely be confirmed in their belief that she was crazy. She wondered where that idea had been born, the one about a judgment on people talking, singing, laughing aloud to themselves as they walked. Why was meditating aloud or murmuring something in public a sign of madness? Even people who walked singing—had it always been that way?

She came down to her house, seeing it as though through other eyes—Cheryl's, perhaps. Jay had been planning to paint it for several years and this year had decided on working during the halcyon days in February. The fall had intervened and changed everything. He had contracted a company in Bluebank to do some structural repairs, too, before the paint job could be begun. The house looked shabby, but most of the houses in town did now. Nobody used precious water to wash windows or hose down walkways. Anyone coming on Gold Flume now would see a town failing, showing that failure in neglect—shops closed and empty, streets wide without cars, houses looking unkempt, over-grown yards sprouting cheat-grass and the short thistles no one wanted to pull, all the dry, seed-hiding stickers designed to catch the clothes of anyone walking by at the slattern end of summer. Town also had seen itself through the eyes of the three hikers and seemed to be sulking in the aftermath of their evaluation.

Jay was sitting tip-tilted on a kitchen chair, his feet up on another, reading a book. His front-yard location showed him available for anyone needing him, but his position and attitude radiated such peace and contentment that only the most urgent business might intrude on it. AnneMarie wished she could take a picture. He had brought out a little side table and a pitcher of packet-lemonade which tasted a metallic sourness, but the pitcher was there and the glass half empty. The day breathed out comfortably. The sun had wandered back behind the mountains and there was a rind of moon high overhead, waiting its turn.

AnneMarie came upon this peace without warning and it flooded her with love for Jay, love for the town, love even at this moment for her life. Depression, even misery, might not be far away, but here, now, the sweet world surrounded her. Jay looked up. She smiled. He smiled.

"Get a chair," he said, "and come on and sit with me."

"I have to soak dinner," she said.

"Soak it later."

"You talked me into it."

They sat until it was too dark to read, neither wanting to go in. Soon the days would shorten further and the first snows would whiten the mountain tops. Fuel would become an overwhelming need and its scar-city a source of anxiety about the Drops, but not yet; not yet.

FROM THE FANTOM
In the future, western movies
Meant to make us miss those days
Will evoke our scornful laughter
At the lives we hankered after,
At the leisure, cleanly ways,
At the ease of horse and buggy,
At the truths of timeless praise.

POSTED BY THE MAYOR: DO NOT DUMP
UNCLEAN FOOD PACKAGING. FLATTEN THE
CLEANED PACKETS, BUNDLE THEM, AND PUT
THEM INTO THE APPROPRIATE DUMPSTERS.

CHAPTER 38

MIKE HAD RUN OUT OF CONDOMS IN FEBRUARY.
Angela was the only one of his girls who demanded that he use one.
Most of his others allowed him to persuade them that they were being
swept away in his sudden, overwhelming passion, that he was too needy,
too enchanted by their proximity to have to hunt around for the damn
thing and put it on.

"Get home quick and wash that out," he told them, "and nothing
will happen."

In February, Angela had said no—not without protection. After
that, she took her mother's pills, reasoning that without her father, what
use would her mother have for them? The pills had lasted until
May. Mike was demanding. Angela had become a little afraid of him.
They had been timing their sex to Angela's periods, or thought they had,
but she missed one in June and one in July. Now, she and Leatrice sat in

Doctor Winograd's office. One look at her face, with its slight cast of darker skin at the sides of her cheek and under her eyes, and he took a breath. Before he could speak, Leatrice did.

"She's got herself knocked up," she said.

He asked the questions about her last period, signs, and symptoms.

"We all know what's happened," Leatrice said. "We just want you to get rid of it."

Winograd had not been their family's doctor. Before the fall, the Brunos had gone to Callan to a group of specialists in a new medical building. Bruno's practice was supported by two orthopedists who did ski injuries and were known to tilt their assessments for favorable judgments when cases came before the courts.

Doc had seen an unusual number of pregnancies and had terminated over half of them, but his position was delicate. "This isn't a scraped knee—" he told them, "it's an invasive procedure that should be carried out in a sterile environment. There's risk connected with it— risk of hemorrhage and infection. Things happen. You should be very sure you want to go through with this."

His glance went from daughter to mother. Both nodded. He went on. "There's something more. Abortion is legal, but a good many people oppose it, violently sometimes. My nurse lives in Granite City, so she missed the fall. I don't have another. I don't want to be shot or have my office burned, either. This means, Mrs. Bruno, that you or someone you trust will have to assist me and that we will need to perform the procedure after my regular hours."

He looked at them again. They were hard women for all their elegant clothes and delicate gestures. They were both physically beautiful, dark, slender and lithe, but both showed expressions of discontent, and in Mrs. Bruno—Leatrice—a dull resentment, pulling at her face. Doc thought that her unhappiness had begun long before this crisis. Angela seemed to regard her situation as inconvenient—a chipped tooth. The phrase "invasive procedure" hadn't penetrated. He thought she had no doubt experienced lots of invasive procedures, and had to castigate himself for the words in his mind. "So, you're both very sure you want to undergo this risk?"

"Yes."

"And that you will be discreet."

"It's as important to us as it is to you," Leatrice said.

"All right, let's see—" He had an appointment book, which he pulled across the desk and opened.

"The sooner the better," Angela said, then, "When will I be able to go out again?"

"Do you mean taking your turn at the Drop or having sex?" He was beginning to lose his doctor's non-judgmental patience and had to work to keep himself in hand. "For the first, two weeks; for the second, six weeks."

"Six weeks!" She erupted. Mike would drop her and probably not without violence.

"Trust me," he said, "you won't want to for a while."

"But I—"

"Shut up," her mother said, stolidly.

Doc told them to come in on the next day, after four.

He hoped the girl wouldn't need an anesthetic. He had nitrous oxide, easily administered and quickly out of the system, but its effects differed so widely that he hesitated to use it. Her procedure should take an hour and a half or so, and another hour for her to rest and for him to make sure that she wasn't bleeding excessively. Min and Ed up at the gas station had locked the pumps the first day and reserved the gas they had for Doc, Jay, and Brad Unger to use. Doc didn't want Angela walking the mile across the bridge and up that hill to the over-large house the Brunos had up Jackass Mountain. Neither he nor the other older residents of the town had become used to the fancy new gated community and the name change, Prospector Heights. At the beginning of that huge storm back in January, the guards of that gate had both gone AWOL, home early to Granite City's trailer park. The homeowners association hadn't replaced them. Doc would drive the women home and it would be after dark, but he thought people might see them and draw conclusions. Still, suspicion has legs but no face, and if the women kept their mouths shut, no one would have a case against him. In a way, Alicia's absence made things easier for him. Alicia was a wonderful nurse, but her moral compass was rigid—the needle didn't move. In a large city, with hundreds of candidates for each job to choose from, that quality of hers would have gotten her fired. Gold Flume had to learn to accommodate itself to a wider range of talents, ideas, and habits than did New York or L.A., he thought. The conditions encouraged flexibility. It was lucky that Bruno, his volatile colleague, had chosen to stay on the other side of the fall. He didn't think that Bruno would respond well to the demands of the kind of medicine the fall demanded. From a box of carefully rationed pipe tobacco, Doc took a hefty pinch, sighed, and filled his briar, luxuriating in its aroma.

The two came on time, just after dark, walking past the house and going in at the back door. The house fronted the river and people walked there on the street from which sandbags and mud had only recently been removed. Doc's front room, where he had his office, was clean and neat. In what had once been a dining room, he had set up his examining and treatment room, cabinets of equipment, glass-fronted and shining. The kitchen and back rooms were piled with supplies from the Drop.

The oven, almost never used even before the fall, was dull with grease. Doc used a small cooker for his solitary meals. Patients often brought food for him to reheat. Lasagna and casseroles could supply a week's dinners. Before the fall, he had gone, every Saturday, down the valley and up over Prospector Pass to Aureole and a Chinese restaurant, where he ordered three dinners and brought back two. Now, he did what they all did, boiling the plastic packets in a pan on the camp-stove. People still brought him the occasional wild salad or a cut from deer, or elk, or wild turkey. These, he grilled.

The women went through this dispiriting kitchen and into the examination room.

"You're on time," Doc said, "good."

He began to explain the procedure, noticing Leatrice wince as he described the process by which the embryo would be scraped away from the wall of Angela's uterus. Angela remained stonily aloof, all but absent from the room and the experience. Doc checked her blood pressure, pulse, and eyes and helped her on to the table. He brought what seemed like some savage-looking equipment, which turned out to be the stirrups that would support her feet. He attached them to the sides of the table, muttering as he did so. The women realized that his nurse usually did all this. They remembered the woman slightly and had dismissed her; she was heavy, broad in the beam, and Brillo-haired.

He didn't speak while he washed his hands, elaborately, and then put on surgical gown, gloves and a mask. This change, the gloves, gown and mask, pulled Angela from her fog and into reality. Doc noticed her sudden presence in the moment. She had begun to tremble.

"It's not too late to change your mind," he said.

She suppressed the tremors, clamping her teeth.

"Move down," he said "and put your feet in these."

She lay spread open before him. Leatrice had begun breathing hard. "Are you up to this?" Doc asked her.

She nodded.

He motioned for Leatrice to wash and put on the gloves from the box at the side of the sink. He injected an anesthetic, waited, and palpated her lower abdomen. They were all silent, intent. He had forgotten to warm the speculum and cursed himself when she jumped slightly. "Sorry."

Angela began to cry. Doc, mistaking her tears for grief at her trouble, leaned over and laid a comforting hand on her shoulder, which she shook off with an expletive. "Get down to business," Leatrice said. Doc sighed and took his place.

He went on deliberately through the procedure, Leatrice steadily handing him equipment and following his instructions. They heard a pounding at his front door. "Someone's out there," he said, "and I don't want to leave this. Could you go and see what the problem is?"

"Are you nuts? We're not supposed to be here."

"Whoever it is knows I'm here. When I don't answer the door, he'll go around back and see the light. I don't want to stop this now—it'll be a few more minutes and I can pause. Can't you go and see what he wants? We can tell whoever it is..."

"We were here first!"

"I know that. If you don't go, I'll have to stop this and go myself."

With a withering look, Leatrice left the room. There was a voice, then, a man's, then their voices insistent. Leatrice came back into the room. "It's Klimek out there. He says his wife is having trouble breathing. He wants you to drive up there with him."

"Tell him to wait for just a few minutes."

"He says it's urgent. I told him we were here first and you were busy."

"Have him come in and wait in the parlor. Tell him I'll come as soon as I can. You opened the door for him when he came in, so please change your gloves again."

"I don't—"

"Do it," Doc said.

"He'll recognize me, I'm sure."

"That can't be helped and he has other things on his mind."

She left the room, returned, changed gloves.

Doc forced himself to slow down, working methodically, finishing. "Let her rest, here. I'll be back and finish up here. Take a deep breath, Angela—I'm going to take the speculum out and get you out of the stirrups. You can get up and then move up on the table and lie back and rest 'til I get back. I'm sorry to inconvenience you. Later, I want to drive you home." He took off his gloves and mask and went to where John Klimek was walking back and forth. "Go sit in my car," he said. "It's out there in front. I'll go get the keys and be right with you."

They drove up the dark hill, Doc's fog lights on. When the fall had first happened and Doc had found himself alone as the medical presence in Gold Flume, he had gone to his basement, unearthed and dusted off his old medical bag, cracked with age and dryness. He had oiled and refitted it with the basic needs of his visits. He had become what he remembered in early childhood doctors were. The picture and the living out of the picture gave him a quiet pleasure.

Along the way, here and there, kerosene lamps, not nearly as bright as the electric lighting, were burning for bedtimes. In the Klimek house and the Isaacs house next to it, the lamps were turned higher. Jay had been alerted and was waiting at the Klimeks' door.

"AnneMarie's up there, with her," he said.

"Any change?"

"No."

"Sorry about the wait—another patient."

Doc went up, hearing the gasping sound as he mounted the stairs. Now and then, there was a gurgling cough.

AnneMarie came to the bedroom door. "Oh, thank God!"

"Do you know how long she's been this way?"

"John said that he came over to us as soon as it started."

Tess Klimek was pulling as hard as she could. As he began to reach for his stethoscope, the sound stopped abruptly. In that moment, she was dead. He listened and heard the final gurgling of fluid in both lungs.

CPR would do no good; a jump-start to the heart would do no good. Before the fall, the call, an hour ago, would have brought the chopper, a tracheotomy, and a trip of thirty minutes to Denver and a trauma center, the stop-gap measures just enough, perhaps, to get her to surgery. He thought that this anguish and helplessness was also the old time doctor's reality. John Klimek had understood what the silence meant and he murmured, "She's been having trouble for quite some time, saying it was flu and that all she needed was rest."

Heart failure, Doc thought, and maybe, had he seen her before, he might have helped, and maybe... and maybe, but probably not. "John, I'm sorry."

"I sat in that car and waited and waited," John said.

"I know," Doc shook his head. "I have a patient down there, now. I have to go. I need to tell you that even if I had gotten up here right way, the outcome would have been the same."

People say things *in extremis,* Doc knew well enough, in fear, in anger, in loss. For a moment he thought Klimek would say something, curse him. The moment passed.

"I'll go get Pastor Fearing," Jay said. "We can take her up to the church. Is that all right?"

John nodded. "John," Doc said. "I have to get back to my patient. I'm very, very sorry." He left, driving back down the hill. As he rode in the true dark, his headlights the only ones in miles, he cursed aloud at the nineteenth century and its unforgiving laws.

On his way up and over to the church, Jay realized that the Drop wouldn't happen until Wednesday. The summer had gone to autumn now, and hot during the day. The emergency addition of a coffin wouldn't be possible for two weeks. The coffin would have to be made here. With what? Much of the wood from downed, dead trees and unused furniture had been burned in the days before the Drop had been established. Old Mr. Thiede and the Shively boy had been buried makeshift—Thiede coffinless, the boy in one of the cartons from the Drop. The only power tools they had were chainsaws. Who was there in town who could make—did the coffin have to be made of wood? They would have to let John decide what he wanted to do with the few resources they had.

To Jay's relief, El Fearing was up, reading by the light of a Rotterdam jar, when he answered Jay's knock and heard the news. He didn't bother to dress but put on a robe over his pajamas. He told Jay to come down to the social hall with him and they brought up a table and set it up in the sanctuary. Then, they got into Jay's car for the five-block ride.

Back at Klimeks' John and AnneMarie had put Tess' body into the back of the police car, wrapped carefully to slide in across the seats.

They had to bend her body a little to fit, and Jay was glad Klimek didn't see that.

The two cars went back up to the church. Tess Klimek was a small woman, looking even smaller on the table they had put in front of the altar.

"I want to stay," Klimek said.

"I'll stay with you," Fearing said.

Jay drove back home quietly, thinking that had he been the pastor, AnneMarie would have been as deeply involved in these matters as he was. Fearing hadn't wakened Cheryl.

FROM THE FANTOM
Cinquain: Only
The old should die.
The cell-borne heritage
Should not throw off its hooded cape
'til then.

CHAPTER 39

IN THE EIGHT MONTHS OF GOLD FLUME'S EXPERI-
ence of the fall, four of its citizens had died. Mrs. Frame and Mr. Thiede,
the Shively boy, and now, Mrs. Klimek. Chris Pantea and his family had
been the only mourners for Mrs. Frame. The Moritzes were too frail to
walk to the graveyard. Samantha Eakers was the only town citizen so far
who might have died a nineteenth century death, having hemorrhaged
after the birth of a child. Doc had used an even more ancient drug, an
ergot derivative, to save her. At other times, the bodies would have been
taken to the morgue at Aureole, cremated there or brought back for
burial at Gold Flume. People went to the graveyard or stayed home as
their relationships directed. Now, Tess Klimek, washed and dressed by
town women, was buried in an adapted wood and cardboard packing
crate from the Drop. Everyone came as they had for the Shively boy.

Mrs. Klimek had been a secretary at the grade school, so the church
was full of kids, vibrating with the world of grown-up ceremony and
drama. The face and body they had seen in school, friendly, engaged,
questioning, was now closed-eyed, disengaged. Billy Shively's body
hadn't been on display. His parents had not been part of their lives. Mr.
Klimek's shocked face stunned them. They had thought that grownups

were free from the anguish they felt at their own tragedies. Shouldn't maturity be a defense against the pain of loss?

Some of the children imagined that it was the town itself that bred these sorrows, and that as soon as they left the valley and went over Prospector Pass and Victory Pass and down-mountain to The World, they would need only to choose among the riches offered them.

John Klimek took the week off, missing a Drop. In his honor, the Wheeler Dealers took their work with balletic precision, unloading in minutes with a minimum of chat. The pilot, one of the regulars, wondered aloud what had happened. No one told him. Telling him would have spoiled the tribute which was theirs to give or withhold.

Mike and Angela didn't go to the funeral. Mike's power had dwindled severely since the blowout up at the cave. Angela was sore inside, still bleeding from Doc's procedure. She had gotten him off a few times, but it was mechanical, and she was angry, so he wasn't at ease when she was on him. He almost never kissed her.

The remaining few of his friends groused and complained. It was still summer. This was to be—to have been—the summer of their liberation, the end of high school, the beginning of trips to Aureole, of going to Denver, of summer barbecues, beer in kegs, whiskey from stores in Bluebank and Granite City where the dealers sold to them at double the price. Mike's mother kept making suggestions: "Why don't you guys go swimming? Why don't you go on a hike?" A hike? To where? Did she want them to be in those stupid shorts like those hiking idiots who had blundered into town? Why wasn't the boredom and stuck-ness he felt mirrored in every face and gesture? He was sick of being the only one feeling what everyone felt but wouldn't admit—that life was about power, and about using it. Hadn't he gotten the sheriff and Winograd off his case? Klimek's wife died. Big deal. He remembered her from the office when he was in grade school. She had talked to him once when he was waiting for his mom to come and take him home when he was sick. It was just a while chatting, but it had been pleasant, not just him sitting there like a rock in the river, inanimate. The next time he was in the office was for sassing a teacher and there was no chat, then.

And now, he had no tobacco, no weed, no hash. There was only the booze they had made from the dried fruit in the packets. People didn't want to give up their sugar rations for that anymore. There was one more stone in his shoe—Chris Pantea. Chris was—had been—the smartest of the kids he had been leading, and Chris had gone over into the dull, dumb, grown-up world, working his ass off on the dig and the Drop. Mike would like to see him destroyed, but he couldn't think of a way to do it.

He sat alone in the cave. It was cool there, but dampish, as though somewhere long-ago rains had collected and gone stale. The smell of the party must have dissipated but he thought he had the smell still, high in his sinuses, sweet as rot, clinging. He realized that the fall, which had been something monumental, unique, historic, had been harder on him than on any of them, those others, the classmates, their parents, the stupid mayor and the powerless sheriff and the dull doctor, and even his clueless mother and big-mouth father. All of them were occupied, like ants, running here and there, full of the purpose of the running itself. They'd broken through the fall and let the river out. Why hadn't it taken its chance and flooded the place? He and one or two others would have braved the mountains and gone away up over into the world—he realized he could still do it. Those damn hikers had done it.

For a long moment, sitting at the entrance, looking out over the scene, he fantasized the trip. He might still go—packets and water in a backpack, a space-blanket, some warm clothes—any of the four ways there were over these mountains and down into Utah, or over the fall and following the river to New Mexico. He might go east and down to Denver. With some money, which was an easy steal from his mother's two or three caches—she thought she was so clever—and once over the mountains, he could get plane, train, car, and out and away. The first part of the trip, the walk over these mountains, would be rugged, but how long could that take—a couple of days? What had the hikers said, three days, four? After that, it would be easy, and freedom...

He was almost ready to announce a plan to himself, to decide which exit he would take, to go to the maps his father had in his damn, sacrosanct office. Then, he would know how and where to go. He saw himself looking at those maps, choosing a route. Then, the whole thing collapsed. Who was he kidding? He traveled on roads, in cars. He had never been up-country in his life. This cave had been discovered by other kids who had led him to it and who were surprised when he declared it his and took it over.

He began to cry. It was lucky no one was with him. The others had gone down to a baseball game that had started pick-up and was now a regular Sunday afternoon event. He cried out of frustration and anger and sorrow, balked at every turn, surrounded by mountains, hemmed in.

After what seemed like a long time, he picked up the things he had brought and left the cave, going down what was now a well-defined trail that had been made by many kids. Since Doc and the sheriff had told him that the cave was old stuff, that there was even a name for it, much of the glamour had left it. He wasn't striking downhill, the way Chris Pantea had done; he was only walking where everyone else walked. He cursed loudly, just at that place where his curses came back to him in an echo that cut itself off as he walked further down, rounding the slope away from sight of the town.

He fisted away his tears, stopping for a while, and then thought about going back to his house. He was tired from the exertion of the walk and his weeping. He hadn't known that shedding tears was exhausting. His mother must be tired all the time. He crossed the bridge and went on to Main Street, hoping to find something to do.

After a while he noticed he was being followed by two kids whom he had seen sitting apart from the group watching the game. They were fourteen or fifteen, hands and feet suddenly too large for their bodies, and operating with wills of their own, dooming the boys, once neatly agile, to shamble and drop things. The shock of this loss of grace from what had been the body-wit of their boyhoods had left them open-mouthed like fish. Fish out of water, Mike thought. He started to dismiss them, but turned instead. "How's it going?"

"Like turds in a crapper."

He thought he knew them—younger brothers of kids he had hung out with. He had no wish to make the climb to the cave again, but he wanted them to know of his claim to it. "You guys been up at the cave over there?"

"Yeah, once."

"Big and dark," Mike said. 'Mercedes' Twat."

The two boys broke out in braying laughter, bent over with it.

"It's hard to climb in," Mike said, "but once you're there, you can stay all day." The boys laughed even harder.

They walked through town's Main Street, up past the town hall and then down a back street. "Unger, you know, the fire chief?"

"Yeah," Mike said. "What?"

"He's got a deer hung in his garage," the blond one said. "Maybe we could go over there and get some of it and go up to that cave and roast it."

"Good idea," Mike said, "but too late for now. He's home, or the Mrs. is. No harm in walking by, though, see about what we could do tomorrow."

They went north up the two streets where the land began to rise. The Unger house had been an old shack, then, a cabin, remodeled and added on to four or five times over the years so that it embodied the history of the town. It was a small house compared to the newer grand ones across the river—compared to Mike's house. They went up past it and back to where the garage was and around to the back, where they might come in unseen, still checking for neighbors' windows. None. They would have easy access and no trouble getting into the garage if it wasn't locked.

"We could tear the carcass so it looks like a bear done it," the dark one said—Mike remembered his name, Chaz. "That'd mean we'd have to mess up the garage some—you know how they do."

"That'd mean what?" Mike asked. He was annoyed that he hadn't thought up the idea first. He had to be on guard not to let his leadership be doubted. They all knew that a bear, unless it was interrupted, wouldn't be content with a pound or so of deer meat. "If it's gonna be a bear," Mike said, "we'll have to pull the carcass down off its hook like a bear would do."

"At night?"

"Won't matter. They're around during the day, too. I don't think night's any better."

They walked around again, casing the garage, staying on the road for as long as they could, then, when they saw it was safe, sprinting over to look in. There was a window on the east side, concealed because the hill rose sharply behind the house. The window was filthy, but they made out the form of the animal hanging from a hook on one of the beams.

"Okay," Mike said, "fade away."

Each of them took a different route and they met lower down on the road.

"How would a bear get in?"

"That garage has got to be locked."

"A bear would pull the lock off. We use a tire iron."

Mike said, "I'm thinking night is no good. You know what happens to dogs when a bear comes around—they go crazy. And the dogs would do the same with us—Unger's dogs would. I say we make it during the day, say during a Drop, when most people are down at the field—or out at the dig. Same bear scenario, only during the day."

The two considered. Mike had no wish to be up before dawn, to make the trip in the dark out of his house—his parents were light sleepers, and he'd have to be out to the road and down and across the river and up to meet with these two. He had been out at night and had the concert of barking dogs tuning up to follow him all the way down his street.

"It'll be two whole days to the Drop. Won't the deer be gone then?" Chaz asked.

"When did he shoot it?"

"Yesterday."

"It'll still be there," Mike said. The two considered, and then nodded. Several people walking by looked at them. "Start talking," Mike said. "You don't want to act suspicious."

The boys began a loud, artificial conversation. Mike wanted to hit them both. Fifteen years old and brainless. "You're not giving a fucking speech to the senate," he spat at them.

They stared blankly at him. How could they act natural when they didn't know what natural was?

"Never mind," he said. "Come up on Drop day, but not together. Go to the Drop first, just to let people see you there, then slip away and come up—not together. Go up to that stand of aspen and then back down to the back of the garage." It was humiliating to have to spell it all out to these calves, but he was stuck with them for the time being and they might be useful in ways he would find for them.

He knew that the venison they would be getting wasn't the aim of this big drill. Followers need a leader, but they also need purpose and adventure. Klimek knew this. He had organized that band of kids with work they thought was important and with just enough adventure and risk to keep up the interest. Two leaders, Mike thought. The sheriff didn't want to lead anybody, and neither did Dixon, the mayor, if you watched her. The pastor, maybe, but he was goodness-crazy. The rest were followers—or maybe there was really a third group and the sheriff and the mayor and old Miz Reimer were in that one. They neither led nor followed, but went their own ways and seemed to need none of the order that his group needed, order that made them follow no matter where it led.

FROM THE FANTOM
I'll never see a freeze-dried meal again
No matter how starvation threatens me,
Without reconstituting all the pain
Evoked by freeze-dried chicken fricassee.
Let mountains be removed, let ages pass,
The memory of beef pot pie will stay;
An aftertaste of plastic, tang of brass
To haunt me to my oh, so, dying day.
The lamb with rice, the block of soup du jour,
The mystery fish that ocean never knew
Repeats at midnight—I have found no cure
For next week's packet—pseudo Irish stew.
In hell I know the Devil's own entrée
Will be the packets, freeze-dried and flambé.

POSTED BY THE MAYOR: PEOPLE
SUPPLEMENTING THEIR DRINKING WATER WITH
RAINWATER SHOULD BOIL IT FIRST. USE THE PILLS
GIVEN IN THE DROP TO KILL BACTERIA IN THE
WATER IF YOU CAN'T BOIL IT.

CHAPTER 40

THE DROP DAY CAME. THE TEMPERATURE WAS IN THE upper eighties and the people waiting wore hats and carried water bottles. As in the winter, they didn't stay to socialize, but got their rations and melted away, some back across the river, some up to cooler houses on the north sides of the streets. The rains had been normal and a few people went across lower slopes into the draws after wild raspberries, strawberries, and the Oregon grape, ground cherries, choke cherries, orache, and wild spinach. The wild asparagus was over, gone to fern. The berry trips were serious, now. People brought back what they could to be canned or made into jelly. Women were asking if the Drop would bring them jar lids and bands. Some women had never made jelly before and needed to be taught how. Commercial pectin wasn't included in the Drop. The jelly had to be boiled down. Women were hoarding their canning jars. Mike heard them fussing over it all, his mother included. When his mother suggested he join her and Mrs. Unger at Chinaman's Gulch, he didn't need to pretend annoyance.

"Biddies!" and stalked off. She would appreciate him later. Venison, and his dad wouldn't ask any questions.

At Brad Unger's garage, the deer hung, aging. The fire chief and his son and his son's friends had skinned and gutted it, with instructions to keep their mouths shut on pain of losing their shares. The entrails had been cleaned for sausage casing, the blood for sausage. What was left was taken up-mountain and buried.

From three miles away, up Willow Canyon, a bear had nosed the updraft and scented the carcass. Two weeks before, she and her cub had sated themselves on an elk calf that had been foot-lassoed in a snarl of barbed wire years old that had once been part of a fence set up by a rancher. The man had died long ago; the ranch was no more. The mother knew that autumn was coming and the berries, though plentiful, were never enough. Caterpillar season was over.

The bear had hunted around the man camps often enough to know that for small forages, pets —chickens, dogs, and cats—the daytimes were good enough, but for meat such as was now on the wind, the night was best. But the need for meat, for building the fat she needed for the winter sleep-and-wake, had made her hunger pull at her caution. She moved slowly, pausing, coming closer.

She made her careful estimate of distance and the size of the portion she smelled, caloric output measured against the energy value of the meat. For her alone, the ratio would have been sufficient, but the cub's needs changed that judgment. The bear began a slow lope toward the source of the delicious aroma. She let the cub follow most of the way. Her pace was steady and she made the two miles easily, crossing the river twice to deter other bears or the occasional mountain lion. The bounding torrent of May and June was now in August's keeping, low and slow in its banks. This had been a big stag. She might tear it up and carry a large chunk away. The place was empty as she came on it. There was a roadway, heavy with the smells of the beings, the forked ones, whose skins shredded and who emitted an unpleasant smell. She avoided the road, staying to parts less redolent. The sun had come up over the mountain but things were still, windless, quiet. The beings were away somewhere. She passed roads and structures and went over the hill to the place the forked ones made to keep the meat. The place was busy with dozens of other smells. The opening way was held with a knot of the hard thing. She pulled the knot away where it was fastened, and it fell to the ground. The opening swung out. She went inside. The deer was pulled up, guts and blood gone, hide gone. She had smelled where parts of it lay away from the main meat, hanging. She might come back for that before too many others took it. She got up on her hind legs and pulled hard and the deer came down all at once and fell on to a place with many things, including the puzzle thing, one she had encountered before, an ice-thing that was ice under the teeth, but not cold and did not melt in the mouth, but stayed jagged and pain-giving, and yet, in the light, looked like ice. When was ice not ice? She had broken the ice-thing and her mouth and face and all the air filled with the fume-stench which was like water, but reek-fumed. When was water not water?

The stench was a concentration of the stench that was on their black roads, defecation of their moving rooms. The stink of it was destroying her ability to smell anything else. There was a chain. She had encountered them before. The thing was hooked to the deer and she pounded it to try to get it off the animal, because it was pulling at something. She slammed the chain down on the flat place where there were the things they had; hook things and pounding things. There was a sudden whoom of air-on-fire and she felt the whoom before the heat and all the other thoughts but to escape left her. Light-heat-airlessness all at once. She tore out of the place she had come in, fur singed, and all but blind and suffocated. She was glad for the black road for her feet, feeling the way to go. She all but ran into the three forked beings who were coming toward her. Stunned, they all stood for a moment, and the bear was able to take some breath and shake her head to clear her eyes. Both were difficult. She had run in the wrong direction, away from where her cub was. She growled in frustration and the ones stood rooted while every dog in the cluster of the beings began to bark and howl and there was noise, suddenly, from the fire that had outgrown the room. The bear turned and ran from the cluster of beings up into the mountain east, intending to circle the place and go down again to where the den was, a cluster of rocks that she had covered with branches.

She ran for a while, but breath was a pull and a push and not enough. She had to stop, often. She became dizzy. Five hundred yards higher than the town and three quarters of a mile to the south, she fell, panting, to the ground and died. By the third day, foxes and coyotes had eaten her and scattered her bones. A mountain lion got the cub.

CHAPTER 41

THE FIRE BLEW INTO THE STILL MORNING AND anyone could smell what had ignited it. Everyone had camp stove fuel stored from the Drop, and had fumy, empty glass containers or cans waiting to be refilled. The call-out was general and everyone came, sending one fire truck to draft from the river while the other put water to the blaze. For a while, the opinion was that the house would go, but the garage was far enough from it and from the houses of neighbors that water sent to the exposures kept the fire from spreading. They had that rare piece of good luck, a windless day.

Three boys had been seen by two neighbors and two of the boys had been identified. The two, Mike Ansel and Chaz Bergstrom, had been seen just before they sprinted away. They hadn't joined the work of cutting the tree near the garage or hauling away flammables from the nearby structures. The fire hadn't spread. The superheated air had gone upward into the day and the paper that might have been stored in the garage, the old magazines and odd wood items and old crates, had all been burned the past winter before the Drop had been regularized. Their absence had saved the house. Half the town was on day vigil in case a wind should come up and make mischief among the ashes. By evening, the fire was truly out and the three boys—Chaz had fingered Vince Holroyd—were in the town hall's holding cell on a charge of arson.

Jay had questioned all three, singly and together, and found out—Chaz was basically honest—that they had been after the deer hanging in Unger's garage. They hadn't been in the garage at all, he said. They had seen a bear tearing out through the broken out entry. They thought the bear had caused the fire. Two deputized men had heard this testimony and broadcast it. It made a wonderful tall story, a gag that would last for years after the boys had long left. A bear, their story went, had scented out the deer, a beautiful one by all reports, and had wandered into the garage. Having heard, and even seen, how humans cooked their food, she decided to try out the idea, had pulled a small grill inside the garage, positioned it under the deer, stolen some matches, poured the fuel stored in its glass container over the material in the grill, struck the match, lit the thing, and sat back to enjoy the prospect of a venison feast. Knowing nothing of grilling technique, the bear had miscalculated the amount of fuel needed to get the grill going. The fire got out of hand. The bear, realizing her mistake, left the scene, unmarked by anyone but the three boys.

This tale was repeated with hilarity and embroidery all over town, growing longer and more marvelously detailed. No one believed the boys' protestations for a moment, but they relished the story the three of them had concocted. Even the Ansel kid, a bad kid, a kid who was far more likely to bluster about the unfairness of Unger having fresh meat, was sticking to the ridiculous bear story. Evidence of the "bear's" destructive ways had been burned in the convenient fire. Now they were all three eating food cooked by the sheriff's crazy wife.

Mike's father had been to the jail twice to talk to the sheriff. After all, there was no proof that the three had started the fire; why not bail them out? He would take responsibility for Mike and he was sure the other fathers would also for their sons. Jay had learned from the other two—Mike was silent—that they had been after the deer, and while Chaz admitted that the idea was his, both boys had declared that Mike was the leader. Jay and the town council declared the two younger boys free on recognizance of their parents. Mike was to stay where he was.

Half the battle between Roman Ansel and Sheriff Isaacs was heard all over the town hall. The one-sided voice was Ansel's, howling at the sheriff. Roman was a member of the council, after all. Read the by-laws, Jay told him. His service gave him no extra privilege. The vote had been to keep Mike for further consideration. Roman had been forced to recuse himself as being an interested party. Jay's words were heard in broken parts because he spoke in a low voice, giving way on no point, simply repeating what had been decided. The Ansel boy was a perpetrator in a break-in, vandalism, and theft in a townhouse in Callan, a suspect in participation in the death of William Shively, a suspect in the arson and destruction of Brad Unger's garage. The boys had been seen at the back of the garage with no reason for their being there. Enough. Ansel threatened a lawsuit. He told Mike the council's decision. They raged together. Mike had been certain that his father would overcome all the objections. The day passed. Another.

And no Angela. Mike had thought she would visit. No one did, except his parents. His mother brought books, puzzles, and even the porno magazines he had been hiding under his mattress, which she handed over to him wordlessly. He couldn't even jack off except late at night because people were often moving through his room where the cage was, and he couldn't tell when someone would wander through. In prison, he thought, there was some kind of dignity; here there was just a kid in a cage. The idleness ate into him like an ulcer and where the membrane of his patience was frayed, hate welled into the wound.

Two councilmen walked through the room, talking. When he had been taken here, people had looked at him as they walked past. Now, they didn't give him a glance and he felt invisible. Sometimes, he made noises to get their attention, but he found that the looks he got were disinterestedly annoyed, as people would be at a chair squeaking. He relapsed into silence, festering.

When he thought of Klimek, Mike thought about Chris Pantea, the Good Boy of the Drop, the dig, and the town. Klimek had enlisted Chris by using his charisma, his authority as a teacher, his enthusiasm that captured all those brainless kids to work like slaves for some old people who ought to be dead, anyway. Klimek had brought Chris, his pet pony, forward, had given him a kind of power that Mike knew he, himself, could never achieve. It wasn't fair—and where was Angela?

Everyone was talking about the schedule. The chopper pilot had delivered it from the state planning commission. The plan was for digging and drilling from the south side of the fall starting in October and expected to last until December, or maybe January. Keeping the boy for all that time, feeding him, supplying him with heat and food and sanitation, was too big a job. Mike heard all these things in voices rising and falling as he lay on his cot, ear to a water glass pressed hard against the wall of the sheriff's office. Isaacs had wanted Mike's parents to bring the food and to add to the supply of fuel, but Ansel had refused absolutely and made daily visits to the town hall to shout and threaten for his boy's release. His "Boys Will Be Boys" justification had been burned off in the heat of the arson charge. Not one of Mike's statements was believed, even by his parents. When he did visit, Roman raged at the boy in the cage. How could anyone raised as he had been, be so stupid? Didn't he know that the town leaders would have been watching him since the break-in? Hadn't he been warned off bad behavior since his activities in the cave? Of course he had nothing to do with the death of the Shively boy, but there had been homemade rot-gut whiskey found in that cave, and everyone knew he had been getting kids to raid the medicine cabinets for their folks' rubbing alcohol and shaving cream, articles not part of the Drop. Everyone knew they had built a still up in the cave.

"I will get you out of here," Ansel declared, "and then your ass will belong to me."

Mike figured he should be in the lockup for two weeks and then, with his father's promises, he would be free until the town was free and then gone. He would take off like that bear nobody believed in.

AnneMarie had adapted Tess Klimek's baking technique and had come to the town hall with muffins for Mike, lunch and supper, and a little candle in a coffee-can affair for keeping the dinner warm. She went down the stairs to the sheriff's office and the cell carefully, carrying the meals she had fixed in what had been their bathroom wastebasket, relined with a clean dishtowel. When she reached the bottom, she noticed that she wasn't panting. Work on the dig had strengthened her. She smiled. Jay came out of his office and took the basket, giving it a look. "Multi-use," she said, sanctimoniously, "ecological."

"Go home," he said. "You are too saintly to be safe in our streets."

"Walk or fly?"

"One more word and I'll launch you. What's in the basket?"

"Tuna salad sandwiches and chicken casserole, and of course, muffins."

"Chow has gotten a big boost around here since we have our homegrown crime-wave visiting us."

She kissed him and left.

She walked up town to the church, having promised to meet Della Pantea and Siri Unger to clean up the downstairs rooms there where the children met. After that, she planned to take a shift at the dig. Her energy was still low, but she had been surprised that she could do these things with what energy she had. She was enjoying cooking again. She had done it on Mike's previous, shorter stays, commanding all the creativity she could muster. Now she wondered why she was moved to do it so carefully and seriously, when the reason struck her and she stood outside the church door for a moment, thinking about it. Young people, even the Ansel boy, reminded her of her own sons and of her own younger self, cooking for them, working her ingenuity all those years ago, pulling and trimming to make the money she had stretch, to bring them variety and pleasure. Now and then, there were words of surprise and delight at their table. How proud she had been in those days, now seen in sunlight, all the normal cuts and abrasions smoothed away. Here she was again, needed, competent, filling her place and expanding in it, taken up. What would she serve her pseudo-son and real husband tomorrow?

Back in the sheriff's office, Jay was separating the meals, noting the care AnneMarie had taken to give each meal some variety—a small cup of juice from their carefully portioned stock of pre-fall food, a little packet of salt, jelly for the muffins, also from their supply, the candle in the coffee-can.

Mike lay on the bunk, playing head-music, his fingers tapping the unheard beat. "Brunch," Jay said.

Mike turned his head to look at the sheriff holding the tray like a wuss. He groaned and sat up. "What slop is the old bat givin' me today?"

Jay was through the cell before he knew it, tray clattering on the floor before Mike could register it. Jay's stinging slap was followed by another and another. Mike's head was flung back, hitting itself against the back wall with a sound that was taken into the sound of his teeth slamming together and a breath pulled in in shock and out in pain.

Again, again. It seemed that the blows came quicker and harder. Mike realized that the sheriff was out of control and that he might die here in blood and broken bones.

Jay had seen not red, but white, and he barely felt the contact of the blows he made, slaps, then punches. There was a roar in his head and he realized he was grunting, trying to speak between the blows.

Suddenly the rage was gone and Jay was at the little sink down the hall from the cell, still barely conscious of his having moved. Everything was slowing, the way it does after an earthquake, coming into focus, a floor solidified beneath the broken crockery and shattered glass.

He looked into the mirror over the sink and saw that his face was grim, but the same, no wolf-eyes or wolf-teeth. Mike Ansel was a prisoner in his care. How would he explain the bruised face, the blood? Jay fought a desire to rush back to the cell, and plead with Mike to keep the beating a secret. He felt sick with self-pity. How much insult did he have to endure from the overgrown creep? He dried his face on the dubious towel that hung on a nail there and went back to his office. Mike was in the position Jay had left him. His face was smeared with blood, his nose lost in blood.

"Come on out and clean up," he said.

The boy stirred. "What will you do to me?"

"Nothing. Don't insult my wife again."

They stood staring at one another. "Son of a bitch," Mike said.

"Yes," Jay said, "I'm afraid so. Keep it in mind."

"You're supposed to be the law."

"You're supposed to be smart enough not to test it too often."

As Jay ate a packet dinner, he tried to hide the bruises on his knuckles, and was relieved AnneMarie didn't seem to notice them. "How was your church work?" He kept his voice level, not wanting to sound too eager.

"Okay. We dusted and arranged things. The floors need more than waxing. There's bare wood in too many places, plywood someone put down in the twenties, waiting for the money to lay something better. There was a fight at the dig."

"Who and who?"

"Kids."

"Anything I should know about?"

"Not this time. Did the Ansel kid say anything about the meals I brought over?"

"Uh—I ate the muffins."

"Both of them?"

"Both."

"You'll just have to get those arrests up and jail a few more people."

"I've been thinking. Doc doesn't have family here. Could we have him over for Thanksgiving this year?"

"Great idea. I'll make my pioneer apple pie, the kind that uses crackers instead of apples. Do we have enough wood to run the oven?"

"There are trips for wood going up every week until the snow flies. By the time this is over, we'll have cut our fire danger in half with all the dead stuff cleared out up there."

He ventured out carefully on the thin ice part of their relationship. "How are your talks going with Fearing?"

"Okay. He's not a therapist, I mean, a doctor, but he does some things doctors don't do—we don't talk about anything medical, brain chemistry, or a whole lot about my past—some, but not much. We talk about—well, about God."

"God?"

"The particle of God that's my will toward health—I know it sounds sappy to you, but that's what we talk about—not talk about, mostly. He's a good listener."

"If he's so smart, how come he married Cheryl?"

"They met in the spring, the season of the Rising Sap."

"How do you know that?"

"Cheryl told me a long time ago, back when they first came, and she didn't know I wasn't anyone special." Jay saw the edges of AnneMarie's lips twitch in a half-smile.

"Is she really as snobbish as all that?" he said.

"Where have you been? She was aiming for much bigger than she got. He was ambitious, too, for a while, but as they say, mistakes were made."

"What were they?"

"His family was very wealthy. Did you know he went to Princeton? He was supposed to be launched. Just after they married, Cheryl got pregnant. El's father was indicted for fraud, tax evasion, insider trading, and slurping his soup. He went off a ferry one night and the body was never found."

"And he told you all this?"

"Heavens, no! Tess Klimek told me."

"Tess Klimek? How did she find out?"

"Didn't anyone tell you that privacy died when the Global Village was born? It's all out there."

"About you? About me?"

"Who you played doctor with forty years ago. Anyway, with no money and the suicide stigma, El's ambition was pretty much dashed. He's done well, here, really, or did until the mountain fell. I don't think Gold Flume will come back from this so soon. What wealthy big shots would want to spend time in a place where they could end up isolated with a bunch of yokels for a year?"

"They tell me it's unlikely for another fall to happen."

"But the idea is there, and that's all people need."

The ice held. He ventured toward the middle. "You seem so much better. Do you know how that happened?"

"To make me better or to make me miserable?"

"Both."

She took a long breath. "Common enough, but it feels like I'm the only one suffering. Parents are dead, people I loved are dead, and the kids grown and gone and even if they weren't gone, their years of need and love are gone, all changed. I tried teaching Sunday school—do you remember?"

"Vaguely, yes, I think I do... some years ago."

"I lasted six months, if you remember. The kids were completely self-sufficient, wrapped up in their own world of iPods and game devices. I was an intrusion in the enclosure they were sharing. When I asked them to turn off their devices, they stared back at me. I wanted to leave after one month, but I hung on for five more, hoping I could get past their indifference. I never felt old until then, old and useless. A cloud came down. Now, I'm necessary, that first, and second, I got off the drugs. If they blunted my pain, they also blunted any pleasure I had and the side-effects were awful."

"Could I have done anything?"

"I don't think so—the problem is a spiritual one; what's the worth of a person? We talk about the value of a human life, any human life, but we don't believe it for a minute." She got up and went to the counter. She had forgotten the napkins, cloth now; the Drop didn't deliver paper napkins.

Jay wanted to tell her about his beating Mike. If Mike told anyone, she would have a hard time with what he had done. When the Ansels visited they would see the shiner and the signature injuries on his right lip and jaw. He couldn't. The loss of self-control was too shaming. He took the napkin and wiped his mouth. "Could you have taken up a hobby?"

"Makework, or so it seemed to me, then. Maybe after we get dug out I will. Now, my job is feeding our criminal-in-training down at the town hall."

"AnneMarie—" The word was suddenly there. "I hit him. I beat him up."

She was silent for a minute and then sighed. "Something he said about me."

"Well—"

"Jay, not much else would make you lose your temper. It's a miracle you kept it so long."

"He was undefended, in my care—"

"He's more than just a brainless adolescent. He's one of those people who has to live on the edge, to harm people so he can feel something."

"The fall has been good for you?"

"I suppose so. There's a good feeling about sharing a pain everyone feels. Too bad our little crime wave can't get his thrills that way."

"You're taking what I said very lightly."

"If you want me to scream and faint, forget it. Every day the kid is here in town is a day he's not at liberty in the wide world."

"The fall is good for that, at least," Jay said. He was surprised at AnneMarie's equanimity with what he had done. "The fall's long-term effects won't be so good. We'll all have been a year or more on welfare. It won't be all that easy getting off."

"You missed a spot on your—here—let me get it."

"So we're all on drugs?"

She winked. Jay felt like kissing her.

FROM THE FANTOM
M'thought that I would never see
Teenagers smiling down at me
With yes, ma'am, no ma'am on their lips
While they collect the next Drop slips.
It's silver lining in our cloud
I almost fear to say aloud.

POSTED BY THE MAYOR: WOODCUTTING WILL
BE DONE THIS WEEK ON PROSPECTOR MOUNTAIN.
ONLY DEAD WOOD IS TO BE TAKEN. SIGN-UP
SHEET IS BELOW. FUEL FOR CHAINSAWS WILL
BE PROVIDED.

CHAPTER 42

CHRIS PANTEA HAD BECOME A LIEUTENANT TO MR. Klimek. At first, it was a source of pride to him, people noticing him, smiling at him, greeting him on the street. Mayor Dixon praised him in a meeting and he had come to represent the son and brother people wanted. As time passed, he felt increasingly uncomfortable. When he saw himself being pointed out as an example, he felt stripped and stifled, his throat closing. His own parents looked on in wonder at his status.

Teenagers had taken over the hard work of the Drop, providing steady, dependable deliveries all over town, but they sometimes gathered after the deliveries to run the streets on skateboards, barely missing women with wash baskets or men with wagons. Chris seldom went with them, having more to do than they did, handling the more difficult deliveries.

On one of these, he was up at the parsonage. His work with the Moritzes was on the other end of town, but Mr. Klimek had asked him to make this special delivery. In July, Klimek had gone to Mayor Dixon and asked if they might not request the Drop to include something extra to be given as inducement and reward for the work the kids did. In October, twelve cans of Coca-Cola were included in the Drop. The pilot told Edwina that someone at the warehouse had taken it on himself to provide the Cokes. The mayor assigned one each to two kids who had served double shifts at the dig and others to those who did the biggest deliveries. One can was to be awarded to Chris. The awards were to be made at the town hall after the weekly announcements. Klimek had thought the package might be safer stored up at the parsonage.

The October day was pure Colorado autumn—aspen and wild maple blazing with color, the sun warm, the air fragrant with just a hint of breeze soft on the face. Chris stood at the parsonage door, and receiving no answer to his knock, went around to the back. There she sat, sunning herself in two chairs she had brought out of the kitchen. Seeing Chris, she turned her full face to him, sighing languidly. He saw it as pose, but that didn't matter. Her face was sullen, but it caught him: her body—she was in tight pants and a low-cut top—full hipped, full busted. In his mind, his hands cupped those breasts.

"Put it in the kitchen," she said, "and bring out a chair. Then you can get some of this—you drink coffee? — whatever this is."

He got the chair and another cup and joined her at the side of the house in the litter of fallen aspen leaves that had blown and settled there. He knew that the sweet air and soft breeze were setting everyone up for the sucker-punch of dry freeze and gossamer snow. Two snows had already fallen and been called away, and this one coming would stay lower and lower on the arms and shoulders of the mountains around the town.

He wasn't comfortable with Cheryl Fearing. She was assertive, and very conscious of her effect, and he had no real reason to be sitting there in the middle of the afternoon alone with her.

"Listen," she said, stretching in the chair and looking at him with amusement. "I know how tough it is to be a star, a stand-out. You start to act. You weren't acting before, but all of a sudden, you have a part to play that someone else has scripted for you. For me, it's Pastor's Wife; for you it's Head Boy, Golden Boy, and you have to figure out what part is real and what's pimping someone else's ideas."

He looked at her, amazed. No one had ever spoken to him that way, person to person, about what he was feeling. Everyone seemed content with roles—his and theirs—more than content, delighted. He knew that if he expressed the discontent he sometimes felt, people, his parents included, would be disappointed. There were parts of his role where he felt he belonged, and that was the source of his confusion.

"But isn't it all or nothing? I mean, how do you do that?"

"I was never very good at it, myself," she said, and studied a ragged fingernail. "I know it takes time, and I'm not real patient. I know marriage makes it harder. The people you marry have these expectations, too."

"But I mean, don't we want people to be uh... the same all the time, like Pastor is Pastor, and Dad is Dad, like that?"

"That's what we want other people to be, but we know we can't be that, ourselves."

Her talk made him feel that he was being let in on a secret, a club closed to the young. Her reputation in town was as a vain and shallow woman. He had heard that gossip for as long as he could remember, certainly as someone you'd never go to for guidance. He also knew that if he weren't male and good-looking, she would have motioned with her head for him to leave the box in the kitchen and sent him off with a wave, or maybe a bouillon packet for his trouble. Chris was tall and had blond hair that curled all over his head. Teachers, male and female, looked at him longer than they did at other students. Only the prettiest girls got so long a look. He hadn't known if they graded him higher than other students, but he suspected they did. The unearned quality of the attention paid him had always caused a vague unease.

She said, "Do you know what's in that box you brought?"

"Nope. I guessed it was something for the church."

"Whatever it is, I guess we'll soon know," and she got up. "It's getting cool. I'm going in." Her tone was like an invitation, flirting. He didn't know what to do, so he got up, carried the three chairs back into the kitchen and left her. She was smiling.

The presentation of the Coca-Cola, hyped by Klimek and the mayor, was an anti-climax. Chris took his reward from Mayor Dixon amid the polite applause. The mayor made a speech. She told everyone that Christmas would be celebrated without any release for them. There was too much going on Outside. Winter was coming everywhere and those whose homes had been destroyed were living in makeshift arrangements and needing the same kind of relief that Gold Flume was getting, without Gold Flume's possibilities. People were healthy in Gold Flume, protected from the worst of life. Outside, where looters had to be shot and hordes of con men had taken food and money for repairs that hadn't been made. As a palliative to the town's need, the state was allowing hunting out of season and rescinding its orders for licensing. At that announcement everyone erupted in laughter. The laugh started as a cackle of scorn. Only minutes later did it stop and allow order to be restored. The five Coca-Cola honorees took the cans and the people dispersed.

John Klimek approached Chris, who was standing in a daydream state in front of the town hall. "It's not the Nobel Prize," he said, "but it's what someone at the warehouse did on his own."

"I wish the reward had been batteries—I would love to use my tablet and cell phone," Chris said. He was aware of the complaining note in his voice.

"To talk to whom? Besides, there'd be too much envy stirred up."

"Christmas will be terrible this year, but did they think we hadn't been hunting here all the time? Were we expecting to see a bunch of the State Fish and Game guys, helicoptered in here with AK-47s to round up the hunters and chopper them out to jail?"

Chris knew that envy might be building somewhere against him. Since his talk with Mrs. Fearing, he had taken his singling out more seriously. He was a great help in town. He knew it—the work pleased him. He liked helping; he liked being recognized with smiles. He liked the fading of the line between generations. He liked being a semi-son to the Moritzes and the other people on the ridge, but Mrs. Fearing had been right about there being a downside to all of it, and the award had brought that home to him. Luckily, there had been the four other kids standing up with him, all younger, glowing with pride, surprised, delighted.

The next day he was up at the Moritzes, who hadn't been at the meeting or heard of the awards, for which he was grateful. While they would have cheered him, had they been there, he wanted no shadow of that to touch them, that he had done things for them for awards or town's regard.

Later that day, he went down to Doc's. The weather had closed in, a light drizzle freezing as it fell, and the way was slippery, the cold not bracing but clinging like a wet garment. Doc was at his door packing pine needles into one of the boxes his medical supplies came in. It was his perk. The packed pine needles burned well in the boxes; loose ones went up too quickly and made a lot of sparks. He was working with a big bag of them, gathered a week before when they were dry.

"Doc—"

Doc looked up, surprised. He hadn't seen Chris coming. "Oh—what's up?"

"I... uh..."

"What?"

"It's about Mr. Moritz, you know, the guy up on the ridge, in those houses up there? I don't like the way he looks."

"Like how?"

"Kind of—uh—yellow."

"And you told him so?"

"Not exactly."

"You deliver food up there, don't you?"

"Yeah, and fuel, and I do things they need. And that's another thing; he always helped. She puts out stuff for me to eat, and he comes out—used to come out and spell me shoveling snow or carrying water or taking in the laundry—Mrs. Sinclair does their laundry now, and I think they pay her with packets. They say they don't eat much. He didn't come out with me my last two visits and this time he didn't get up when I came in. He always does that, and he looks yellow."

Doc took his four boxes, which were the size of bricks, and tied up the bag of pine needles. "Come on in," he said.

They went into the cold house. "The thing is," Doc said, taking a box and putting it under the waiting wood. He was breathing heavily in the cold. He lit a pine cone to start the fire. "I can't just go up there and walk in and start treating him. If he's conscious and in his right mind, I have to be called by him."

"How can I work it? I mean, the guy needs help."

"Have you talked to Mrs. Moritz?"

"I don't think she notices it. She's a little blind and a little deaf and she sees him every day, so I guess she stopped looking."

"Does your dad still go out to the dig site every day?"

"Most days. He says it's interesting geologically. You don't get so many chances to see what's underneath a half-mountain that slides off."

"Are you interested in geology?"

Chris watched the cardboard begin to take fire. He shrugged. "Not really. My father wants me to go to a technical school, CSM maybe, where he went, or even Stanford, if I could get in, and major in it."

"Follow in his footsteps?"

"That was okay with me before, but now—"

"What's changed?"

"I've been up there at the Moritzes and the Dentons and working with Mr. Klimek, organizing deliveries and matching kids to the people they were going to deliver to. I like doing it. With the babies and old people, some of the kids don't like the smell—I don't mind it—I mean, it's just part of your body, and I get past that—I want to work with people, even sick, old people—"

"Which is why you've come down to see me."

"What should I do?"

"Go back up to the Moritzes and talk to him. Get him to ask to see me. Is there anyone you can send down here?"

"I'll get someone to go up with me."

"I'll be waiting to hear."

Chris left Doc's office with the idea of going over to the Shivelys and getting the Shively kid to come up with him. Billy's brother had attached himself to Chris after Billy's death. Chris had asked him to help with loading deliveries going up to the ridge, the youngest kid doing it, and proud. Chris' praise had helped to blunt the effect of the rumors that painted Billy as a dope addict and his death, a murder.

Chris walked the block along the river, now showing lace edgings of ice at both banks, and then up to Main Street, thinking to go up to Mr. Klimek's house where the Wheeler Dealers went to hang out and pick up assignments. Sam Shively might be there, or maybe he was still at home. He paused, trying to decide, the directions being opposite to each other. He saw Mike Ansel coming toward him. How had Mike gotten himself out of the lockup? Chris took a breath to speak but he never got the word on that breath because Mike moved to him, almost at a run, and smashed a fist into his face.

The move was so sudden and the effect so blindingly painful that Chris wasn't thinking at all. There was a loss of balance, another blow, and another, and he was on the ground. Time passed. He didn't measure it, but went through the stages of shock, pain, weakness, and nausea, eyes blood-blinded.

People had come. He heard voices, a good many voices. He had forgotten what had happened, how he had come to be lying on the ground. Then, someone asked him how he felt. He didn't know. Someone said, "I seen it all." Then dark.

CHAPTER 43

He was back at Doc's. Hadn't he just left Doc's? Wasn't he supposed to do something, be somewhere? It was important, but what was it? Words wrangled their way out of his mouth, but they made no sense. Dark again.

Then, he was home. Doc was there. It was night. His mom was crying. His dad was furious. Was it something he had done? He told them he was sorry and this time, the words came out muffled, slurred but understandable.

Doc said, "I think we can get by without having to chopper him out. His airway's okay and I'll watch him for swelling. There'll be some dentistry needed and some rhinoplasty. The collarbone is broken in place—we'll have to stabilize his arm and shoulder while it heals. He's going to have quite a bit of pain—I'll leave you with medication for that when I go, but now, I'll just sit here for a while."

There wasn't much of anything for Chris to feel in the first few days. Sometimes there was daylight, sometimes there wasn't. He slept and woke and ate soup. His dad helped him to the toilet, and he was dizzy and couldn't seem to balance himself. On one of these trips, he suddenly remembered that Mike had come at him when he was on his way to the Moritzes' and had hit him. He stopped.

"Dad! I'm supposed to go up and see the Moritzes. Mr. Moritz isn't well and I went—I was supposed to—"

"Let it go," Ron said. "There was nothing you could have done. Doc was here with you for a day and the next day he sent somebody up there. Moritz was too far gone. He died the day after that, and there was a funeral. Mrs. is staying with someone until she can go to relatives."

"I was supposed to—"

"It's a hard lesson, the one that people die, people we value."

"I thought if I got up there in time—"

"He was a very old man. I think that if we'd gotten him choppered out and to a hospital, they would only have prolonged his dying, not given him any kind of a chance."

"Where's Mike?"

Ron Pantea growled and helped Chris down to the toilet seat and left, waiting for a call when he was finished, but Chris could hear him cursing outside the door. Ron was a quiet man, ordinarily, not given to great expressions of joy or rage, even-tempered, sometimes more than Chris or his mother wished him to be, but there he was, growling. "The bastard. I blame the sheriff, too. Why was the kid out? The bastard should have been in jail." The mutter went on, but the mutterings didn't answer Chris' questions and when he was finished and called his father to help him up and back to bed, "Where's Mike?" he asked again.

"He's gone. There's still some flow in the river. We think he got some money from his family and got a kayak and went in the river through the notch and out. He might even have gone up Prospector and over the pass. Of course, the folks aren't talking. I blame them, too. They knew their kid was a loose cannon. Why didn't they have him under control? He could have killed you."

"Does Doc say I'll be okay?"

"Yes. Do you know why he attacked you? People who saw what happened say he went at you with no warning."

"I don't remember exactly what happened, but things had been bad with us for a long time."

"You were with him when he broke into that condo—"

"That was back last year, I—uh—things—"

"That's not my point. You were friends. What broke that up? Not that I'm sorry. The kid's been bad news for years."

"He envied me."

"Explain that; I don't get it."

"In his eyes, I had it coming."

"Give me that again, slowly."

"He saw me as a big name around here, for my age—our age. Mr. Klimek tells everyone how great I am. Then, the stuff that was going on up at the cave came out and the Shively kid died. Kids told me that. No one wanted that kid up there, anyway—he was too young. He— "

"So it wasn't about the cave and the boy—that you told us."

"I don't think he knew that I ratted about the cave."

"What was it, then?"

"That was the thing—everyone was telling him about how great I was, but I was up there, too. I got there when the party was winding down. Kids were screaming and people were vomiting. I was no better than anyone else—I got out earlier, that's all. I knew they made that stuff they drank, what they distilled from pine needles and sap."

"Good, God—turpentine. It's a wonder they're not all dead."

"Some of them were sick—their folks didn't know what it was—flu, they thought. I don't think anyone drank that much because the stuff was so awful. I got in late and left early and all of a sudden I'm Mr. Big Shit."

"You didn't tell anyone until the night of Harbison's elk feast—"

"I wish people would stop putting me up as a model."

"They won't stop. The best thing to do is to thank the people and let it go."

A wave of nausea rose in Chris.

"Doc left something for you—you look a little green."

"You'd better get the bowl...."

CHAPTER 44

JAY HAD GONE UP TO THE ANSELS' THE EVENING OF the attack on Chris. Doc had not been sure, then, if Chris' injuries were life threatening or permanent. Janeen Ansel had been telling people that Mike had been unfairly picked on by Chris and by people in town. When Jay arrived in the police car, dressed officially, her first emotion wasn't anxiety but anger. She knew that Mike bullied younger kids, but also that he was a natural leader, like Roman, who bullied people. It was what strong men did. Roman Ansel might rule the roost, but he wasn't stupid, a drunk or a miser. They lived well or had lived well before the fall.

The sheriff told them that there was news from the agency organizing the town's relief. It would be months before the fall would be cleared and the highway open. Mike would be released but he was to be at home by dark every night and was to report to Sheriff Isaacs twice a week. He was to sign up every day for a full shift at the dig. The Ansels agreed. Mike had been released.

Ansel had come to the door at Jay's knock, Janeen behind him. "I need to talk to Mike," Jay said.

"Mike isn't here."

"Do you know where he is?"

"No."

"Do you know when he's expected home?"

"He's usually here for dinner," Janeen said. Roman moved his foot over her instep and pressed down.

"I'll wait," Jay said. "There's been a serious situation."

"Can you tell us what it is?" Roman had gone stiff and precise in his speech. His consonants could crack ice.

"You know how gossipy town is," Janeen said. Roman let that go. Encouraged, she said, "He doesn't go to the cave anymore."

"I can wait here, or in the car."

Ansel had weighed the choices and after a long minute, said, "Okay, come in."

Jay described what the three witnesses had told him. Although they weren't close to the attack, they had all been shocked, staring at the boys because of its suddenness and ferocity. Chris Pantea might die, and then Mike would be arrested for manslaughter. He would be choppered out and sent to an appropriate facility.

Janeen began to weep and Ansel growled at her, then leaned in on her foot. The wails came harder and louder. She was keening with loss. Mike had been a longed for child, the answer to years of trying and blame, and he was now tangled and helpless in this net of law.

When she quieted, Jay described Chris' condition. Ansel had listened with no change in his demeanor. Receiving no answers to his questions, Jay rose to leave, telling the Ansels that if Mike returned and they didn't bring him in, they would be liable to prosecution as accessories after the fact of assault with intent to do great bodily harm.

Mike didn't appear and the next day, Roman noticed things missing from the garage. He thought Mike must have gone home immediately after the attack, when neither of them was there. Some cash was missing from Janeen's cache. The house was large enough that even had they been home, Mike might have come and gone unheard and unseen.

Chris had spent two days at Doc's and then had been taken home on a Stokes litter from the firehouse. He was in great pain and had been doped much of the time. He saw double and had bouts of nausea.

The Ansels heard these things when they went out or, unwillingly, from Harbison at the Drop. There was no word from Mike, but they didn't expect any. Janeen cried several times a day, annoying Roman enough so that he slapped her.

Janeen still kept the house in the hyper-orderly way Roman liked, nothing out of place. When Roman was out one day, she opened the door and went into Mike's room. As orderly as the rest of the house was kept, mess and dirt had been Mike's Declaration of Independence. The room was musty and overlaid with the strong smell of male feet. There were clothes dropped from wearing and half-eaten food in and under the bed. She found nun-chucks and two shurikens, the purpose of which puzzled her. The looks of them were menacing.

These days, there was little chance of finding porno under the mattress. All the porno he had, she had sent to the lockup for him. More must be on Mike's computer, lying dead and useless along with all the other boxes, modems and ancillary gadgets that surrounded it in a struggle of wires. Janeen felt the tears again and moved through the room, attacking the things in an orderly sequence as Roman had instructed her in the early years of their marriage. There were those clothes on the floor and others wadded on the floor of his closet, summer things. Janeen picked them up to wash and felt a weight in the pocket of a pair of jeans. With a squeamish feeling, she went into the pocket and came up with a set of keys. They weren't house keys. They were keys to suitcases, she thought probably for ones they had in the upstairs closet. She had also seen, shoved under the bed, a metal box that had a lock. What was he doing with all those keys?

She paused. She would commit a small rebellion against Roman's directive. She left the room and went across the hall to the closet where the travel things were kept, camping equipment, suitcases, emergency things, and the camp stoves they were now using for heating. There were seven suitcases of various sizes. Janeen pulled at one of them, surprised at its weight. She had trouble with the heavy key ring but finally got the key that fit and opened the suitcase where it rested on the shelf. It was full of things she didn't recognize—clothing, electronic equipment, costume jewelry, and a pair of women's alligator cowboy boots, all thrown in haphazardly.

Two others were filled with the same random collection. Four were empty. She went back into Mike's room and sorted through the keys until she found the one that fit the lock box which she had retrieved from under Mike's bed. Inside was an envelope, empty. From its shape and distortion, she thought it must have contained money. And there was a watch. She picked it up. It was heavy, a Rolex. She smiled. These watches were imitated in many different countries. This was certainly a good knock-off. She looked at the watch. Roman had told her once about Rolexes. She stared at it. It had weight, heft. Where had he gotten such a thing? Where had all that jewelry come from? It was not of one kind, as if from someone's collection and taste, but a jumble, and clothes—and those boots—they couldn't have been from the condo— she hadn't believed he had masterminded that. The girl—that Angela, looked like the ringleader, the boys following her the way adolescent boys will follow, sniffing and huffing. The three had been caught. Hadn't everything been returned? Where had all this come from?

For a long second, breath in, breath out, she thought, "I'll ask him when he comes in...." but then came the stroke of knowing: he was gone. She said, "I may never see him again," and she wailed in the messy room, that den of his, smelling of leftover food and lust and feet.

Did Roman know where Mike had gone? He must. As usual, her husband must have acted on his own, an indication that he thought her too stupid and inept to be of any use, giving her work, and her wishes, no value.

Janeen had been very good at some things in college. Her physics professor had wanted her to major in physics, for which she had a natural gift and an open delight that he seldom saw. Her English professor had wanted her to major in that. Roman had promised her that she could go on after they married—why not? Women have good careers, nowadays, but he needed someone to keep his apartment in order, to cook and, later, to keep the household accounts, to entertain. Then, there was the big house, then, a bigger house, and by the time they had moved to Gold Flume, and he had his job as head engineer at the ski area, she had disappeared behind him.

How many times had she wept in those houses, cried down the hallways as she vacuumed? The sorrow and loss she felt turned to rage. Roman knew and he must know now that he had raised a bully because he was a bully. And she, pushed aside, had let it happen, had let it all happen.

The first September snows had fallen, forgotten the next day in the benison of the sun. Early in October there had been three, and the peaks were white. The first big snow came on the day after Mike had gone. The last week in October was the first of the winter season of a hard frost and a two-foot deep, dry snow. Roman spent the morning in his house office, the room warmed by the camp stove. This heater he carried with him while Janeen fed a fire of fuel from the previous Drop. In the afternoon, he went out, saying only that he would be home for dinner, which, as always, he expected to have ready for him.

In the days of warming ovens and chafing dishes, that had been an easy task; now it was almost impossible. When she didn't meet his expectations, he might strike her, but she found it was his disapproval that chilled her more. That self-satisfied look around the perfectly ordered house had made her feel superior to all the women she knew.

What was that superiority, after all? What was this perfection when her son was gone and gone without respect for her? Roman had no respect for her either. She had carefully preserved herself from this knowledge for years. The fabric—she thought of a burqa—had been ripped from her, in Mike's escape.

Janeen finished the dinner preparation and went to the door. She shivered in the stinging cold, dry and sharp as rancor. She had washed the pots and pans she had used to prepare the meal. Roman didn't like to see any dirty cooking equipment left out. She had two dishpans of water, one wash and one rinse. She combined them and carried the larger one to the front door, the door they used now that they didn't drive their cars. Roman was a thinking man. He had drained the gas tanks of both cars and flushed the systems. When life returned to normal, the cars would be drivable without having to be cleaned of congealed oil. It was this forethought, sensible, rational, and practical, that had earned her respect and had kept her thinking that he must be right about all of his other judgments. Why, then, had he chosen her: stupid, unthinking, irrational? She took a breath of the icy air and instantly regretted it. She hefted the full dishpan, three gallons, and threw the contents down the front steps. It would be dark when he came. She went back into the house, got the camp stove heater from Roman's study, and grinning with guilty pleasure turned it up to high, and went into the dining room.

She had noticed some crumbs on the rug. She had to go hands and knees with the little crumber they used at meals. He hated mess of any kind, crumbs, dust. He had often told her how well-run homes existed even before electricity and modern conveniences. When the rugs were perfectly clean, she settled herself before his heater and took out the book she was reading for book group. It was Melody Reimer's choice, a little sugary, she thought.

The light left. She lit the lamp and began to get the meal on the table, two packets of reconstituted vegetable stews, rice, three-bean salad, compressed bread. Outside there were cries for help. "Oh, my," she said.

He was lying on the icy flagstone apron below the four flagstone steps to the house. She had taken several minutes choosing the right clothing to wear in the cold night. She heard him call for help, his voice muted by the walls between them. Scarf, hat, gloves, which she put on carefully, finger by finger, and then changing her mind and taking out some mittens. By the time she came to the door, the shouting had slowed. She opened the door.

"What were you doing in there?" he demanded.

"I had to get the right clothing to wear. You know how it distresses you to see me not in the appropriate outfit for what I'm to do."

"Are you crazy? I was calling for help. You must have heard me."

"Of course I heard you," she said pleasantly. "Dinner's ready."

"Help me. These steps are all icy."

"What makes you think I can do any better than you are doing?"

"Get the damn ice chipper. Use your head for once."

"Why don't you just slide down to where there's no ice and then come in the back way?"

"Listen to me. Concentrate. I'm hurt. Get the ice chipper. It's in the garage, and come and—no—get a rope from the garage. I'll make a harness and you can pull me up."

"You're much heavier than I am. I might get pulled on to the ice myself."

"Well, hitch the rope to something else then, and I'll pull myself up."

"What should I hitch it to?"

"Will you, for Christ's sake, get the goddamn rope and bring it here."

"I'm not smart enough to figure out these things. I might make a mistake and get the wrong rope. Remember you have three or four sets in the garage and I might bring the wrong one. Besides, it's dark, and if I light the lantern, it will be quite a while before I'm able to see around to where the ropes are. Tell me where to look."

"You know where I store the rope."

"Really, I don't. Tell me so I don't make a mistake."

"Haven't you thought I might be badly hurt?" Why was this happening?

"I assumed you would tell me if you were. That's just logical."

Roman had slipped badly, and his left ankle and right knee were sending shafts of pain through his body. He knew it would hurt even more trying to get a purchase on the ice with his arms. Twice he had levered himself up the bottom step, ready for the next, and slipped back. He gritted his teeth. "Go inside and get the lamp. Light it. Go through the kitchen and out the kitchen door to the garage. From where you stand, the ropes are on your left, on the second shelf from the bottom. The ropes are in coils. Bring the middle-weight one here. Then I'll tell you what to do."

Janeen went back into the house, took off her hat, coat, and mittens and took the lighted lamp to find the lantern they used for outside. She went to the pantry where they had hung it, took it down, lit it, adjusted the wick, put her hat, coat, and mittens on again and walked slowly through the kitchen to the door, which she opened with care, went into the garage, turned right, and made her way very slowly around the walls. Their two cars, covered, stood waiting for the end of the town's isolation. Roman was neat; she would give him that. Nothing was out of place that she might trip over. At last she came to the three coils of rope, carefully placed where he had said they would be. She picked up the middle one, inspecting it carefully. She didn't want him dead, just gentled, made aware of his human need. Mike was gone. Her principal reason for silence and compliance must be away over the fall. She had tried to keep him from following his father's example and had failed. She sighed and took the rope back through the kitchen, mimed taking off her coat, hat, and mittens, mimed putting then on again, and went to the front door with the lantern.

He was lying on his back and in the light of the lantern she saw how close he was to the end of the throw of ice. He could roll two or three times and be able to crawl around the side of the house in the snow and be at the back door in moments, yet he had made all this fuss about ice chippers and ropes. Well, he knew best, didn't he? She was grinning.

FROM THE FANTOM
Thanks to Doc and Sheriff Jay
And Melody, and let us say
Amen to Pastor and Pantea,
To Dixon, Klimek, Tess, and Rick
Who've kept the Town and made it tick.
To every shovel at The Dig
Take a bow and make it big.

POSTED AGAIN BY THE MAYOR: PLEASE BOIL ALL
WATER FOR DRINKING. THIS INCLUDES SNOW
WATER. EVEN THE CLEANEST SNOW IS FULL OF
POSSIBLY HARMFUL CONTAMINANTS. TYPHOID
AND CHOLERA HAVE NO SEASONS.

CHAPTER 45

FOR THE PEOPLE OF THE MIDWEST AND EAST, CLOUDS
tell the story, sending the news of coming weather ahead in the sky. But
Colorado has a nature profligate with its heaps of earth and its vast history in rocks. It often gives its immense bowl of sky every cloud that
wind and water make, all at the same time. With no TV weatherman,
the forecasts the town needed were no longer being given. People hung
clothes on wash lines with sun and a sweet breeze and took them down,
still wet, when a storm poured over The Hungry Mother or Jackass
Mountain or through Whiskey Gap, or fell, straight and sudden, from
a sky blue and open as a baby's eyes. Rain fell in torrents or not at all,
with no way to intuit or predict.

A snow fell for two days. Then came a day of sun, sparkling on the
drifted powder. Had the road been open, skiers would have flocked
to the slopes, to the dry, light, champagne powder, feeling their skis

beneath them, but barely hearing them. There was another snow and another in such quick succession that two Drops had to be canceled, the scheduled one and a default one, then, two more snowfalls and another two scheduled Drops.

There was a panic in people's eyes and voices. They realized again that their existence was determined by wind and weather and in the hands of strangers. People who habitually planned ahead had saved food packets and fuel rations against such a time. Others had traded the packets and the fuel for work done or favors. The packets had replaced money and the usual relationship between the provident and the improvident reestablished itself; people were going hungry. More children showed up at neighbors' doors to beg.

Jay had stopped a small group of them on the street, noticing that the house-to-house processions looked like Halloween, which Edwina had decreed would be a town party. The groups of two or three had started out merrily enough, but there were rejections at many doors.

"We all started out the same," some people told the kids. "Why did your folks waste their rations?" Soon, the kids' moods had flattened or gone weepy or truculent.

"What's going on, guys?" Jay's tone was friendly. They told him. "The Linnehans gave us something and the Draguls and Mrs. Fitten and Mrs. LeDoux." One of the older boys said, "Why don't you give us something, Sheriff?"

"I'll give you some advice," Jay said. "Try not to be angry at people who don't give you anything. Everybody's a little bit scared. We all know that as soon as the bad weather is over the Drop will be started again— but—" He looked at the kids, trying to gauge how much they understood about the dependency now being mirrored in their elders. "You know how you get when you're looking forward to—say—a birthday.

You think maybe it won't come, or maybe everyone will forget. The whole town's that way, now. Do your folks really have nothing to eat?" Two of the kids nodded. "You two go up to the parsonage and tell Pastor Fearing that I sent you. Go ahead." The other four stood looking at him. "Divvy up what you've got and go on home," he said. "Tell your folks I said you've done very good work. The Drop will come back as soon as the weather eases up." He didn't tell them he hoped their parents would stop trading packets and learn to build up a supply. He thought he would also tell AnneMarie to stop giving packets out at everyone's sob story.

The town's weather changed again. The snows stopped and people were filling their buckets for water. The threat stood just above the bell on the fire house and the flagpole on the roof of the town hall, a gray band of overcast sealing Gold Flume so that with no way in or out, the sense of being imprisoned was all but overpowering. No Drop was made.

Now, carefully guarded and stingily used wood piles were put piece by piece into the maws of everyone's wood stove. To Jay, it was the smell of childhood autumns, evocative of times and people long gone. AnneMarie came to stand at his side as he stood on the porch and breathed in its air.

"I have a surprise for you."

"What might that be?"

"Onion soup—no, not the packet stuff with all the chemistry. I got a bunch of wild onions last summer and put them away in the tool shed all wrapped up."

"What about the sherry?"

"We still have half a bottle—"

"Darling, you make my heart pound."

"Jay, what if the next Drop doesn't come? I stew about it. It haunts me. People will go crazy and act like Neanderthals."

"Oh, not you, too. Why are you giving Neanderthals a bad name? We have to believe that whatever agency runs this knows our situation and will keep sending help. The whole town goes through this every time it's windy or snows. We're dependents, let's depend."

"I have a confession to make."

"If it's about you and Fearing escaping together in a balloon, forget it. I'll shoot it down."

"You have nothing to worry about from us—it's that I've stopped thinking about things going on out there in the world. I'm anxious about the Drop, but I've not thought about the kids or about anyone or anything outside of our little mile and a half square kingdom right here, and when I think about outside, it's with fear. Part of me doesn't want the town opened up ever again. Outside is full of wars and disasters, looting and crime."

The word "crime" reminded Jay again of Mike and the white heat of his own rage, uncontrolled. He had let himself lose his professional cool. He had allowed himself to be goaded into a stupid and shameful position of weakness. Janeen Ansel had seen the boy's black eye, cut lip, bruises. She had said nothing, but surely Ansel had been told. Jay hadn't seen Mike since having let him out of the lockup. Weeks had passed. They must be saving their revenge until the liberation of the town.

"Where were you just now?"

"Thinking about our one-man crime wave."

"What made you lose it?"

He sighed. "My cup just spilled over."

"He said something about me, didn't he?"

"It was about his arrogance and his love of risk. Some of the swimmers in the gene pool are snakes. Some are alligators. The snakes understand how to get along, the alligators don't."

They linked hands as they stood.

By the next day, the overcast had been swept away and a windless, bright blue lifted above them. Surely, now, the Drop would be made; the authorities would be conscious that there had been a lapse in their flights. Last winter there had been enough food stored on people's shelves to fall back on when the Drop was delayed. The town was coming into this winter with freezers unplugged and larders empty. People who didn't save packets would be in danger, and so would the town.

Jay wasn't a man who practiced anxiety. He had, with AnneMarie, who did, gone through the falls, broken bones, and illnesses of three rambunctious children, and the four years of AnneMarie's despair, with calm dependability. Now, he was shivering in what was more than the November cold. Might they have been forgotten in bigger calamities? He breathed deeply in and out several times, the way the article on anxiety said to do.

He had been in Aureole, in a doctor's office, with AnneMarie and had picked up the magazine, leafing through it idly—Ten Ways To Deal With Stress. He had thought: The ways we used to do it aren't in style now: booze, cigarettes, dope, fighting, sleeping in, porno, grass, religion, candy, and apathy. He was smiling when his eye traveled down the list— all the usual advice, but there was one suggestion he hadn't seen before, and it was about breathing. They were scraping the bottom of the barrel with that one, he thought. Everyone breathes. But as he read the article, he found himself following the method it described, breathing from what seemed like another deeper place, lower in his body. Four or five of these long, slow, deep breaths did seem to clear his mind. He had used the technique now and then over the years and found himself advising it in situations of tension: domestic calls, accidents where families or witnesses were hysterical. He used it now, replacing the pictures that had formed in his mind with the simple counting in and out of deep breaths.

At ten a.m. the next day, they heard, from the distance, the sound of their salvation. The snow had banked in the streets and hadn't been cleared from the field, but today, there was no thought of Wheeler Dealers getting the rations. Everyone with legs that could hold weight was pounding down to the chopper field to see the Drop. People fell into their lines like dancers in a well-rehearsed routine. They cheered when the rotors blew snow over them. The pilot, not one they had seen before, looked young and embarrassed by the attention he was getting. He helped unload, an act unprecedented. No one asked for news anymore, or seemed interested in the mail, which had shrunk. The work done, he thanked them for their organized skill and took off, racketing the air, up and gone.

People went home, jubilant, but Jay noticed that for the next few days, a depression lay on everyone like a fog. Why? The information print-out that Mayor Dixon received noted that there would be a Thanksgiving Drop of turkey and fixings, frozen, the cranberry sauce and sweet potatoes not freeze-dried, not in packets.

What had brought them low and what had crossed Jay's mind was the consciousness of their dependence on a distant fallible, fickle, faceless source of their lives. They had been giddy with relief at the Drop, and depressed with the fading of the 'copter's sounds.

Some people had taken up hunting immediately after the fall. The Drop had refused all the council's requests for ammunition. Gun owners had looked over what stocks they had and some had given their guns and ammunition to the better hunters among their friends for the promise of a share. Private hunts had gone on all year, but a week after the rein-statement of flights, Edwina Dixon called a meeting and suggested that the town get up a communal hunt, meat being portioned out to all the inhabitants. Weather had been the prime factor in the canceling of two Drops that month, but instead of waiting for the snow to stop and then sending the chopper, the authorities had insisted on maintaining the schedule. There were shortages and uncertainty. Why not pool all the ammunition and guns and let those superior hunters direct a big, coordinated effort that would include all those who wished to take part, wisdom and experience guiding the hunt? The kills would be shared. If enough animals were taken, there should be meat for everyone. These mountains teemed with wild sheep, elk, deer, bear, mountain lions, coy-otes, raccoons, and wild turkeys. There were enough of all these ani-mals that the general wild populations would suffer no decline. Jay was thinking that a successful hunt would re-establish a feeling of control and independence in people made insecure as children by the capri-ciousness of the Drop.

There was, in terrain like this, danger of falls and accidents. The hunters would have to be experienced, acceptable to hunt leaders.

The response was immediate and universal, until the question arose of who those leaders would be and who should assist them. For a while it looked as though the arguments would damn the project, but in the end, the hunters were chosen by vote.

Guns and ammunition appeared from closets and garages all over town, some so old and out of use that they had to be rejected. This caused some bitterness. Brad Unger, who had been chosen as hunt organizer, told hunters used to firing away at whatever moved that they would have to count every shot.

Jay wouldn't be going. The hunt would take several days and the town needed an official presence. John Klimek and most of the Wheeler Dealers would go. Fifty men formed groups of ten, to drive the quarry into Chinaman's Gulch and fire down on them. There was little sport in the plan, and none in the way they spoke of it.

The leaders of each ten had hunted these mountains for years and knew the terrain. What no one knew was what the weather would do. There was no confident TV meteorologist to stand before the map of the nation and show everyone what was to come. The hunters had to have plans for cold and snow even as they looked into the innocent blue-eyed sky, smiling with sun.

There were days in this November country, even in winter, and between snows, when they had sweater weather, mild as May, with May's little soft sigh inquiring into any leaves still on the aspen. The hunters all knew enough to trust nothing in the warm day. They packed as though they were moving to live up Jackass Mountain, to its pass. Their packing made them very slow, moving west through forests of pine and fir, finding they were following, in the old snow, the passings of deer and elk.

There were two mountain gulches where the animals wintered, one as low as the town and warmer because of its shelter from the north and west winds.

The bears would be in retirement in dens further up, a semi-hibernation. The plan was for the hunters who had guns and ammunition to fan out in a circle around each gulch, not shooting until everyone was in place, slowly closing the rim and driving the animals down to the ambush.

FROM THE FANTOM
The days are closing
Even the weasel regrets
Its winter ermine.

POSTED BY THE MAYOR: GOOD HUNTING!

CHAPTER 46

CHRIS PANTEA WAS IN A GROUP OF MEN HE DIDN'T know well. He had nagged and pestered his parents and Doc to let him go on this hunt, having set himself to recover in the months after the attack, his jaw just out of the splint Doc had made to keep the bones from moving. The Wheeler Dealers had been separated, one or two in each of the groups. He wasn't a hunter, and this seemed to please the men because it made him docile and pliable, doing what he was told and offering no alternatives to what had been decided. He hoped he could stay the course, not weakening or having to hold up the group or make them suffer for his weakness or incompetence. He had no gun, but if he slipped or tripped and fell, or if he was out of place when the shooting started, he might cause someone to be injured, or even killed. The possibility of his getting hurt or killed himself bothered him less.

He and Mark Harbison did much of the carrying, setting up and breaking down the camps as they moved, cooking and gathering wood. He noticed that Mark was annoyed at being a gofer, following orders, when he had hunted so often with his father. Chris' ignorance was a personal slight.

"We camp here, camp's made up and then changed without any sense, further up, further down, further north..." Chris said. Mark shot him a look but said nothing. Chris had to seek out one of the knowledgeable men to ask him what the moves meant. Some of the moves seemed reasonable, others like whim. Bud Considine considered.

"You do both," Considine said. "Think and plan and do that, but there's also hunch. After lots of hunting seasons, you learn that hunch can be as good as the best plan there is. Sometimes we want our scent to reach the animal and sometimes we don't. Slope, aspect, wind direction, water—it all figures in even before we see the game."

Chris gathered from scraps of talk among the men that this hunt wasn't like others they had gone on over the years. For one thing, there was no drinking, no sense of being liberated from normal controls. The men sat around the fire on the first or second evenings, but the talk wasn't loud or rowdy. This hunt was work, not sport, the need for game urgent, not a recreation.

On the second day, in the morning, they came on the tracks of a mountain lion, the hunt's dogs giving voice and promptly silenced by their owners. A few yards on, there was evidence of a kill, an area stamped around and the pulled out clumps of feathers of a wild turkey, which must have put up quite a struggle—its feathers were all around the circle.

Someone spotted a bear down range, moving slowly, out of hibernation in the mild weather. The hunters shot it and in field dressing it, found its gut and meat full of worms, and had to let it go. Men from the other groups made contact using mirror signals. Chris was impressed by the ingenuity of the technique and the hunters laughed.

"There weren't always cell phones and beepers and locating equipment," one of them said. Chris' face fell, and the hunter shrugged to moderate his comment. "People always forget the tech skills they leave behind. They ran large hunts long before there were mirrors, and I don't know what they did, then."

Their team slept well, protected from the wind in a snow cave made between three ideally spaced aspen whose fallen leaves, after the snow had been cleared away, were heaped nicely beneath their ground cloths. They were to be the highest wing of the hunt, closest to the end of the tree line and driving the game down from the east and north toward the group coming up into the secluded draw. They had been climbing for a day to come back down when the signals would be given.

"We might not be in sight of each other all the time," Andy McNeil told the team, "but every ten minutes, we'll give signals as we go. We need to go down together, more or less. Don't hurry. Make sure you have good footing. We have rope if you need it."

A hard wind had blown at the recent snow and there were bare places across the faces of the downward slopes. In other places where the snow had been driven, it was banked in crusts, slabbed, and treacherous.

Chris was at the far eastern edge of the group, keeping in sight of the desert-camo outfit of Mr. McNeil, to his right, hearing the whistles and calls of men coming in a relatively straight line on down. Ahead of him was the Shively kid, Sam, who had been sticking to Chris like cheat-grass bristle. They had been paying such close attention to their footing on the crusted slope that they weren't conscious of a rock formation ahead of them. The kid had gone down to it and, to Chris' surprise, turned and came back up the slope to where he stood, trying to plan their route around the spine of rock.

"There's a kid down there, a big kid."

"What?"

"In the rocks, sleeping. There's a little snow on him."

"Are you making this up?"

"No—he's there. He's in between that big rock. He wanted to get out of the wind, I guess, so he went in there and fell asleep."

Muttering with impatience, Chris moved down closer to the rocks. The footing was murderous. The boy couldn't be asleep. He must be from one of the teams further down; too young. Damn kid.

McNeil and the group were well ahead by now, and Chris whistled. McNeil looked back upslope, saw Chris and Sam, slowed, but didn't stop. The kid led Chris to a boulder, behind which was a well of cleared ground on its lee side and wind-slab on both ends. In the well, the sleeping body lay curled.

Chris' mind reached out to try to make reason. He stopped and looked down at the body. Someone was testing him, ridiculing his inexperience, with a manikin. He stood, thinking-not-thinking, stupidly, then, realized he hadn't breathed for too long and pulled in the icy air. This was a dead body, frozen. This dead body belonged to Mike Ansel. The Shively kid began to tremble.

"It's dead," he said, and his face got ready to cry.

A whistle. Chris tried to whistle but his jaw felt the pull in a sharp ache. He gave a call. Call back. "What's up?"

"We're coming. I got my foot stuck, is all. We'll be there in a minute."

"Don't hold us up. Do you need help?"

"No—we're okay."

He recovered the world after a breath or two. "Sam—listen to me," he told the kid. "If we give the alarm the hunt will be over and this body will be picked up and taken back to town."

"But—"

"The others will blame us. If we hadn't been at this end of the group, if we hadn't gotten stuck up here, we never would have found the body at all." Mike Ansel was causing trouble even after he was dead. "We never saw him," Chris said to the boy. "We were never here. Do you get that?" For an instant he thought of telling Sam facts about Mike, but realized that any more explanation would only make things worse. As it was, the kid would cling even more. "We need this hunt," he said, "and the guy is dead. Telling won't help."

"What about after?"

"If you want to, okay," Chris said, "but how will that look? Still, if you want to" —

"They'll blame you, won't they?"

"Yes."

"I won't tell," Sam said.

"Good boy," Chris said, "but now we have to hustle."

They made their way carefully around the rampart of rocks and came into line, with Mr. McNeil's camo to his right. "Sorry," he called. McNeil turned to see him, stopping carefully to do it. "My foot got caught in some rocks," Chris yelled.

McNeil whistled and Chris heard the other whistlers take it up down the line.

Soon they heard sounds and saw the quarry moving ahead of them, some of it large elk, deer, rabbits scurrying, foxes skimming. Whistles sounded from the group coming across to them, closing the circle, moving carefully so as to avoid the river. Other whistles sounded from the planned places.

The hunters were carrying an assortment of guns, varying in range and capacity. They had made strategies that would warn off anyone from firing at random. Chris, gratefully unarmed, had his moment before the firing began, when a huge elk burst out of the bushes directly in front of him and bounded away down the hill toward the grove. The animal had been so close that Chris had felt the wind of its passing and was all but driven into the wall of the animal's side as it passed. This took less than a second, but it seemed longer, even longer than the time he had spent looking at the body curled against the rock.

The plan was for those without guns to stay back and uphill when the firing started and to lie down in their designated spots. Because of this, Chris didn't see the ambush or the actual killings in the grove. He heard shooting, individual shots, and then volleys on and off and then silence and a last pop here and there, and then whistlings signaling the cease fire.

Then the work began. They had eight deer and six elk, and a coyote which had been driven into the bullet-rain and been killed. The full complement of hunters went down to see what had been done. Chris remembered a movie he had seen, name forgotten, of some plains tribe celebrating victory in the hunt. The exaltation here lasted far more briefly than it did in the movie.

"We'll field-dress all this," Brad Unger said. "Who's got the sleds?"

"Wait a sec—" It was Rick Harbison, a hunt leader and Chris' boss at the dig. "You field dress too much, you lose too much of the meat. People will use every scrap we can get, even the intestines for sausage casings. We've got enough man-power—we can bless the snow. Pulling the sleds will be lots easier."

Voices were raised in protest. The terrain was difficult and even with the light vinyl runners, the work would be an exhausting drag up the hill and then, precipitously down to the river and across the river to the town.

"No one's going to have to go into the river," Rick said impatiently. "There's a bridge—"

"That's out of our way..." someone said.

"It's not a mile; and no one needs to fool with trying to get across the ice that's there and maybe go through. We have fifty guys. I say we cut now and quarter and haul it all up tomorrow and the next day."

Protests erupted. Field dressing should be enough, some said. Who'll really make sausage and ground meat, and all the specialty stuff made with lesser cuts and scraps and added fat?

"Many of the people I know, and some who'll get things from others who do. We owe it to the town and to the people who gave up their ammo for this."

The argument went back and forth and then they noticed that the sun had gone down and that it was afterglow and they overruled Brad Unger and voted to quarter the animals and divide the hunters, using the sleds and ropes or ropes alone, four men to each deer and six to each elk, each animal's edible entrails to go with it.

They cut until they couldn't see to cut, knives dulling and not enough saws. They slept in shifts alert for bears, mountain lions, coyotes, bobcats and all the other animals with an interest in what they had done. The smell of blood and entrails must have alerted a mountain full of predators. The men ate from what they had brought, too tired to cook.

They woke a little after first light to find that six of the hunters were no longer there and must have left just at first light. The night had been cold, but not freezing, and the quartering hadn't been finished. McNeil looked at Chris, grimly. "You won't know who's a hunter until a time like this, no matter what he's said or done before. It'll take two days to get this back, and the six will all have good excuses."

"Maybe I should go back to town and get some more people to help us."

"Not a bad idea, if they'll come. I hope you're not using that as an excuse to disappear. I'll see if Brad thinks we can do this as we are."

They pan fried deer and elk liver, which seemed to Chris to be as delicious a meal as he had ever eaten.

"It's the cold and the work that does it," Harbison said. "It's rich stuff, though, don't eat too much of it."

They ate the brains with seasonings their wives had bound in small squares of cloth.

There were eight vinyl 'sleds,' slightly convex, with holes placed for ropes. The finesse lay in how the quartered animals were tied on. The hunters pulled and rested, pulled and rested, and changed places, front to back. As the terrain became steeper and more rock strewn, they sent men ahead to scout the easiest way up and clear what they could of rocks and debris, testing the snow ahead of the group. The hardest pulls were up front, the last sliding on the snow packed by the animals and men in front of them. They sweated in their clothes that would go clammy in the cold when they stopped and night caught them halfway to town.

Chris had never been tested physically before. Work in the dig had been planned to accommodate kids and women and seniors, long and slow on the relatively level terrain of the riverside. This work, lasting as long as the light lasted, was calling on everything he had and as it went on, he became anxious about falling and pulling some essential muscle or tendon that would make him an inconvenience, or worse, to the other men.

At dusk, they built a big fire, because there was danger of hypothermia in their sweat-soaked clothes. Some of the men took off boots and socks and dried the socks at the fire, watching them steam as they dried.

It was there, lying in the fume of the sweat that rose from beneath his collar that Chris realized that the old Westerns he had depended on for his understanding of the desire to hunt had trivialized the scenes of the warrior-hunters being greeted by the tribe at their return. There had been all that ululating and singing and dancing as the hunters arrived. He had remembered those scenes for years. In that movie, the hunters had been spry and triumphant and fresh in feathers and war-attire. It was wrong, all wrong. The hunters would have been limping and spent and stinking and blood-spattered and with burns from fire and blisters and torn outfits and broken weapons with no wish to sing or dance or brag, only to take off their smelly clothes and sleep the sun around. He thought he had done all right today. What a relief that was. He hadn't been hurt out there, either. He hoped he would have another day without shaming himself.

The next day, three more men left, claiming injuries. Chris, himself, felt barely capable of working another day, but the worst of the trek had been done and Harbison sent him on ahead to get help from town.

So it was, that the sheriff and Mr. Klimek and the mayor and others came out with sleds and sledges to help the hunters home. As they were moving the quartered animals to these sleds, McNeil came close to Chris and nodded. "Good to hunt with you," and moved away up the line.

Chris hadn't known the McNeils well. They lived up in a new subdivision of five-acre estates in a huge house with a tennis court. His simple statement was Chris' eagle feather and would give him a smile before sleep for days to come. He needed the words to stand as a barrier against the picture he had of Mike Ansel's body curled up for warmth in the sheltering rock.

FROM THE FANTOM
Thanksgiving's coming, give your thanks
For rivers kept within their banks,
For chicken packets from the Drop,
For stars above the mountain top,
For these conditions which are all
Resulting from the goddamn Fall.

POSTED BY THE MAYOR: CONGRATULATIONS
ON A SUCCESSFUL HUNT! SAVE THOSE PACKETS.
WINTER IS COMING.

CHAPTER 47

THERE ROSE THE ISSUE OF THE DIVISION OF THE meat they had brought. How should it be apportioned, who should get the best parts, and who should have the meat that would be ground into hamburger or set up for stewing. Whichever way it went, Brad Unger said, the apportionment would be seen as unfair. At last the decision was to do it by lottery, a separate lottery for each animal, people signing up for deer or elk and allowed only one ticket. The meat having been cut carefully and all the lotteries going on at once, quick work was made of the distribution of the animals. The internal organs and brains were given away to anyone who wanted them, few arguing over tongues, sweetbreads, kidneys, Rocky Mountain oysters, or intestines.

For a while, Rick Harbison had wanted to deny tickets to men who had left the hunt after the shooting was over, but there were wives and children and old parents to be considered and Edwina talked Brad out of the idea—too much weighing and measuring of each man's contribution and too much promotion of bad feeling. The next hunt, if there were one, would have hunters only and not duffers.

The lottery worked well. Some people took their cuts in pans, went home, and cooked them; some froze the meat, packing it in snow and pouring water over the snow to keep the meat in blocks of ice until Thanksgiving, five days away, or until Christmas.

For most people, the idea of fresh meat was too tempting to hold off and the smell of it roasting in woodstove ovens or lying on grills rose from the town, striking Pastor Fearing—standing uphill of the marvelous odor—to declare that he felt like the Lord, feasting on the smell of the sacrifices. The Fearings had received the lower leg of one of the elks. He went out to the garage and with a hatchet hacked it into pieces for soup meat. There was also the hoof, for aspic if she wished to use it. Cheryl cursed for parts of two hours.

That evening, AnneMarie came up bringing a cut of the elk brisket they had won. "I knew you got only bones," she said to Fearing, "and we can't eat all this ourselves. You've helped me so much, I feel I owe you something money can't buy."

"I really..."

"We'll take it," Cheryl snapped. "Too much Christianity is as bad as too little."

Jay hadn't been all that delighted with AnneMarie's generosity, but he didn't say anything when she cut a piece from their portion and told him she was going up to the Fearings. She had come so far, rising to the challenge of the fall, and had done so well that he didn't want to damp down any of her spontaneity. He had seen what solidarity meant to the dig, when the whole town was menaced, and he had noticed as he helped the hunters to town how they had formed a solid group, becoming close in the hard work they had done. He had enjoyed watching their body language, give-take, looking to make sure of one another's position and safety, waiting without consciously waiting for someone slower or with a heavier load.

And El Fearing certainly hadn't been blessed by the gods of chance. Someone commented that if Pastor worked for God as often and as hard as he had, surely God should return the favor. When this was picked up and repeated to Fearing, he said, "God didn't come to the drawing; I think He went skiing instead." Jay was aware that before the fall, Fearing never would have joked that way. How many changes had there been in this hard year?

The pilot of the next day's Drop carried the message to Mayor Dixon that given steady weather, implementation of plans for the removal of the fall would begin on the Callan side. When that was done, there would be contact between Gold Flume and the world.

Edwina had received this message and decided not to broadcast it. Everyone had gone through a dozen cycles of hope and disappointment through the year, but somehow the word had gotten out and she was besieged again, yet again, by people importuning her for day and time.

The town had lost a year of business and even if it got the word out by January, plans would have to be made to get the tourists back. The Drop would have to continue for a while until revenue started to come in.

Rumor ran its vines through town again. Gold Flume had been forgotten once; could people be sure that someone in the state government in Denver was really paying attention to its problems? Jay tried to give a bland response when people asked him what more he knew about their situation. Couldn't electric lines be dropped? Phone lines? Generators?

"Why would I know any more than you?"

"Well, you're being told things."

"As soon as I'm told," he said monitoring the words he didn't want to remember himself as having said, "I'll tell you."

The mild autumn days at the washhouses were long over. Back in September and October, there had been some pleasure in being out in the benevolent weather, working away together, chatting, gossiping, regaling one another with songs and jokes. Now, wood heaters had to be set up, not only to heat the water they used, but also to keep people from freezing as they worked. Wash days had to be canceled twice because the creeks that fed their basins had frozen. People did small things at home, using melt water. Some people kept their sheets for months between washings. AnneMarie was working next to Melody Reimer, their washboards balanced on the rim of the ore cart. "We used to want to be closer to nature," she said. They were waiting for the fire under the cart to heat the water. "Now, we're closer than we ever wanted to be."

"The women back then had servant girls," Melody said.

"I used to envy people who had servants, but I don't anymore," AnneMarie said. "You had to worry about them, their health, their honesty, all that stuff. People go on about the gap between rich and poor, but they don't know what a gap there was in the old days. I don't look back with any nostalgia at all."

"Lots has changed," Melody said, warming her hands in the armpits of her jacket. "They didn't have tranquilizers back then." She suddenly realized she was in the middle of a mine field, that AnneMarie was— "Well," she went on, seeing the trip wire too late.

"There was one—"gin." AnneMarie pulled the wire away.

"And Mother's Friend."

"You're dating yourself."

"Lydia Pinkham's—twenty percent alcohol, and you got serene after a couple of tablespoons of that. Do you remember Marie Kimball?"

"Faintly. She was very old by the time I got here."

"You'd come to her door and be zonked with a breath of gin coming out of her any morning you stopped by. There were lots of others, a nice, steady tipple all day. I think they must have been half gone most of the time."

"We have that now, or did. Look at Lowayne LeDoux, the Warings, both of them, how many more? We have more alcoholics in Gold Flume than people know about." AnneMarie looked thoughtful. "I guess I was so busy with my own troubles that I never thought what it must be for any serious alcoholic after the fall. Are they still eating the rugs off the floors and the paint off the walls?"

"I think Doc does something."

There were only four women at the ore cart that day. The other two were talking about their dogs.

There was a Drop the next day, the Thanksgiving Drop, the strangest they had yet received. Besides turkeys, dozens of them, and the fixings, marshmallows and sweet potatoes, chestnuts and stuffing, there were coats and hats, old and new, blankets, stuffed animals, bags of charcoal briquettes—very welcome, candles—the scented ones that made Jay say, "Smells like what's waiting on the pier when the fleet comes in."

"What's going on?" Mayor Dixon asked the pilot. "What's all this?"

"You're famous," the pilot answered. "Someone found out about this town and you're now The Town The World Forgot and people started donating all this. Some sent money, which was what got you the super-sized turkeys and the eggnog; there's gallons of the stuff. People sent Bibles, too. There are a hundred Bibles and half as many decks of cards. That's the bad news. The good news is that there's been pressure being exerted to open up the road. You were on a list, but with all the publicity, I think they'll get to you sooner than they would have. The next bad news is that you'll probably be famous when they do open the road, interviewed, you and everyone in town, here, and your fifteen minutes of fame, fifteen seconds, this time, is on its way. Maybe they'll make a movie."

Boxes and boxes had been unloaded and the pilot waited no extra moment with any more explanation but was up and gone and the field was left with the unaccustomed load that was on no list and was thus not part of the quick, efficient distribution which was such a source of pride. Bibles. Playing cards. Bundles of coats and blankets.

"I wonder if the eggnog has rum," AnneMarie said later, when Jay told her that six gallons were being distributed in sips for the whole population. "If so, it should be saved for the alcoholics."

The women of the town looked over the collection before them. Almost all of the local wood had been used for heating in the cold spells between Drops. Electric and gas ovens hadn't been used since the fall. Wood had been scavenged from all the lower skirts of nearby mountainsides. Cuts from any hunting were small enough to grill or stew. What was to be done with twenty-pound turkeys, a hundred of them? What was to be done with the coats and boots and blankets and kids' toys and the playing cards?

Roman Ansel remembered that there was some rebar at the back of the firehouse. Since breaking his leg on the ice on his front steps, he was on crutches, but he told Brad Unger to go back and find the rebar, and with Harbison, the two began to construct spits in front of the town hall. They improvised handles at each end with tree branches cut to size and drilled to fit at both ends of the spits. The Wheeler Dealers brought in rocks, Ron Pantea passing on which would best be used. The men took turns at the cranks until they worked together. Fuel from the Drop was soaked into the rocks and the turkeys were spitted. People walking by got the idea and passed the news. Anyone who wasn't bedridden was soon out with plates and utensils as the sun went down. Even old Mrs. LeDoux, who never left home, was there in the line that moved past the spitted birds, to vats of gravy and bread stuffing, yams with marshmallows, eggnog, cider, coffee—oh, coffee. Pies, breads, cakes, and people ate standing. Some had brought chairs or camp stools. Kids sat on the cold ground, wadding the donated coats beneath them. They ate, drowsed, ate again. They took cloth, paper, plastic to wrap leftovers, bones for soup, the odd yam, food to be saved for later.

The grilling and eating went on long into the night. People were loath to go home, but stood waiting until they were sure all the food was gone. The tables which they had set up for past events had long since been taken for firewood. Some people moved to the edges of the space and spread the donated blankets and clothing and went to sleep before they had finished lying down.

Chris Pantea found himself facing Janeen Ansel, who was carving the last slices of the turkey she had been overseeing. Behind her a row of women were fixing bags of stuffing for the trips home. Her looks shocked him. She had been stylish, an older woman, but rounded and sensuous and along with Cheryl Fearing, a woman who had taken a warm, sweet, secret place in his fantasy life. Her body had been both full and lithe, under the soft flowing clothes she wore. He could remember looking after her, long looks, back last spring as she walked out of church wearing a flowered dress with a low neckline, a breeze forcing the cloth to her thighs. This woman looked pulled, her face stretched over its bones, her hair tight back, nothing lithe or flowing under the coat she wore, now too big for her. In his fantasy, she would have sought out the warmth of the fire behind her, moving back toward it. Now, she stood away, as though it didn't matter to her whether she was warm or cold.

Was that because of Mike? How could she know? Had the Shively kid, Sam, told? That couldn't be. If he had, the sheriff would have been all over Chris for not reporting it. Mike. And this was his mother. Mike was dead. Mike had been a bully and a user, frightening at the end, and a second rate human being. She must have known that and loved him anyway. Chris shivered, hoping superstitiously that she couldn't see into his mind, to where there was a body folded into the cup of the rocks. Chris knew where Mike was, and a mountain lion and a bear would know it and some crows. Insects would know it when the weather changed. He hugged himself for warmth. She must have thought of her son going over the mountain or up and over the fall, and thought that he would call or write to her later from some safe place away from the law. She was waiting in the ache of her loss.

Chris had reasons to think he was a good person. People had told him so. He saw their approval every day. Does it matter, though, if love says that being a bully doesn't matter, if love says that a person can be Mike Ansel, and still be loved and wept over?

If so, what was the use of goodness? Angela: was she feeling Mike's loss? For an instant, he envied the curled body in its final place. He thought of the dead people mourned on TV, teenagers or murder victims. "Everyone loved him." "She was so funny and friendly. We'll never forget..." Never? Is the drunk teenager or victim of violence never dull or mean like Mike, or someone who could be lost in a crowd of two? He knew that he was justifying himself. He also knew that Sam would see telling as Chris' job, and that if he told even a year from now, there was nothing illegal about his silence. They had not touched the body. The guilt of his inaction he could bear well enough.

He looked over at the people still eating. Tomorrow, they would all be sick. These people were not used to real food anymore, not used to eating to satiety and past it to the belching bellyful of past feasts. Almost a year ago, the grownups lay in the chairs and groaned, only rising to go to the TV to watch football. Mike's body would be found some day, or the bones. He recognized his mood as dark when it shouldn't be. Everyone near him was laughing and talking while the stars left their identities to fade without an imprint in the pre-dawn and the air lifted to get ready for the day.

FROM THE FANTOM
Some got sirloin
Some got bones
Some went singing
Some gave groans.
You got filets from the hunt
Who pulled that Thanksgiving stunt?
Hearts that melted miles away
Blessed us this Thanksgiving day,
Made us feel a victim's shame
Eat your fill, dear, all the same.

POSTED BY THE MAYOR: ANYONE NEEDING
CLOTHING FROM THE DROP, PLEASE COME AND
PICK IT UP. WE ARE DONATING THE UNNEEDED
FOR THE METRO DENVER CLOTHING DRIVE.

CHAPTER 48

ANGELA HAD BEEN GOING WITH CHAZ BERGSTROM, who had just had his sixteenth birthday, He had been on the hunt and was eager to take over from Mike Ansel. He brought most of his allocation of meat and enough wood and extras to impress her and get approval from her mother. They smiled at him and asked no questions. Angela was happy for the change. Chaz was easier to satisfy than Mike had been. His sexual needs were simpler and he didn't pout or whine about seizing the power or respect he deserved. Mike had been crudely needy about power. Chaz was a fantast. His big word was 'create.' "I'm gonna create..." "When I get an idea, I'll create..." "It'll be an idea for— for something new that no one has ever seen before." Only once had Angela said, "What's that idea?" And he had stared at her in shock.

When Chaz was angry he yelled, but he forgot his anger quicker than Mike did.

Her father's anger was a dry one of gritted teeth. "It's your own fault," Leatrice Bruno told her. "They all want to be rock stars, men, and with thousands of cheering fans. Your father went into surgery for that reason. He was good with his hands and he could lord it over patients and nurses and even other doctors. Why do you think he left us, to stay where he was and not be choppered back here? He could have hired a chopper. He said the higher need required his presence. You know what crap that is. Gold Flume has no cheering section and he would have to do routine stuff like Winograd, who he called 'that pill-pusher.' Whatever they want, the truth isn't it."

"If I could just get out of here, I could get something better than Chaz Bergstrom."

"He's good practice, don't forget that. You'll go to college and there'll be plenty of men, but you can choose to go upscale, or bargain basement, a diamond or a rhinestone. Some women prefer rhinestones, they're lower maintenance. Oh, and you're better with less make-up. Men don't like faces left on the pillow at night."

"Oh, Mo-ther!"

On December first, there was a Drop with more than they needed, some of it Christmas things, and the pilot left a printed notice with the mayor. The agency that dispatched the chopper said that charity items would have to stop. "As though we asked for them in the first place," Edwina growled. There was more, another notice: Earth movers had finally been freed from other work to begin clearing the fall. It might take a month, but there was work beginning. There would probably be some kind of hoopla when the machines broke through. Drops would continue for some time after, but no one knew for how long. It was all part of an already determined relief plan. The Drops they had made had cost the government millions already. Citizens should get a plan to ready themselves for going off emergency supplies. The dole, Edwina said. They felt the sting again.

Each day for four days there were flyovers, some high, some low, none acknowledging the people below them, none with markings. The council met again, huddling around Melody's campstove, each aware of a fume, the chemical expression of their individual unwashed bodies.

"The environmental guys must have been studying the river, how we've changed its place, here," Edwina said.

Rick Harbison sounded impatient. "It was done to save the town. It was a terrific thing that took a hell of a lot of creativity and work, with no modern equipment. There's been no back-flooding or cave-ins. The redirection of the river's bed was well planned. I'm proud of what we did."

"I think the flyovers must be concerned with that, at least in part," Ron Pantea told him. "They're reading maps and charts, and they've found that the river's location doesn't agree with the maps anymore. Heads are being scratched."

A big snow put off the Drop that week and people stayed home. Jay and AnneMarie had been out at the dig before the snow, cutting some tree roots that stuck out of a place along the edge of the fall. They had brought bundles of kindling and arm-sized branches back, making three trips, and were burning them in the fireplace, a luxury, as the evening came on.

"We aren't clearing the streets out front. Nobody seems to be," AnneMarie said dreamily. "We did before; why not now?"

"We're waiting to be rescued," Jay said. "What do you bet nobody will show up at the wash house, either?"

"I will. They said it may be a month or more before they're through and can get in power lines and set them up. The waiting is sure to make things worse."

"It's hard, I admit," Jay said. "I go out and listen for sounds and I don't hear any—no shuddering of engines eating the rocks."

"In a way, I wish they hadn't told us. The days have suddenly gotten longer," AnneMarie said. "John Klimek says he wants to keep the Wheeler Dealers going after this is over. They won't be delivering food, but there's plenty of need around town for things teenagers can do— help for old people, work on the river walk. Old and sick people have had things better during this year than they ever had before. People on the ridge told that to Chris Pantea. People without kids or grandkids used to have trouble getting food and drugs from the mall. They were depending on neighbors, some as old as they were. Pastor wants it, too. Do you see that happening?"

Jay paused for a moment. "No, I don't think so. I hope I'm wrong."

"Are the men going to bring us the wood we need for the washing fires tomorrow?"

"If they don't, I'll rout them out one by one," Jay said.

The wood was there, and women showed up, but the mood was pettish and no one laughed or gossiped. AnneMarie recognized the impatience. They had waited out last winter's hard days, a snow-spring, a hot summer. They were adept, but they had made do, found new resources in themselves and each other, and had been proud. Outsiders—the pilots of the Drops—might see them as demanding and dependent, but they knew how much wit and care it took to heat water and stay warm on the small supplies of fuel, how much effort and ingenuity there was in varying the unvarying packets of freeze dried food. Soon, soon the world would open up again, but when—how soon? Jay had read somewhere that more prisoners in captivity became ill in the days of their delivery. He tried to reason with himself. It might be months—the authorities had given them optimistic dates, but it would seem to take forever between the breakthrough and the time the highway would be usable— before electricity would be re-established. His job as sheriff had shown him what happened to people denied what they had come to believe was theirs. He hadn't been above the fray, either—he had battered Mike Ansel. He had wanted to kill Mike Ansel. He kept trying not to think about that. What had AnneMarie said? Higher highs, lower lows. Very few people had learned resignation. AnneMarie had returned to him, depressed sometimes, anguished sometimes, but real to him, real in the world. The people outside wouldn't understand what the people here had done. The dig had been monumental, and so had the response to fire and accident, the Wheeler Dealers. Skiers and tourists would return and people would again be the store owners and ski-lift operators, the hosts they had been. They would try to take seriously the complaints over slow maid service at lodges and at late shuttle busses. The kids would go back to their technological nests, their interests narrowed to their fingers texting messages to one another, cocooned into themselves and their chosen realities. They were avid for it—he was avid for it—just a trip to the mall or the other side of the fall. Did the mall still exist, or was it under the mountain? He had asked several times, but hadn't gotten a straight answer. How bad was the destruction beyond their little wedge of the world? When the world was open, would there be a place to go?

The evening came down at four in the afternoon, while the mountains above them still glowed. Gold Flume had a very long twilight. He walked back to the office in the town hall, passing the river— their soothed dragon, noticing its height. Everyone did that, now, automatically, in case the way might be blocked by falling earth a mile down or a boulder slid from a mountainside.

He did his evening patrol up, over, and around the town. Snow was going to ice on the streets where people hadn't cleared it. They would have to use fireplace ash to keep the sidewalks from becoming skating rinks. Even as he passed First Street, he looked up and saw one or two people up the hill chipping ice from their walkways. He smiled. He and AnneMarie had cleared the snow from their steps, walk, and sidewalk before she had taken the laundry up the hill to the sluices and the ore cart. The new prestige was that cleared walkway, that stretch of sidewalk, and how quickly it was done after a snow. The wash had been hung out to freeze on the line until the next sun warmed it.

Two snows came, one after the other, all but burying the town. People didn't venture out for days, some staying in bed to keep warm. Doc was looking out his window and saw Sheriff Isaacs pass in the police car. He thought for a moment that he might go and flag the Sheriff down. There were people up at the ridge that he needed to visit. There was so much snow on the roads that the car might not be able to make the hill. People had become used to walking everywhere, but few developed a liking for it. He would go when the ice melted and the way was open for his car. He thought for a moment about the old people up there, that they had hung on longer than he had thought they would, with limited medicine and mobility. When the road was opened and electricity restored, he had told Jay, people would go back to watching TV and using their computers. They would be able to do something about villains like the Ansel kid. Enough booze and cigarettes would keep the addicts evenly supplied and on this side of madness. The Brunos would probably split up and there would be a wave of separations and divorces, too, he thought, people having seen one another in a different light—the kerosene lamp.

There began to be flights of choppers over the town. People could hear them through the day, their sound magnified in the ear-trumpet of the valley's end. At the next Drop, a man in a suit emerged from the chopper and asked to see the mayor. He had a clipboard, an iPad, a cell phone, and a harried look—all business. His agency was a five-figure acronym. Edwina, who had been at every Drop, came forward. The Acronym man looked past her.

"The mayor—"

"I'm the mayor."

Acronym talked to the air over her head. "I'll need a meeting with the officials of this town," he said, using *town* as a word of contempt.

Edwina called for the one-bell clang that summoned the council. They went up to the frigid second floor of the town hall to wait. The mayor didn't use the heater. She saw Acronym shiver.

The council members came pounding up the stairs. Someone had come. Help was at hand. Acronym began with questions. How many people had been killed in the fall? How many remained? How many had been injured, and what were their injuries? How many other deaths had there been? Why had the river been diverted? Didn't they know that they had broken the law by diverting it? Did they know that the environmental effect might be serious? Who had made this decision? He opened his briefcase. These are the papers that must be filled out—in triplicate, and these, involving the diversion of the river, in quadruplicate.

Edwina took the papers, dazed. There was a sheaf of them. "How long will the Drop continue after the town has been opened and services restored?"

"We're not the agency that is concerned with that part of your situation," Acronym said. "You'll have to take that up with FEMA and the other agencies that regulate those matters. The environmental effects of this alteration are extremely serious."

"We didn't cause the fall. Had we not diverted the river, the town would have become a lake," Harbison said.

"Didn't you think of what the effects would be on the areas downstream?"

"No."

"Fill out the papers."

"You can simply clear away the fall and re-divert the river to its old bed," Harbison said.

"There's too much material to move."

"That's why we diverted it in the first place."

"There will be a hearing." The man rose, went quickly down the steps of the hall, out, and quickly down the streets to the field and the helicopter, got in, and was borne away.

FROM THE FANTOM
"Hope is a beautiful thing," say some sages I've heard of.
"It's the waiting that spoils it."

CHAPTER 49

THE MAYOR AND THE MEMBERS OF THE COUNCIL spent the afternoon filling out papers. Who had ordered the diversion, the question ran, who had participated in it? For what purpose? Was it to create a private property financial improvement? Did it have commercial backing or interest? What environmental advisors or agencies had been involved in the decision? What toll had been taken by the diversion? Wildlife? Fish? Agricultural? Wild plants? Had the group or agency promoting the diversion applied and received permission and certification from the six agencies listed below?

"Weren't we told that we were on our own because all their mechanical resources were being used—*utilized,* they said, in other places?"

"We were heroes," Edwina said, "and that's that. We saved this town. We'll tell them to re-divert or go to hell."

When she told Jay about the questionnaires, he went down to his office to look at them. He knew it was a mistake as he went in. Rage built in him as he read. Who were the people purposely trampling the law for selfish ends? "So we go from 1880 to a modern day law court. The time we spent at the dig will look like heaven on earth," he told AnneMarie later.

"There are lawyers in town—"

"Not our kind. Hanchett does bankruptcy, Lucas works with real estate."

"Funny how I forgot their old roles here. Hanchett brings the water from the fire truck and Lucas runs the sluices for the washhouse. The authorities can't do anything until we're dug out anyway," she said, "and by then, they may be busy with whatever else is going on outside. It may be years before they get to us. With luck, we'll be dead by then and so will everyone who made the decision to save our lives, and the whole thing will have disappeared."

"It's the idea of the damn questionnaire that gets me. We were heroes— we did heroic things."

"Sergeant York died unhappy, and so did Robert E. Lee. We won't die unhappy; we'll die forgotten, the way almost all decent and heroic people do."

"I'll look forward to it," Jay said.

The first Drop in December, the pilot reported that work had begun on clearing earth, rocks, and detritus from the Callan side of the fall. People claimed to hear the sound of heavy equipment. Soon, the sounds were a fact, and then a source of near panic. Would they stop? Would some other tragedy call the machines away and leave Gold Flume bereft? What if the diversion they had caused to the river would close them away from rescue? Mayor Dixon tried to stop the rumors, but they were as constant and widespread as the snow that settled lightly and packed itself hard as granite.

On December 20, in the early afternoon, a yellow earthmover appeared at the front of the town hall, cracking the concrete street in five places. The driver climbed down from his perch and announced to the gathering, sudden as a flash-mob, that the road between Callan and Gold Flume was open for one-way traffic and that vans with TV and media crews were on their way into town.

The crowd was dead still. Here and there people scrambled out and away, but the rest stood shocked, sleepers suddenly awakened in strange beds in a city not their own. From far away, they heard the sound of engines, a sound that but for the chopper had been absent from their lives for fifty weeks.

"Somebody said you were having trouble with the river," the man said. "If you show me where the narrowing is and there's some ground that's not a high bank, I can open it up a little."

"You mean before the diversion?"

"I don't know anything about that—I just heard..."

They told him things were stable and he nodded and climbed back up into the cab of the engine that was the size of a mountain cabin and turned, back and forward, chewing up a line of willow shrubs the garden club had put in in 1976. The yellow brontosaurus lumbered away down the newly opened road.

A helicopter flew over them and another and then a line of vans moved slowly into town, cars following them. The opening was narrow, the first reporters told the mayor. Trucks would be widening the way for several days and it would take that long for power lines to be brought in and service established. Food Drops would continue, but they had asked the authorities and hadn't gotten an answer as to how long the help would last.

Other reporters had followed, carrying in their minds the stories the town was meant to tell. Depending on the slant of the media they represented, the reporters expected that people had fragmented, had cooperated, had made great town feasts, had fought over the food packets. There was a black market; there was generosity and open handedness. There had been looting and murder. Someone must have mentioned men breaking into Ms. LeDoux's basement way back when the booze had first run out, but the questions had been changed to ones about stores being destroyed by looters. Someone had also mentioned the town's all-but-total church attendance and the reporters took the words and sent them back with everyone praying for a miracle and/or everyone pharisaically grateful for his or her individual salvation. The visitors told the mayor and council that had the fall been only a few degrees to the north of where it now lay, the town would have been destroyed. Wasn't this town like Brigadoon? Brigadoon had been blessed to be kept from the materialism and greed of the world. How did it feel to be without those curses? Who was the hero of this story? Surely there was that single shining soul who emerged as the natural leader, here?

Eyes turned to Jay. "I think that would be Roman Ansel," he said, "the chief engineer at the ski area. He was our leader."

"Where is he? Where can we find him for an interview?"

"I imagine he'd be at home." Edwina's gaze met Jay's. "He's a modest man, a private man—" They were gone in moments.

Edwina grinned at Jay. "Pants on fire." she said.

A word from the mayor was recorded and pictures of the most photogenic people in town, but most were quickly away over the bridge and up the hill to the Ansel house.

"The Sheriff has depths I never saw in him before," Edwina said to Ron Pantea.

When they heard the story, John Klimek laughed. Chris Pantea was indignant. "Mr. Ansel never was any kind of a leader except for helping to engineer the dig. Town leader? Mr. Klimek, and you, Mayor Dixon, and Sheriff Isaacs, and Chief Unger, you're the real leaders."

"Don't let that bother you," Klimek said. "You should give the fish to the person who needs to eat it."

FROM THE FANTOM
Look how eagerly
The proud warrior woman
Lets go the bucket.

CHAPTER 50

THE MEDIA MADNESS LASTED FOR TWO DAYS AND then the reporters were gone. Jay saw his own weary frustration reflected in other town faces. People knew they wouldn't be able to give a true account of what their year had been like. Had they been brave and resolute? Yes and no. Had they been fearful and clenched? Yes and no. Were there no lessons to be learned from their experience? Who knew? Ten years from today, when they did know, no one would want to hear what those lessons had been. Even if someone wonderful in town—someone with a gift, would try to tell what had happened, only a narrow sliver of the experience could be lifted away from it. How could a sliver describe a house?

Waiting for the power lines to come in was much harder, now. People were in a fever of impatience for hookups to allow them to boot up their computers and turn on their devices. They waited for batteries, for oil and gasoline that would allow them to drive the newly opened road to get more, to go to the mall, which was, indeed, still functioning near Callan. On the third day, the road was clear enough for bicycles, ten of them, to be ridden into Callan for supplies and for Brad Unger to drive the fire truck there and come back with gasoline and oil for other trucks that would bring still more. Three contingents of women were driven into Callan in the second wave of trucks. They had clothes for the laundromat and dry cleaners. They were avid for fresh food. They came back puzzled and shaken.

On the day after the fall, a fine particulate material had been raised and deposited on the Callan side. The town had been covered in the toxic dust, as someone said, fallout from the fall. It was a powdery, gray-brown grit that could be stirred up at a step. By a fluke of slope, aspect, and wind direction, Gold Flume had been spared much of this dust. The town had also been spared Callan's economic collapse. The closing of the ski area in Gold Flume had thrown hundreds of Callan's people out of work. No choppers had dropped food or supplies to those people, the maids and nannies and waiters and salad-makers dependent on Gold Flume's success. The women had become aware, as they shopped, of a low level, softly spoken resentment in the Callan people, as though the dust had been their doing. The women had expected greetings and congratulations, some expressions of the wonder the reporters had shown. The Callan people told them that even though they had worn masks, particles had been too small and had clogged the masks through, and particles had gone into bronchi and lungs. People in Callan had died, while in Gold Flume, there had been a year of clear skies and clean houses. Had they not been told that the lungs of many of Callan's people had been scoured and ruined? It took dozens of trucks to cart away tons of the dust, dampened by water so it wouldn't blow. The water supply had been compromised. Yes, Callan had had a Drop also, but only water and only for three weeks, while people swept and shoveled and swore. Nobody's car left out of a garage had paint on it. All the while, Gold Flume had been getting fed and tended, and supplied with all its needs. The people of Callan had seen the choppers week after week, bringing what Callan needed, not to Callan, but to Gold Flume, and why?

Because Gold Flume had the ski area and people with lots of money and influence, while Callan and Bluebank claimed the many people who serviced Gold Flume's spas, galleries, and upscale restaurants.

"My friend, Julia, told me this," Melody Reimer said, talking to AnneMarie and the others in the sewing group on Wednesday afternoon. Melody, the genius of the Drop, had been suggesting responses to the paper stack that the mayor was collecting. "I never knew that Julia envied me," she said, "or saw me as any different from her, or my life from hers. She said their house had been all but unlivable, dust forced under closed windows and through keyholes and under doors. It scratched where you tried to rub it off, the windows ruined, furnaces and vents choked, and all the while, the choppers, which could have been used to spray the town with water, were all flying past on their way here—"

"With frankincense and myrrh and gold," AnneMarie said. "I haven't been to Callan, yet, to the mall. For some reason, I don't want to go. It's the funniest thing—as though if I go, I'll never be able to come back. Something, fall or flood or death, will stop me from getting home, ever again."

"That will fade," Melody said. "Soon we'll all be talking about how we found out about the fall, the way we talk about 9/11, or if you're old enough, Kennedy's assasination."

"It did hurt, that feeling I got in Callan," Della Pantea said. "People didn't understand. They didn't know about the dig or how cold we got when the fuel rations didn't come."

AnneMarie recounted what had been said to Jay that evening. People had brought batteries from Callan and their cell phones and radios and CD players were keeping everyone in their houses again. "Callan and Gold Flume were created together—gold and railroads—the valley opens wider at Callan, so there were cattle, too. The people of Callan were always richer than we were."

Jay had been told that the Dust Bowl times had made everyone equal, all those people who had endured it in equal poverty. The Depression had leveled the valley towns in the same equality of want and hopelessness. Only when the skiing came in did Gold Flume shake off its darkness. Jay had known this, but wanted AnneMarie to make her point. They were standing in the bathroom—lights and running water and there was heat coming from a furnace up through vents in the floor. They were barefoot in the middle of winter.

"We shared experience, all of us, as valley people," AnneMarie said. "You said *valley* and everyone knew lots about you right away. The way Melody put it, there was a big difference between us and everyone else. It hurts to think we're so set apart."

Jay was conscious of the warmth of his feet and ankles. In moments he would be standing under the abundant hot water of his shower. The pump had been primed, the system flushed. Which song should he be singing under the spray? Then he thought about how dirty he had been, how cold at the dig. Then, his thoughts moved over, turning on their own.

"I'm going to miss our unity, the way we worked together. Even the phantom writer will be gone. No more postings on the board outside the town hall. I wonder who it is."

"You don't know?"

"I think it's someone older than thirty—just the associations and words he uses."

"He? Your writer is a woman. You must know who."

"I always thought it might be John Klimek. Sometimes I thought it was Tess, until she died."

"No, heavens no."

"Then who?"

"I knew by what she mentioned but more, what she left out. A secret woman. A hiding woman, a well-educated woman."

"Who?"

"Janeen Ansel, of course. I knew it months ago."

"You amaze me. When did you work this out? Did someone tell you?"

"In all those postings there must have been fifteen or twenty people mentioned by name and all the town council except one. No mention even obliquely of Harbison's elk feast, or any of the picnics she wasn't at."

"You really are splendid," he said.

"I still feel set apart."

"Any returnee feels something like that," Jay said. He picked up his toothbrush absent-mindedly, forgetting it in his hand. "I got it when I was back from Vietnam, my year there.... People—young people—didn't like the war. Some were hard on the soldiers. Even if that hadn't happened," he noticed the toothbrush and put it down. "The strangeness would have been the same. We had had experiences, and not all bad, that changed us, and we felt we couldn't explain them or share them with anyone but another vet. My readjustment wasn't <u>from</u> the anxiety or even the terror of the war, but <u>to</u> the dailyness, how ordinary life was."

"I wish I'd known you then."

"I'm glad you didn't." He rinsed his mouth.

"You never talked much about your Vietnam days. Was it because you thought I wouldn't want to hear about them?"

"They go on a lot about PTSD now, but some of what I felt was plain guilt and shame—not because I did anything terrible over there, but I saw terrible things, and because—sometimes I felt I had let buddies down or didn't measure up, or because I was scared about feeling that I didn't care as much as I wanted to about people who died. Back here, I didn't fit into the old body or the mind I had left."

AnneMarie nodded. "I feel a little like that—a Me I haven't been for years and a Me people weren't expecting. I'm not back; I'm here, but I'm someone else, now."

"I hope that woman loves me and the life we have here."

"She's learning."

———————————————◆———————————————

At 1:07 p.m., the digital clock on her oven began to beep. Della Pantea ran into her son's room, hoping to find him there. Lights were on. Heat was on. Chris had left for the Drop, she saw. She went out into the street without a coat, slipped on the icy walk where the way hadn't been swept, and went down hard. Their next-door neighbor, Siri Unger, came out and ran to her.

"I don't think I broke anything—I just need to rest a little here, before I get up. Go back home and turn on your lights. Make us some tea on your stove. The 1880s are over."

They heard people shouting down the block. "I'll drink tea with you, Della," Siri said, "but I can't stay long. I'm going up to spend an hour in the bathtub."

Della noticed Siri was in a robe and slippers. "Thanks for coming," Della said.

Lights were being flicked on and off, heat was flowing up through vents. In their excitement, people forgot that they had been told to unplug appliances and not to turn them all on at once. After an initial surge, the power went out again, and Gold Flume returned to dark, but lights came on later with a brown-out, slowly brought up to full strength. Once again, Gold Flume lived in the twenty-first century.

They had all expected elation, a lift as great as what they had known together when the dig had broken through. For this moment there was a separation of feeling—joy—some people danced in their newly lit houses. Some were impatient, growling as they re-started computers and re-programmed all the electronic devices that had defined their days. Pastor Fearing wondered aloud to Cheryl whether any good things the town had learned would stay with it—the sense of community, the loss of some of the class differences that had formerly marred town life. Cheryl snorted. "Class? Of course we need to be different. How else would people want to rise in the world?"

Edwina Dixon sighed with relief. She had liked and missed being a small town functionary, a part-timer, with long afternoons for reading her guilty pleasure romance novels and gold panning up Whiskey Gulch. There would be time again, the view, and the $180 a year she got out of the gulch's gold. This past year had been full of hard work, sleeplessness, and hard decisions. Thank God it was over.

Some people kept lights on all night, waking now and then in warm houses to assure themselves that the past was past. Women smiled in their second sleep, dreaming of burying the jerry-made washboards and blowing out the fires under ore carts, their fingers finding the assurance of the corona dials: a wash cycle, a rinse cycle.

AnneMarie Isaacs lay exhausted in Jay's arms in a post-coital coma. He couldn't tell her that he had secretly ascribed her recovery to the needs of the fall and that he was worried about what the return of modernity would do to her. Seeing her smile in a light that wasn't the glow of a kerosene lamp but the shadowless glare of their track light, he asked her how she was.

"I'm not going back," she murmured. "I'll keep seeing Pastor Fearing. He told me that he's happy for our talks. He says he seldom gets to do real pastoral work. People don't expect that kind of guidance from clergy these days."

"Funny, that's what Doc said, that most of what he's handled in the year would have been sent off to specialists. I guess it's the same with me—law enforcement—the heavy stuff—goes to Aureole." He began to fade toward sleep. They lay curled into one another, drugged with happiness.

At the Brunos, Angela and Leatrice were up late, packing. They looked without affection at the cobwebbed corners and the uncared for furnishings, the spotted rugs and gritty floors. On all the bare surfaces there was a rim of grease from the overflame of the kerosene lamps. The kitchen hadn't been attended to. "Your father is not coming back," Leatrice had told her daughter. "A minute more in this dump than I have to be is a minute too much. I'm sure you feel the same."

"Where is he?"

"I called the hospital where he was supposed to be, but I couldn't get anyone who knew anything more about his living arrangements. I'm sure he's not alone."

"Is that men, or just him?"

"Maybe some men make the effort—if the goddamn mountain hadn't fallen on the road with him on the other side, we might have stayed together for a few more years, but I doubt it. I think he'd have taken off. If he'd wanted us, he'd have hired a chopper for us. He sees himself like a Christmas tree, with us as ornaments, us and other women. He liked it when you were a kid."

"Did he like me?"

"He liked to show you around. You were cute and perky. As soon as you got boobs, he saw you getting looked at by boys. Competition. They're always telling the women to let their children go. You never hear that said for men, but let me tell you—enough. Let's get packed. We have to get someone to get us out of here. The car's a loss."

That morning Brad Unger faced a crowd of people at the firehouse. As chief, he managed the only working trucks and equipment in town. Everyone wanted gasoline and motor oil for cars that had been drained last year. People who had been orderly and disciplined for the Drop forgot that knowledge and all but mobbed the building. Brad called Edwina and Jay, who came quickly and found a furor they hadn't experienced since the earliest days of the fall. Jay got back into the squad car, turned up the sound, and pushed the broadcast button. A shriek of feedback stopped everyone in mid-cry.

"Trucks will be arriving with supplies of gasoline and motor oil later today. Go to the Drop site tomorrow morning and form your regular lines and positions. Nobody is going to get anything today. Go home. Enjoy the return of the electricity. Get ready for a belated Christmas. Mr. Klimek tells me that school buses will be in town on the day after tomorrow and will be going to the junior high and high schools. School will be in session. Please disperse and go home." He waited until the streets outside the firehouse were empty and drove the squad car back up the hill to his house.

He'd noticed Roman Ansel in the crowd, and had thought of asking him about Mike, but there was a different quality about the man since he had broken his leg on the ice a month before. Jay saw a blurring of his outline, something he recognized now and then in old people or stroke victims. He had gone for Doc after Janeen had come to his house to get help for Ansel who, she said, had fallen. They found him lying on an apron of ice at the bottom of the front steps. The scene had puzzled Jay. Ansel was a perfectionist. His garage, when they went there to get a tarp, was neat as an operating room. Why had he allowed these steps to be in such bad shape? His leg was fractured. They had carried him in the tarp to the garage. Doc had come and splinted the leg. Jay had expected Janeen to be more solicitous than she was.

Their son had gone, probably risking the river or hiking up over the far side of the fall. Roman and Janeen would be waiting for him to contact them, but that wouldn't happen until he thought it was safe. Jay wondered if Mike had told them anything, whether they had given him food and clothing and money, or whether he had simply taken off, one step ahead of arrest. There was no point in asking. Whatever Gold Flume had loosed on the world, he would soon be standard issue in some prison or other. Jay found himself looking at Ansel longer than he might have, until Ansel found the look and stared back at him.

At the parsonage, Cheryl was sitting stiffly at the dining room table, writing out a list for the belated Christmas materials: candles, a box of tinsel and ornaments for the church. Her siege of weeping had retreated. Years ago, she would have masked her misery with a little more make-up and pretended that she wasn't frustrated, disappointed, and yearning for a life just out of reach. No more; let him see it all. He had told her about the vision he had had, the chance for perfection for the people of Gold Flume. What foolishness. The people in this scenic wilderness were now as far from Eden as they had always been. She had seen her husband as a failure. Now she saw him as a fool. The sessions he was enjoying so much with the sheriff's mad wife had confirmed it. The knowledge made her lonelier than ever.

FROM THE FANTOM
I'm signing off my interesting blog
Of things that happened in this almost year.
I've heard my name be guessed at there and here—
I'm old or young, a scold, a pedagogue.
We broke a mountain, suffered heat and cold,
Selfish and unselfish, fearful, bold,
Some weak got strong, some cowards were unveiled;
Some watched addictions break their awful hold
To leave us as we were, our tale is told.

CHAPTER 51

CHRIS PANTEA WOKE UP EARLY ON THE BEGINNING of the world as it had been. He dressed and went from a newly warmed room downstairs to his breakfast. As she had last December, his mother fixed a long-saved, padded plastic bag with his lunch. Last night they had gathered his books and equipment ready for school. He was to have graduated last June, but, of course, none of the Gold Flume students had. The group, eighteen in all, took the bus carrying both junior high and high school students to Callan. As they rode, they studied the cut they had dug through the fall, marveling at the work. Their year away made them all feel like strangers. The junior high students got off at the stop in silence, making a group that moved together up the walk, past the flagpole from which the American and Colorado flags lay open in the light breeze. The high school students looked after them, knowing that they, too, would leave the bus in a silent clump, maybe muttering to one another about having to encounter former classmates who had gone on to other lives. The class they were to have graduated with was gone, of course. Younger brothers and sisters were now in their places, but the old jealousies and rancors were still there, left behind.

There was the school, looking bigger. With no eagerness, the Gold Flumers left the bus and walked, resolutely, toward the school entrance: CHS, home of the CHS Mountaineers, whose football trophies lined the left wall of the entryway and whose logo was an unconscious copy of the fascist bundle of stalks. The Flumers came with low expectations. They had heard from mothers and fathers who had been outside that there was resentment in Callan and Bluebank. Their year away and the anguishes and triumphs they had known had separated them from people beyond the fall. They had heard that those people felt the town had been coddled by charity and made dependent while being freed from the grinding news of the world's other traumas. They were judged as people who had opted out. The valley, they had been told, had suffered, too. The mall had been filled with fine dust thrown off from the fall. Stones and gravel had broken windows with the wind. The river had gone down and soured in places during the summer, rank with dead fish.

The principal, Mr. Guidry, met the group at the door. His attitude gave Chris the feeling that the Gold Flume students had caused him time and trouble. They were to be tested, he told them. Whoever passed would join the present seniors to be graduated in the spring. Those who failed would be placed in the appropriate classes.

The words came as a shock. No one had thought that the group might be split up, that they were to be separated, left to face incomprehension, disinterest, even hostility by themselves. Chris made a weak protest. The seniors, four of them, since Mike and Angela had gone, had been ready to be graduated last spring. Was it fair to keep them back? Perhaps they could cram, together, for a test that would allow them to catch up on what they had missed from the last seven months in school.

There was no such test, Guidry told them, with weary patience. They weren't even caught up with those students who were now seniors, a year behind, and even with testing, graduation was impossible. Some might even be sophomores.

Chris knew he hadn't kept up with the high school curriculum. The classes Mr. Klimek had set up were only three to four hours a day and didn't meet when it snowed, or was too cold, or was a Drop day. All their pleading made the group seem as though they thought themselves superior to the Callan and Bluebank kids, and secretly they did. They had been involved in all kinds of projects—practical and vital things. They had learned new skills and had seen them work in an adult world. Here, their mastery was ignored and their experience set against them. They felt themselves victims in a way they never had in the fall. When the group met for lunch, they sought out Mr. Klimek, who told them he had no power to change a decision made by the school administrators. They went home and complained to their parents. Everyone was being left back.

Chris heard the school's special language, the coded talk of each group, its tribal tongue of in-group references, all new, since the fall, other secrets, other styles. Within the week, parents had been drawn into the controversy and there was argument and rancor.

"These kids have experienced things no school could teach," Rick Harbison declared at the meeting called to make the school's position plain, "They've been on engineering projects college students would envy, math and physics made real in application, hands-on—the dig, the wash houses, wagons they've made out of scrap wood—their help in organizing and delivering goods and food for 300 people on a regular basis—these kids have taken part in discussions involving city planning, waste management, and seen the math work for all of them. I'm an engineer; I know what I'm talking about. They were to be graduated last spring. Let them be graduated here, now, by special dispensation. This could be done if you and the school board choose to do it."

The administration was adamant. No test was to be given, no exception allowed. At the meeting, the arguments broke up into sputters of indignation on both sides. From their feelings of pride in what they had done to save the town, Gold Flume's people received the full shock of their distance from the rest of the valley. All of the one-time seniors chose to stay out of school and begin tutoring for GEDs. Chris saw his plans for college withering away. He had been accepted at the Colorado School of Mines, but not without graduation from high school, and not with a GED.

Slowly, the word went out that this year's ski season would be spectacular. People calling in to Aureole's Chamber of Commerce about the area's condos and lodges were told about snow depths and the probability of wonderful weather. All the lifts would be in operation by the end of January, and rates would be lower. There had been no artificial snow being made, Roman Ansel told a TV reporter, but the snow levels at the four principal lift areas—Thunder Alley, Backbowl, Shooting Star, and Hidden Gulch—were their highest in years. Mayor Dixon said that all services including those for fine dining and luxury accommodation would be fully in place for holiday vacationers who loved Colorado's champagne powder snow. All the ski and sports magazines in print and online were sent articles on Gold Flume's readiness to welcome its guests. The media had stressed the isolation of the town and its scarcities. Now, everything had to be done to make the snowy streets seem quaint and the slowly recovering inventories, adventurous. March was the season's height, but everyone wondered if the Chamber of Commerce would have the word out on time.

There had to be constant assurance that the slide-off of a mountain wouldn't be repeated. The town's geologist, Dr. Pantea, went on TV to declare that as a man with an intimate knowledge of Gold Flume and the mountains surrounding the Ute Valley, he could affirm that the mountain-fall, uncommon in this situation, was most unlikely to be repeated. Edwina Dixon called him the next day, shouting over the phone, "Unlikely? Uncommon? Why not say 'we sorta hope'?"

"Ms. Mayor, no geologist could say what you would want him to—that he or anyone could know absolutely and promise. I'd be laughed out of the profession. Unlikely will have to do."

Their late Christmas came with lights and the town's annual celebrations—tourist-inspired, but now accepted as a Christmas tradition: a sledge-pulling contest and caroling through the streets.

People were still partly dependent on government food shipments, but because trucks could get through, the packaged food was fresh or frozen—hams, turkeys and vegetables, salads and fruit.

For a while, phone lines were overloaded with calls from relations and friends. Jay and AnneMarie got calls from their families in California and Texas, both wanting to hear more than that Gram and Gramps were okay. How had it been? What had that year been like? Had they kept a diary, letters, thoughts put down about what had happened? Both of them talked to the kids and grandkids but couldn't capture any of the flavor of their experiences to describe them. Later, their eldest, Lucy, told Jay: "Dad—what's happened to Mom? I haven't heard that voice in years. She's so—she's so **back**, like back to who she used to be."

"No one ever goes back to a used-to-be. She is better, though."

"How did it happen? Was it all that work she had to do, scrubbing all those clothes and stuff?"

"I think the drugs helped for a while. Later, they made things worse. I think your mom was depressed about many things—"

"Our leaving?"

"I think she expected to have all you kids and the grandkids around her as we got older— her friends moved, many died, or got sick."

"But she knows I couldn't stay—Andy—"

"Staying in Gold Flume wasn't in the cards for any of you. We both know that. I'm not talking about what she wanted to feel, but what she did feel, and knew she shouldn't feel. How do you tell someone that you are angry about her dying, when you are supposed to be sad but philosophical? People think you are stupid not to know and accept that loved ones die."

"What about her faith?"

"Agnostics and atheists can yell at a non-existent God and feel vindicated in non-belief, but your mother is a religious woman. It all fell in on her—a physical message in her menopause, a spiritual one that was much worse. What if the brain wants a shot at fixing itself? Anyway, she's coming to terms with things, if anyone ever really does. Keep in touch more, will you? Call us up."

"And you?"

"I'm not immune."

"What do you do?"

"I use movies and comics—W.C. Fields—very sophisticated stuff— bloopers, people losing their pants, falling down in various ways, pie-fights, food fights. A good food fight scene will keep me going for months at a time."

"So you haven't had your fix all year."

"The comedy went local."

"Keep going, Pop."

"Thanks for the call, sweetheart."

———————◆———————

The road between Callan and Gold Flume was being widened, a plan set before the fall. Tourists had been complaining of traffic jams as they came into town. Jay was out at the site, having talked with Rick Harbison and Sheriff McMasters about speed limits and pull-off spots along the road. It was bright and sunny after a snow. Along with the ski-buses and cars carrying ski racks on their roofs were groups of planners, engineers and builders looking at the site of the fall and making measurements that they set on the iPads they carried.

Harbison had gone up to where the river had been diverted. He was gone for a long time. Jay saw Considine up in one of the earth-movers, stopping to let a line of cars through. Considine saw him, turned off the machine, and climbed down, walking to where Jay was parked.

"Hi, Sheriff, looking for someone?"

"Yeah, have you seen Harbison?"

"Up the road a bit. I can get him on my cell—"

"I'll wait; it's nothing urgent. I didn't know you were on this crew."

"I just got this job. Do you remember our last time on this road? It was the morning after the fall and you had a couple of delinquents to go up to Aureole. We got turned back. I can still hear the kids laughing."

"A lot's happened since then. Whose rigs are these?"

"It's an outfit down in Denver. They do some of the heavy stuff on government projects—the whole Midwest and Inter-mountain area. It's huge. They took me on right away. I guess they were a little red in the face."

"Why?"

"This town was supposed to have been opened up six months ago. The requisitions, the work orders—all the paperwork got scrambled online somehow—someone must have pushed the delete button, I guess."

"We got deleted?"

"We did. Flights went out, regular deliveries for food and fuel, but nobody picked up on the disconnects until last week when some watch group from the government started wondering why all those 'copter runs were still being made and thought it might be a scam. They were going to shut down the deliveries until someone actually decided to come on up here and see what was going on, a reporter, I think. Nobody had given the order to open the road. I went out and down to Denver, thinking to get something in heavy equipment, and I found out that the highway was being widened, by the same company."

"So we were supposed to have been opened up in June?"

"June, July, sometime in the summer."

"And the pilots of the choppers kept telling us that crews were all busy in other places."

"They were, but those places were all being taken care of by other companies. I guess everyone assumed that everything was out on loan. We had rigs idle in Denver all the while." Considine shrugged and began to climb into the cab.

"Would you do me a favor?"

"Sure, Sheriff." He seated himself and put his hand on the ignition.

"Let me be the last person hearing this." The motor caught and the great beast stuttered.

"I guess it would cause a real stink," Considine yelled over the sound.

"I guess so."

CHAPTER 52

MANY PEOPLE SAID THEY WOULD KEEP THE PARTS OF life they had found valuable in their year of exile—church attendance, neighborliness—reading to the family, town meetings and celebrations, walking more. Some made the effort—most did not. The kids went tribal again, texting and talking to one another almost exclusively on their electronic equipment. People who had lost weight by working and walking stopped working and walking and gained it back. Cars that had been drained and put up for the duration were filled and put back into service. Those that had been left were towed away to Bluebank and Callan and rehabilitated. The pregnancy rate fell back to normal as people began watching late night TV. The wash houses were slated to be dismantled, but more immediate needs took precedence and they were left to rot away and erode until they looked like the far older sluices and breakers of Gold Flume's mining past.

Chris Pantea and the other students began to be tutored by a woman hired by their parents. Colleges at which they had been accepted rescinded or continued their status differently, but Chris, who was to go to Mines to major in geology, changed school and major, a secret disappointment to his father. He would get a degree in social work, then go to graduate school in business administration. The Harbison girl, also affected by the fall, would major in geology.

In May, Mrs. Moritz moved to a nursing home in Aureole. The other people on the ridge left, bound for the homes or cities where their children lived. All important shopping was now done at the mall three miles outside of town, and the Gold Flume of its jubilee year relapsed into its dependence on the automobile. Town shops had all returned for tourists and skiers. The eight restaurants and six bars in town re-opened to catch the best snow season in a decade. The recovery of the economy was hugely aided by articles in ski and sports magazines, the excellent work of the town council.

Angela and her mother had left two days after the opening of the road. With two of the three participants in the past December's breaking and entering at the condos in Callan gone, and Janeen Ansel turning over all the contents of Mike's suitcases to the sheriff, Jay Isaacs thought that an agreement might be arrived at in regard to Chris Pantea's involvement. The news was good for Chris.

"It looks like there won't be any charges for your adventure into delinquency," Jay told him. "The condos were destroyed in the fall. They're under God knows how many feet of rock and soil. I don't see any interest in following on your case. As to the problems up at the cave and the Shively boy, we'll send out a bulletin about Mike Ansel and hope they catch him somewhere."

Chris took a breath to speak and then let it out. Then he said, "I think everyone who was in the cave feels sorry. There was all that noise and crowd. When I was there, people were all drunk or sick or stoned— there must have been twenty of them, and the cave really isn't that big. No one knows exactly what happened."

The Fearings divorced. Cheryl eased things for El by telling him that her misery was directly linked to his failure instead of to a general dislike of Gold Flume. He had been prepared to put in for a placement that would more closely fit her ideas of the good life, but he knew that wherever it was, it would be a place much like this one, maybe without the tourists. When she left, he noticed with a pang that no one expressed either surprise or sorrow. She sank away and in less than a week after her exit from the parsonage, three women were coming regularly with casseroles and pasta salads. Now, with the electricity restored, El did a competent wash, and Melody Reimer and the church women laundered the choir robes and took care of the ceremonial items. He missed Cheryl, but not as badly as he thought he would. AnneMarie Isaacs took a class in Spanish and continued her talks with the pastor. They started a book club, one with a very serious spiritual slant. At first they thought others would join it. Some did, to sample, but soon dropped out. Teilhard De Chardin killed off two.

Doc missed the house calls and the bedsides. Even people who had praised his skill began to return to specialists over the pass in Aureole. He had been frustrated at the number of addicts the fall relieved of their drugs of choice who went back to them as soon as they were available. AnneMarie patched together a program of relaxation and soporifics to sleep and eased herself back into the world.

Melody Reimer had been talked about as a possible mayor, but two years after the town was opened, she moved to Arizona to stay with her sister.

Over time, the tourists and skiers came back in more than their original numbers, and the town recovered its economic health. Pastor Fearing called what had happened the Jubilee Year. As it retreated into memory, people stopped referring to it at all.

The kids forgot it first. The year had no context for the rest of their lives or futures. As most grew up and went away to colleges, they were, at the beginning, surprised that no one had heard of Gold Flume as the town that had once had a year separated from the world by the fall of a mountain. On telling of how the townspeople had diverted a river and saved everything, they were greeted with shrugs. People thought about Gold Flume as a ski town, a place where rich people came on vacations. A year later, a helicopter service began running flights for extreme skiing on the ungroomed heights at the east side of the Hungry Mother. With money pouring into the town, the council conducted a makeover, complete with new antique-looking streetlights and an outdoor skating rink where the chopper had landed for the Drop. The pictures of the Drop that had been taken were buried in home collections or on the walls of the Hi Grade or Finnegan's Wake.

Geologists came to study the fall. A sociologist came and wanted to study how the town had kept itself from anarchy. The grant application was denied so the study never took place. Edwina Dixon served another term and then retired. She was succeeded by Rick Harbison and then by Rick's brother, Dan, who had grown up in Gold Flume and had come back. He wasn't interested in promoting, as he said, "a meaningless accident of nature."

The edges began to blur in people's forgetting. When they would remember again, years later, the event would have changed to something dear and distant, spoken of with a wistful smile.

Joanne Greenberg